Damnation Inn

*A collection of dark stories
for that fireside drink*

First Published in Great Britain 2017 by Mirador Publishing

First edition: 2014 (published as *Damnation Alley*)
Second edition: 2016
Third edition: 2017 (Revised, Extended and Uncensored)

Any reference to real names and places are purely fictional and are constructs of the author. Any offence the references produce is unintentional and in no way reflects the reality of any locations or people involved.

A copy of this work is available through the British Library.

ISBN: 978-1-912192-81-6

Mirador Publishing
10 Greenbrook Terrace
Taunton
Somerset
UK
TA1 1UT

Damnation Inn

IXIDORR HACK

Contents

Introduction by the Author

Please allow me to introduce myself, as the fella said. As a writer I go by the name of Ixidorr Hack, but I am a Psychiatrist by trade. I'm not as new on the literary scene as you might think; I have been writing for a very, very long time—since a teenager, in fact—but it is only now I have decided to put my more recent works into an anthology for publication.

There is a strong psychological component to my tales. My tales nearly always start off very low-key so that you don't know what genre I am writing from and I gradually build up the strangeness to a point where I finally go off the rails, and the climax has absolutely no semblance to the beginning—you wouldn't believe it's the same story—so that the reader might think two completely different people wrote the work. I should have sufficiently exhausted all eventualities and taken the story to its absolute extreme so, I hope, there is nothing more beyond that extreme. I would like to share that approach to writing and my apocalyptic vision with you and let you decide. All I ask of you is you write a review of my humble book, for better or for worse but, most importantly, as long as it is honest.

I suppose it's all good and well being Jekyll but you've gotta let your Mr. Hyde out once in a while. I remember one of my medical superiors in the days when I was still doing my Psychiatry training noting that as a Psychiatrist I'm always 'calming things down' but as a horror writer I am 'stirring things up', allowing me to maintain the perfect balance in life, an 'equilibrium', if you will. So I guess I won't give up the day job just yet.

I use music in my stories, what I consider the cherry on top. You see I love Rock music, always have. I believe the song should be relevant to and fully compliment the work, and the work in question should live up to the song. I like to call my deliberate song placements Hack Tracks. There's even a Hack Black Track in there somewhere.

Why horror, you may ask? Most people don't think much of horror fiction, but like every genre it too has its virtues and shortcomings. I have tried discussing and critiquing the Horror genre at various points in this anthology, in a number of stories.

Mostly, I am here to entertain, and to a lesser extent educate, but perhaps not so much moralize. I hope you appreciate my anthology of horror stories, the time and effort it took to put them together, where nothing is as it seems and madness figures greatly and Hell blazes close on the heels. Here are 21 Ways to be Damned.

Choose at your peril.

Wishing you dark dreams…

IH
October 2013

Acknowledgements

Contretemps, Paris: *To my Beautiful Wife, How can I expect you to forgive me for hurting you when I can't even forgive myself?*

Margin of Deceit *is dedicated to MJVR, who inspired this piece of fiction and to whom I would like to show what any writer worth half his salt can achieve if properly motivated…*

Deadliner: *In my futile attempts to address the Emma Dilemma. Keep you forever wondering why I wrote this… or maybe you already know!*

Birdwatching: *2011: the Year of the Lovebird. In loving memory of our own cute, darling, little tum-tum things. RIP. Xx*

My eternal gratitude to my Beautiful Wife, Hannah, for putting up with my nonsense, and also to my two good friends, Anthony & Guy, for encouraging and actually appreciating my nonsense, as well as my third but equally important good friend, Jamie, for providing constructive criticism on my nonsense.

And to my family, Ye of little faith. Now you can finally believe me…

List of Tales

The Indescription: A London copper forced to migrate to Wales at his wife's request suffers the most indescribably terrible night of his life.

Vampire Season: On the last night of a successful run of a play, the leading man meets with the surprise of his life.

Winter's Chill: A family on a drive to relatives on Christmas Eve encounter a strange presence in the middle of the road.

Healing The Sick: An ailing grandmother eagerly looks forward to a visit from her handsome GP.

The Haunting of Herman Hinkle: After killing his unfaithful wife, Herman Hinkle finds out that she just won't stay dead.

Harbinger: A seemingly innocent holiday in Lanzarote awakens an ancient evil with terrible consequences for all.

Invention of the Devil: A late-night cable station specializes in extreme torture.

Birdwatching: A lonely schoolboy is given a pair of lovebirds as a welcome home gift with which he grows an ever-increasing fascination.

Margin of Deceit: A fling between two hardworking medics hides unspoken secret pasts.

Shetani: A letter to the British PM explores the darker side of Africa.

Getting His Dues: A re-telling of a classic Kashmiri folktale.

An Act of Faith: A man contemplates his own beliefs during a journey on the London Underground.

Contretemps, Paris: Whilst waiting for a flight back to England, Dean Hayes loses his girlfriend at Charles de Gaulle airport, but the truth is far removed from anything anyone could have imagined.

Lonesome October: A group of teenagers spin out their favourite urban legends on Halloween night.

Black Lung: A treatise on the wonderfulness of tobacco.

Deadliner: A mad drinking contest between two writing buddies leads to an even crazier conclusion.

Hiding in the Light: Decades later, a writer recalls the tragic story of his finest and funniest friend from their teenage years until their ways parted unexpectedly.

Neighbourliness unto Edification: Having moved into their dream house, a couple develop an unhealthy obsession with their neighbours.

Hartigan Strange: A retired police detective writing his memoirs recounts his most puzzling case.

Charterhouse Road: An apparently ordinary house in the suburbs possesses a truly extraordinary and terrifying garden.

Picturing The Unimaginable: A group of wealthy individuals gather to bid for a clandestine collection of dark art.

BOOKEND: Tales Told A Thousandfold (Inicio)

The sign for the street name reads DAMNATION ALLEY but I take no notice. I trudge down the dusty, cobbled street, unsure how I got here, the sky apparently dyed with the fiery hues of sunset, the air shimmering and heavy and uncomfortably warm. Seething and churning, the sea below the edge of the quay has turned blood-red, reflecting the last lingering light of day. I spot a building to my right, a tavern of medieval design, overlooking the crimson sea. The rusty, beaten sign hanging over the tavern door bears the painting of a three-pronged pitchfork together with the name of the establishment: DAMNATION INN. The stonework of the tavern is badly-eroded, crumbling, as though perpetually scoured by heat and wind, and the windows cracked and textured with centuries of grime, making it impossible to look inside.

Still uncertain where I am or how I arrived here, I push through the ancient oak doors and cross the threshold. The inn is curiously dark inside, bereft of neon, lowly-lit by flickering candlelight, and as my eyes adjust to the prevailing gloom, I manage to pick out numerous figures in the place, drinking or smoking or talking or laughing. Most of the punters I cannot identify – could be anyone off the street – but the few faces I do recognize causes old, quiescent memories to be carried up to the surface of my mind, bringing on an overwhelming swell of shock, awe and nostalgia. I am staring at Jim Morrison who is taking swigs from a half-empty bottle of Jack and loitering near the jukebox, where Paint It, Black, *courtesy of Jagger and Richards, spins round endlessly... Oh, and there's Jimi Hendrix shooting some pool with Kurt Cobain, each enjoying a doobie of epic proportions! Michael Hutchence, cigarette in hand, strolls up to them, and whispers something amusing into Cobain's ear, causing him to smirk. In the far corner, I watch Brian Jones challenge Keith Moon to a darts contest and drop a suspicious-looking pill into* each of their beer glasses. Sitting across from them, Sid Vicious tightens a tourniquet around his arm...

In fact I am staring so ridiculously hard, Jon Bonham nods back at me in cheery acknowledgement. I wave back slowly at him, mechanically, still gawping like a lemon.

What is this place? This magical place, where I find myself in the presence of Greatness. Surrounded by these Rock Legends who happen to look as young as the day they died...

"Can I help you?" asks the Innkeeper, who bears more than just a passing resemblance to the record producer, Brian Epstein.

"What is this place?" I ask, this time aloud.

"Damnation Inn."

"How did I come to be here?"

"That isn't important," the Innkeeper informs me. "All that matters right now are the tales."

"Tales? What tales?"

"The punters here have some interesting stories to tell you," he explains. "Sit ye down, and we can begin. First, let me slake your thirst."

I see the bronze plaque behind the bar and briefly shudder: ABANDON ALL HOPE, YE WHO ENTER HERE.

The Innkeeper pulls me a pint and directs me to a barstool at the counter. I turn to the man seated beside me, tapping me on my shoulder, eager to talk by the looks of it. One by one, I listen to the stories my fellow customers are keen to impart, these anonymous people with their tales to tell, tales as close as the next page...

The Indescription

"Great is the hand that holds dominion over
Man by a scribbled name."

Dylan Thomas (1936)

It was exactly five o'clock on a hot Friday afternoon when the terrified man staggered into the lobby of Tolwyn police station.

Stumbling forward, he managed to make it as far as the duty officer before his legs gave way and he collapsed asprawl the reception counter. "Help me," he panted, groping the counter for support. "Please, you've got to help me..."

The police station was quiet at the time, except for an elderly lady, who was explaining to PC Gareth Neville how she had been accosted in the street by a young delinquent and her handbag and pension-book forcibly snatched. The unseasonable September heatwave was playing havoc with everybody's concentration, not in the least PC Neville's, who listened to the old lady with detached boredom as she ceaselessly grumbled on about the declining moral standards of the youth of today. He would provide her with an occasional sympathetic nod to show that he was still paying attention. His colleagues, too, wished they were elsewhere, aestivating the day away in more leisurely pursuits (flycasting, say, or taking in a spot of sunbathing), instead of spending the afternoon as pot roasts in this oven of a police station. There was no air-conditioning to speak of, and the limited supply of portable fans placed strategically around the station could do little to dispel the baking heat. Sergeant Powell sat in his office, busy preparing a crucial report for the regional ASAC and, in the adjoining conference room,

PCs Evans and Haddon were themselves buried in their own drift of paperwork when the fright-stricken man made his dramatic entrance.

"Help me!" he repeated, pronouncing it *Hellp mee.*

Sergeant David Powell put aside the monthly audit he had been compiling and went over to attend to the newcomer. "Afternoon, sir, what can I do you for?" he asked amicably.

The man confronting him began to sob.

"There, there," Powell said, soft and soothing, "it can't be all that bad."

"Bad?" he burst out. "You don't know the meaning of the word. You'd think different if you knew what I'd seen?"

He certainly presented a perfect picture of wild-eyed panic and near-utter confusion. His long, greying hair was plastered over his forehead in sweaty tangles and, from his clothes, he looked as though he'd come runner-up in some sort of mud-slinging contest. His glasses were National Health issue and they too were streaked with mud, the left wing broken and repaired with duct-tape, a visible crack running up one of the inordinately thick lenses. His dirty, draggled appearance aside, his dress-sense left quite a lot to be desired: his green cardigan and brown donkey-jacket were already so tatty as to make Michael Foot, on whom he obviously seemed to model himself, a rural fashion icon. Or so PC Haddon thought, amused. *Who could forget those priceless duffel-coat buttoning embarrassments, hey boyo?*

The emotional outburst caused all present, including the old dame, to turn in his general direction. Only Sergeant Powell remained strangely unmoved and continued in calm, measured tones. "Let me be the judge of that," he replied. "First, can you tell us your name?"

"Err… Thomas…?" The man seemed to be having difficulty in remembering who he was. He hesitated, searching for his full name. "Thomas Dwyer." *Tom-mus Da-wehr.*

"Now, Mr. Dwyer," Powell said, and PC Haddon was sure he detected a glint of recognition in the sergeant's eyes. "Tell me what happened."

"*M-M-Monsters…*" he murmured, trying to bring the words to the surface. "I was attacked by monsters."

"Monsters, was it? What kind?"

Probably an armed robber or a lager lout or maybe the old fogey's notorious bagsnatcher, PC Haddon thought, returning to his notebook. He felt as hot and bothered as a pig in a pen and wanted nothing more than to finish his report about a stolen Ford Escort Cosworth found burnt-out and abandoned in a field on the outskirts of town.

"Monsters, man," Dwyer exclaimed almost incoherently. "Monsters from Hell... *Cwn Annwn*... The Hounds of the Otherworld!"

PC Haddon looked back sharply. *Monsters from Hell? Hounds of the Otherworld?* What was this fellow chatting about? Was Otherworld synonymous with Underworld here? Was he referring to some gangland fracas? Had he got himself into a nasty scrape with some mob kingpin? Did some heavies decide to pay him a visit and work him over? If so, then why couldn't he just come out and say it? Why, for petessakes, did he have to be so bloody euphemistic about it? That really was one of the big problems adjusting to life in these parts: the people talked a whole lot of waffle to mean something else entirely.

Haddon saw the old lady's face show concern as the sergeant beckoned the newcomer towards the conference room. "Tell me all about it in here," Powell said as he led him through, putting a consoling arm around the man's shoulder.

The conference room wasn't as impressive-looking as it sounded. Although markedly less cramped than the set of interview rooms that flanked the corridor further along, it was nothing more than a poorly-furnished, chestnut-panelled chamber with a broad, formaldehyde table in the centre, around which were placed six plastic chairs, two of which were already occupied by Evans and Haddon. They could see the station car-park from where they were sitting, sunlight shining off the windscreens of the cars outside. Perched on a filing cabinet in the far corner of the room whirred the spinning blades of the best fan the department could afford, offering some respite from the stifling heat. Across the back wall hung a large poster-map of the Welsh territories, the near wall proudly embellished by a bronze wyvern displaying indecipherable runic inscriptions. Shelves of labelled boxes ran along the length of the adjoining wall, filled to capacity with redundant protocols and old, disused case-files. Behind the door, a water-cooler needed replenishing.

Most of the staff meetings were held here and all high-ranking visitors were ushered into this room spacious enough and private enough to conduct their official business in relative peace and quiet, without undue distraction. Thomas Dwyer didn't look much like a civil servant to Haddon and the constable wondered why the fellow had been granted a special audience in the conference room. The acceptable environment aside, the fearful look in the old lady's eyes told Haddon that something big was going down. He didn't know if he should stay or not, but decided he might as well. Clock-off time it indeed was with a willing wife and weekend waiting for the taking, but curiosity had got the better of him and he decided to stick around and hear the man out. It was too early to tell if this tired, dishevelled man's experience would warrant a call to the boys at CID or whether he would end up being classified as yet another routine case for the local bobby. But, for now at least, Dwyer looked like a promising candidate.

"Fancy a cuppa?" Sergeant Powell asked politely.

The man shook his head, seating himself down on an empty chair. He removed his spectacles and began to wipe the lenses absently with an old rag. He succeeded merely in smearing the mud worse than before. Rhodri Evans closed the door.

"You sure? We can make some if you want, no problem. Always does a power of good. Steadies the nerves."

"No thanks!" Dwyer said in disgust and despair. Without his black frames and cracked lens, his eyes assumed a cast of frank suspicion. Round and restless, they reflected a state of jittery agitation that comes only when someone is on the verge of losing their mind. "How can you possibly expect me to eat or drink at a time like this?"

"Now, now, don't get so wound up," Powell said, gently patting the man's shoulder. "I know you've been through a terrible time, but you must try to remain calm if you want us to fully appreciate what happened to you." He pulled out an incident report form from the uppermost drawer of the filing cabinet and grabbed himself a seat. "Now, shall we begin?"

Dwyer said nothing for a moment. Then he proceeded to tell his story whilst trying to wrestle with his emotions. He spoke slowly in a voice, though easily excitable, betrayed a fair amount of misery.

"I went up to Friend's Grove for a little poaching," Dwyer began uneasily, "you know, for my *mis-sus* — she *all-ways* cooks rabbit stew on

Sundays. A popular thing in our house, is rabbit. Anyways, hunting never hurt a hair on my head before, has it? Going out and about. The fresh air, the exercise, do me some good, my old missus always says. I mean, I don't hunt for fun like those posh fools do and I never trespass on other people's land. Me, I'm alright, you see. A *jenu-inn* sport. A real nature-lover. I never put a foot wrong. Only rabbits is all I hunt and I really look forward to it. Once a week, nab me a rabbit or two. *Ree-lax-ses* the mind, you know.

"I took my shotgun with me — I *do* have a licence for it and I'll show you if you like. Fires buckshot, it does. Nothing extravagant. Never causes much pain to the poor *ann-ee-mull*. Well, there I was a-walking up to Friend's Grove. Not that far from where I live is Friend's Grove, up Midden Hill Road."

Powell gave a faint nod of agreement.

"Half-an-hour's walk is all it takes. Lovely day, clear skies, no need to take the car. Let's just walk and look for some good-sized warrens, I'm saying to myself, expecting a good tally. I didn't mind how long it would take, as long as I caught myself a prize specimen.

"Luck was on my side, I could feel it in my bones... And, would you *bell-eve* it, I got lucky! Square off the mark, out in the open, glimpsed between the blades of grass, I found me one. Speckly-grey in colour. Big and juicy as a rabbit should be. The finest prize specimen if ever there was. Better for stuffing and displaying on your mantlepiece than making stew out of. Just begging to be bagged. Lucky me, hey?" He gave a hollow laugh before continuing, evidently perturbed: "But I had no idea what horrors were lying in wait for me. I should have known something was wrong from the start — it was all too easy, you see. The rabbit saw me spying on it and scampered away. So I went after it. Followed it off into the woods. I think that was when I noticed the signpost was all wrong."

"And what signpost would that be?" Powell asked.

"You know, the one that said *Fiend's Grave* when it should say *Friend's Grove*... Fiend's Grave like it was a sick joke or something... Of course, I thought nothing of it. Why should I? A couple of kids messing about, what else could it mean?... But I'd learn about my mistake later on. Oh yes, I'd learn my mistake, alright!" He was getting hysterical again. "Fiend's Grave, it said — I don't think I've been there before and I know this town like the back of my hand... *Fiend's Grave!... Fiend's Grave, I swear it, FIEND'S GRAVE!"*

Powell decided to restore order. "Let's not be a big girl's blouse now, shall we? What time was this about?"

"I don't know," Dwyer said uncertainly. "I'd say about eleven this morning—I really can't remember."

The sergeant scribbled this down. "Then what happened?"

"I followed the rabbit is what," Dwyer explained with a little more composure, "like a bug-collector who's chasing after a rare butterfly. Instead of a butterfly-net, I had a loaded gun with a *dee-cent* range and a target that was so much bigger and simpler to catch... Except I couldn't get close to it. I tried to, but I just couldn't keep up. It wouldn't let me. It seemed to be always one step ahead of me. A fast, nimble thing it was. Outsmarted me at every turn... I should have given up sooner and told my missus there would be no rabbit this weekend, but I really didn't want to disappoint her...

"How was I supposed to know the rabbit was playing me? Deeper into the woods it was taking me, because the deeper I went, the darker it got. Brought me there on purpose, don't you doubt it for one second. Always one step ahead of me, always out of firing-range. Like it *knew*... Like it could think like a man. I know it sounds crazy, but it was like it knew where to take me. That, by taking me into the dark, it would spoil my aim and every chance of shooting it."

"Couldn't it be that it just wanted a safe place to hide?" Powell suggested.

"No!" Dwyer retorted back. "It *knew*, I tell you! Too clever by half! It was the feeling I got about it and I've been hunting rabbits for years. It just wasn't behaving like no ordinary rabbit. Rabbits aren't as fond of the dark as badgers are, and rabbits never venture far from their burrows. My little friend meanwhile was a long way from home and trying real hard to get me lost. We were well into the woods now and I was still nowhere near catching the blasted thing. Was developing into a real worrying situation. A *prop-per* mission. You understand, it wasn't only the rabbit that was giving me grief, but the woods themselves. *They didn't feel right.* They seemed normal enough on the surface, but I couldn't see any other living creature or hear any of their familiar cries around me. No birdsong, no squirrels rustling leaves, none of the common woodland noises you would expect to hear—you get my point? I felt all alone. The woods looked so dark and empty and threatening... Like a *tomb*... All the while, I'm fretting about the ghostly silence, wondering where all the other creatures have gone... Like they've all scurried away on holiday... Or they've all *died*... Or *waiting for something*... By now, I was getting quite scared.

"Then something happened that pretty much tipped me over..." He paused, his eyes darting about mistrustfully. "One minute, the woods are regular, the next, everything's *different*."

Powell interrupted him. "What do you mean *different*?"

"Different, you know what I mean. *Diff-ferrunt!*" he punctuated. "I don't know where I was, I can't explain it. It was like the woods changed in front of me, in a blink. As quick as it takes to click a camera. I didn't recognize them anymore. Like Friend's Grove was no longer there. Like I was somewhere else," he slowed in chilling emphasis, "*somewhere dark and ee-vill*...

"The trees were different, taller somehow, and all strange, twisted shapes that swelled out in places with... what could only be *faces*. Like there were people trapped inside. Screaming *faces*, only their screams were trapped in with them. The *roots*... they were alive and *moving*— moving, I say—snaking over each other, creeping along the ground and reaching out for me."

Haddon's jaw dropped in disbelief. What was going on here? Was this man serious? Despite his doubts, he, as with the rest of his fellow officers, had become strangely engrossed by the newcomer's tale. Even Sergeant Powell had stopped scribbling.

"There's a stream which runs through Friend's Grove. Fenella's Brook it's called, after the wise woman who used to live there in the olden days, helping weary travellers with her special herbs and potions. Springs up from the hills it does. Has healing properties, some claim. I don't know about that, but it definitely beats those rip-off, mass-market pick-me-ups when you put your head down to drink. Such a *mag-niffy-cent* spot in the summer for a stroll or a picnic or a little loving. I'd go up there with my missus in the days when we were still courting. Young and frisky she was then. Nowadays, even climbing the stairs is too much bother. Rheumatism, the doctor says. Mind you, I got a touch of it myself..."

"What about Fenella's Brook?" prompted Powell.

"'Ey?" Dwyer responded distractedly.

"Fenella's Brook. You were going to tell us about Fenella's Brook."

Vague puzzlement passed over his face, advising he not relive his ordeal but retreat to pleasanter reminiscences. His eyes suddenly widened in terror, his lips trembling as he spoke.

"The brook was gone. Fenella's Brook was *gone*. Where its clear, refreshing crystal waters had once been was now filled with muck. Dirty, filthy *muck*. A thick, wet, flowing river of sludge that stank worse than a septic tank that's blocked up bad. A smell straight from Hell. And there were things *living* in it. Actually *swimming* in it. I don't know if they were fish or not—I thought they looked more like eels—but every so often they'd come up for air, then sink back under.

"The same goes for all the other animals. I'd seen nothing like them before. They were so different, so horrible to feel anything but loathing for. In some cases I didn't have a clue what they were. The foul river attracted a lot of insects, mainly the bluebottle variety. Believe me when I tell you, they were as big as bats and busy wallowing in the muck, laying eggs wherever they could. I hated to see what would come hatching out since it was bad enough seeing how the full-growns moved. Because their wings were too small for flight, all crinkly and zigzagged with pulsing veins, they could only move by dragging their fat, swollen bodies behind them. Dragonflies buzzed around... only these weren't no ordinary dragonflies. They were huge and clumsy and deformed like they were the work of a deranged god who chooses to make monstrous creations for his own cruel amusement. The woodlice could have been cockroaches for all I cared, except they acted more like an army of ants; I saw them surround a sorry, frightened thing that was more rat than mouse and I knew what they'd do to it. God forbid if I were ever to run into a wasps' nest in this place. There were stoneflies the size of starlings and there were beetles that weren't quite beetles. There were creatures that looked like a cross between a bull-frog and a grasshopper—I don't know how and I don't want to know. All I can tell you is they were smoky-green and their proportions were all wrong... and, I swear on Mother Mary's life, they were all croaking out my name...

"I was really crapping it now, getting downright scared. Everything around me was wrong and I badly wanted out. I was cursing that bugaboo for bringing me here, but, most of all, I was hating myself for ever falling into its trap. You see, it no longer resembled that innocent rabbit I was telling you about. Just like everything else in these woods, it too had changed. It could have fought a tomcat and won, it was so big. And so savage and ugly and unnatural-looking like it was diseased or *mutated* or the result of some mad experiment. Its fur was all dark and mangy. It was difficult to tell its front from its back because it had *too many legs growing out of it*... like it was part-spider or something; imagine a hare with spider legs. It had teeth that could bite, hooks for teeth that could have chewed your hand clean off... But the worst feature was its eyes; it had eyes, not rabbit's eyes like it should have had, but *human eyes*... Real human eyes that were watching me up close and personal. Watching me like it was trying to size me up... Like I was the main course at a banquet." Then Dwyer leaned forward, his eyes bulging wider until Haddon thought they would pop right out of their sockets. "*And that's when I saw them*... Coming out of the woods... Coming at me... Swarms of them... shiny as coal, slimy as slugs... charging at me — poor, old me! *Creatures as black as night itself*... I was so shocked as they came at me, I nearly dropped dead from fright there and then. I screamed and dropped my gun. I knew no bullet could ever harm these things and, even if it could, what would be the use? There were just too many of them. I ran. I had to. I was running for my life. Oh God, did I run? I ran and ran and ran till I got into town, huffing and puffing like a greyhound at the races!" He shut his eyes as if to block out the memory.

"What was it that came at you?" Powell inquired.

"Monsters..." Dwyer replied, losing his composure, sobbing more loudly. He remained upset and unpredictable as ever. "The Hounds of the Otherworld..."

"Can you describe them for me... these *monsters*?"

"I already told you, man. They was *indescribable*: shapeless and purest black."

Haddon shook his head in defeat. Was that it? Was that what he'd stayed behind for? Was this why his dinner was getting cold? All on account of a statement made by a bloke with the same naff taste in clothes as Michael Foot? A miserable poacher, at that, whose experience in the woods came off sounding like the mounds of these hounds? What had started out as an interesting case had rapidly degenerated into a penny dreadful, so shockingly dire, it added up to one of the worst cock-and-bull stories Haddon had ever been forced to endure in his entire career. And he'd certainly heard a lot of cock-and-bull stories in his time! Dwyer, in some ways, really took the biscuit, maybe because nobody in their right mind would barge into a police station at five o'clock on a Friday afternoon and spill out this kind of hooey unless they were really asking for it or perhaps just completely soft in the head. The latter probably applied to Dwyer who looked like he might have a few unresolved issues, a couple of loose screws. *Man*, it could be so *damn* frustrating sometimes when dealing with cranks and crazies. And, my goodness, had Haddon seen his share of both! *You take them seriously, give them your complete, undivided attention, then they pull their pants down and spray diarrhoea into your ear and chuckle about it afterwards with their mates...* We got one over the pigs, didn't we? *they'll tell their mates... No respect, that's what it was, no respect for the law!... Don't you think we've got better things to do than listen to this tasteless twaddle?* It was always easier handling cranks because, at the very least, you could book them for wasting valuable police-time. In most cases, it would deter them from committing any future felony. But, with crazies, it was not so straightforward since their deluded convictions ran deeper than their logic; a police reprimand did no good. A load of old tripe, you could opine of Dwyer's fantastic tale, yet, the worst of it was, Dwyer actually believed it. You couldn't fault him on his earnestness, only the wildness of his story. Haddon doubted the Specials would get involved (they wouldn't touch this case with a piece of bog roll), neither did he expect the local Bill to take an active role. He didn't want to appear callous, but, taking the story purely on its merits, he presumed Powell would dismiss Dwyer by giving him a much-needed slap on the face and the telephone number of the nearest loony-bin. *Creeping trees, insects the size of birds, rabbits with human eyes, slimy, shapeless monsters as black as night itself — I mean I ask you!...*

However, he was surprised when the sergeant's expression grew grave, meaning to pursue the matter further. *Just for the record*, Haddon supposed, *a simple police formality.* "How long do you think you were in the woods?"

"I'm not sure. An hour maybe. Two at the most."

"And you've only just got back?"

"I don't understand…"

"You expect me to believe you spent the best part of a day in the woods and you were only gone two hours?"

"I tell you it's true," Dwyer cried adamantly. "It makes no sense, I know, but you *have* to believe me. It happened like I said."

PC Haddon hadn't failed to notice the essence of apples on Dwyer's breath, almost masked by the general odour of mud and sour exhaustion. Cider, Haddon thought, and judging by the whiff, a great deal of it too. For all practical purposes, he drew his own conclusions, confidently formulating a reliable reconstruction of events: in a nutshell, Dwyer's little adventure kicks off at the pub round about eleven where he downs a few-too-many, goes rabbit-hunting somewhat worse-for-wear, loses track of time, and lands a run-in with some freak shadows which, in turn, he misconstrues as obscure monsters. Case closed.

But Powell didn't think so. The question he followed up with caused Haddon to look at him peculiarly. "Time runs different there, right?"

Powell must have meant well because his comment sent a bright rush of relief and understanding through Dwyer. "So you *do* know what I'm talking about!" Dwyer exclaimed.

"I might do," Powell remarked mysteriously. "But let's not get carried away just yet."

"You have no idea how much it means to me… I thought I was going senile."

Senile, you say? Senile? Why ever for? Make Maltesers in your spare time, do you, sir? Haddon thought with stabbing sarcasm. Evans, on the other hand, had maintained a neutral, noncommittal attitude throughout.

"Righto, I think I've got everything that I need," Powell said, wrapping up the interview. "Feel up to going home by yourself or would you prefer an escort? I bet you could use a brew right now."

It took several strong mugs of tea to settle Dwyer's jangled nerves before he felt brave enough to leave. He refused an escort, as well as Powell's offer of having him checked out by the police surgeon.

When he was gone, Sergeant Powell turned to Evans and Haddon. "I realize this may sound funny coming from me, but I'd like you, lads, to look into Mr. Dwyer's story. If you could drive up to Friend's Grove and try and find this elusive place called Fiend's Grave, I would appreciate it very much."

They were in the lobby when Powell assigned them the job. Evans stood in the doorway to the conference room, Haddon by a rack of pamphlets. On the staff notice-board, above, were tacked numerous internal memos. Public information posters had been put up around the ochre-coloured walls. SPEED KILLS, some said, and DON'T DRINK AND DRIVE. Others read: COMBAT CRIME BY CALLING CRIMEBUSTERS and FIGHT DOMESTIC VIOLENCE WHERE IT HURTS and JOIN THE NEIGHBOURHOOD WATCH SCHEME AND MAKE TOLWYN A SAFER PLACE.

"Oh, but Sarge, you can't be serious…" Haddon objected. "It's my weekend off. I've made plans."

"I'm afraid you're going to have to break those plans of yours," Powell maintained. "You know we're short-staffed."

"Why can't Rhod go by himself?"

"I'd like both of you to go. It won't take long, I promise."

His assurance did little to lift Haddon's sinking heart. The clock at the main entrance stated that it was already half-six and Haddon felt more than frustrated that his shift was about to be extended further. Powell appeared to sense his disappointment and added more kindly: "Do it for me, please. I'll return the favour some time."

Haddon nodded reluctantly. "Do you actually believe that fella's story?" he asked, astonished at his superior's interest in this ludicrous affair. "I mean, it could just be a nasty case of the DTs."

"I wouldn't like to say," Powell replied worriedly. He seemed far from his usual stoical self. "But that's the fifth person in the last month, who's come into the station insisting on having seen such weird creatures in the same fictitious place nobody else can find. Evans will brief you on the way up. There's definitely something shady going on, you can bet on it, and I'd like to know what. Poke around a bit, see what you can find. Report back by nine if you have no success." His attention was now focused on a pretty young lady at reception, accusing her husband of assaulting her with her own vanity-box. "I'll handle her. See you in a short while, lads."

As they prepared to depart the building, PC Neville, who'd only just finished with the disgruntled old lady, crept up to Haddon unawares and whispered conspiratorially: "Wait up, man. Before you go gallivanting off, beware of *Cwn Annwn* and the Time of the Wild Hunt."

West of the Marches lies a strange and lonely country. The sinister-sounding Black Mountains forge a frontier to a place where the hills rise stark and shingled and the vales grow green and wooded. One can ramble around for many miles and never tire of the atmosphere as it awakens the senses, fires up the will and fortifies the soul, satisfying the needs of both the simple pleasure-seeker and the more dedicated countryside-enthusiast. The stretches of cultivated farmland and the rich pastures upon which the livestock graze only enhance the enjoyment of the long walks since these are as pleasing to the eye as any view from a hill. Brooklets trickle silver through the glades, and the occasional barn stands vacant in the corner of some fragrant, brier-bordered meadow in which couples have been known to meet and make love under an August moon. No doubt one should feel alive, liberated, a free spirit, walking this land, in touch with Nature itself, yet one cannot escape the nagging feeling that not all is as it seems. For, in spite of its fabulous rustic beauty, this is also a principality steeped in superstition and the gravest, blackest secrets.

Tolwyn is located somewhere in the Twyi Valley amidst the huddle of mining towns of the Brecon Beacons, most of their pits now closed and used as landfills. Only up until recently the prodigious colliery-wheels were fully operational, each giant revolution conveying a bountiful supply of coal capable of sustaining whole families for months on end. Reduced to sad, hulking monuments of rust, silhouetted against a backdrop of economic ruin, they now persist as a silent reminder of former prosperity and progress, times of pride and passion that once united entire communities to one great single purpose: to provide for their children while preserving the memory of their forefathers. Nowadays, in a morass of broken comradeships and lost livelihoods, the workers have been left to their own devices. Without a steady income, many have fallen prey to drink and despair, wistfully whiling away their remaining days in the local social club. The more motivated amongst them look for employment elsewhere, and, if necessary, are not afraid to migrate beyond the border in their eager quest for a decent working wage. Some try their hand at self-sufficiency, meticulously tending to their allotments in a bid to prove that there are no obstacles posed by the land they were born in. Others indulge in age-old customs, practising arts long-thought dead and forgotten. And strictly forbidden.

Prospects are marginally better along the coastline, particularly with its thriving tourist trade and fishing industry and the revenue generated by such popular university towns as Aberystwyth and Bangor. But, there again, those on welfare outnumber those in the employment sector.

Northwards, the villages and solitary farmsteads dwindle away as the terrain becomes hard rock and achieves the grandiose. A plethora of peaks chokes the horizon and there exist valleys of primeval forest that remain unexplored to this day, untrodden by man, unfelled by any axe, perhaps untouched by the briefest hint of sunlight. It is even claimed that the constant midnight of certain coombs conceals colonies of dark, degenerate creatures unrecorded in any Nature index. Only a handful of rut-ridden roads and curse-muttering rivers connect these remote regions, the few far-flung settlements avoided at all costs by the lone traveller. For queer are these places and queerer still are the people. Strangers are shunned, the inhabitants quick at showing open hostility to any outsiders. There is talk of witchcraft and dark legends and tales of terror that would chill even the most fearless of dreadnoughts.

The stories are many, but the admirers are few. These so-called legends are usually handed down over generations to a people who are often reluctant to share their esoteric knowledge with the outside world, exiled from the rest of us by their own choosing, committed wholly to their ancient beliefs and their conscious ignorance of civilization. Fortunately, a more reliable source can be found in the irrepressible curiosity hound, for whom these backwaters are awe-inspiring and a regular haunt. It is therefore not unreasonable to assume that they may indeed hold the key to unlocking the tantalizing secrets inherent to these parts, for they have actually been there and seen the evidence for themselves. Such connoisseurs of the macabre always have some dread encounter or another to relate, a personal experience that excited them in all its ghastliness or threatened to drive them to the very edge of lunacy. They will then knowingly point toward the strange, olden ruins which crown so many of the Cambrian hills, morbid curiosity satisfied. Since, here, lies the answer, in these sinister remnants of a past best left unmentioned.

These circles of standing stone, now badly eroded, once central to the old ways.

Supposing one were to find out the awful truth…

PC Haddon was unwinding at THE WHITE SWAN, trying to erase a hard day's tedium from his mind, when Hywel Glendower sauntered over and passed a peculiar comment his way. "It wasn't always called Tolwyn, you know."

Haddon had been married nearly a month to Glendower's daughter, Sian, and it would be a good three days before Dwyer would stumble into the police station. He glanced up from his beer-glass, somewhat unsettled by his father-in-law's gruff tone.

"I didn't quite catch that."

"I'm saying our town wasn't always called Tolwyn," Glendower repeated glaringly, causing Haddon to cower inwardly. Haddon immediately wondered what he'd done to upset Glendower, then realized the old man was probably only trying to make conversation. It was amazing how common an error this was when speaking with Glendower, whose towering presence not only dwarfed Haddon's own by a good seven inches, but also scared the living hell out of him each time, and once again Haddon paused to wonder how this boorish man could, in any way, be the father of his beloved Sian. Sian, who was a slightly taller-than-average, blue-eyed blond babe, miles better-looking than any Catherine Zeta-Jones and certainly no highfalutin bitch… and this man, this huge man, this giant of a man with his leathery skin, white, shoulder-length hair, prominent brow, double-barrelled chin and dark, piercing eyes, who looked at least a hundred years of age, a rugged, youthful hundred years, mind you, but still old enough to be her great-grandfather. Maybe she was adopted. Haddon decided not to ask.

"Won't you join me?" Haddon said politely, intimidated as ever, feeling an interrogation coming on.

Glendower grinned, showing off a couple of his gold teeth. He grabbed a stool opposite. "You know, I think I will." He called over to the barmaid, the very buxom Bernadette who looked rather ravishing, dressed as a serving wench. "Give us a drink, dear." He checked Haddon's almost empty glass. "Care for a refill?" he asked, in response to which Haddon nodded. "Make that two ales."

Haddon had already consumed six pints, and suddenly didn't feel quite as merry as he had moments earlier. Glendower had something of a sobering effect on him. Still, another drink wouldn't hurt, especially when tackling a man like Glendower. Render the dialogue between them more agreeable.

At the counter, Bernadette rang the bell. "Last orders!" she decreed. There were a few disappointed groans from a group of men gathered in the furthest booth, but most of the crowd went about their conversations uninterrupted.

Haddon caught some of the friendly chatter that drifted across the room, though could make no clear headway of what was being discussed. It was a packed house tonight, and the prevailing mood was one of sweeping exuberance interspersed with vibrant laughter and sporadic bursts of drunken singing. Haddon had to admit he was rather taken by the local inn, which provided a welcome change from the drinking establishments he and his former colleagues used to frequent back home. Wine bars, mostly. *Talk about pretentious.* He remembered meeting Sian for the first time at a colleague's leaving-do in a Kensington wine-bar/bistro and presently thinking what a dive it was by comparison, with its 'trendy', ritzer-and-spritzer clientele, who were snobbish and stuck-up and, generally, a bleeding pain-in-the-arse. Moneyed, mineral-drinking poseurs the lot of them. Incredibly, he'd never got round to asking Sian what she was doing there in the first place. Nor, for that matter, what he was doing there himself. Did he once honestly believe he would fit in famously with all those shallow, greed-fixated bright young things? *Afraid so.* Done up in a mock-Tudor style, THE WHITE SWAN was as small, quaint and lively as any social ought to be. A proper working man's club. Wooden beams supported the ceiling, and the long bar possessed real, black, vintage pull-pumps that seemed to be a sorely-missed item in most modern pubs. No slot machines, no noisy jukeboxes, no woeful karaoke nights, just the wild bacchanale of good, honest, hardworking folk. The comforting smell of smoke and sweat and spirits.

Bernadette came over with the two pints of ale, placing them on a coaster each. "Will that be all?"

"Yes, my dear," Glendower replied with a mischievous grin. "Now you run along and keep my customers happy, you hear?" He slapped her playfully on the rump and she withdrew, giggling, as any saucy wench accustomed to her boss's bawdy behaviour does. Besides, in Haddon's opinion, she didn't seem much like the type who would protest. "Nothing wrong with a bit of harmless fun, what do you say, my boy?" he added.

Haddon smiled weakly. His mind went back to his wife. She seemed content her hubby spend his evenings in the company of her dad, which was fundamentally okay (father and son-in-law should invest some time together, get to know each other as family), except it rarely left time for much else—like sharing some valuable quality-time with his new-found bride. At the moment, their relationship wasn't exactly going according to plan; just lately, the spark between them had faded and they seemed to be stuck in some sort of hiatus. He'd fallen for her in a big way ever since he'd found her caught up in the London tourist trap, had proposed to her within days of their first encounter and subsequently tied the knot less than a [record-breaking] week later. Not so much a snap decision as rash, some might have called it (and those who knew Haddon knew him never to be impulsive), but it had been peaches and roses back then, and Sian had been everything Haddon could ever have wanted in a girl. He hadn't had much experience of the fairer sex—he had only ever dated two women in his entire twenty-eight years on this planet—and when Sian made her feelings to him known, he had been unable to resist. Her looks had floored him the instant they made eye-contact, looks that could have graced Page 3, but it was her adventurous spirit combined with a sweet homeliness and her rather inexplicable interest in him that won him over. He considered her perfect (well, almost, save for his slight, niggling qualms about her Welsh upbringing) and he had wanted her more than anything. His little diamond in the rough, he used to think of her. *What's it like beinn' marrit to the morst boot'ful girl in the wurld?* Sian would often ask him in bed late at night. He'd never figured out if this was a sign of insecurity or whether she was just being adorably vain. *A treat, my sweet!* he would always reply by way of compliment. But now, with their arrival to her home town, they were seeing far too less of each other and, when they did, they hardly spoke, as if they'd run out of things to say. They had also begun to argue a lot lately which didn't bode well for things to come. Perhaps they were going through a bad patch, and things would eventually pick up. To round it off, he just didn't like her old man. Glendower looked like the kind of person who, if you got on his wrong side, would gladly snap your spine in half.

"One for me," Glendower said, bringing his pint-glass up to his lips, "and one for my brand new son." He pushed Haddon's glass towards him. "Now drink up, my boy. There's no fine ale than there is here." Glendower gulped his down heartily, whilst Haddon raised his in a formal salute before sipping slowly. Admittedly, the local brew wasn't bad, but neither was it anything worth bragging about. Haddon had tasted better.

"Give my little girl a good pump of your hose after," Glendower said quite unexpectedly, and Haddon spewed his drink out in a fit of violent coughing.

Did he hear him right? Did he really say that?

"You alright, my boy?" Glendower asked as if nothing untoward had been said.

Haddon nodded moments later, eyes streaming as he brought his coughing under control. "I'll make it..." he spluttered. He took another sip of his ale to lubricate his throat. Haddon always found it hard to take the undignified way in which Glendower spoke of his only daughter. It defied belief. Was this how the Welsh spoke of their loved ones, or was this merely Glendower's usual brand of humour? Haddon wanted to believe the latter, but he couldn't be sure. You could never tell with the Welsh, with their eager willingness to offend or be offended. Glendower did it to him every evening. Made him feel all flushed and uncomfortable. Tact hadn't yet caught on in this town, it seemed. On no account could Haddon simply sit around and allow his wife to be insulted in such a way—what he and Sian got up to in the bedroom was between them and them alone, and definitely nobody else's business, and they most certainly didn't need any encouragement from his father-in-law—and, one of these days, he planned to put the old man in his position. He wouldn't have minded knocking the old man's block off right now, if only he didn't feel so threatened by him. Haddon decided to defend Sian's honour some other time.

"Only kidding," Glendower said, as though he had read Haddon's thoughts. He grinned broadly, adding: "If you don't learn to lighten up once in a while, you won't survive half a minute in this town."

Somehow, Glendower's reassurance didn't have the desired effect it should have had. Haddon remained quietly wary, one particular question at the back of his mind resting uneasily. Could it be the old man wasn't so much teasing him but actually *testing* him? Vetting him? Seeing how he'd respond? Looking to see if he would make the wrong move? Testing whether Haddon was worthy marriage material or only in it for Sian's body? On which note, Haddon thought it safer to change the topic of conversation. "You were going to tell me about Tolwyn..."

"Ah, yes, I was, wasn't I?" Glendower said with the look of someone about to embark on a long nostalgic journey. He seemed surprisingly better-informed and smarter than most of the natives. Perhaps on account of his age. But also far too volatile. "Tolwyn: I'm something of an authority on the subject. Know much about its history do you?"

"Just what little I gathered from Sian." It had been shortly after he and Sian had got hitched when she persuaded him to move down to this godforsaken town. All because she loved him and she happened to be born here. She was supposedly experiencing the agonizing throes of *hiraeth*: longing for the old country. Back to a simpler time, she had said, and he, like a fool, had obliged. He'd gone into the reference department of a London library to uncover more about her beloved hometown, but had surprisingly found scant-to-no-mention of it in the various guidebooks. Even the most recent Ordnance Survey maps had conveniently ignored its existence. Which, in itself, was puzzling to say the very least.

"I bet she didn't tell you it used to be called Touen," Glendower said, deliberately tapping the side of his nose with his forefinger.

Haddon tried to appear on the surface interested. "What's the relevance?"

"Well, in Celtic mythology, *touen* meant a druid place of dark rituals and human sacrifices. The weaklings of the community, those unwell or injured in battle, were regularly offered up for slaughter to the powers of Nature. Druidism believed that the only way to preserve a man's life was by letting another burn in his place often inside huge figures made of wickerwork. You could look at it as a bit like balancing the books. A blood pact between the human and supernatural worlds."

Fascinating stuff, I'm sure, Haddon mused, bored already.

"The Roman general, Paulinus, stopped these pagan acts of worship in 52AD. Caesar himself had made a detailed record of the rites of the ancient druids in his journals during his campaigns almost a century earlier. Some say that the druids had become corrupt and impure which led to their eventual downfall. I say they branched out, became *heterodoxical*."

Heterodoxical? Haddon thought disdainfully. *Nice, fancy way of putting it! Personally, any religion that advocates the burning of people in pyres deserves all the flak it gets.*

"The Romans may have passed their own laws," Glendower explained, getting into his stride, "but they never changed the name of the town. They had no time to—how could they? Not after an entire legion of Roman soldiers vanished. Quite literally. Disappeared without a trace. *No-one knew where they went.*" He grinned, a cold mocking grin that seemed to magnify what he had just said. Haddon felt the hairs on the back of his neck prickle. "The Danes did not dare invade. Then came the Norman Conquest, but they too left in a hurry." Glendower continued, growing serious again. "Once more, our rain and mountains had saved us. But we knew the peace wouldn't last. Things were about to change in the late thirteenth century. That scheming tyrant, Edward I—Edward Longshanks to his enemies—was about to do his worst. He defeated Llywelyn the Last in battle and seized our land, annexed our people. Slaughtered thousands, subjugated the rest, made slaves of them. Ruled over us with an iron fist. The bastard even tried to wipe out our very Welshness. Of course, there were many national uprisings in the centuries that followed, including my ancestor Owain Glyndwr's famous revolt in 1403, but sadly he must have realized they stood little chance of stopping the rot set in by the English scum. We still suffer today because of it... present company excepted."

Those last few grudging words trampled Haddon where he sat. "That's very big of you," he remarked, lying through his teeth, disguising the sarcasm in his voice with some difficulty. "I can't thank you enough for making me feel so at home." *And many thanks for your very colourful diatribe, prejudiced though it was. No love lost there then. How can anyone not admire your political candour? Good to be direct with one's fellow man. Very illuminating. Diplomacy was never your forte, was it?* Haddon had clearly exposed Glendower for the flaming Anglophobe that he was. *So what else is new? I'm a flaming Taffyphobe and proud of it, your daughter's company excepted.* Significant still, it added one more glorious black mark to Haddon's list of reasons for hating Glendower and, in general, having to live in this dump of a town. "Why you telling me all this?"

Without warning, Glendower leapt from his stool. "Why…? *Why*…?" he bellowed with barely-governable rage. "I'll tell you why!" For a moment Haddon thought Glendower was going to thump him — the inn had suddenly gone silent as though in anticipation of this outcome — then he saw the landlord check his temper, his surly expression mellowing out, much to Haddon's relief. The aggression was gone from his voice when he next spoke, and again Haddon marvelled at how a policeman like himself could be intimidated so easily by this brute. "There's nothing to see here…" Glendower reassured his customers. "Just having a chat and a quiet drink with my new son, that's all." Everyone went back to what they were doing. Glendower picked up his stool and sat himself back down. Haddon returned to his ale, sipping it shakily. "Because it's important that you know," replied Glendower with the solemn tone of someone intimating a great family secret.

Fair enough, Hadden thought, trying not to give away his trembling exterior. The old man had certainly got his attention. *I'm not complaining.* "You just go on right ahead. I won't interrupt you again."

"I am a Glendower from a long line of Glendowers, descended from our Silures forefathers. There have been Glendowers who rallied the nation against the English overlords, Glendowers who set sail for the New World, Glendowers who fought in the Great War and lived to tell the tale, Glendowers who laboured down the mines night and day only to see their coal snatched away and their villages ruined, Glendowers who guided their colliery band to the regional finals and won, Glendowers who signed petitions calling for Welsh independence and took us one step closer. So I am a Glendower through-and-through in whose very veins courses the blood of heroes, martyrs and warrior-kings."

"I guess, I ought to feel privileged," Haddon said, sounding dubious. "I had no idea I was in the presence of such esteemed royalty."

His scepticism went unnoticed. Glendower lectured on. "Christianity may have spread its wings far and wide, but rumours persisted hereabouts, claiming that black druidism was far from dead. Reports of an underground movement, committed to the old ways, forced to conduct its midnight ceremonies in secret. That is, until 1745 when the squire of the parish, William Shepley, rooted out all those involved and sentenced them to the gallows. Every activity which he perceived as deviant or not in keeping with his Christian beliefs, he stamped out with a ruthlessness unseen even in the highest ranks of the clergy, and the town's name was finally changed to Tolwyn."

Good for him, observed Haddon. Then a thought crossed his mind that he had not really considered before. It concerned the local church which stood boarded-up on Gadfield Road, and it suddenly occurred to him that he had never once questioned its abandonment. It had been closed since he'd arrived in Tolwyn and there were no signs suggesting that it was being renovated. He himself wasn't much of a church-goer (he'd got married at the registry office in Chiswick, a quick ceremony, boycotted by his middle-class parents who hadn't approved of his choice of wife, her being Welsh having something to do with it), but what of the local priest? Haddon didn't know of any in Tolwyn, of either faiths. If so, where did all the Christian worshippers go on Sunday mornings? Out of town, perhaps? *Were* there any Christian worshippers in this town?

"The title of druid still survives in these parts," Glendower declared, yielding a disconcerted glance from Haddon. "You mustn't jump to conclusions. Druidism is not what it used to be. The term now only ever applies to the annual festival we call *Eisteddfod*, a competition of Celtic poetry, drama and music of which I am a chairing member and chief adjudicator. At the end we always stage a play that features many regular faces, including your Sergeant Powell's as indeed it did my little girl's."

"Do you mind elaborating?" Haddon said at the mention of his wife.

"I, myself, am in the play, *Hywl Glyndwr*, gentle narrator and First Emissary. Sergeant Powell depicts both Pwyll and Arawn interchangeably, the Prince of Dyfed and Guardian of the Otherworld respectively. Rhodri Evans's role is just as crucial: Pwca, the shapeshifting rogue who leads benighted travellers astray. My little girl used to portray *Ceridwen*, Beautiful Sorceress, Enchantress of the Lake and Goddess of Dawn and Rebirth, before she went off sight-seeing in London and met you."

Haddon could not have been more impressed, despite being of the ilk that cryptic lore never really amounted to much. More to the point, he had never imagined Sian might have hidden talents. Now he knew. *Sorceress, Enchantress, Goddess?* Was that Sian's contribution to this bardic Welshfest? Haddon could scarcely conceive of her overcoming her natural shyness, let alone performing drama in front of a live audience, and was mildly astonished she'd never broached the subject whilst they'd been out dating. Maybe she had thought it unimportant. "What's the play called?"

"*The Indescription.*" Glendower noticed Haddon's peculiar frown. "I know, strange though it may sound, all the same, an ingenious piece of writing."

"When's it held?"

"Around this time of year. Very soon, actually. Other towns tend to hold theirs seasons apart, but we prefer harvest-time. Gives us hope when the crops are bad."

"Worth a look, I suppose."

"Well-said, my boy. You know, there might even be a part in it for you."

"No, I couldn't—"

"—Impose? Not at all, my boy, not at all. Rehearsals might nearly be over, but I'm sure they can still fit you in somewhere."

Although it had seemed like a good idea at the time, exciting even, for a second or two at least, thinking it through now, Haddon didn't feel much up to the challenge. "Don't get me wrong. I don't mind a spot of amateur dramatics. I just don't think I would be suitable for—"

Glendower didn't let him finish. "Then, it's settled," he said, beaming. "Let's toast to your participation. Need I mention, we could do with some new blood."

Haddon was stumped. In spite his best efforts to the contrary, he'd just got himself cast in a play and, considering he'd never acted before in his entire life, the prospect filled him with dread. Haddon wondered whether he should flat-out refuse, then thought the better of it, lest Glendower should take exception and blow his top.

However, Glendower wasn't about to blow his top. "How's about my little girl then?" he said. Instead of instructing Haddon he get a few tips off her, seek out some of her acting skills, the landlord, father-in-law and respected man-about-town asked with a wink and a lewd grin: "Going to get your leg over again tonight?"

Haddon had been totally unprepared for this remark, and he produced a grin of his own—a fool's grin—an awkward, cringeworthy grin more out of shock than humour. He just couldn't help it. What was it with this man? Why was he deliberately acting like a pimp? Did he have no shame? Didn't he have any respect for his daughter? Worse still, was it possible he was eavesdropping at their door at night? *Give it a rest, for chrissakes, and stay out of our private business! Try getting your jollies elsewhere!*

He didn't realize the rest of the inn had overheard their landlord. When the place suddenly erupted into coarse whistles, roars of laughter and lusty cheering in support of Glendower's carnal blessing, the shock was complete.

"What was all that about?" Haddon asked Evans in the near-empty police car-park. They were climbing into their Vauxhall Astra, the official vehicle, a chequered black-and-gold stripe running along both sides. The early evening air was shimmering, the sky lavender-blue, the sun gilded with fire. Haddon could only squint against the sunlight. The polished chrome of PC Neville's cherished motorbike glinted invitingly nearby. PC Brydon's death-trap, a sickly pink Morris Minor, looked unnaturally hale, ready for action. The only other vehicle in the vicinity, Powell's ordinary white Montego, shone with the light of Heaven.

"What was all what about?"

"You know, Neville and that stuff about the Wild Hunt."

"Oh…" PC Evans said absently.

"Well?"

"Well, what?"

"Well, aren't you going to tell me about it?"

"I will."

"When?"

"Later..."

Haddon sighed in exasperation as he turned on the ignition, flipping down the sun-visor in the process. He didn't need this right now. The interior was hot to touch and his bum was burning. The only thing that seemed more perishing than the heat was Evans's inability to form complete sentences. Loquaciousness was a paradox with him, a contradiction in terms. Many a night Evans could be seen in the mess-hall playing solitaire in silence, avoiding all conversation and company. One might have mistaken him to be a deaf-mute, save for the fact that sometimes, when the conditions were right, he would be known to talk utter *bollocks*. Examples were far and few between, but a favourite amongst the men was the time Evans got sick-drunk on New Year's Eve and went on at great lengths to discuss the insides of a ping-pong ball whilst he was busy heaving. Gauging information from him for routine, mundane, prosaic matters was a similarly galling experience as it could take you a lifetime before he told you who he was, where he was and what the hell he was doing here. Was he really good for anything, except talking Bollocks?

As they began their drive out of the car-park onto Station Road, Haddon wondered why Evans was being so reticent about Neville's disquieting comment, but chose not to inquire further. *Not just yet*, Haddon told himself sagely. *Best not to push him. Better to wait until he's ready.*

They passed the small railway station where a solitary figure, dressed in an immaculate blue business suit, was standing on the far platform. Perhaps waiting to catch the 19:05 to Swansea.

It'll be late, Haddon guessed, smiling slyly. *The trains are never on time. You'll be waiting for another half-hour if you're lucky.* He recalled his first day in Tolwyn, almost a month ago. He'd taken three trains from London, and none of them had been on time, resulting in a loss of a day's worth of wages. *Too many signal failures this time*, according to British Rail, another classic from the ones that brought you the wrong type of snow and the dangers of autumn leaves on the line. Privatized or unprivatized, BR or Railtrack, or whatever those useless, incompetent pricks were called these days, would never change their transport policy: *Poor Service, High Prices.* Or was it, *High Prices, Poor Service?... Whatever happened to the Great Western Railway? At least, it was more efficient. Or, for that matter,* Ivor the Engine.

"Fag, Mitch?" Evans offered, sprinkling Old Holborn into some rolling paper.

"No thanks, I have my own." Keeping control of the wheel, Haddon pulled out a B&H from its pack and lit it up with Evans's box of matches. He drove past the local branch of Lloyds-TSB on the High Street, and Woolworth's and the town's Burger King, newly opened for fast-food junkies. People queued outside the local cinema, which was re-showing *The Remains of the Day* starring the *true* Prince of Wales, Anthony Hopkins, successor to the crown held by the late Richard Burton. That idle scrounger and insufferable prat, Prince Charles, didn't know the first thing about Wales; *what had he ever done for the country?* as Glendower had once remarked. *If you suddenly got rid of the monarchy and their royal estate, the Windsors would be at the dole office because they've not done a decent day's work in their life and are therefore so bleeding useless at everything!* Welsh devolution was a welcome relief and many centuries overdue.

Along the way was the old Elizabethan inn, THE WHITE SWAN, where Haddon had been enlightened only yesterday that beefy Bernie was giving big Bernadette the old sinful treatment, as the bishop said to the netball team in the girls' changing room.

Fitting into this strange society was equivalent to a migraine headache for Haddon. He craved personal space, but circumstances never seemed to allow it. After their nuptials, he had searched frantically for a decent place for himself and his wife, but had found none. There wasn't a single apartment available in the whole of Tolwyn so Sian had suggested they stay at her family home for a while. Glendower had been only too happy to accommodate them (rent-free, of course) in the plushest guest-room at the inn. They'd accepted it graciously. However, Haddon still didn't much relish the idea of having to kip under the same roof as a man who was unnaturally keen that Haddon shag his only daughter.

They left the High Street, turning right onto Duke Street. The Magistrates' Court and Council offices were situated here, and there was less traffic and fewer pedestrians. The parking lots were almost vacant, probably awaiting an influx of young clubbers who would undoubtedly make the police dance to their tune later on. *And where are our invaluable pen-pushers all this time? Why, at home, of course, lounging around the house while some poor copper gets a broken bottle in the face... I mean, you can't expect anybody in administration or the judiciaries to work on a Friday evening, can you,* Haddon thought cuttingly, *especially when they're supposed to be off-duty? Even the overtimers finish early. Only the domestics hang around to mop up the remains of the day.*

Another right turn. The beginning of Gadfield Road. The steeple and tower of the derelict church loomed into view, and once again Haddon noticed how old and abandoned it looked, much like those tumbledown warehouses on Potter's Lane long-shutdown and awaiting demolition. The stone facade was filthy and weathered and crumbling and thickly covered with moss. The windows were boarded-up, blindfolds to a blind man. The path from the missing gate to the actual building was completely overgrown. Rather than feeling pity for this decrepit Christian edifice, Haddon was instantly repelled by it, yet struggled to define why. He puzzled over why the church-goers had left it to ruin so. Was there something symbolic behind its state of decay?

The town centre began to fade away as streets of slant-roofed, terraced houses took hold. Children played tag and hopscotch and pitch-and-toss on the pavements, and, like so many children do, stopped only to follow the progress of the police car as it cruised by. Men, drinking and chatting on the front stoops, too adopted the same curious gaze as the children. There were no women about, probably indoors preparing supper. The side-streets sloped uphill with rows of houses that were indistinguishable from one another, grey-stoned two-up, two-downs that exuded a pleasant lived-in look and an overwhelming sense of family. The westering sun drew long shadows from the people and buildings alike, the accompanying heat as oppressive as ever. Haddon considered it a rather homely scene, conforming to both expectation and old tradition, a way of life that was a dying rarity in the big cities. He could even imagine heaps of coal piled up on each doorstep during the winters gone by, the inhabitants wallowing in their daily ration of warmth in those far-off days before the globalization of gas and the inevitable pit-closures that would bring poverty to the community. Boys in flannel-shorts riding their bicycles up and down the street. Little girls in pretty dresses skipping and giggling and disclosing secret crushes to their best friends. Their fathers, in string-vests and braces, smoking and joking and enjoying a cold one in the sultry early evening air. The engaging aroma of mince-and-onions wafting up through the open kitchen windows. The sound of a TV somewhere, blaring out *Pobol y Cwm*. Washing drying on lines in the backyards. Outside toilets. *Oh, Nana Myfanwy, those were the days!*

Haddon returned to the mystery itching his curiosity. "You going to tell me or not?"

"What about?" Evans asked.

"About the Wild Hunt?" Haddon said, feeling a sense of déjà vu. "The suspense is killing me."

Evans glanced at Haddon with an uninterested eye. "I'll tell you..." he answered, trailing off.

Haddon was getting distinctly pissed-off. "When?"

"After I've finished my fag," Evans replied lazily, his makeshift cigarette dangling limply from his lips. His perm was a tragedy to look at and one of the handlebars of his outrageous moustache was slightly longer than the other.

Haddon groaned inwardly. You just couldn't win with him. There was nothing amicable between them, that much was for sure. Nor, likewise, between Haddon and the rest of Cymru. Evans did his very best to get on Haddon's pecs, which he more often than not succeeded in doing without even trying, but it was only because the mentality of most of the Welsh defied belief. Haddon had been informed before he'd unwisely moved to Tolwyn that the Taffymen were relentless sheep-shaggers, crazed rugger fanatics and appalling close-harmony singers. What he hadn't been told was that they were also a bunch of slothful, dull-witted country bumpkins, who didn't give a damn what happened in the rest of the world as long as they got their beer and fags on time. True, Wales wasn't all that bad. It boasted a fantastic landscape, employed numerous wind-farms which could harness infinite reserves of natural energy, and was, as one BBC scientific correspondent put it, in the event of a devastating nuclear strike on London, the only region in Britain apart from the Scottish Highlands that could survive the fall-out. But that didn't compensate for the fact that the Welsh were wankers — in general, sad, uncultured *twats* — and if Haddon had his way, he'd arrest the whole bally lot of them (Sian excluded) for ever being born. Their lack of worldly sophistication was legendary. Their national dish, rarebit, was basically cheese-on-toast. The defining ingredient of laverbread was—*get a load of this*—seaweed. And the Welsh accent: *I mean, what kind of confounded gibberish was that supposed to be?* A tribute to Stone Age man? The grammar was totally wonky, the letters *a* and *e* were phonetically interchangeable, the consonants between vowels were lengthened, and strange fricatives were in operation, for example, *ll* was spoken *cl*. *And that's just for starters!* Haddon always felt he was speaking to someone with a leek lodged terminally up their backside, let alone saying the town names which could take you a year to pronounce and required at least half-a-pint of phlegm in your throat. Take *Llanfairpwllgwyngyllgogerychwyrndrobwllllantysiliogogogoch*, for instance. Even *Rwy'n dy garu di* (or, in normal-speak, *I love you*) sounded about as romantic as a rape threat. No use complaining to the Commons Welsh Select Committee or *Cymdeithas yr Iaith Gymraeg* (the Welsh Language Society); they didn't have a clue what was going on either. *There ought to be a law against a name like Hywel*, Haddon declared. The people, the dialect, the culture. *Troglodytes, I'm surrounded by troglodytes!*

Haddon didn't want to sound racist, but, God, he *hated* this country. He had spent the last few days trying to pluck up enough courage to ask his wife if they could move back to London. This brave deed he had to do without upsetting her. For fear of retribution. They'd had a bit of a lover's tiff over his less-than-flattering comments about her father, and Haddon had been terrified that she would run down the hall and tell him. Luckily for Haddon, she hadn't, and they'd slept apart on the same bed last night. He'd found it hard to nod off, chewing over their relationship in his mind—whether it was over and that he should have listened to his parents. He hadn't made love to her since they'd frolicked in the hayloft of the old barn in Leighton Field. That had been a poignant moment for both of them (beautiful though it had been, and very different, Haddon had felt a certain finality about it, a strange, sad feeling that they'd never make love again, which he had found rather worrying), and since then, she had refused any sexual advances, turning him down gently, despite Glendower's "pimping" attitude concerning his daughter. Haddon wondered if there was something intimate going on between father and daughter, or whether she was seeing someone else.

Further up, the terraced streets gave way to a consortium of more upmarket houses, mainly large semi-detached. Quieter streets. Clean, litter-free kerbs. Primly-trimmed hedgerows. A car in every driveway. Two-point-four children and a modest mortgage. A roost reserved solely for middle-income earners and retired couples, Haddon reckoned. *I guess, the closest we'll ever get to the 'Burbs in Tolwyn.* He noticed how many of the houses in the area were up for sale. The streets too were quiet—*deathly* quiet to be exact—and it was this very air of vacancy that perplexed Haddon. Where was everybody? *Coming from a country where it's supposed to rain every other day, you expect at least somebody to be out and about on this hot Friday evening.*

I imagine they're round the back sunning themselves or holding a barbecue on the patio...

Don't be so sure—

A lone telephone box, the type that had been disbanded in favour of the newer, modern BT phone-booths, stood gleaming-red at the junction of Gadfield Road and Tolwyn Pass. It seemed to somehow enhance the overall effect of emptiness, and Haddon got a strong suspicion that Tolwyn was a town living in the past. Stuck in the old ways, averse to change. Almost as if the former occupants of this short, suburban belt had become disenchanted for some reason and had resolved to move to a more affordable, less contemporary neighbourhood.

Now that makes perfect sense.

Does it?

[Living in the past...]

He couldn't have been more right, as he would soon find out.

The houses dispersed as the two constables headed out of Tolwyn. Exiting Gadfield Road, they cruised through open countryside, along Tolwyn Pass, destined for Midden Hill Road. The sky had taken on a delightful auburn colour. As the sun continued its steady descent, Haddon continued to sweat gallons.

Evans stubbed out his roll-up and started building another, the contract between them broken, much to Haddon's exasperation. The irritation, the frustration, the despair. The man was constantly testing his patience. Why had Powell sent him on what was obviously a wild goose chase with, of all people, Evans? Haddon was meant to be off-duty, not spending his Friday evening trapped in the same car as El Weirdo, running up another fool's errand. He considered this crummy case he'd been assigned to, The Case of the Slimy Monsters, the ultimate insult to injury. *If you don't mind, Sarge, I should be at home with my wife, kissing and making-up, investigating The Case of the Girl with the Big Tits!*

Before you could say *Supercalifragilisticexpialidocious*, the job was done and the rollie in his mouth, Evans puffing away merrily. He flicked the ash out of the window. He said nothing for a while, which infuriated Haddon even more. Just when Haddon was about to clip him round the earhole, Evans dispensed with his unique brand of procrastinating and decided to talk: "I believe you wanted to know about the Wild Hunt?"

Yes, a lifetime ago, Haddon thought, annoyed but also grateful. *If it's not too much bother.*

"It's an old tale, deeply rooted in Celtic myth…" Evans began in a dreamy, laid-back tone.

"And?"

"First, I think I must tell you something about the history of our little town."

"Don't bother. Mr. Glendower was kind enough to enlighten me on the subject the other night. A history lesson I won't be forgetting in a hurry."

"So you know Tolwyn has a bad history?"

"I do indeed," said Haddon, demanding: "Please get on with it."

"Legend says that the Wild Hunt is the time when *Cwn Annwn* are unleashed."

"*Cwn Annwn?*"

"The Hounds of the Otherworld, owned by gods and acting as psychopomps, forever in search of fresh souls to ferry across to the Other Side. Their death portent to anyone who hears them is the beagling sound of bloodhounds."

"Where would we be without good, old-fashioned, lame-brained superstition?" Haddon said wryly. Despite his reservations, he found himself smiling. *Don't stop him now. He's on a roll.*

"It's part of our heritage," Evans said with pride.

"I'm not doubting it," Haddon observed. "But it's only a legend. And, with all legends, means diddly-squat."

"That's not what Thomas Dwyer thought," Evans challenged.

"And you know what I think of Thomas Dwyer…" Haddon replied curtly, immediately regretting his choice of words. It showed downright unprofessionalism on his part to dismiss Dwyer straight-off as just another emotionally-unstable hospital-case without properly investigating his claims. On the other hand, neither did he wish to be drawn into an argument, particularly on this puerile nonsense. "What I'm trying to politely say is, how is any of this pertinent to our present situation… you know, the problem of finding Fiend's Grave?" Then he added querulously. "You got something useful to say or do I have to hire a private detective?"

"I've been here all my life and I can tell you I've heard some of the strangest things… things where the rules of common sense don't apply… things that would make your skin crawl…" Evans was staring at Haddon eerily. "Fiend's Grave is supposed to be one of those places. Tales of mindcrushing terror and bloodcurdling horror."

Not quite the answer I was hoping for, Haddon thought, *but what can you do?* The poacher's ravings were at the forefront of his mind and the constable would never forget the craziness of it all. "Go on…" *This had better be good.*

"Well, over the years, people have gone missing, never to be seen again," Evans informed him. "Hitchhikers, hill-climbers, hippies, bikers, *even policemen.*"

"You're kidding me, right?"

"No, on the level," Evans resumed, dragging deeply on his rollie. "There was this bobby called Wilkes. A nice enough fellow he was too. Hardworking. Always made the most of his beat. Had just moved here like yourself… Well, he went out on a call one night, you know, in that terrible Winter of Discontent… *and he never returned…* Just never came back from his call. I remember, we searched the whole town for him and we never found him again. *Never*, I say!"

Probably got peeved-off with Tolwyn and did a runner back to England, Haddon resisted remarking. Could it be that Evans was pulling his leg, what with the queer look and that spooky voice? If he was trying to unnerve him, then it wasn't working. Haddon shot him a peculiar look back. No policeman would be daft enough to go missing. Then Haddon remembered the Roman garrison that supposedly disappeared under mysterious circumstances. Really? Was it possible…?

"Here one minute, gone the next. Like the earth just opened up and swallowed him whole."

"Is that so?"

"Not only that, but my sister once saw a horrid-looking *ellyllon*—a poison elf—that stood outside her kitchen window… just watching her, it was. She ran outside with a broom and, when she cornered it in the alleyway round the back, it disappeared. I say, simply vanished into thin air…"

Yep, it was the Return of the Bollocks. *He's got to be yanking my chain. Either that or his sister was on something, probably illegal… Mushroom elf, more like.* And Evans too for that matter if he believed her. *I mean, is that the best he can come up with?* "Ever seen any of it yourself?"

"No, and believe me, I don't want to," Evans said, and Haddon thought he actually saw him shiver. "You stick around here and you'll hear some of the strangest things."

Haddon didn't intend on sticking around here. He was a tough, ambitious young man, who saw himself promoted to Detective Inspector at Scotland Yard, ten years from now. Top Brass. He was only here because he was doing his homesick wife a favour, but sure, he'd leave this crazy place alright, where the local constabulary sounded as preposterous as the panic-stricken plonker who'd entered the police station earlier. There certainly couldn't be anything normal about Evans either, who was as eccentric as he looked. He wondered if Powell was as nutty as Evans.

The auburn colour of the sky had deepened to a murky-red and the sun had already begun to dip below the distant hills when Haddon swung the car onto a long, flat stretch of country road, which he promptly assumed was Midden Hill Road. The trees, shrubbery and fields fell away, ceded by wilder, untamed grassland. A sense of wrongness about time and place bit into Haddon's contemplations, but he ignored this uncanny feeling, blaming it on his lack of sleep the previous night.

"Read science fiction, do you, boyo?" Evans asked, out of the blue.

"You know, stuff about parallel universes, alternate dimensions and mysterious time-slips?"

All the time! Haddon thought, finding it impossible to curb his sarcasm. *I always make it my daily duty to read science fiction every evening. Honest! AS IF...!* His mind went back to secondary school and he vaguely recalled reading material by H.G. Wells and John Wyndham, and he remembered that he hadn't thought much of it at the time. *At least, they weren't Welsh*, he chuckled inside. *So what do you say to that, Mr. Griff Rhys Jones?* "No," he said bluntly. "What's that got to do with the price of bread?"

"How about horror? H.P. Lovecraft?" When the expression on Haddon's face suggested that he hadn't a clue what he was blathering on about, Evans added: "He was a horror writer, quite outdated now."

"He wasn't Welsh, was he?" Haddon quizzed.

"No, an American," answered Evans. "You don't have anything against the Welsh, do you?"

Haddon was rumbled. "God forbid, no," he said in mock horror, resisting the temptation to burst out laughing. What could be more amusing than making fun of the Welsh? And Griff Rhys Jones. "Just joshing. In answer to your question: no, I've never read any of his work."

All he had ever covered on the subject of horror was a novel by Denis Wheatley called *The Devil Rides Out*. Total sash, of course, even worse than the science fiction. The only respectable asset Wheatley possessed was that he wasn't Welsh!

Evans failed to notice the smirk on Haddon's face and proceeded to roll up another cigarette in the glove compartment. "You see, I've read a lot of Lovecraft, mostly during the lonely night-shifts back at the station. Did you know for someone who changed the face of horror, he was heavily influenced by his long trips to Wales? Some of his settings are very reminiscent of the more remote Welsh villages. The dreaded *Necronomicon* by the mad Arab Abdul Alhazred, whose text Lovecraft made frequent reference to, contains material that isn't that much different from the ancient customs of the Celts. His favourite theme seemed to be about unnameable, indestructible creatures called Cthulhu, Dagon or Yog-Sothoth, capable of eating humans whole or sending them round to Arkham Asylum. You'll be surprised to know our folklore contains descriptions of similar creatures... But shall I tell you the really weird part?"

"No, what?"

"It's been rumoured that such eternal monsters *do* exist, transported into our world from some distant, faraway place, outside all known space-time continua."

Haddon eyed him askant. "What are you saying?"

"My point is that it could be possible that the disappearances in Tolwyn might be connected to such Universes co-existing and colliding."

Haddon might have thought Evans was only joking if it were not for the look of utter conviction on his face. The guy was dead serious and, considering he was supposed to be a long-serving police constable, it completely flummoxed Haddon. Was this what the police force had come to? Was this what they were teaching the new recruits these days? What use exactly was a forensics' team at a crime scene when you could simply ring up the psychic hotline and ask Nerys Nibblebottom to come over, gaze meaningfully into the aura of a victim's personal effects and tell you who the bloody killer was? And, whilst you're at it, why not consult Mystic Meg for a reading into the police department's chances of catching the killer? But, hey, why stop there when you could ask Ali Bongo — or some other clown from the Magic Circle — to conjure up the killer for you right there on stage? What was Evans going to tell him next? That alchemy was hugely underrated? That astral projection was actually an outmoded form of transport? That automatic writing was the work of ghosts who had been graffiti-artists in life? Evans was probably the sort of chap who still believed the Earth was hollow or that Icke-bloke was indeed the new Messiah.

When Evans noticed the incredulous look on Haddon's face, he decided to expand on his conjecturing. "I know that lad, Thomas Dwyer. Bit of a fruitcake though. Used to be a peacenicker way back in the '60s. Took lots of acid and, in my opinion, that made him a bit daffy. He's been in the station a number of times with reports of the unexplained. Last week, he arrived claiming he'd seen a couple of UFOs in the northern sky. They turned out to be a couple of advertising blimps. But, this afternoon, his testimony corroborated four other eyewitness accounts, including those of a schoolteacher and Williams the Postmaster, all respected members of the community, all claiming to have got lost in some make-believe place called Fiend's Grave. They saw the same black, shapeless creatures in the woods. Enough to earn Mrs. Gwynne early retirement. Check the files in the station if you don't believe me."

Haddon's opinion was rather difficult to describe in words. He recounted a witty comment by Noel Coward (another man who was thankfully not Welsh): *Never trust men with short legs; brains too near their bottoms.* Would a swift punch in Evans's happy sacks suffice instead? Checking those nonsensical files served Haddon no purpose. Haddon had faith in the sane, sensible world and genuinely believed that Evans was more barking than usual. The basketcase had probably spent too much time reading that horror drivel until it had sent his logic to Coventry, as too, perhaps, had the rest of the town. Everyone seemed to be behaving like gypsies with their barmy runes and riddles. First, Glendower and his Indescription malarkey, then Neville and his warning about the Wild Hunt and now Evans and his monster mania. Maybe mass hysteria was sweeping across Tolwyn, or the entire townsfolk were normally this doolally. *You can never tell with the Welsh.* Enter Haddon, the Last True Cynic, in the Neverending Battle against the Bollocks. Of course bizarre things happened in the world, agreed, but they could all be adequately accounted for by cool, collected reasoning. It was becoming an overwhelming necessity that Haddon should stuff Wales and scarper back to London, pronto. He'd let his old trouble-and-strife know how he felt, tonight. She could either like it or lump it. "So where's this Friend's Grove of yours?"

"Oh, just a bit further on," Evans said. "I hope I'm not inconveniencing you in any way."

No, of course not. I love it when you talk tosh. Really makes my day! Aloud, he said: "Let's stop faffing around and get this over and done with." He felt like a drink more than ever. A B&H could tide him over until then. He fumbled around in his top pocket, only to find his cigarette-packet empty. He crumpled it up in disgust and tossed it on the floor. *Great, just what I need! Having to resort to pinching one off Old Porn Face.*

"Nearly there, boyo."

And don't call me Boyo! I hate it! I loathe it! I despise it! Even worse than the patronizing tone in which Glendower referred to Haddon as 'my boy'. *Makes me want to strangle someone each time I hear it! Now that wouldn't be good for public relations, now would it, HEY BOYO?*

As darkness kept on falling, Haddon formed the impression that they'd been driving on this straight, deserted B-road for miles, without actually getting anywhere. It wasn't so much they hadn't passed a single vehicle or signpost along the way, but more that odd sensation of disorientation in time. The sun was almost completely sunk, a blood-red glow over the hilly horizon. Its scarlet retreat bordered ever-deepening layers of dusk. The heat of the day was dissipating fast and a freshening breeze drifted in through the open car-windows.

Maybe Evans felt a similar kind of uncertainty for he inquired along the same lines: "What time do you make it?" His watch was at the menders and the clock in the car hadn't been reset, its display continually blinking 00:00.

Gripping the steering-wheel with his right hand, Haddon flipped over his left wrist to check his digital. The read-out remained largely unglimpsed as a black furry object straddled onto the road directly ahead. It came out of nowhere, suddenly transfixed by the sound of the approaching car. If Haddon had been paying marginally less attention, there would have likely followed a grisly thump. But he caught its movement just in the nick of time and instinctively slammed on the brakes. In a long, drawn-out screech of burning rubber, the police car came to a mad, juddering halt barely one yard from the black thing, which had frozen rigid in the middle of the lane. As the two constables were jerked back in their seats, Haddon was the first to identify the culprit.

"A cat!" stated Haddon shakily. "A *stupid* cat!"

The black tomcat was staring at him through its white, luminescent eyes, apparently unfazed by the commotion or the terrible possibility that it had come dangerously close to getting mown down, to becoming roadkill.

Then Evans said with a nervous whisper, "Never let a black cat cross your path."

"What?"

"This is to ward off bad omens," Evans forebode, forking his fingers in the sign of the evil eye.

"What the hell's the matter with you?" Haddon snapped at Evans in furious vexation. How could the man be so blatantly primitive? Haddon still couldn't fathom where the stupid animal had come from and why it had done so—more to the point, what in the world it was doing so far out of town. "Look, it's only a cat! What's it going to do? Purr loudly and change into one of those black, slimy monsters?" For an absurd moment, "black, slimy monster" was precisely what Haddon had thought when he'd hit the brakes. Then his rational self had reasserted itself, allowing a more practical appraisal of the situation. A cat Haddon could deal with. But Evans was not only aggravating him, his old wives' prattle was creeping him out as well. *Better not give yourself into his lunacy. Take charge of the situation. Let Willem over there know that jaywalking is a bookable offence.* Haddon poked his head out of the window and gestured tersely to the black cat. "Shoo, you stupid moggie, before I really do run you over!"

The cat sat back, almost smug, unmoved by Haddon's warning. For a short while, it refused to budge, its preternatural eyes fixed upon Haddon as if marking him: *I damn you, sir!* Then it opened its mouth to reveal small, sharp fangs and, hissing contemptuously by way of reply, trotted off with an air of arrogance into the grassland.

"That showed it," Haddon said, more than satisfied. He felt a little smug himself. He'd triumphed over the feline, given it a little taste of his authority. There was never a more lazy, selfish, unsociable a creature as a cat, and they certainly needed to be taught their place in the general scheme of things. Preferring to snooze a dozen times a day than hobnob around like any normal pet. What else were cats good for aside from preening themselves? At least, dogs had personality. *Damn thing's probably gone off to victimize a lowly field mouse.*

Tromping on the gas-pedal, Haddon turned the ignition-key to get the stalled car rolling again. His efforts came to no avail; the engine merely groaned and spluttered, unable to start. He tried again with the same result. *Isn't that just dandy? Now the car's giving me hassle.* Perhaps the jolt had knocked loose a spark plug or broken a connection to the battery, or maybe he'd just inadvertently flooded the car. Whatever the cause, he'd fix it in a jiffy. No use relying on Evans; the worthless git didn't know the first thing about driving, let alone car maintenance. "Back in a sec."

Pulling the bonnet release lever, Haddon stepped out of the vehicle, into the gathering dusk. The breeze was cool and pleasant on his face. He walked round to the front of the car, confident he would identify the problem without travail. He lifted the bonnet, blocking out the view of an extremely anxious Evans. There was still enough daylight for Haddon to check the working components within.

He fiddled around with the various connections, testing their integrity with the thoroughness of an experienced mechanic. It didn't take him long to find that everything was in relative working order, all shipshape and Bristol fashion. Puzzled, Haddon lowered the bonnet, and puzzlement instantly turned to startlement.

Evans was nowhere to be seen. He had inexplicably vanished from the passenger seat.

Haddon's initial reaction was one of indignation: *Now where's that dim-witted oaf got to now?* But perturbation was swift to follow. Haddon looked back the way they had come and far ahead toward the dark, distant hills, but Evans gave no discernible clue as to his whereabouts. He had simply vanished. *Vanished.* Haddon saw only plain, grassy flatlands on either side of the road and that copse of trees in the foreground. *That's odd*, he thought, mystified. He could have sworn those trees weren't there before.

He peered in through the driver's window as though expecting Evans to reappear in the passenger side by some divine miracle. When nothing happened, he speculated that maybe the old bugger was hiding at the rear of the car, ready to jump up and give him a nasty scare. Implausible, yes, but not entirely outside the realms of possibility. You certainly couldn't put it past Evans. A real nuisance was Evans sometimes.

Narrowing his eyes and nodding slowly, Haddon called out: "I know you're there, so get out from behind the car!"

No response.

"Look, this isn't remotely funny, so show yourself! Or, I swear, you'll have a lot to answer for!"

There was still no acknowledgement to his summons—no Evans popped up from the back of the Astra.

"Damn it!" Haddon thought grumpily. *He wants me to walk over so he can play his silly prank.* There was no way he was going to give Evans the satisfaction, but what choice did he have? *The man's worse than the cat!* "Enough's enough! The game's over!"

Still nothing.

Reluctantly, Haddon strode over, his fists curled, knuckle-white, expecting Evans's idiotic face with its mop of perm and its handlebar moustache to emerge grinning above the boot of the car any moment.

Any moment now…

Yet his astonishment came from the no-show. No Evans was lying splayed out facetiously on the ground. Neither did Haddon get the chance to open the trunk or check underneath the car. He might have done so if it were not for the stark observation that struck him dumb. He could so easily have missed it, except Haddon was a perceptive fellow. Haddon felt the first real pangs of disquiet.

The road had changed from black tarmac to dirty-brown cobblestones. Hundreds of them, stretching out into the distance.

Where had they come from? Or, more accurately, how had he missed them? In spite of the nagging consternation that now had a firm hold of him, his rationality proved as resourceful as ever. *What if those cobblestones were there before and I didn't notice them, just like the woods? I slept badly last night and now my mind's playing tricks on me.* He laughed as though this were the solution to the oddities, but it wasn't a laugh of contentment. Roman roads came to mind.

It wasn't just the road or the trees. Daylight was fading fast, the sky approaching deep violet. The moon was out, a pale full moon that hung low over the hills.

Please explain to me how it can be past twilight already? Absolute sunset didn't occur until well past eight in September. And hadn't Sergeant Powell demanded they be back by nine?

Haddon checked his wrist-watch. "Christ!" he breathed, further profundity clouding his thoughts. He read the digits again and again, not believing what his eyes were telling him.

10:47.

Almost four hours had elapsed since he and Evans had left the police station. That had to be impossible; they couldn't have driven for so long. It was the same as driving from London to Cardiff. *No, the watch has to be wrong,* Haddon thought, trying to take solace in his own reasoning. But nightfall suggested otherwise.

[Time runs different there, right?]

His brain raced. Evans had disappeared in this God-awful place — practical joke or not — and Haddon had the irresistible urge to head back to Tolwyn. That is if the car worked. But what about Evans? Haddon couldn't leave him here in this grassy wilderness. And Sian — how could he have totally neglected to have called her? Haddon had never worked this late before without letting her know; she would be worried sick.

How about radioing back to the station, calling for assistance? Haddon thought earnestly. He slapped his forehead with his palm. Yes, of course, that was it! His mind leapt at this stroke of inspiration. An obvious suggestion, yes, plain to see, but still — *nice one, Mitch! Nice one, me old mucker! The Sarge'll know what to do. He should be able to advise me. After all, it was him who originally sent us out here.*

Haddon picked up the mike from the com-set and thumbed the transmission switch. "This is Alpha-Bravo-Foxtrot, do you copy, over?"

Static greeted him.

He sought the police hailing frequency again. "This is Alpha-Bravo-Foxtrot calling. Do you read me, over?"

More static, pure and simple. *Doesn't anything in this car work?*

Almost unannounced, the police scanner came on-line. The crackling cleared a fraction and Haddon made out a faint, incoherent voice. *"Ataphwai k'gai... Wghoit rsna zoul... Adanogh ngh'aana kryon... Yothuth rhatghna krahdaar..."*

"What is this...?"

"Nyarh opahgn... Ssagosghiat mnep'gha..."

Haddon tried fine-tuning the frequency, got no improvement. He could still make no sense of the garbled message whatsoever. It was definitely a language alright, though one he fell short of recognizing. It wasn't Welsh, that was for sure. Something Continental, perhaps? A broadcast from the Eastern Bloc? Or, rather — ?

Must be atmospherics distorting the sound. Yes, that was a fair possibility. Except he realized that it was a clear, cloudless evening and the "voice" on the police CB was, in actual fact, *multiple, overlapping.* An ensemble of faceless voices whispering in a patois of archaic syllables.

The mobile...! He could use the mobile.

Haddon turned off the CB and went about rummaging through the glove-box. He brought out his Vodaphone and urgently dialled in the number for the police station. The phone on the other end gave a few rings, then, while expecting to hear Sergeant Powell's reassuring lilt, those voices—those singular, collective voices that had plagued the radio-link—were once again clogging up the line, this time on his personal mobile.

"Nqmai ul'rha… Dhudas krsa wpguh'thyrag… Mnghlf drfylopeth drehep rrhas… N'gah-Kthun… Azareth phga zoond… Saggai hethoth yaddiqqh iagghdoi sila'aaktheth…"

On any other occasion, Haddon might have mistaken these wild whisperings for a dirty phone-call, what with the heavy breathing, but, at that present moment, he was alone in the dark on a deserted country road, with no viable means of contacting the police station while simultaneously grappling with the sudden disappearance of his partner. Alarm bells began ringing in his head. The dim, incomprehensible voices continued on his cellular, putting the frighteners on him. They seemed to brim with an ancient evil, like gods speaking in forgotten tongues, whispering and muttering and chattering and sneering. Suddenly afraid, Haddon dropped his mobile-phone like he would a poisonous snake, and took a step back. Diminished by the high grass, the populous voices floated up to him as if reaching up from the black wells of Acheron.

Then, just when Haddon thought things couldn't get any worse, someone let out a shrill, hideous scream that pierced the night with all the vicious thrust of a sharp knife. The mobile went dead at that instant and Haddon regressed to a stone-statue, the cold agony of that shriek chilling him to the core, his thoughts as frozen as the rest of him. It took a while for his senses to return as he tried to locate the source.

The noise had emanated from the woods.

It might have been an injured animal's cry for help, but Haddon knew with alarming certainty that it wasn't. There was no disputing the human element. It had been Evans, and he sounded as though he was in trouble. Deep, serious trouble. By the sound of the scream, the kind of trouble that frequently got someone hurt… or possibly even *killed*.

Haddon considered his options and realized there weren't many. What should he do? Go after Evans? That would have been the right thing to do, the obvious thing by standard police procedure, but

Haddon suddenly didn't feel like it. To him, it seemed like the worst idea imaginable. *You really want to go chasing after that scream?*

What if Evans was lying hurt and helpless somewhere in those woods, relying wholly on Haddon to rescue him?

Sod the Welshman! It's his fault for getting into whatever trouble he's in! Let him deal with it himself. As for you, I suggest you get the hell out of here!

No, he surely couldn't leave Evans in whatever mortal danger he was in, even if a part of him was insisting that he head back home. *I'm an officer of the law, for heaven's sake, and I have an obligation to my uniform —*

This isn't the time to be playing Dixon of Dock Green! *If you know what's good for you, you'll leave, and right now!*

Use your damn initiative! How's running away going to look on your record?

Are you out of your mind? Because whatever's got Evans might still be out there, and it'll get you too...

However appealing dereliction of duty appeared at that moment, Haddon wasn't one to leave a fellow officer stranded in the middle of nowhere, in dire need of assistance. Almost against his better judgement, he rushed off in the direction of the scream.

Why Evans had gone to the woods was beyond Haddon? To take a leak, perhaps? Why not by the roadside? How he'd got to the woods undetected was an even greater mystery. Haddon had been under the bonnet for less than a minute and the group of trees was at least a good five-hundred yards from the car.

Haddon got to the edge of the woodland and contemplated whether he should go on further. The branches soughed in the early autumn breeze, and Haddon hesitated. The darkness beneath the foliage yawned at him like the gaping maw of a netherworldly titan, bidding him ominous welcome. *Won't you please reconsider?* his heedful half pleaded. *We don't have to do this.*

Yes, we do...

With mounting apprehension, he entered the company of trees.

He ran through the woods, his shoes trampling twigs and fallen leaves, totally oblivious to the nettles that tore at his uniform and grazed his shins. Branches whipped across his face. Although a torch or flashlight would have come in handy in such a situation, he was now somewhat indifferent to his dark surrounds. The world had stilled around him, high-octane tension welling up deep inside him. He didn't think. He didn't want to think. He had to get to Evans as quickly as possible.

A second scream, louder, fuller, a resounding indictment to pain, split the silence that lingered like a suffocating shroud. Again, Haddon's emotions were assaulted by that cold, illimitable dread as he wondered how anyone could possibly sustain such a scream for so long. There was no detracting from the haglike quality of it, and that fear of impending peril, of certain doom, was stronger than ever. *I didn't hear that! I really didn't! I swear to you, I* didn't!

Yet he had, and he knew it. That traitorous inner voice was having a ball. *You wanna bet? Play it again, Sam, and you just can't miss it!*

If Haddon had paused for just one brief moment and glanced upon the old, weathered signpost at the clearing, it is highly unlikely that he would have ventured into the woods; he would have simply packed his bags and left. It wasn't so much the terrible scrawl that read FIEND'S GRAVE, but the way in which the individual characters had been painted in what appeared to be a dark, dripping substance. Haddon would most certainly have realized that they were written in blood. A further intuitive guess would have told him that it was Evans's blood. And he daren't touch it for he'd have known it would be warm.

Fresh.

Haddon's head was rapidly filling up with the worst cases of his policeman's lot in London. They came to him as a series of unpleasant flashbacks, the brutalities of man he didn't care to be reminded of. It explained primarily why Sian had suggested a change of scene, why she'd pressured him to move to a more rural environment for police-work, a task which would, for all intents and purposes, require him to deal with the less dangerous criminal. Sian had been scared for his safety and rightly so. She had also said she wasn't prepared to become a widow so young.

PC Haddon had certainly faced plenty as a young constable in the days when he was constantly being shifted from one department to another. (Problems with manpower, was his superiors' excuse.) A fairly broad cross-section of crime, to sum up his experience. Oh, he'd seen his share of illegal stuff, alright: from the offie-raids to the bank-robberies, from the neo-fascist propaganda to the Paki-bashing, from the road rage to the motorway rape, from the high-class vice to the child porn on the Internet. He'd even worked the city slums, busted half-dead low-lifes on heroin possession or scouted through garbage skips for day-old babies left for dead by teenage mothers either unable or simply unwilling to look after them. His stint in the Riot Squad had been a particularly nasty experience: trapped in a burning police-van by anarchists who would rather hurl obscenities and petrol-bombs at you than talk things through like proper human beings; he, like those policemen, would have surely died in that blazing wreck if reinforcements hadn't arrived in time to disperse the angry mob.

However, Sian's decision had been the upstart of two major incidents. The first one had involved PC Haddon investigating what appeared on the surface to be a routine, domestic disturbance. When the police burst into the contentious residence, they discovered a badly-beaten girl pinned to the bedposts by four-inch nails embedded deep in her wrists; her suffering and accompanying histrionics had been unbearable. Her drug-crazed, psychopathic boyfriend was standing over her, and there were no second guesses as to what he intended to do to her with that mean-looking machete.

The other major event that upset Sian had been a triple homicide in a busy nightclub in the East End of London. A man had walked into the club brandishing a sawn-off shotgun and, in typical gangland style, picked off three rival hoods. The ensuing panic led to the deaths of a further half-dozen people who were mercilessly crushed underfoot as they tried to escape the carnage. In apprehending the gunman, a policeman had been shot, and Haddon clearly recalled his colleague's terrible screams as he lay bleeding on the floor, clutching his wounded stomach, a hard-bitten man screaming in the wild, uncontrollable paroxysms of a toddler in a dentist's chair. PC Caldwell died in hospital later that night.

And what of the reports and files and cuttings Haddon had browsed through as an eager recruit? The horrors of Saddleworth Moors, Myra Hindley and Ian Brady receiving life-sentences for their sadistic crimes; Peter Sutcliffe whose exploits in a small Yorkshire community reproduced the savage notoriety of Jack the Ripper; Dennis Nilsen caught only when the decomposing remains of his gay victims blocked the drains and stank out the neighbourhood; Michael Ryan's murderous broad-daylight rampage through Hungerford; Fred West and his torture, murder, then burial of over a dozen young girls, including his own baby daughter, in the cellar of his house in Gloucester; the horrendous killing-spree in Dunblane which would hasten a bill through Parliament implementing a nationwide ban on all illegal firearms; and, in more recent times, suffer the little children as a paranoid schizophrenic strides into a nursery school in Wolverhampton to tend to a day's worth of child murder...

The Hall of Infamy. The endless tales of mindless turpitude. Essential reading for the budding policeman, powerful enough to build character or details deemed so distressing as to permanently fracture your faith in the goodness of Humanity and leave you forever wondering about the intentions of Heaven—how any Great and Merciful God could sit back on His celestial throne and willingly let Evil thrive in such vast, unassailable numbers. Make-or-Break Time for the Uninitiated.

So Haddon had moved to Tolwyn. To get away from the filth, the corruption, the general degradation and the constant risk of death at every corner. Sian had seen to it. Haddon should have been delighted with the change, but, looking back now, it was precisely the hard toil Haddon missed the most about London. Anyone who thought joining the police force would prove a cushy number—a vocation any wally could do—needed to seriously rethink their future. It was a tough job at the best of times, no matter how many stripes you attained, requiring grit and determination and a cool head in the face of danger, but there was also a certain amount of satisfaction to be had from protecting the streets from the scum of the earth and enabling the good citizens to rest easy in their beds at night. In Tolwyn, Haddon got none of the pleasure he had derived from his work back home. He just didn't get the same buzz here. Moreover, he understood he wasn't doing his career any favours by staying here.

What difference had Haddon made since arriving in Tolwyn? What important arrests had he participated in? What great case had he solved?

His last "great" case had involved the burnt-out Ford Escort Cosworth. Not even a high-speed chase to warrant the whole thing worthwhile. Mind-rottingly dull. Worse, it was a Friday night and, although it was his weekend off, Haddon had been appointed The Case of the Slimy Monsters when Powell knew for a fact that he was supervising a skeleton crew tonight and Haddon might prove more valuable tackling the drunken brawls that would inevitably break out after the pubs and clubs shut than chasing imaginary monsters. Now there was a man who really needed his priorities sorting out. How more petty could police-work get? *Not to press too fine a point, but what the hell am I doing out here in the middle of nowhere? Get it together, Sarge, or I'm lodging a formal complaint to Head Office. In triplicate.*

11:32 PM.

He had lost radio contact with the police station.

He felt the trembling dark of the woods around him.

And he still had the little, trifling matter of his missing colleague to contend with.

Those screams had dredged up old unwanted memories, grim moments in his life when Haddon had narrowly escaped danger himself or witnessed first-hand the terrible consequences of criminal transgression, ugly reminders of man's dark heart and our own eventual mortality. Evans's screams only served to put everything neatly into perspective.

It was all up to Haddon now.

There was movement in front of him as a dark shape, darker than the surrounding shadows, suddenly wandered into his path, nearly tripping him over. Haddon somehow managed to retain his balance as he skidded to a standstill in a spray of rich earth. He released a small squawk of alarm. Then he spotted two white, luminous eyes peering up at him low on the ground, recognizing them immediately. They belonged to that conceited cat that had stalled the car. What was with the damned thing? Was it following him or something? A surge of spiteful rage swept through him and he kicked out at the black ball of fur. *Why don't you get off my case?* Before his foot could make contact, the cat darted into the undergrowth as though anticipating his reaction, leaving Haddon to punch the air in frustration. *Get lost and stay lost!*

Haddon resumed his advance through the wooded nocturne, fleet of foot, quickening his pace. Evans couldn't be far now.

He heard the refreshing sound of a spring up ahead, trickling and babbling and gurgling, and soon he was splashing through running water, maintaining reasonable purchase over the smooth, rounded pebbles. He crossed the stream and noticed the ground had begun to rise uphill. Where was he? Was Fenella's Brook where he was at? He thought he was, even though he hadn't been here before. It then occurred to him that he must be at Friend's Grove — where else could he be? — except he found nothing friendly or vaguely uplifting about the place. The atmosphere was mirthless at best, almost illusory, and the silence hung thick and heavy. Apart from the trees that sloped proportionately to the incline and the cat he had lashed out at, Haddon felt alone and terribly afraid. One would have expected the September woods to be rife with wildlife, yet there were no birds nor bugs, no other sounds to speak of, save for the gradually receding burble of the stream in the background.

Dwyer was right, Haddon thought with dull apprehension. *You can feel it. It's like something's waiting to happen… Like the calm before the storm or the lull before the panic, the way everything's normal just moments before a car-wreck or like when you're going off to bed not knowing you're never waking up again… It's coming, whatever it is. And it's almost here…*

Again, he experienced that compelling urge to retreat, to turn back, to run away, but he suppressed it with a drastic mental effort. He was no longer in the position to relinquish this undertaking. He continued to climb upwards, at times forced to scrabble on all fours. His boots liberated loose stones, which clattered down the hillside, striking the water below with a faint *splosh*. He knew he had to get to the top because that was where he would find Evans. He knew that for certain, knew it beyond the shadow of a doubt. He didn't know how he knew. He just did.

He pushed onwards, slowed down by the steepening gradient, mortally afraid for Evans, at the same time more afraid of what might be waiting for him at the top…

Higher and higher he scrambled.

Then he was there; he'd reached the top, soon on the brink of uncovering the fate that awaited him there.

Like the bare patch of a balding man, the crest of the hill was a grassless, treeless barren that overlooked an expanse of dark, hoary grove. A disappointment in many respects, if it were not for the awesome sight he beheld, ahead of him.

Haddon found himself at the edge of a ring of standing stones. Mighty silhouettes pitched against the night sky, sleepless sentinels keeping the watch, they crowned the summit like the apex of an ancient temple. He realized that these must be the "strange, olden ruins" he had heard so much about, apparently commonplace in these parts. Catching his breath, he crept forward, scrunching scree, to examine these sky-flung obelisks. The moon floated high in the sky, a great orb of white light which, because of the banks of passing cloud, provided him with only short bursts of illumination. Touching the corner of the nearest monolith, Haddon was amazed to discover its surface was smooth and perfectly-even as though it had been recently cleaned, polished, restored. Inscriptions were chiselled into the stone, strange hieroglyphics that he knew no layman could ever decipher. The symbols somehow reminded him of the sinister voices he had heard on the police scanner, and, as he dwelled upon their possible connection, those cold fingers of dread closed around his neck.

But where was Evans? The column-cinctured crest appeared deserted, a shadowy flat slab of dolomite at the centre of the arena.

"Welcome!" a voice said, with such suddenness, as to make Haddon jump. It was like someone introducing a surprise birthday party. There followed a short series of fizzles, and torches clasped on the inside of the stone pillars sprang to life. They blazed of their own accord, a bright border of flames that lit the centre stage.

Four dark, dwarf-like figures [Ellyllon?] confronted Haddon. Where they had come from he hadn't a clue, but he thought it wise he put as much distance between himself and these elves. Then he realized they weren't elves but four small children dressed in black, ceremonial robes. Except they weren't ordinary children. Haddon remembered an article he had once read in a newspaper about a medical condition called 'progeria'; the similarities were unmistakable. Their faces were old and wrinkled, the hair atop their heads wispy-white and limited to tufts and whorls. Their genders were impossible to make out—but that wasn't entirely true, was it? One of the children Haddon did recognize, much to his alarm. She resembled his wife, Sian—a young-old version of her, her beautiful features a hideous, twisted caricature. Maybe it was only a sickly niece of hers, or an illegitimate daughter, perhaps, kept secret from the rest of the community for reasons too obvious to go into. *Or what if it was indeed Sian herself, changed by some bizarre act of nature?* It didn't bear thinking about. The dwarves/elves/goblins continued to watch Haddon as the flickering torches cast dancing shadows on their leprous countenances, accentuating their dark sockets, demonizing their grins.

His tongue felt as rough as sandpaper and the fast, steady beats of his heart accurately reflected his fear. *Get me away from here, please!*

He noticed each of the four was carrying a double-headed battle-axe, the blades glinting luridly in the torchlight...

Are they for me?

Somehow he didn't think so.

Then, all eyes turned towards the raised block at the centre of the stone-circle. Upon it, above an ocean of gleaming bluestones, lay a human form. A familiar figure, unclothed and unconscious. When Haddon saw who it was, he suddenly knew something awful was about to happen, something ugly and utterly unspeakable. He wanted to scream out to Evans, to tell him to get up, but the sound was trapped in his throat. He also accepted it would do little good. Evans was out of it—it was probably too late for him now, anyway. The centre-slab undoubtedly composed an altar of sorts—that much Haddon was sure of. In the same way he was sure he'd unexpectedly wandered into some sort of illicit, pagan ceremony.

"Welcome to our humble lair," the nearest child said again, without turning round, his voice full of malice. "We have been expecting you."

Expecting me? Why should you be expecting me?

"Do not be dismayed, for this is the Time of the Wild Hunt," another child spoke up as though reading Haddon's thoughts. "Bwcibo must be appeased."

"The Lord of a Million Concubines!" said the first in the same cackling, maniacal voice.

"The Shining One!" said the second, accompanied by shrill laughter from the others.

"The Blinder of Time!" added the first.

"The Eater of Worlds!" said a third child-druid with even greater glee. "The Devourer of Starry Dimensions!"

"The Bringer of Doom, the Avatar of Wretchedness!" the final member of the coven, the Sian-child, declared.

"Hear our Prayer of Pain, feel the Pleasures of Torment," the first druid recited more solemnly, "the Sacrifice of Flesh... the Rites of the Unholy..."

Then they all chanted in a chorus of evil verse: "O Father of *Hywl Glyndwr*, the Essence of *Pwca* shall flow for Your Awakening!"

Enormous horror filled Haddon as he stared, shocked speechless, at the ritual that was about to unfold before him, a course that he did not want to envisage but had little choice in the matter. His absurdist, vaguest, wildest fears were about to be realized. He shoved his fist into his mouth as they *did* exactly what he thought they were going to do. And there was nothing on earth he could have done to have prevented it. Arrested them, he would have, except they weren't your average run-of-the-mill kids.

Allocated a limb each, the axes came down in quick succession, each dismembering Evans's naked body with the wet, gristly crunch of a meat-cleaver performing an emergency battlefield amputation. There were no tourniquets available. Arms and legs gave away as easily as chicken wings, a dense rush of dark gravy spewing out, splattering over the glittering stones heaped around. One barbaric stroke later, this time by the ringleader, and Evans's head was lopped off his shoulders as cleanly as any luckless Spaniard's might have been, courtesy of Henry Morgan's cutlass.

The decapitated head rolled towards Haddon, the lifeless, blood-streaked ball coming to a stop by his shoes. Haddon stepped back in physical revulsion, feeling the upheaval in his stomach, wanting nothing more than to turn back and run from this scene of gory gratification, but unable to move, his legs like treacle.

The battle-axe came down bonecrunchingly again, hacking through Evans's chest, cleaving the ribs apart. The leader of the child-druids — who possessed more than a passing resemblance to Sergeant Powell — thrust his hand into the open chest and ripped out what could only have been the heart, holding it aloft. "We give You the Dark Passion of Pwca."

As they each took a bite from the extracted organ, their eyes turned skyward expectantly. *"Pgnesrn k'yel... Yuthnw ptgesn k'yai..."* they chanted, reverting to the same ancient tongue that had haunted the police radio. The child-druids were apparently fluent in the language. *"Hrystn baie g'dawr... Zalwr my'nak fhtagn... Nrtesn Nyarlahotep..."*

Haddon followed their gazes and saw storm clouds gathering overhead, a scud of dark, rogue clouds crowding together directly above the place of sacrifice. Their speed was unnatural, unthinkable, meteorologically impossible. In a different section of the sky, the full moon looked on impassively.

Looks like rain.

But the cloud formation was anything but indicative of rain. Their grouping converged on a swirling central focus. The circle of clouds had patterned a passage to some faraway, upperwordly place—a vortex, perhaps, to the vast Infinite and the great Beyond.

The gems piled around the altar began to glow. They throbbed with a pearly-blue inner light as though individually powered by tiny reactors. Haddon watched, part-fascinated, part-terrified, as light-beams shot upwards from the pulsing stones, taking droplets of Evans's spilt blood with them, trapping it inside a tall column of light. His blood dripped forever upward, defying gravity, sucked up by the skybound vortex, like strawberry 'shake through a straw. It was into this very focal point, this rift within the swirling clouds, where the blood and light were swallowed up.

What was this aerial spectacle, this whirlpool in the sky?

A portal to the stars? A gateway to another dimension? Was this place a secret outpost of some distant, transcosmic entity?

"O Olden One," the child-druids chanted together amidst the whirling noise and the light-display. "We have brought You the Chosen One for the Eternal Suffering! Let him submit to the Fear of the Indescription!"

All of a sudden, the commotion ceased. The visuals ended and the clouds were gone. The altar-stones were as dry as bone.

There was only the hill-top and its girt of stone monoliths bathed in moonshine.

The children's eyes turned back in the direction of Haddon, their intentions malevolent and all too clear, their mouths glistening with the blood of the human heart they had just consumed.

Haddon knew he was in for it now.

The initiation was over. Whoever–or *whatever*–had been up there beyond the clouds had fed well and now lusted for more.

Haddon could have run, but seemed somehow incapable. The brutal slaughter of his partner had left him in a horrendous state of shock. His face was pallid, his lower lip in quivering overdrive. He fully expected the four young butchers to come towards him, to carve him up with their steely red blades, to finish him off in one last gratuitous act of receiving Hell.

Yet, as it turned out, he would not be granted this small mercy. Instead, he was forced to witness an even greater obscenity.

The child-druids looked to the heavens again with renewed interest. "O Olden One," they cried out in unison, "we surrender to Your Will. Bless us with Your Power so we may claim our prize!"

Message sent. Received. Acknowledged by a higher intelligence somewhere across the stars or beyond dimensions. The response came swift on the heels. Lightning hurtled down from the same invisible focus in the sky and speared the druid-worshippers where they stood, blitzing their mouths with unfathomable accuracy. As each swallowed gigawatt upon gigawatt of current, their heads glowed like halogen lamps. Enveloped in individual spheres of electrical energy, their bodies jigged about like mindless puppets, skin and clothes crackling with charge, emitting furious sparks. The effect was both spectacular and frightening. Haddon watched, entranced, as the lightning split the air in a perfect pyramidal formation, electrocuting each intended target with a power that was staggering in its intensity. Fat spluttered. Flesh smoked, burned, competing with the smell of ozone. A further bolt of lightning struck the corpse at the altar–Evans's corpse–or what remained of the corpse, a headless, limbless torso. It twitched, trembled. *Moved.*

As the pagan priests continued to absorb, channel the lightning like superconductors, their wrinkled faces shimmered, rippled, seemed to melt, then darken, coalescing with their robes. Tenticular growths sprouted out from their bodies as their faces became no more. They were all changing into blobs, grotesque, gelatinous beings, with the colour and consistency of tar. The growling, keening sound of beagles accompanied their noisome metamorphoses. They were the blackest, indefinable creatures Haddon had ever seen, waking or asleep.

He knew what they were even before their transformations were completed: these were the black, slimy monsters of Dwyer's nightmare.

Cwn Annwn. *The Hounds of the Otherworld. The Howlers of the Night.*

Haddon had found them, and he didn't like what he saw. When he had first heard of the myth, he had pictured a pack of bloodhounds set loose by their master, racing across the moors, paws digging up soft clods of earth, hides appearing almost black in the misty night. Think red eyes, noses attuned to the scent, mouths barking and snarling, canines bared, poised to strike, wound. On the trail of a trespasser, a poacher perhaps, who is blithely unaware of what is coming for him.

Not this.

Haddon's attention went back to Evans's reanimated corpse, drawn towards the huge aperture in the chest which had magically transformed into a second set of jaws. "Bring me the Chosen One!" the thoracic mouth boomed with malefic authority. "It is time to enjoy the thrill of the chase…!" Evans's head which had lain inert at Haddon's feet too shuddered to life, eyes flicking open, fixing on Haddon. "*Cwn Annwn… Cwn Annwn… Cwn Annwn…*" it rasped in a parody of phantasmagoric insanity.

That finally did it for Haddon. He broke free of his gripping paralysis and fled. He tore down the hillside, sliding painfully where the shingles were many and the purchase poor, in a frantic effort to get away from the league of monsters. He could hear them in hot pursuit, their screeching as mindrattling as metal fingernails dragging down a blackboard, their seething, stewing, slithering, slobbering, sloshing, squishing, squelching bodies swarming after him.

What these shapeshifters were, he dared not contemplate, for he knew he would find no sensible answer. Unearthly spawn of some kind? Human-alien hybrids? Whatever they were wasn't important. The important thing right now was that the game [*Time of the Wild Hunt*] was afoot, and Haddon was the prize.

He stumbled down the slope and slid twice, feeling the sharp shale snatch skin off his back. Reaching the foot of the hill, Haddon ran into another spot of bother. He landed in what he first thought was wet cement. Except for the smell, of course. The smell was bad, the smell was lethal; it was like living next door to a sewage works, except a hundred times stronger, and Haddon had the palpable urge to puke his guts out. He resisted the rising tide of bile, nevertheless. It didn't take him long to figure out where he was. Fenella's Brook had apparently become a wide rill of sludge, a stinking, festering tributary of goo. Haddon got up, his hands and trousers dripping muck. Thoroughly disgusted, he tried wiping away some of the muck on his sleeves, but managed only to dirty his uniform further. He had to somehow negotiate his way through this sludge without upchucking. He was shin-deep in it, almost wading in it. He lurched forward, grimacing, forced to pull his foot free of the mulch with each sucking stride.

This is what it must feel like being a sanitation inspector, working the sewers, he thought, repulsed, retching. *Dimly-lit tunnels of rats and polluted water. Dealing with human waste day in, day out.*

Haddon stepped on something soft and slippery, and remembered Dwyer mentioning there were creatures living in this muck. Strange, eel-like bottom-feeders. What putrid life was this that dwelled exclusively in this cesspool of creation? Haddon knew no sane naturalist would know, neither want to know about the lives of these unnatural, fulsome creatures. Even in the dark, Haddon could see bubbles form on the surface of the ooze, and the thought of its indigenous species taking a bite out of him got him moving again.

Soon he was on the other side, only to discover his clothes were ruined, completely fucked; he had shit all over him. His uniform was plastered with the evil-smelling muck that he knew no laundry-service would ever be able to clean. He paused to notice the flow of the sludge, another disturbing sight. The ordurous river slurried up the hill, mocking gravity with a flagrant disregard for its long-established laws.

The screeching of the *Cwn Annwn* was more distant now, but still audible. What if it was a deliberate ploy so as to give their prey a false sense of security, and they actually got quieter the *nearer* they got?

A short breather, and Haddon was off again, trying to retrace his steps out of these intimidating surroundings. Hell, they were worse than intimidating. Everything around him was past weird, almost too bizarre to be true.

As if I haven't seen enough already...

Haddon might have been lost in a hypnagogic dream or standing in a forest on an alien planet. The trees seemed well over fifty feet tall, having swelled to a mad, over-nourished luxuriance as though their roots were constantly sucking up vile, vitreous juices from the earth. The angles too were all wrong, freaky and distorted, because the trees were either growing aslant or consciously leaning over to take a closer look at him. Yet the extreme aspect was their gnarled trunks.

Nothing could have prepared Haddon for the sight of the screaming faces knotted into the tree-trunks. Dozens of actual faces were carved into each trunk — no, *fused* into each trunk — and Haddon could see their tortured expressions stilled in the act of screaming. Muted screams of agony that implored for a way out from their ghastly incarceration. Dwyer had been right on that count too. It was as if man had merged with bark by some dark, sorcerer's spell. How had it happened?

Haddon would never know how close he came to finding out.

Something slid around his leg, and Haddon was suddenly yanked backwards. He hit the ground with a hard thud, and pain flared in his head. "Oooph!..." he murmured, momentarily stunned, seeing stars. He was dragged face-down in the dirt for several yards before the instance of shock abated. His senses revived, he sneaked a quick glance over his shoulder. One of the tree-roots had wrapped itself tightly around his ankle and was vehemently pulling him back towards the base of the mother-tree. A mouth awaited there, a huge, toothless, gumless opening in the bark, that vied to swallow him alive.

He kicked out at the root-creeper with his other foot, but it wouldn't let go. It possessed the taut resilience of rope.

The greedy, seamless mouth yawned ever wider.

Somewhere, the screeches and sloshes drew nearer.

More creepers were sliding sinuously in his direction when Haddon remembered his Swiss army-knife. The one he always carried with him in case of emergencies.

Like now would be a good time.

He brought it out of his trouser-pocket and fumbled with it for a moment, almost dropping it. *Now wouldn't that be a turn-up for the books?* Making soft, cawing sounds, he worked loose the blade, then went in for the kill. He swung back full-tilt and stabbed the living root that shackled his ankle. Black fluid that looked unsettlingly like blood in the dark sprayed out of its wound, and the creeper reacted instantly by releasing its hold on his ankle. Mewling in hurt and anger, it retreated, slithering away with all the other creepers that had been heading his way. The hole in the trunk gave up the ghost and closed its mouth.

Haddon got to his feet hurriedly. Large insectile wings droned by his head, and Haddon ducked, hoping against all hope not to see what had made that noise.

What kind of place is this, where the trees attack you and hold you hostage for all eternity? Where sludge substitutes for spring-water and druid-children turn into monsters?

He knew where he was, [*Fiend's Grave, baby, Fiend's Grave! Whoopee for me! Let's have a big cheer for Fiend's Grave, everybody!*] but didn't want to admit it to himself. As sure as he knew that, if he put an axe to any of the trees, the wood-flesh would bleed.

He was suddenly aware of being watched, a horrible, unshakable feeling of being scrutinized by a thousand pairs of eyes, by shapes sensed but unseen. Strange, moving shapes that deliberately stayed outside his field of vision. Shapes in the air, like the one [*giant dragonfly?*] that had brushed by his ear just seconds earlier, and furtive shapes in the undergrowth [*Armies of carnivorous woodlice. Beetles that weren't quite beetles. Wingless blowflies dragging their fat, bloated bodies behind them.*] feeding and breeding and growing and mutating. Outlines of shapes that lived and breathed, but did not conform to any blueprint set down by Nature.

Haddon was thankful of the dark, since he would not have to see them.

PC Evans was history now, a goner, a fatal victim of Fiend's Grave— *may his soul rest in peace.* He had bought it, and that was the absolute truth of it. He hadn't deserved to die the way he had—a damn shame— but there was no point mourning his loss just yet; there would be plenty of time for that later. No, there was still someone very dear to Haddon, who was still very much in the land of the living, who still needed special looking-after and probably all the encouragement in the world to make it to that funeral on time. *Yes, you've guessed it: Yours Truly.*

Haddon got going again, knowing that running away was the best thing he could do, knowing all-too-well that creatures of a different, disturbing, indeterminate nature [*the black, shapeless kind*] were on his tail. He could hear them somewhere far back in the woods screeching and sloshing and squelching.

He wanted to believe that he was simply dreaming, that he was stuck in a realm of dark deliriums, that the woods and its infestations existed only in his mind, and that, if he tried hard enough, he would eventually wake up to the world that he had always known.

But the wake-up call never came; he didn't come round from his hellish fantasy.

He met an old friend, instead. It sprang out from one of the trees and bundled Haddon to the ground.

"Where do you *think* you're going?" it demanded with a fierce hiss.

Flat-out on the moist earth, Haddon's eyes widened when he saw what had stymied him. The terror exploded in him like an overheated pressure-cooker. He managed only a soft squealing whisper that had been straining to break free for a long while. The cat was back, but like Dwyer's jinxed rabbit, it was considerably changed... and not for the better.

As with everything else in Fiend's Grave, it too presented a corrupted, uglified version of itself. It could now talk, and its face had somehow [*Oh, dear God, no!*] taken on the features of Hywel Glendower.

Face-to-face with Haddon—upside down, mind you, like a ghoul gloating over a corpse—it peered down at him with those familiar glowing eyes. White cat's eyes on a half-human face that looked almost like a latex-mask. White hair covered most of its pointy ears and flowed outrageously down its back. The feline whiskers, which bristled below the half-human nose, were curled upwards by one of Glendower's godless grins, the lips pulled back to reveal a cluster of teeth, huge, spiked teeth, a couple capped gold, glinting. Slicked with slaver that gave them a rabid, murderous edge, they were easily capable of ripping out Haddon's throat and close enough in fact for Haddon to smell the foetor off its breath. A globule of drool extended down from the catty ogre's jaws, stretched soundlessly like a strand of spider's silk and dropped casually into Haddon's mouth...

URRRRGGGHHH!

Gagging and spitting in downright disgust, Haddon shuffled away from the grinning monstrosity, digging his heels into the earth to give him the necessary thrust. He expected the cat to pounce on him any second and start tearing him to shreds, but when it didn't, Haddon stopped scrabbling. Having achieved some degree of distance between himself and the cat-thing, Haddon boosted himself up on his elbows to see what it was doing.

It hadn't moved. It was just sitting there, smug as a Cheshire cat, watching him with its glowing eyes.

Now Haddon was allowed to see the rest of it, if he could only just for one minute distract himself from its bright, glow-in-the-dark stare. It was a giant of a cat, a beast of both sinewy beauty and inconceivable abomination, built as though it had in some way plundered the physique of Glendower and incorporated it into its own form... which it most probably had. A product of evolution gone mad. Although its hide seemed well-groomed, as sleek as a black panther's (except for its mane of white hair, of course), its size was proportionate to that of a Bengal tiger's. Perhaps bigger. It looked formidable enough to wrestle a Doberman, even a pitbull, and walk away the victor.

"*Miaow...*" it purred harmlessly and licked its paws. No, *claws*.

Terrified though he was, Haddon was also at his wit's end. "What the fuck do you want?"

The Glendower-cat-thing considered this for a moment, its eyes growing dull. Then it answered with a question. "What do you think?"

"How the hell should I know?" Haddon said, confused, in emotional disarray. He couldn't believe he was talking to a cat, let alone one with the face of his father-in-law. He was surrounded by madness, utter madness, complete and utter certifiable madness, and he had no idea how he was going to get out of it with his sanity intact. "I want to know what's going on?"

"The Indescription dictates The Time of the Wild Hunt."

"I've gathered as much. What's it mean?"

"Can't you hear them?" it hissed, pricking its ear expectantly. "They want your fear... your life... your soul... There is *no* escape..."

Haddon could certainly hear them, louder than ever: the mephitic monsters and their dry screeches and wet sloshes as they signalled their presence. A symphony of the damned. It wouldn't take long before he was in sight of them. Dreaming or deluded, did he want to be in sight of them? "No escape? So wh-wh-where do you fit into all this?"

"I am the First Emissary," Glendower declared importantly, kattitude and all. "And, as First Emissary, even I must serve a higher power: the Olden One. A power not of this earth."

"Look, I couldn't give two figs about your higher power!" Haddon roared in confusion and bitter desperation. "I don't like it here anymore, understand? You've had your fun, now let me go! Please, won't you let me go?" He felt like sobbing. "I just want to go home... I swear, *home*... Home to my wife, home to London."

The cat-thing's eyes blazed fiercely, Glendower's temper more than evident. "Take a care what you say about the Olden One! I might be the First Emissary, but I am not the Olden One. The Olden Ones ruled this planet long before the first Celt raised a spear. Who do you think killed off the dinosaurs? The Olden Ones may have retired to the stars when the world was young, but one day They will return and, when They do, we shall welcome Them back and help Them reclaim what is rightfully Theirs. We are but pale imitations of Their Likeness. They are our real Lord and Masters, our Gods, so show some respect, *boy*! Or your suffering will go down as the stuff of legend, indeed!"

Haddon remembered the crazy ceremony up on the hill, the manner in which the clouds had parted, how something beyond the normal range of vision had sucked up the blood of Evans. There, Haddon had sensed a presence. Was that what the cat-thing referred to as the Olden One? A being from a bygone era that thrived on random chaos? Some extracosmic consciousness that lurked somewhere among the darkest stars, or roamed the trackless wastes at the very edge of the Universe, or perhaps even reaching out from the unplumbed gulfs of dimensions far beyond, through the re-enactment of a mythical pact with an age-old cult?

[*Christ, I'm beginning to sound like Evans.*]

[*Yes, and we all know what happened to Evans...*]

And the Hounds of the Otherworld were *what*? Direct descendants of the Olden One? Monstrous spawn of this Supreme Evil? Haddon had in his possession some explanations, but they were as mentally indigestible as the cat-thing that confronted him. He thought he would go mad just delving on them. "Why me?"

"Because we are dying and our land is dying with us. You are the Chosen One. You were selected from a score of candidates. We needed a suitable donor, and you came along. The seed you planted in my little girl will carry on our line. Our days of glory shall return."

"Sian is pregnant?"

"Even as we speak, your seed is growing inside her."

The disclosure hit Haddon hard. His faith in his wife wavered, crumbled.

[*I have been under the spell of Cerdiwen the Sorceress and Enchantress*]

The Sian-child. The child-druid who had looked remarkably like Sian. *Is that what Sian really looks like? None of the gorgeous, perfumed, leggy blondness I fell in love with; no, sir, that's just an illusion to seduce the normal, everyday bloke, right? She's in fact one of those old, wrinkled druid-meanies, who make a nasty habit of turning into those hideous, black slimeballs? Am I any nearer the truth? Are you honestly telling me that my marriage was all one big sham, a pretext by which to lure me here in order to impregnate what passes for your daughter? Is that what you're saying? That, that little munchkin, is what I've actually been porking all along and is what I've in all gross probability sent up the duff?* Haddon thought it so, and he suddenly felt sick to the stomach. *Oh my God, I made love to a monster, and I didn't even know it! I must be losing it, yep, I'm definitely losing it!*

"Despair not, my boy. Soon you shall become like us. An immortal. A member of a far superior race. Servant to our Olden One."

"What if I don't want to be part of your race?"

"You must! You see, the seed we speak of is *you*. You *are* the seed."

Haddon tried to comprehend the information laid before him. "Let me get this straight. You mean to tell me she's going to give birth to *me*, the man she slept with? *I am my own father?*"

"In not so many words, yes. You shall be reborn. Reborn into a new world — *our* world. Granted access to the keys to the kingdom."

[*Goddess of Rebirth*]

The concept itself was staggering, mindblowing. If Haddon had understood the cat-thing correctly, he would emerge several months down the line from his wife's birth canal. *As what, exactly?* An alien halfling? Before then, he would have to be content with being just an embryo, a mere foetus. Haddon didn't much fancy the idea of floating helplessly around in someone's amniotic sac. He tried to envisage the environment which would contain and sustain him as he developed, and found himself further repulsed. What were the chances that the amniotic fluid would be black, like petroleum? *But, hang on a mo, aren't we getting ahead of ourselves?* How could he be both living, unformed, in Sian's oily belly and yet still be standing here in these woods as a full-grown man?

Had to be physically impossible, even by the metaphysical standards of this mad place. Besides, it was a matter of human consciousness — it surely couldn't exist in two places at once. *So what gives?*

"The seed will not survive unless you have committed yourself to the Final Reckoning," the cat-thing continued. "Only you can complete the ritual. Only you can perform the task which is required of you."

"What task?"

"You liked my little girl, didn't you?"

"What task, dammit?"

"Once more she has proved her worth. Gave her some lessons myself, you know."

Oh, what joy! What bliss! What memories you must have! "What task, you inbred bastard?" Haddon screamed. *"What task?"*

"How dare you take that tone with me?" the cat-thing hissed back, enraged. The conversation was evidently over. It got up from its haunches, hackles raised, flashing its eyes and baring its deadly fangs as if preparing to attack. "Go now and embrace your destiny, or I might do something that I may later regret."

Haddon was no match for it and, like a good, little choirboy, he obeyed. Moaning cravenly, he stumbled away into the creeping, intertwining murk of the woods. He ran full-pelt, not wanting to incur the wrath of Glendower or the slimy monsters or the sinuous root-creepers. Getting out in one piece, avoiding any more of these nameless creatures, remained his top priority.

When he had disappeared from view, the cat-thing sat back again, pleased. "If you thought you had it bad, just see what we have in store for you. You will find, my boy, there *really* is no escape," it said and chuckled fiendishly. The trees chuckled with it.

Haddon didn't know how long it took him to clear the woods, but it was a hazy chain of sensations that got him in sight of the abandoned police car. And he didn't stop at the clearing, either. He kept running until he was about to sit in the car when he received another shock, one that might have stopped his heart from beating altogether.

Like the other car accessories, the courtesy light wasn't working. Furthermore, if Haddon hadn't been in such a hurry, he might have seen the ill-defined shadow sat slouched in the passenger seat. Instead, he slammed shut the driver's door and felt for the key in the ignition. It was still there, and Haddon thanked his lucky stars for showing him some compassion. Sweating like swine on a spit, his breath coming out in burdensome gasps, he turned the ignition-key, his fingers trembling, mind fearing the worst. There was a low, grinding noise. "Come on you pile of junk, start!" he bawled desperately, smacking his palms against the steering-wheel. He wanted to leave this abhorrent place before those disgusting slime-monsters came shlopping out of the woodland for the express purpose of shlurping him up. He tried again with the ignition and, this time, the engine roared to life. "Yes, oh, yes!" he exclaimed with a great whoop of triumph. *Are we ready to Rock 'N' Roll or what?* Then in softer, soothing tones, absently sweet-talking the car: "Just a bit more, baby. Just a teeny-weeny bit more... *YESSS, ANNNND WE'RE OFF!*"

In a terrific trail-burst of smoke and skid marks, Haddon hovered a loud, erratic U-turn, bringing the car safely back onto the road once the ungainly manoeuvre was done. "We're cooking now! Yes, we've hit the jackpot and we're *Boogie*-ing on down!" The relief was monumental, almost orgasmic.

He switched on the headlamps to lend his vision better road access. The country road lit up and the dials on the dashboard gave off their own reassuring green glow.

It was about then that Haddon realized he wasn't alone in the car.

Unable to turn, he sensed someone beside him, reclined next to him on the passenger seat. The dark figure, who had remained silent throughout Haddon's excited rant, suddenly moved, and Haddon felt a horrible pang of panic. The fright-stricken scream did not emerge, though, stuck firmly in his throat like a fishbone.

Then the shape spoke up in a voice that Haddon both recognized and loathed in equal measure. "About time too, boyo."

Haddon nearly lost control of the car in sheer astonishment. "Evans...? My God, Evans...!"

"You were expecting someone else?"

Haddon hazarded a glance. Sure enough, it was Evans with his unmistakable moustache and unflattering perm, as usual smoking a home-rolled cigarette. For the first time since moving to Tolwyn,

Haddon experienced something he would never openly admit to: actually being glad to see Evans.

"I've been waiting here all evening for you," Evans said stolidly. "Caught me napping, I'm afraid. So where have you been?"

Waiting for me to return? Haddon thought wildly. *I've just seen you get chopped up by a gang of homicidal kids, who incidentally turned into those black, slimy monsters we talked about earlier. Then your body got possessed by God-knows-what... I saw the whole thing, man, I saw you DIE!* "You wouldn't believe me if I told you."

"You smell bad."

Evans was right. Haddon looked awful and smelled awful. His uniform was ripped in many places and covered all over by a mixture of blood, sweat and muck. His face ached in a snarl of cuts and bruises. Worse, he had scraped his back badly when he'd slid down the hill. "Tell me about it."

Hey, hang on a minute...! the sceptic in him puzzled. *Headlights...? A car at night...? Night...? It was night-time? Call me paranoid, but how could PC Evans have sat here all night and not gone out to look for me?* Haddon snatched a glance at his watch. There it was, 1:37AM. No way could Evans have sat here all evening, not for six hours, without raising the alarm. Suddenly, Haddon had a leery certainty that something was still amiss. Why shouldn't he be cautious, after everything he had gone through? He had been to Hell and back.

"So you've been in this car all this time?" Haddon said, throwing Evans a suspicious glance. "I don't buy it, matey!"

"I radioed back to the station at nine yesterday evening," Evans explained, stubbing out his roll-up. "Old Powell told me to stay put, so I've been waiting for you since. He was planning to get together a search-party, you know, if you didn't show up by two. So what happened? Why did you run off like that?"

Some the tension dissipated then, and Haddon felt a great weight lift from his shoulders. No longer mistrustful, Haddon considered where to begin. *Take a bit of sorting out, this will.* Was it possible he had gone to sleep at the side of the road and had experienced a short nightmare? *Say, a nightmare patched together from the various conversations I've had over the past few days?* That would definitely account for the anomalous quickening of time and the freaky sideshow monsters. No, that couldn't be it. The journey from the moment the cat had stepped into the road to the point he had come back to the car had been so vivid, so *real*, that Haddon could only put it down to some elaborate hallucination. That seemed the more likely explanation. However, as explanations go, Haddon still found it rather implausible, because it indicated he must have a sick, ailing mind if he was suffering such perverse hallucinations. Haddon could say without a shadow of a doubt that his higher faculties were intact, his judgement totally unimpaired. No alcohol, no drugs, no family history of mental illness. And it didn't even begin to explain his general wear-and-tear.

Having no-one else to confide in but Evans, he decided to relate his tale briefly.

"Fiend's Grave, hey?" Evans said when Haddon had finished. "But I never saw any woods. Only grass, lots of it."

"But they were *there*... I was *there*, I swear it!"

"Don't worry," Evans replied with a slow, satisfied nod. "I like it. Proves my theory."

"What theory?"

"That you were transported to another time or a parallel universe. I can't be sure, but those monsters you encountered were probably 'shoggoths'—Lovecraft coined the term. I prefer to call them 'Broodlings'. Can you remember if they were covered all over with eyes and mouths?"

It seemed Evans was still singing *Looney Tunes*. Once you got him started on this kind of stuff, he was unlikely to stop. "What the hell are you talking about?" Haddon countered in incredulous dismay. "There are no such things as different dimensions and parallel universes. Can't you think of anything more down to earth?" *The last person to ask. Beware the Bollocks!*

"More down to earth, hey, boyo?" Evans said thoughtfully. Then a frown of wisdom crossed his forehead. "How about a juxtaposition of dimensions, the possibility that a fragment of a parallel universe merged with our own?"

For an instant, Haddon thought Evans was taking the piss. But the look on his face suggested he was as serious as ever. "For chrissakes, try to be sensible for a change! Or kindly shut your coal-hole! You're obsessing over a subject matter which is madder than the madmen who write this madness!" Then he corrected himself: *He's not the issue. He's not the one beset with demons; you are, when the demons are in your head. You're the madman who witnessed all that madness. So stands to reason, you're not crazy. Stark raving mad, perhaps, but not crazy!* Haddon shook his head to clear away these negative thoughts, deciding to let the matter rest until he was back at the police station, in the comfort of its shadow-dispersing, artificial lighting.

He concentrated on the deserted road back to Tolwyn, the straight, cobbled road in the middle of the ungroved grassland, grey and bleak and desolate in the waning moonshine. *People have gone missing, never to be seen again. Here one minute, vanished the next...* A consideration that Haddon didn't need reminding of. Especially from himself. "Look, matey, I don't pretend to know what's going on. All I'm asking for is a simple, rational explanation, you savvy?"

Evans sounded disappointed, genuinely miffed. "So you don't believe in my Broodlings then?"

"No!" was Haddon's gruff, frustrated reply.

"That so?" It was precisely then that the hand clutched Haddon's left arm, the nails digging deep into his flesh, and a dark minatorial voice at his side thundered: "*You know, you shouldn't drop your guard so easily, otherwise you'll live longer!*"

Terror seeped through his body anew as Haddon swung his head sidelong to see another nightmare unfold. It wasn't Evans anymore, but a xenomorphic travesty of the human shape. Swelling up to several times its size, Evans's face abruptly split open from brow to chin like an over-ripe melon. The attendant sound was far from subtle, closer to the ripping of heavy-duty plastic than anything else. Underneath, the flesh resembled a kind of living Jell-O, as pliable as Plasticine, contorting and stretching, liquefying and blackening. Tendrils erupted from his uniform, slithering and squirming and sloshing, reaching out for Haddon...

The panic didn't vocalize, but his reflexes remained relatively alert. He pulled his arm away from the grasping hand, hustled open the driver's door and, regardless of the car's speed, leapt out. Haddon landed hard on the cobblestones, rolling over a few times, before coming to rest on his back. He heard a sudden metallic thud, followed by the sound of cracking glass.

Trembling like a bundle of loose wires, he got to his feet and saw that the police car had slid into a ditch, the driver's door hanging open. *I don't know how, but it's happening again!* his mind wept. *Do something, dammit!*

Haddon did. He began to run, blindly, abandoning the dented Astra.

What if you're experiencing another funny-do, and Evans is actually in the car hurt?

No, he's one of them!

How do you know? What if you're wrong? You want to risk it?

Haddon conceded to logic, stopped running, looked back at the ditched car. *I'll just go back and peer inside. If I don't like what I see, I'll—*

He was deliberating whether to return to the police car when his left arm began to sting. To burn. To rack with pain. He raised his arm and discovered with irrevocable revulsion that he'd taken Evans's hand with him whilst evacuating the car. It clung to his arm like a giant leech. And it was no longer a hand. The tiny monstrosity twitched with infernal life while rapidly reverting to black ooze, eating away at his uniform and the underlying flesh as effectively as battery acid.

With a horrified yelp, Haddon tore off his uniform, the brass buttons popping off in every direction, and flung it to the ground. Clad now in a white vest and dirtied, defiled royal-blue trousers, his eyes happened to go skyward at the moon. Or, to be more exact, *moons*.

Haddon stared agog at the twin moons in the heavens as his perception unravelled and the world lost all meaning. The feeling of motion-sickness was overpowering. Yet Haddon tried to console himself with the knowledge that this was all happening in his mind—that none of it was real in any sense. The moons were glowing like the luminous eyes of that ubiquitous black cat as if watching him from above. Haddon could imagine those dark, ellipsoid craters at the centre of each oblate sphere as being pupils. Watching him with cold, derisive laughter. Watching him the way a cat toys with a mouse. Watching him with all the devilish glee of Glendower.

[*Chair and Adjudicator and First Emissary to the Olden One.*]

And the sky too. It looked surreal and pigmented, as though painted deep purple by an artist's brush-and-palette. It looked as if it might very well fall off the edge of the horizon and shatter into a gazillion pieces.

Jesus Christ, where am I? What is this place? What in God's name is going on? Why are you doing this to me? Questions, questions and more questions, the answers eluding him to every extreme. *GET ME THE HELL OUT OF HERE!*

The fiendish woods had been terrible enough, Evans's transmogrification into a morphing, shapeless non-entity beyond frightening and the sky's degeneration into a kiddie's picture a far cry from reality, but Haddon was about to experience a sight that would leave an everlasting impression on him, for what little life remained. It made even less sense than anything that had transpired before it.

The cobbled road behind began to undulate, rising and falling like a carpet, as if something underneath were trying to force its way out. It came in one long sweeping wave towards him and then, two hundred yards from where he stood, the cobblestones began to loosen—loosen with the harsh, mechanical, grinding noise of overstressed concrete—and fly off... They flew off as though spring-loaded from beneath. First, one... then, two... three, four, five... finally, in furiously rejected clusters, clattering around him as they fell. Haddon watched, petrified, as something enormous emerged from the egresses. What he thought at the outset was some kind of fungous, polypous growth turned out in fact to be the nuclei of writhing, ebony-black tentacles, their girth enlarging and swelling to the size of ancient oak boles, their texture that of wet, super-squidgy liquorice.

As the black, surging formlessness displaced cobblestone after cobblestone, Haddon fled, his heart way up in his throat. A confusion of thoughts whirled in his mind. PC Neville warning him of the *Time of the Wild Hunt*... Thomas Dwyer crying out: *Monsters! ... Armies of them! ...* Evans lecturing: *Different dimensions, parallel universes... You should believe in them! ...*

Haddon took a quick dekko over his shoulder and caught a vision that he thought was only possible in those old Quatermass movies or in the daft struggle between Steve McQueen and the extraterrestrial blob.

[*All definitely not Welsh*]

The road behind was a river of black. Not just black, like the sunken shaft of a minepit, but a colour vastly blacker than black, the very antithesis of light. Pure 'anti-light'. Glistening slickly by the glow of the attentive twin moons, the knobbly, tentacled lifeform—one couldn't even begin to imagine how big it was—tossed the patrol-car into the air like it were a mere Matchbox model, and gobbled it up, roof-first. Haddon saw the unfortunate Astra disappear into the colossal tongue of animate tar and estimated the creature to be immense, immeasurable even, possibly a collective, full-scale version of the monsters he had encountered in the woods. A creature unto itself, screeching into the night.

Haddon didn't dawdle around on this lonely track of flying cobblestones, either. He ran from the amorphous, gargantuan being — this black blasphemy from below and beyond the boundaries of the known Universe — in a state of apocalyptic terror. Haddon ran and ran and ran.

Haddon reached Tolwyn Pass as the sky was beginning to lighten. Time had become a meaningless constant for him, fast, measureless time where minutes passed in seconds. Feeling as though he had run a marathon, Haddon at last glimpsed Tolwyn, nestled in the valley like a peculiar gem. He picked out the distant courthouse and the tall steeple of the church, two such landmarks rising darkly above the spectral sprawl of roofs and chimney-pots and telegraph poles. Bisecting the township, the furrowed strip of the branchline disappeared altogether at the town centre only to re-emerge on the south side before journeying onwards.

Haddon should have felt a certain relief (he had left the giant jet-black mass far behind him), but he realized things were still not quite right even before he got into Tolwyn.

The red telephone box on the corner of Gadfield Road was the first sign of trouble. In the space of a single night, it had become a dead glassless wreck. As Haddon tried contacting the police station, he discovered the phone didn't work; he held the handpiece close to his ear, listened intently for a humming tone, found none. The result of vandals, Haddon would have normally assumed, no big deal… if it were not for the rest of the road. There was no-one about, certainly no great surprise, since no ordinary person is expected to be up and about this early, except maybe the occasional taxi or police car or the habitual party-animal. But with regards the few cars that were parked in the driveways, they looked to be in the same dilapidated state as the telephone box, broken-down rust-buckets that hadn't been driven in years. Many were missing engine-parts and tyres and windshields, and their paintwork had almost completely eroded away. The houses too on this smarter end of Gadfield Road appeared utterly deserted, and Haddon didn't need to break into any of them to know he would find each property unoccupied. Their general outward neglect, the rank dirt clogged on the sash-windows, told him everything he needed to know.

"Come out, come out, wherever you are!" Haddon yelled into the disquieting silence, laughing out loud. He yelled again for good measure, then intermittently. If there was indeed anyone about, they would have likely glanced out of their windows by now to see who was causing the commotion. Turn on the bedroom light, draw the curtains aside, peer down into the street. Normal human behaviour. But nobody did. Nobody at all.

Probably because there are no curtains to draw, nobody around to look down from their window. Undoubtedly, the given truth of the situation, the absolute and unalterable truth. Tolwyn was dead and deserted. There was only dirt and decay to keep Haddon company.

The exact same thing applied to the terraced streets farther along; just the eldritch, empty-looking shells of houses as inanimate as the cobbled streets around them, untouched buildings of a forgotten past. Perhaps not so much forgotten as forsaken.

Lungs as red-hot as pokers, stomach burbling with acid, mouth filled with the taste of tin, legs aching from sheer exhaustion, Haddon wandered through the ghost-town like an explorer stumbling across an extinct, uncharted civilization. *Ruins of the Minoan empire, say, or maybe the Mayan.*

Is this is what I came back for? he thought with dull, jaded despair. *To languish in the Land of the Lost?*

Thank you very much, Sergeant Powell, for a most interesting tour of your Darklands. Please wake me up when it's over.

Haddon craved rest, but most of all he craved reality. He knew he wouldn't find it here. It appeared as if the Tolwyn he'd known, like time itself, had been contaminated somehow by whatever dark forces were at work. Whatever affected the woods now affected the town. Something evil had taken over the place, turned the land into corruption. Haddon couldn't deny feeling like he had slipped through a membrane into another dimension, one which bore only a faint resemblance to the world he knew, one where time was rapidly winding down and an ancient evil held court.

The answers he desperately sought would soon come to him as he tottered towards the town centre.

Just when he was beginning to think he was the last human alive on this entire planet, Haddon heard singing. Well, at first he thought he did. Voices in chiming unison, singing. Then it dawned on him that what he was actually hearing were people chanting.

He drew nearer and established it was coming from the church, the same church Haddon had seen derelict and abandoned not so long ago. Except it didn't look particularly derelict now, nor abandoned. It had been miraculously restored, and Haddon had the sudden urge to run inside and join the congregation, ask the people for help. However, a stronger dread stopped him in his tracks. He simply had to look at the church to notice that things weren't exactly pukkah.

The whole building had been painted black, and it wasn't a trick of the dark. The arched windows were no longer boarded-up and light poured out of them in brilliant swatches, illuminating the stained-glass murals in their vivid fullness. There were no beauteous saints or angels to speak of here, only scene upon scene of unnameable creatures crawling up from the Last Circle of Hell. The inverted cross of Black Mass embellished every window. Huge, horned, hooved devils gnawed greedily on the heads of imprisoned soldiers. All manner of grotesque, loping monsters had tied-up a naked, semi-conscious maiden with the obvious intention of raping and torturing her. A winged chimaera snatched a newborn baby from his screaming mother and carried him off into the godless night to feed its already-gorged young.

The lighted windows glared at Haddon like a multitude of alien eyes. The black stonework seemed to shimmer with life, rippled like flesh under dusky, glistening skin. The incantation rose higher in pitch as the flock inside reached some kind of diabolic frenzy.

"*Yuphregsn wy'hyten...*" went the unhallowed canticle. "*R'yelah ogas mytemn... Phtegn drohetep g'yai... Dlos'tai fhtagn zei'dfhg Hyehaotepf...*"

It hardly required a great genius to figure out that the language coming from the church was the same as that broadcast on the police band and that which had formed the spoken address of the child-druids. From the noise, it sounded as if the entire town had gathered in the church for this very sermon.

The purpose? To praise the Olden One? To confirm their faith in this faceless, outerworldly being? To summon Him forth?

Haddon was on the verge of deciding whether he should get a closer look, maybe peek in through the stained-glass windows, when the double doors burst open and the creatures he thought he had left far behind came pouring out in unassailable numbers. An exodus of black, shapeless monsters. *Broodlings*, as the erstwhile Evans had labelled them. Haddon turned on his heels and ran. Ran like a sprinter straight off the starter's block, ran like he had never run before, ran as if his life depended on it.

Was this nightmare ever going to end? he thought as he fled, wild-eyed, face limned with panic, his sanity like flour sifting through a sieve. *I really can't take much more of this!*

They rolled after him, screeching and squealing and sloshing. On the High Street, he noticed the sign of Glendower's den of iniquity had changed radically overnight from THE WHITE SWAN to THE BLACK RAVEN. He passed the local cinema, which had begun to play something called *The Remains of the Dead*.

They came out of everywhere, from every entrance, from every available threshold: the bank, the cinema, the library, the newsagents, the post office, the Burger King bar, the hairdresser's salon, even the sewers. The circular covers of the manholes rattled on the bone-dry cobbles as the horde of viscous, tarry blobs came streaming forth like a rendition to a video-nasty, the nightmare getting worse reel by reel. Like monstrous black amoebi, the Broodlings tumbled in his general direction as if sensing him by smell alone.

Terrified beyond rational thought, Haddon turned left on Station Road and arrived at the police station, praying that the creatures weren't lurking there too.

His luck was in. By some extraordinary quirk of fate, the police station was a monster-free zone. Almost as though preordained.

He ran into the lobby of the police station and bolted the doors, then barricaded himself in with the heavy wooden benches. He heard them pile up outside the doors, scratching, squelching, sloshing, screeching.

Thank God, there weren't any windows. It bought him some time, at least.

What could he do to defend himself against these jellified abominations from Hell? Was there a chance of escape round the back or was he being just a bit too optimistic? No, he deliberated, they would most likely have the building completely surrounded? With lightning speed, he locked all the other doors down the corridor, then waited and debated over his next move. High time he thought of a way out of this mess. There *had* to be something he could do. There just had to be or —

I'm going to die, aren't I?

Don't be ridiculous!

Who's being ridiculous? Unless I think of something pretty sharpish, I've had it!

There was no use denying it, and it struck him with the force of a loaded gun. Through all the madness he had been forced to endure, he had not once considered the possibility of his own death, and now it had become almost inevitable. Contemplating it was like waiting for the hangman. No man wants to believe that his death warrant has been signed, dated and delivered. Haddon wasn't ready for it, would never be ready for it. As a policeman he had faced death a dozen times, yet this time it was different. This was real, this was happening. Haddon's pulse raced erratically, his heart hammering haphazardly in his chest. The walls seemed to close in as the dust-softened, cobweb-festooned lobby took on the sinister charms of a sealed crypt. How long would those barriers hold out against the mob of shapeless things?

Not long, he supposed. *I'm as good as dead, and you know it... Soon... Perhaps sooner than you think...*

You're not, dammit, so shut the fuck up!

He would have wept had the reception counter not attracted his attention. Like everything else, it too was covered by a thick layer of dust, collected maybe over centuries. Atop rested a corpse-candle, the only source of light in the sepulchral gloom. There were no light-switches or telephones in sight. So much for calling the big guns for emergency assistance; it seemed he would have to see this through on his own. Beside the candle lay a closed book and a shiny object, which Haddon figured to be a long, jagged shard of glass.

Presently, he crossed the lobby to the counter and was somehow compelled to look at the book. It was an omnibus of some kind, bound in leather, as fat as an encyclopaedia. Maybe it held all the answers to his problems, a way out of here. Haddon stared at the title on the cover which seemed to be written in the same ancient, esoteric language that had blighted his night. Then, without warning, the strange symbols re-configured into untranslatable Welsh, switching over eventually to plain English. The title of the book was now clearly readable: THE INDESCRIPTION by Hywl Glyndwr.

Curiosity lent Haddon a helping hand as he opened the volume to the contents' page. No, pages, to be precise. He scanned the list which overall comprised nearly four hundred chapters, set down in chronological order, the wording in fine print, the vellum old, flimsy and yellowed. The first chapter read: DOSAI 158BC. FENELLA MEYRICKE 974AD constituted the two-hundredth chapter. The three-hundred-and-ninety-third chapter was marked: WILKES, Geoffrey 1979AD. Somehow the name had a familiar ring to it, but Haddon couldn't recall why. The next entry belonged to SIMMONDS, John 1985AD, the penultimate: BRAITHWAITE, Alan 1991AD.

Entry 396: HADDON, Mitchell 1997AD…

Haddon felt the terror strengthen its rapport, felt the glue holding his mind together separate.

My name! How can it have my name?

Haddon riffled through the pages, the book flipping open to the relevant section with inordinate ease, as though intentionally. The chapter began with the following text:

September 1997. Six years since the last sacrifice, Thomas Dwyer straggled into Touen police station a desperate citizen in a dashing ploy to capture the untarnished curiosity of a young police constable by the name of Mitchell Haddon, who glanced up from his notebook at the new arrival.

"Help me, please," Dwyer murmured, acting the victim impeccably. *"You've got to help me!"*

"Afternoon, sir. What can I do you for?" Sergeant Powell asked, attending to the newcomer.

"Monsters!" Dwyer replied. *"I was attacked by monsters…"*

"Tell me about it in here," Powell said consolingly, leading Dwyer into the inner sanctum.

Haddon looked up again, and this time, there was no doubt in my mind that Mordyll Di and Arawn-Pwyll had drawn our unsuspecting Londoner into the intriguing mystery of Fiend's Grave...

What the hell was this? Some kind of diary of events? Why was Glendower [*gentle narrator*] writing about him?

Haddon flicked through the pages, randomly pausing at another passage:

... And the Ellyllon held up high, as homage to the Olden One, the Dark Passion of Pwca and, thus biting into the Apple of Lost Eden, they cried as one voice, "O Olden One! We bring You the Chosen One for the Eternal Suffering. Let him endure the Fear of the Indescription."

Haddon, the Chosen One, looked upon the Ceremony of Gorsedd in unrivalled lamentation, unaware that he would be facing Cwn Annwn, the Time of the Wild Hunt and the Fear of the Indescription before finally choosing the Path of Infinite Torments...

Haddon read it again and again, not believing what his eyes were conveying. His whole ordeal was written down here for him to read. How was such a thing even possible?

Bad Omens and Black Magic.

But this was much more than just bad omens and black magic. This was impossible. This was insanity at its most infernal.

Drawn on by a fatalistic compulsion, Haddon realized what he must read next. Feeling like a medieval soothsayer about to pronounce his own doom, Haddon skipped to the last passage of the chapter and read:

The Bible of Godless Parables was closed. The story of the Untold had been told.

Haddon knew all and chose to have no choice in the outcome of the Fear of the Indescription. As the Broodlings of Annwn crashed through the gates of the Last Citadel of Order, the righteous perished by the will of his own hand, and his soul was lost for a hundred thousand years until claimed by Bwcibo in the Sanctuary of the Damned.

And where there is an ending, there is always a fresh beginning...

At that moment, the confusion cleared and it occurred to Haddon what it all meant. An instant of crushing revelation. The script had been written in the past tense. Yet it had not happened. Or had it happened? Maybe it was going to happen.

These written accounts must relate to the missing people, all those unfortunate few who had vanished in the general vicinity of Tolwyn, never to be seen again. Disappeared under mysterious circumstances. Apparently, sacrificed as an offering to the gods. It was all coming together now. Fenella Meyricke had probably been one of the middlemost sacrifices. Haddon recalled hearing the name PC Wilkes from his long chat with Evans. But there were hundreds of names on the list, chosen approximately five to ten years apart, stretching forward from the distant past to the immediate present. Sacrificed. Murdered. While, to the public, swept under the carpet as 'Presumed Missing'.

And Haddon served as the immediate present.

With a combined sense of futility and finality, Haddon realized it was the end of the road. A calmness descended over him, the artificial calm of shock and acceptance, of knowing that nothing he did now would ever matter. What he was dealing with could never fit conveniently into any formal police report, *oh no*, for he had somehow leapt beyond the shores of reality to the mountains of myth and madness. To a world beyond comprehension, beyond definition, beyond description. As the enormity of it sank in, he recognized he was lost in a nightmare of someone else's creation, the anteglories of a cruel, malignant imagination. The victim of an evil conspiracy, of which his so-called wife had played an unscrupulous part. Sian was as guilty of duplicity as Evans, probably more so, since she had actively sought him out, had been the one who had suggested marriage as well as pleading with him they move down here. He had never suspected her hurry might harbour a hidden agenda. He had been too enamoured by her to complain. He had been completely... *bewitched*. She had used him, strung him along and in no uncertain terms set him up for a mighty fall. The Welsh tart had seduced him with her dark designs of desire, lied and cheated her way into his heart, and eventually stolen his essence in order to add to a dimension-crossing race of creatures which had conquered death and fed on fear. He had paid the price for bein' marrit to the morst boot'ful girl in the wurld. His mistake, his folly. Then, her repugnant father had pre-written Haddon's obituary with unerring clarity, accurately foretelling his last bitter moments in Tolwyn's Chronicles of the Dead. Glendower had manipulated Haddon from the start, exploited him like a cheap, expendable puppet. Because that was what he was, *literally*. A helpless puppet, an ill-fated character in an elaborate stage-play, hosted by Glendower, performed in honour of the Olden One, the unterrene Termagant. This had all been one big show, not to mention, one big set-up. It was the end of the road for him — that much he was sure of — and Haddon numbly surrendered to the inevitable. He knew his ordeal, his night of unprecedented torment, would soon be over.

All I ever wanted was to get out of this shithole. Now, it seems, I never will. Reborn, Glendower told me. I shall be reborn.

What malefic secrets had the community kept from the outsider? What black arts were practised in accordance with strict druidic customs? What unnameable horror existed in some far-flung corner of space, on some sightless, Stygian world, waiting for the day It would return and enslave all humanity? Haddon had a reasonable inkling, just as he knew he had been lured to one last encounter with the Olden One's ageless acolytes, keen on ensuring his final immolation.

This was not for the mortal mind of Man to question or understand. It was purposely designed to remain an undescriptive, so to speak.

Haddon shut the book and looked back grimly, resignedly at the barricades he had erected at the entrance to prevent admittance to the hungry monstrosities from the nether abysses. The door was creaking and bending inwards, the wood straining to its limits under the weight of the squishing, squelching masses outside. There followed a loud thrashing noise at the door, the sound made when a battering ram is used to break down the besieged castle gates.

Gestating in a wombful of black ichor didn't much sound like his idea of marital bliss. Imagining himself crawling out, squirming and screeching, from his wife's prolific birth canal as some gelatinous, blobbified changeling too failed to uplift him.

Not quite the bright, sensible future I hoped for...

The door caved in an instant later and the candle guttered, extinguished. Haddon saw them, silhouetted against the sunrise, spill inwards in search of his condemned soul. Mad things that were once people, physically corrupted over uncounted centuries. Transposed, cartoon-like, upon the writhing, semi-vitreous form of one of these unspeakable creatures was the gorgonian, bastardized face of his beloved wife.

Hello, darling, you look kind of different. Is that a new makeover you've had?

All of a sudden, Haddon had an unnatural desire to laugh. Not a humorous laugh, mind you, but the sort of laugh one hears from a committed patient in the maximum security wing of a psychiatric block or when a crazed killer admits delightedly that he's bludgeoned his whole family to death. *It's a fair cop, guv. It was just for larks.*

One man's ordeal had come to an end. Haddon understood what course of action he must take in order to save himself from the black, hellish miscreations, [*Only you can do what must be done. Embrace your destiny.*] and, as they advanced with their shrieks and sloshes, he picked up the beckoning splinter of glass, raised it to his neck and glided it like a straight-razor across his throat.

Down in Tolwyn, everything was as normal as could be. It was three in the morning and most of the people lay tucked up in their beds, fast asleep. A few clubbers hung around on the streets of the town centre, affording only a few minor skirmishes with the police. And, at THE WHITE SWAN, Glendower went back to banging his daughter.

At the police station, life was quiet as always. Sergeant Powell sat engrossed in conversation with his deputy, PC Evans, in the mess-hall whilst the radio chugged out *Puppet Man* by Tom Jones, a step above any of the young pretenders. Now there was a man who was definitely Welsh! If there was anything better than Bassey the Beautiful Mongrel Lady, it was none-other-than the Granddaddy of Rock, Tom Jones — the Olden One.

"It seems our English friend isn't with us anymore," Powell was saying as he put down the statistical report he'd been idly perusing, earmarked for police headquarters the coming week.

Evans sat, hands folded behind his head, feet resting on the coffee table. "You know, I almost miss him."

Powell nodded contemplatively. "Strange man, I must admit. Arrogant. Judgemental. Cynical as a French floozie. Thoroughly unlikeable. Hated us with a passion. Never gave us the respect we deserve. Well, not to worry. They've got to learn, haven't they? *Never underestimate the Welsh.*"

"Right on," Evans agreed pleasantly. "He'll soon come plopping out of Glendower's girl a changed man."

"As one of us, a Cymran," Powell said with cool satisfaction. "Won't feel so hostile towards us then, I'm sure. Should be more amenable, receptive. He'll come round to our way of thinking soon. Give him time. Might even take to humming *Men of Harlech* with the rest of the boys."

"Or maybe dabble in a little druid worship on the side," added Evans.

"One less Englishman in this country, by Jiminy," Powell remarked. "Care for a spot of tea, sir?" he mocked in a perfect butler's voice.

Evans was on the same wavelength, his impression of the English gentry passable. "Rawther. I'd be most delighted, my dear fellow."

"I'll just check if the water's still hot," Powell said, returning to his usual accent. Eyes shifted to the other side of the room and the electric kettle, top removed, on a tray consisting of three empty mugs and an empty teapot-and-cosy. Powell opened his mouth as if to speak, but instead of words, a long, black, serpentine tongue flicked out and darted to the kettle opposite with the smooth, stretching sound of wet elastic. The absurdly extended tongue dipped into the liquid, then returned, snapping back in his mouth. "Tepid," he informed Evans with unflinching composure.

"Great play this year." Evans resumed.

"Indeed," Powell said. "Excellent performances all round. Yours especially I liked."

"You flatter me."

"No, really. We couldn't have done it without you. You always make the whole thing look a cinch."

"Nothing to write home about," Evans said with some modesty. "I've been chopped up so many times, it's become kind of fun. Does sting a bit though, afterwards."

"Take it from me, you were born to play Pwca. You performed excellently."

"I've never known a poet as the likes of our Glendower," Evans pointed out. "A visionary if there ever was one."

"True, W.H. Davies, Lowri Dafydd and John Cowper Powys are mere shadows to Glendower's dark gift. Only Dylan Thomas, and dear Danni Abse's treatise on the Pathology of Colour, go anywhere near his brilliance. Arthur Machen's not bad, either. We should expect a high yield."

"So what now?" PC Evans asked casually. "We get his daughter to pick up another Cockney?"

"Soon, my friend. When it's time."

Evans said nothing for a moment, then a slow, impish grin spread across his face. "Want to?" he asked, sounding less like a kid hinting towards a dare than a man propositioning an old lover. "You know, for posterity?"

David Powell smiled back, catching his drift. "Do you have to even ask? Been a victory-salute of ours, the first Britons, since I can remember. You know I never tire of hearing it."

Emboldened, Rhodri Evans gave it his all. "Oggie, oggie, oggie!"

"Oi, oi, oi!" they chanted together and burst out laughing.

Outside the window, the red, bloated harvest moon rode high in the sky, looking over a land that was positively flourishing.

May 1997-November 1997

Vampire Season

"*I love acting. It is so much more real than life.*"

The Picture of Dorian Gray (1891)
Oscar Wilde

The show was a success. An absolute success.

Linked arm in arm, Jeremy Hobbs and the rest of the cast bowed their heads in a modest display of thanks as the red velvet curtain fell on stage. Ably supported by the orchestra below, the last movement of the score was delivered, a streaking scherzo that swelled to a crashing crescendo. The atmosphere was electrifying, the rapturous applause of the audience supplementing the bouquets of roses tossed in appreciation of the cast's sterling performance. It had been a long evening at *Le Mercury* for most, but the play had finally wound its way to the end.

Vampire Season had received favourable reviews and, for the first time, the critics raved. Might the producers take the show to Broadway or the West End or maybe even sell the film rights, they speculated. *A fine actor in the making*, approved *Variety* magazine of Hobbs's unforgettable interpretation of the Duc de Devereaux.

Hobbs didn't need to tell them why. *Don't Englishmen make the best villains?* Take the likes of Sean Bean or Alan Rickman or Jeremy Irons or Gary Oldman: actors who possessed class and embodied quality and brought a certain gravitas to the role, playing opposite the usual American airhead of a hero. *Some might even say that a movie is as good as its villain.*

And Hobbs had certainly learned from the best. Not to say that it had been an easy ride. Hobbs had shone in a role that demanded the pinnacle of theatrical talent. Rewarding still was the knowledge that against all odds he had proven his father wrong.

An educated man and moderate disciplinarian, Terence Hobbs had always advocated reading as "the nutriment of the soul" and, from an early age, all three of his children ploughed through book after book in the hope of one day finding their "great passion". Jack found his, a fascination with crime that would later lead him all the way to law school. For Carol, the youngest, it would be journalism and a job at *The Whitby Times*. Jeremy's interests lay elsewhere: theatre and the world of drama. He remembered the nativity plays and school pantos and how the parents afterwards would praise Jeremy's remarkable flair for acting. *Hi-diddle-dee-dee, the actor's life for me!* This was what he wanted to do. Whereas his classmates were quick to pass rude comments about the Lit teacher's androgynous looks and complain constantly as to why they had to "learn this useless crap" for homework, Jeremy was lost, utterly captivated by the immortal lines of playwrights past and present, the situations and scenarios, the scenes and the settings. He had caught a heavy dose of the acting bug.

His father was the first to point out the downside of his "great passion", that acting was neither a sensible nor worthwhile choice of career. There was little-to-no job security; the majority of actors never made it and only a handful reached the top. Furthermore, it was Jeremy's duty to do the smart thing and uphold family tradition by studying accountancy and undertaking an apprenticeship in the firm of *Dempster and Hobbs Chartered Accountants*, where his father was a semi-retired senior partner. However, Jeremy had no head for figures and resented the fact that his future had been pre-decided, and irrespective of his father's will, he packed his bags and set off, Dick Whittington-style, to seek his fortune in the big, wide world. The memory of his father standing on the doorstep insisting Jeremy come back immediately or he'd never be allowed to set foot in the house again supplied Jeremy with all the ammunition and determination to fulfil his potential.

He enrolled in drama class and paid for his fees by working part-time in an auto-mart. Jeremy took to the road soon after, scraping a living doing bit parts in cheap, shoddy commercials. There were no financial contributions from his father, who expected his son to find out the hard way how misplaced his enthusiasm about acting was. A series of absurdist comedies followed, but even a sizeable role in Harold Pinter's *Waiting for Godot* failed to ensure any form of recognition, and the work soon dried up. Not that Hobbs had any shortcomings, unlike those terrible actors who forgot their lines in the midst of a performance, much to their embarrassment and hilarity of the audience, got booed off stage and are told by their director they'll never work again. Such misfortunes befell others, not him. No, the problem was one of competition. There just weren't enough opportunities available to the struggling actor on the English theatre-circuit.

So Hobbs travelled south to seek his fortune.

To London, the very seat of theatre. And it was in a wine-bar in Westminster that he met another out-of-towner, going by the name of Ruby St. Clair. *Smashing girl! And if I might be so bold, ravishing!* Born to embrace danger and fearless in her approach to life, Ruby got a wild rush from rambling the misty streets late at night, alone and unescorted, this despite hearing the darker stories of London, of Hackney drivers who preyed on girls in their cabs, of gangs that mugged entire carriages of commuters on the Underground, of loons who kidnapped, tortured and murdered the ordinary, unsuspecting tourist simply for kicks.

Well, there they were in the wine-bar, talking about the vibrant experience that is theatre and Ruby suggested he audition for a part in a play she had been writing for a new, independent theatre company. *Vampire Season* was planned for release three months down the line in a fashionable Parisian night-spot, not far from the legendary Grand Guignol.

Hobbs did just that. He bought plane-tickets with his remaining funds and, like Hemingway and Miller, journeyed to Paris, the City of Lights, to audition for the role.

Adopting the intense approach of method-acting, he beat thirty other hopefuls to the role of Duc de Devereaux, a lead that, although he didn't realize it at the time, Hobbs was destined to play. What more could any actor ask for than a role that is both sexy and scary? When he got down to rehearsing his lines, however, he was disappointed by the tackiness of the script, with its almost minimal emphasis on the avant-garde. Was he making a mistake, plumbing new depths? It read like just another of those dull, boring, unoriginal vampire stories that flocked the bookshelves and the film industry. *Vampire Season* purported to have derived its gothic flourishes from a Mervyn Peake novel, but on closer inspection Hobbs saw little evidence of it. A penny dreadful would be a more accurate a source; the *mise-en-scène* alone reminded him of the children's book illustrations of Rackham.

Set in a medieval chateau, *Vampire Season* was the tale of a vampire who terrorized the villagers of Chamonix in the French Alps and brought upon himself the wrath of the whole of Christendom. The sole, singular aspect of the plot was the ambiguous ending: Crusaders went up to the castle to capture the Count, but were never seen again.

From the outset, Hobbs was certain the play was doomed to failure, that it would sink unnoticed below the mire, that this would indeed be the final nail in his coffin. Regardless to say, he gave it his best shot, did it notoriously well and, lo and behold, the play was an instant hit and Hobbs an up-and-coming sensation. *Un-bleedin'-believable!*

Surely now, Hobbs could look forward to better things, greener pastures. *Goodbye poverty, toodle-oo obscurity.* Rising up from the same humble beginnings as Gielgud and O'Toole. If only some caring, considerate producer were to give him the opportunity to act in *The Tempest, The Crucible, The Mousetrap* or *The Ladykillers*, Hobbs would set the table on a-roar. Would it be too much to ask if Hobbs were offered membership to the Royal Shakespeare Company with a chance to perform at the Old Vic or the Globe? Was his ambition to work in *Les Miz* or *Phantom* so far-fetched? So what if they were musicals? He could do a pretty good Danny Kaye and was unusually enlightened on the whole subject of vaudeville since first watching Kaye bursting into song in *The Secret Life of Walter Mitty* and then there was, of course, George Burns's old darling in *The Sunshine Boys*. Fair enough, as an actor, Hobbs wasn't in the same league as Kenneth Branagh (whose vanity often got the better of him, believing himself to be the reincarnation of Laurence Olivier), but who knew where Hobbs would be a decade from now? Most of all, though, he could ring up his father, whom he hadn't spoken to in over seven years, and tell him about his top-billing status. *O Ye of little faith!*

God, it felt good to be the star and a vampire with a taste for triumph and a theatrical taste for blood. Under the glare of the spotlights, Hobbs bowed again and, in one last fitting gesture, he furled his long, black cloak before exiting stage left. *What a turn-out, what a performance, what a night! That's what you call showmanship! Wasn't it Shakespeare who said, in his infinite soliloquy, that the world was one big stage and each of us merely players?*

Backstage, the party was in full swing. Corks were popping, champagne was flowing and the cast members were carousing with the rest of the production crew. Hobbs pushed through the milling throng, the hubbub of voices offering him the heartiest of congratulations, toasting his laudable success, urging him to mingle and socialize. He reciprocated their gratitude with similar verve, vigorously encouraging them to make the most of a night that dawned on a bright future for all of them... *à votre santé!*

Dominique LaVerne, who'd played the helpless heroine, stopped him. "That was *magnifique!*"

"The same goes for you," Hobbs said, returning the compliment. "I couldn't have done it without you. Who else could I victimize with such passion and cruelty?"

"What about us having dinner tonight?" she asked expectantly.

"I'm afraid I'm going to have to do a raincheck," Hobbs replied, pretending to regard his watch. "Some other night, perhaps?" He frowned with puzzlement. "You haven't seen Ruby, have you?"

"*Non, mon ami*, I haven't seen her all day."

Hobbs registered the slight look of disappointment on Dominique's face. "It's not what you think, I don't even know her." Except, Hobbs wished he did. He wished he knew Ruby a whole lot better. Dominique was all good and well, but Hobbs longed for Ruby. Tonight, it seemed wasn't going to be that night. *You might have expected the playwright to have turned up on the last night of her play!* Where was she? What could have happened to her? Ever since he'd met her, Hobbs had become smitten by her — that stunning figure and those flawless good looks, her short raven hair and the dark luminescence of her eyes and the sweet lure of her voice that could subdue a man at ten paces, the enigma of how little he knew about her: where she was from, where she lived, whether she had family, if she was seeing someone. Ruby did her best to give nothing away and kept her private life a secret from everyone. But, instead of averting Hobbs's gaze, she managed only in filling him with a greater sense of intrigue. And, oh, those succulent lips: Ruby by name, ruby by kiss.

Let it go! Hobbs deliberated with a sigh. *If Ruby wanted to get to know you, wouldn't she have done so by now?* He decided to take Dominique up on her offer. After all, she'd been pestering him all week. And, as the leading lady, she was entitled to a little attention from her leading man. "All right, *ma chérie*, a restaurant of your choosing."

Dominique's eyes lit up and she pecked his cheek, delighted.

"First, I need to change into my clothes. Otherwise, I'm liable to scare the restaurant staff and all the punters."

"I'll see you soon," Dominique promised and re-joined the celebrations.

Hobbs waded through the crowd, progressed to the hallway. Selina Bossis met him there.

"Jeremy, kudos on a job well done."

"Thank you."

"And no prima donnas, this time."

Hobbs laughed. "I've given them up for good."

"I've got your schedule for the coming week."

"Now would not be the best time," Hobbs told his red-haired agent. "We'll go over it tomorrow. Why don't you join the others for a drink? Enjoy yourself, tonight. You deserve it. We *all* deserve it!"

"Don't you want to know what I've lined you up for?" she asked with some enthusiasm. "I've booked you in for an interview with Jean-Paul Durnier on his show *Le Théâtre Nationale*. He wants to meet you tomorrow."

Not quite Francois Truffaut, but Durnier was still a popular talk-show host, adored by millions of listeners. This was precisely the kind of exposure Hobbs needed in order to get into the mainstream. "You're a peach, you know that, Selina? Tomorrow, it is!"

Hobbs left her beaming. He wandered down the corridor, past rows of signed, gilded photographs of actors who had attended gala-night at *Le Mercury* over the years, some famous like Jacqueline Bisset, Alain Delon, Jeanne Moreau and Simone Signoret, others Hobbs hardly recognized. Their eyes seemed to follow him down the hallway.

This sell-yourself-promotion-malarkey was certainly draining, but Hobbs knew it had to be done. He couldn't work as a vampire all his life. It wasn't healthy; one got stereotyped. Expand the field, broaden the horizons, demonstrate a little versatility, maybe even have a crack at scriptwriting.

The reporters waiting outside would undoubtedly be more concerned about the next venue for the play rather than his next project. Pose for a few publicity shots (a chore Hobbs felt was synonymous with his growing success), then get down to the business of entertaining Dominique.

He liked Dominique. She was young and friendly, not to mention a well-endowed brunette, who dreamed of owning a vineyard and appearing at the Cannes Film Festival. He found her jealousy of his continual fixation with Ruby somewhat amusing. Make the most of the evening, and if the rumours about Dominique were true, he'd probably wake up next to her tomorrow morning. *The things thespians have to do in the name of talent!*

Snickering, Hobbs opened the door to his dressing room and entered. He kept the door slightly ajar, warming to the sound of collective mirth that drifted down the corridor from the stage-set. No-one could have hoped for a better night than Hobbs. Adulation well-deserved for his finest hour. To think, only a year ago he was just another disillusioned, unemployed actor. From relative obscurity to flavour of the month, with the sky positively the limit. He glanced at himself in the dressing-table mirror, the buzzing glow from the single fluorescent deepening the lines and enhancing the ghoulish features on his thin, cadaverous face. He bared his false fangs and improvised in sinister Slavic tones: "I am the Duc de Devereaux and your blood is now *mine!*" It produced the desired effect; the overall sense of menace could not be denied. His red lips curled into a self-congratulatory smile.

He switched on the radio, caught a soft snippet of the song: *Bela Lugosi's Dead* by Bauhaus.

By Jove, he was good! Hobbs considered of himself. He looked the part, acted the part, made the part his own. *A bleeding natural!* Hobbs thought, chuckling inside at the pun. *A lot less Christopher Lee and a little more Lord Ruthven ought to do the trick.* The future had never seemed so bright and rosy, ready for the picking. A few more roles as meaty as that of the despicable Duc de Devereaux and he could die a happy man.

Preparing to wipe off the make-up that made him partway to being such a convincing vampire, he was applying lotion to a cotton ball, when an echoing cough from somewhere nearby made him spin round with an involuntary start.

He had company.

There was another person in the room, presently emerging from the sequestering shadows behind the door.

"What the hell are you doing here? Don't you know my dressing room is off-limits to—?" Hobbs broke off when he saw the person in question.

The visitor was dressed in a completely identical outfit to Hobbs, right down to the cape and ruffled shirt. The face too, though shrouded in gloom, looked remarkably like his own. Hobbs wasn't just rattled; he thought he was seeing double. *A doppelgänger?*

Then, it occurred to him. *Of course!* The visitor was probably a devoted fan, a wishful-thinking dress-a-like, who saw Hobbs as an idol. *I don't mind it in the least, but why do they have to be so damned sneaky?* "You liked the play, huh?" Hobbs said, making absent small-talk. "Autographs are later on so if you could please go and wait outside like all the others." The intruder didn't move, didn't speak. *Hey, this isn't funny!* "I think you didn't hear me," Hobbs said, getting annoyed. "Don't you know stalking's an offence?" Hobbs leaned forward, reached for the internal phone. "I'm calling secur—" Once more, Hobbs froze, on this occasion, not understanding what he was seeing. Or more precisely, what he was *not* seeing.

He whisked a bewildered look at the stranger, then back at the mirror.

Whereas, Hobbs could see the unwanted guest in the room, the mirror lacked any image of his presence. According to the glass, there was no-one in the dressing room except Hobbs.

That's because vampires don't cast reflections.

Suddenly, the room seemed darker, colder, more cramped than usual. The walls appeared to close in, and the wigs and costumes on the racks rustled as if swathing invisible bodies. The laughter from the ongoing celebrations sounded oddly muted and faraway. The song on the radio took on a tinny quality. Hobbs was held captive by the penetrating stare of the stranger, who stood still and silent, his skin paler, his lips redder, the hollows beneath his eyes deeper.

"What do you want?" Hobbs croaked lamely.

The stranger spoke, his voice low and ageless, impeccable save for the vaguest hint of a Black Sea inflection. "Are you not going to ask me who I am?"

No, because I already know...

"Not a bad likeness."

A compliment from the stranger. Hobbs should have been honoured, but he wasn't. He was terrified. He was confronting a figure [Le Diable au corps] immortalized by French superstition, a character Hobbs had just moments ago portrayed on the stage. Who was impersonating whom and who was the understudy here? *Vampire Season* — surely the story wasn't factual? "You can't be real..."

"Ah, but I am and you know I am."

"What do you want?" Hobbs repeated, the truth too stifling to bear.

"I came for *you*," he replied with the cruel clarity of a crypt-keeper. "I am the Duc de Devereaux and your blood is now *mine!*"

There was a chilling irony in the way Hobbs was now at the receiving end of those words, words he had rehearsed a thousand times before. He had to do something, otherwise he *really* would end up flavour of the month.

Hobbs's fingers fumbled for the protection of the gold crucifix his mother had given him on his tenth birthday, whipping it up from the dressing table and holding it aloft in front of him. "Stay away, foul demon!" Hobbs babbled in warning, wild-eyed. "Don't come near me!"

Yet his gesture did little to impede the stranger's intimidating advance. He snatched the crucifix away from Hobbs's trembling hand and slung it aside, casually. "It's about how strong your faith is."

Faith? Faith in what? Hobbs thought, overcome, soporified. It was only when the stranger's mouth closed round the actor's neck that Hobbs surrendered to the sickening realization that his own faith rested exclusively in his accomplishment as a vampire.

Curtain-call.

Once again, Jeremy Hobbs would play the role of the vampire. This time, for real.

February 2002-March 2002

Winter's Chill

"Bah! Humbug!... If I could work my will," said Scrooge indignantly. *"Every idiot who goes about with 'Merry Christmas' on his lips, should be boiled with his own pudding, and buried with a stake of holly through his heart..."*

A Christmas Carol (1843)
Charles Dickens

The car shuddered, spluttered, slowed, crawled to an untimely halt on the snow-swept country lane. The engine completely cut out, gave up the ghost. "I think we have a problem," Stanley Henslow informed his family, perplexion mixed in with embarrassment. He tried the key in the ignition several times, but the engine refused to turn. It wasn't as if they had run out of fuel since the gauge for the petrol tank registered half-empty.

"We should have got the train and taken a taxi from the station!" Belinda Henslow, his nagging harpy of a wife, snapped back at him. "It was *your* damned idea to drive this ancient heap!"

"There's nothing wrong with the car!" Stanley protested, despite knowing he didn't have a leg to stand on. "It's a classic."

"Well, your classic car has just broken down miles from nowhere," his wife reminded him. "And you didn't even bother buying a TomTom."

Stanley was loth to admit it, but Belinda was right. It was Christmas Eve and they were visiting his in-laws for the holidays, an annual tradition. Except this was the first time they'd driven there. Previous years had involved the indignity of travelling in cramped, overcrowded trains, where you had no choice but to stand for most of the journey. Stanley had hoped that buying a second-hand car — in this case a stone-grey Rover Metro from the days of yore — all he could really afford on his assistant librarian's salary — would mean they could travel in relative comfort and at their own pace and leisure. But, as if Fate were mocking him for the gullible chump he was, not only did the goddamned Metro turn out to be a veritable pooping ground for the birds, but it had now broken down at a critical juncture. He should have suspected from the car salesman's proper Del-Boy attitude and the fat wad of cash he flashed at them and the dodgy fellow's stark refusal to provide them with any sort of warranty, the car might not be entirely fit for purpose, even if it had *allegedly* passed its MOT. Maybe Stanley should have approached his father-in-law, Cedric Fothergill, retired President and now primary stakeholder of Chilton Frozen Foods and greatly feared by his former employees, for a loan in order to buy a more roadworthy vehicle.

However, when the time came, pride had prevented him from doing so. Cedric had never liked Stanley, made him feel small and worthless, a straggling garden weed in the Grand Design of Life, wholeheartedly believing his daughter had married beneath her. More to the point, Stanley did not wish to be owned by Cedric, who would never let him hear the end of it, if Stanley had indeed borrowed money from the old curmudgeon.

Stanley peered out of the windscreen, scanned his surroundings, assessed their current situation. It was certainly beautiful out there: Christmas-card-beautiful, snow-globe-beautiful, born of fairytale enchantment. For once, this part of the world would be celebrating a White Christmas. As big, fat crystal snowflakes fluttered silently down from the ashen-grey heavens, a soft, twinkling whiteness blanketed the fields on either side of the country lane, betraying each dip and contour of the land, stretching away to the distant horizon. There were no signs of habitation, of life — most of God's creatures, great and small, probably in the swaddles of hibernation, acorns squirreled away for winter — apart from the occasional sharp squawk of a crow. Stanley and his family could have trekked across the desolate snow and taken refuge in a farmhouse or cottage, if one had been in easy reach or even vaguely visible. However, there was none. Only field upon field shrouded in a sheer, untrodden whiteness, and a copse of conifers in the west clothed to its very unseen hollows in snow.

"Don't just sit there, do something!" his wife's prickly voice came from somewhere faraway.

Stanley suddenly realized he'd been sitting there for the best part of five minutes without saying anything, just staring at the magical, snow-dreaming Dickensian scenery outside the windshield. He glanced at his wife in the passenger seat, her mouth downturned in a sour expression, and twisted round to check on the kids in the back, eight-year-old Becky and five-year-old Adam, who were looking at him expectantly, small innocent smirks on their faces. "Of course, my dear," he murmured, snapping out of his reverie, taking a moment to organize his thoughts, deciding what he must do. He could have looked under the hood, but he didn't know the first thing about car maintenance. Instead, he rummaged through his coat pockets and brought out his mobile phone. The phone indicated limited satellite coverage, one bar for a signal. Prioritizing, he rang the RAC.

He was glad when he eventually got connected to Customer Services even though he experienced a great degree of embarrassment for calling out the RAC within the first seventy-two hours of purchasing the car. The helpful lady on the other end asked him all the relevant, routine questions: insurance policy, make and model of the car, the current problem with the vehicle. When it came to informing her where they had broken down, she became strangely quiet. When she spoke again, the friendliness was gone from her voice, and Stanley could have sworn he detected fear.

"Church Falls, you say?" the lady at switchboard asked.

"Thereabouts," he reiterated, checking the roadmap. "Old Church Lane, I think. We can't be that far from Church Falls."

"I see," the lady said coldly, and paused. Stanley imagined he could hear her thinking: *How in God's name can you be so irresponsible to get stranded out there?* When she did finally speak, she reluctantly told him: "There will be a breakdown van with you in the next two hours... *if you're still there...*"

The oddness of her afterthought caused Stanley to start, leaving him wanting to know what she meant. "Why wouldn't we still be here? Where do you expect us to go?"

"On *no* account leave your vehicle…"

Before he could ask why she sounded rattled, she had already hung up.

"How long will they be?" Belinda demanded.

"The Engineer'll be here in a couple of hours," said Stanley and considered his next move, still reeling from the curious manner in which the lady at Customer Services had behaved. "I think I ought to call your father, tell him we're going to be late."

He geared himself up to the challenge. After several rings, a gruff voice answered: "Yes?"

"Season's Greetings, Mr. Fothergill," Stanley spoke formally, since he felt uncomfortable using the old man's Christian name.

No reciprocal greeting, no pleasantries. *No surprises there*, Stanley supposed, imagining the powerful dread Cedric's antediluvian sense of self-righteousness must have instilled in those he had once worked with, making them want to find a rock to crawl under and die. Cedric took no prisoners, hired and fired at will, including the entire HR department. Cedric's successor at Chilton's must have been glad to have seen the back of him. "Why aren't you here yet? We expected you hours ago!"

"We've hit a bit of a snag…"

"Don't tell me you're lost?"

Stanley kept his voice steady, trying not to sound awkward or intimidated, not wishing to stand on ceremony. "Unfortunately the car's broken down just outside Church Falls."

"You should have taken the train!" Cedric barked, reflecting his daughter's opinion. *Similar minds think alike*, thought Stanley. "We have a robust rail network."

"Of course, I'll keep that in mind for future reference. We shouldn't be delayed too long. The breakdown service should get us moving again soon."

"Don't you dare go putting my daughter's and grandchildren's lives at risk!"

It may have been an innocuous enough comment, but just as with the RAC Customer Services' advisor, the conversation had taken on a distinctly creepy turn, which had nothing to do with Cedric's formidable personality.

"What kind of danger do you think I'm going to put them in? Bore them to death with my stories of indexing and cataloguing books?" Stanley said, and immediately regretted the fatuousness of his comment.

"Are you trying to be funny?" Cedric responded belligerently. "Your duty is to protect your family. Be careful like you've never been careful before. I don't want to be attending your f—"

Stanley was suddenly listening to the whirring tone of a lost connection. The phone had cut off. He tried ringing again, but got no signal.

"What did Dad say?"

"The usual…" It wasn't so much what Cedric said, but how he said it. Like the lady at Customer Services, Cedric had delivered a warning. Stanley had sensed actual fear within that pompous, bullying voice. *I don't want to be attending your* — what? *Funeral?* Was that what Cedric meant to say? Stanley laughed inside at the foolishness of his own imagination, but he could not escape the slight chill that radiated up his spine. He desperately wanted to know how that sentence finished.

"I feel sick," little Adam said from the backseat.

"Now look what you've done," Belinda said scathingly, giving her husband a withering glance. She turned round and spoke in soft, soothing tones to their son, who looked green and distressed. "There, there, Adam, sweetie…"

"Why's it my fault?" Stanley said incredulously.

"If you hadn't got us stranded in the middle of nowhere, we wouldn't be in this mess!"

As usual, Stanley had no comeback.

Adam heaved into the plastic bag his mother provided, tried to vomit, but nothing came up.

"I'm cold," Becky suddenly complained with chattering teeth.

Stanley avoided his family, hated coming home, preferring to pour his heart out to the local barmaid. He was sure Belinda was cheating on him while he was at work, not that he ever confronted her, but there was no jealousy or objection since he just didn't care. The two-bit whore he called a wife unfortunately wore the pants in the household. Their son, Adam, was a total wimp, a sickly child, probably rightfully bullied at school, mollycoddled by his mother to his detriment. Becky was a miniature version of her mother, a proper little madam, spoiled rotten and stuck-up. Belinda believed Stanley only stayed with her for the sake of the kids, but in reality Stanley would have left his family a long time ago if he could afford the divorce costs and alimony. He was forced now to play happy families, to look after the kids against his very wishes. *All the fun of the fair!*

"I'll see what I can do, darling," Stanley told his shivering eight-year-old daughter. The engine had cut out. Switching on the fan, Stanley hoped that whatever residual heat he could salvage from the engine would keep them warm while they waited patiently for roadside assistance. As the engine cooled down, however, snow would begin to accumulate on the bonnet and the windows would ice over, and they would then have to be fully reliant on the warmth from their woollen scarves and gloves and thick winter coats. He imagined the worst case scenario: what if the RAC man didn't turn up, couldn't locate them? Considering they had not seen any passing vehicles, Stanley did not fancy the prospect of spending the night in the car with these *people* he called his immediate family.

All tuckered-out from building their snowman, creating snow-angels on the ground or from ice-skating on the frozen lake, Stanley imagined most of the population would now be sitting down with a glass of Harvey's Bristol Cream, snug and toasty in front of the roaring Christmas fire, to share Victorian ghost stories or perhaps watch traditional feel-good Christmas fare: Alastair Sim's definitive Scrooge or James Stewart saved from the brink of suicide by his guardian angel who proceeds to show him how incomplete the lives of his friends and family would have been if he had never been born. They would tell you Christmas wasn't a season at all, but a state of mind, a *feeling*.

Winter lies long in the remote country, and darkness comes early at this time of year. As twilight descended, a terrible blizzard roared out from the north, scouring the land with gale-force winds and threatening a foot of snow. And, up ahead, out of the blizzard emerged a dark figure, a human silhouette, who immediately began to advance towards the stationary vehicle.

"I'm getting hungry," Becky moaned.

But Stanley wasn't listening. His eyes were fixed on something dead ahead.

Something was coming out of the blizzard. He had originally thought the figure might be a projection of his over-taxed imagination, but he quickly dismissed the idea when he noticed that Belinda followed and corroborated his gaze. Indiscernible at first, a vague outline, due to the whirling maelstrom that obscured the landscape and reduced the world to its elements, but as the figure drifted towards the car, Stanley realized it was an actual person.

Who would be stupid enough to venture out on a night like this? Not someone sane, surely. He wondered if there was a mental asylum nearby, whether they were missing a resident. Some whack-a-doodle psycho-killer, perhaps. Should he be concerned?

The wind howled powerfully and pitilessly, buffeting the car, bouncing fluffy snowflakes against the windscreen.

As the person continued to approach, Stanley identified her as a woman... and not just any woman. She was *incredibly* beautiful. Dark blond locks, graceful looks, milky complexion, the face of a porcelain doll. All she was missing were the wings of an angel that ought to be sprouting from her back.

And what the hell was she wearing?

She wore only a long white silk dress, too thin and unsuitable for this bitterly cold weather. No coat, no stole, nothing to wrap around her shoulders, to keep her warm. She looked as though she were blithely waltzing home from a night at the opera at the height of summer.

After a moment's speculation that she might be in the same boat as them, another driver whose car had unexpectedly broken down amidst the suddenness of the snowstorm, Stanley changed his opinion when he became aware that she was barefoot. *Walking through the snow, barefoot.*

But by far the most peculiar aspect of her approach was her footprints in the snow. Or, more correctly, *lack* of...

That had to be physically impossible, didn't it?

As she drifted eerily round the front of the car, almost floating across the snow, her movements serene and hypnotic, she leaned forward and tapped the driver's window with her long polished fingernails. "Can you help me?" Stanley heard her say, a voice as angelic and musical as her looks.

With her bent forward like that, Stanley's eyes were drawn towards the delectable, dipping valley of her round, ample cleavage above her low-cut neckline, the hardness of her nipples protruding through the delicate silkiness of her glamorous evening dress. He experienced a rare and pleasurable stirring in his crotch, plucking a cracker he had once heard from down the pub: *Sex is very much like snow — you don't know how many inches it's going to be or how long it will last!* Somewhat guiltily, he shot a glance at his wife, and realized that Belinda hadn't noticed the bulge developing in his pants but was merely staring, mesmerized, at the beautiful apparition outside, rendered speechless for once.

"Let me in..." the Woman in White uttered softly, her golden locks flecked with snow, her skin bereft of make-up or colour, exceedingly pale, perhaps from the prevailing hibernal cold, perhaps not, and her lips, rose-red, unnaturally red, without any trace of lipstick.

Stanley suddenly recalled an old Japanese myth, peculiar to the hill folk. Of an evil, spectral being called Yuki-onna, the Mountain Snow Woman, the spirit of a woman who perished in a snowstorm. Legend claimed that her ghost, manifesting as a naked, inhumanly beautiful woman, would appear before lonely travellers trapped in winter storms, leaving her victims frozen in place with her icy breath. Myths were what they were: myths. But Stanley knew that, with every myth, it arose from some event rooted in reality, the story itself modified and distorted, exaggerated and embellished over the centuries, reinvented, until it eventually lost any sense of credibility and served solely as an entertaining yarn, parable, allegory or tall tale. But there was no escaping the fact it began from something real, contained a grain of truth.

"I'm scared," said Adam nervously.

Becky too appeared spooked, afraid. "Don't let her in, Mommy."

"There's something seriously suspicious about that woman," Belinda said, passing judgement, breaking the spell. "I don't trust her." More sharply, she added: "Stanley, don't look at her, just ignore her, and maybe she'll go away." But Belinda's eyes remained poised on the presence outside.

"Let me in, *please*..." the strange, nameless woman, inadequately dressed for the raging, bleak midwinter's night, repeated, her request growing more plaintive and seductive in equal measure.

But Stanley experienced none of the fear his family presently felt. He was captivated by this voluptuous, ivory-skinned maiden lost in the blizzard, not caring whether her dress sense took little account of the sub-zero temperatures and wind chill factor or that she left no visible tracks in the snow. He revered her siren's lurid beauty, those dark, fabulous eyes that could see directly and deeply into his soul, read his every thought and desire... and those lips, *oh, those lips*, profoundly red and yearning desperately to connect with his...

His hand went to roll down the window, obviously under her thrall.

"What do you think you're doing?" Belinda demanded, alarmed.

"Just helping out a damsel-in-distress," Stanley replied naively.

"*Just hold it right there, mister!*" Belinda exclaimed, stopping her husband from making what she foresaw was a terrible mistake. His hand hovered, trembling, over the door handle.

He blinked at her, his expression disquietingly blank.

The haunting wail of the wind reached into the secret listening hollows of the night, flakes of feathery snow swirling and tumbling across the windscreen.

"*Stanley Henslow, don't you dare open the door!*" warned Belinda dangerously. "If you thought your life so far was a living hell, you'll discover I can make you suffer until you wish you were *dead!*"

Stanley considered his options, *really* considered them. He was nothing more than an outsider in his own family, trapped in a cold, loveless marriage. Even his own children, no matter how young, didn't listen to him, paid him little respect. Without intending to sound like a Grinch, Stanley didn't care much for Christmas, either. He had read somewhere that many of the traditions observed during Christmas began long before the Birth of Christ. Exchanging gifts between family and friends, giving alms to the poor, and decorating trees with candles were originally rituals performed by the ancient Romans during Saturnalia, a festival in honour of their god Saturn, in preparation for the New Year. Germanic and Nordic tribes, too, held a festival called Yuletide to celebrate the Winter Solstice, wherein a Yule log would traditionally burn in the hearth and people would gather around the fire and hold a great feast. These pagan winter rituals were allegedly hijacked by the Roman Emperor Constantine, a recently converted Christian, who wished to incorporate them in a celebration of the Birth of Christ. Eventually, over the centuries, the Catholic Church managed to make December the Twenty-fifth solely about the Birth of Our Saviour, ousting any celebrations once meant for pagan gods. And Christmas continued to evolve over time, and as we entered living memory, Christmas grew more and more commercialized, a veritable gold mine for Big Business. Nowadays, it wasn't so much about Charity and Giving but *Gimme-Gimme-Gimme*, not so much a Celebration of the Birth of Christ, but just another excuse for Gluttony, Inebriation and Fornication.

Stanley struggled with indecision no more. What did he have to lose?

[*your duty is to protect your family*]

He first turned to Belinda, his voice incongruently kind and full of gentle humility. "I sincerely beg your pardon, Belinda, but I really can't be bothered to obey you anymore." With similar humble affection and contriteness and sorrow, he addressed his children: "I'm sorry, kids, but you don't mean that much to me..."

From the confused, stunned expressions of his family, Stanley realized his deliberate, less-than-fatherly sentiments had wounded them... and it felt *soooooooo* good!

He resolved on a course of action that would prove much cheaper than any marriage counsellor, nor would he have to bother celebrating the Christmas holidays ever again. Whatever personal restraint or self-control he possessed melted away as he proceeded to open the driver's door. Before him stood the glorious, fantastic creature, whose singular provocative loveliness nobody could ever refuse. "You're welcome, my lady. Come on in. I'm yours for the taking..."

He heard Becky's frightened protest. "*Daddy, noooo!*"

"*You'll kill us all!*" Belinda shrieked, dismayed, utterly mortified.

Strong gusts of wind blew powdery snow into the car, instantly chilling its inhabitants.

This was not a woman in trouble, Stanley knew now. He saw her lips form a smile as celestial sweet as it was deliciously wicked, revealing pearly white teeth and upper canines that appeared unusually pointy and menacing. The smile continued to curl up into a grotesque Chelsea grin.

Stanley gave into temptation, willingly offered himself up to her.

For the Henslow family there would be no silent night, or peace on earth, or goodwill to all mankind. There would be no jingle of sleigh-bells, no children carolling, no angels singing tonight. No dance of the sugarplum fairies, no cooing of white turtle doves. No Spirit of Christmas, no fat bloke with a snowy-white beard and jolly red suit climbing down the chimney, no customary roast turkey or mince pies to gobble down, no egg-nog to imbibe, and least of all no Midnight Mass to ring in the Birth of the Saviour ever again. Even a kiss under the mistletoe would metamorphose into something unromantic and hungered, as sublime and unique as the tiniest snow crystal. *Rum-pum-pum-pum*, went the little drummer boy.

The ivory-white, ridiculously-underdressed woman moved with a speed no human could be capable of, readily accepting his invitation. In a flash her mouth was positioned by the side of his head as she whispered sensuously into his ear, *"Your soul is now mine!"*

To the high, terror-stricken screams of his wife and children, the blood-drinking demoness sank her fangs into his neck in an unholy, virginal kiss. Only, Stanley registered no physical pain, instead experienced an unprecedented bliss in which he could picture all eternity.

'Twas the Night before Christmas, and the orange RAC van trundled down the country road, maintaining a cautious speed, its plough cutting a clear thoroughfare through the gathering snowfall, its headlights piercing the pale haze of darkness ahead, unable to make significant inroads on the severely reduced visibility. Brent Saxton, as a RAC Recovery Service Engineer, normally enjoyed his work. He travelled far and wide within his designated catchment area, which incorporated a lot of rural parts, and he gave it his all wherever his expert help was required. Very rarely could he not fix a problem. But this was a job he was not looking forward to. He did not like the idea of being caught up in the blasted snow or driving to, of all places, Church Falls.

There was something sinister about the village of Church Falls. Rumour had it that it was a place where reality was at its thinnest, serving as the mouth to another world – if there were such a thing.

Historically, Church Falls had got its name because witchcraft had thrived there over the centuries and ultimately survived, at the expense of Jesus Christ Our Lord. Brent wasn't a religious man, but he had heard stories from the superstitious folk of Church Falls who insisted that the Devil walked amongst them, sometimes glimpsed in graveyards on Walpurgis Night and All Hallow's Eve, holding dark communion with the witches of the forest. They claimed all manner of unspeakable abominations abounded. They hung garlands of garlic on their front doors, loaded their guns with silver bullets, kept rabbit's paws, grew four-leaf clovers in their gardens, wore only their birthstones, resorted to counting crows, and believed sneezing risked their soul escaping their body. That was the kind of backwater mentality one encountered in isolated communities, full of religious nuts and suffering a high suicide rate... *or, perhaps, it wasn't always suicide...*

Now Brent was going back to Church Falls, though fortunately only to its periphery this time. It had been a while since he was last called out there for a tow. He thought his winch might have a role to play again, upsetting his professional efficiency score.

What kind of trouble were these latest imbeciles in? *Let them freeze to death!* he felt like saying and turning round. *They should have known better!*

Suddenly, his headlamps picked up something up ahead.

Brent slowed down his RAC van and came to a stop behind the obstruction.

There was the car, half-buried in a snowdrift. Yet its headlights were on, an obvious drain on the battery. Curiously, the front two doors were swung wide open like outstretched wings, giving the vehicle an air of abandonment... *or maybe doubling as a tomb.* The wind hurled snow against the doors, sculpting the final deposit in soft, dune-like patterns.

How could anyone be stupid enough to leave their doors open on a night like this? He had a horrible suspicion he might have to call for an ambulance to have these people checked over for frostbite, or stretcher them away in body bags... that is, if they were still in the car. Or maybe there was nobody in there, the occupants hopefully having found temporary shelter in the nearest farmhouse. The car certainly seemed deserted.

What if something—some monstrous aberration of nature—*took* them? The thought just popped into his head, and Brent fought the urge to turn the van round and go back the way he had come. Yet, his normal reasoning re-asserted itself, and he chastised himself for falling victim to local, medieval superstition. But the original, unpleasant thought persisted at the back of his mind and Brent was unable to dispel it completely.

He clambered out of the van into the cold winter's night. *Let's get this over and done with.*

It was freezing: according to the thermometer it was minus-seventeen out. He began to walk over to the snowbound Rover Metro, pulling up his jacket collar against the wind as it whipped flurries of snow into his face.

He heard snatches of music coming from the car, growing louder as he approached. The radio was apparently on, and Brent recognized the track as *Ring the Bells* by James.

Each step a conscious effort through the deep snow, Brent trudged to the open door of the passenger's side... and looked in.

At first he thought there was no-one in there, but when he shone his flashlight, he was greeted by four occupants, a family of two adults and two children.

Something abhorrent was happening to them...

They did not acknowledge his presence initially, for their heavily-clad bodies were twisting and writhing in their seats like snakes—even the kids—and their faces appeared to be swathed in a tight, transparent membrane. Brent quickly realized that whatever was happening to them, they were being *reborn* in some obscene way. He stared, transfixed, fascinated and repulsed, as, one-by-one, the amniotic sac split from the apex and slid down their heads, producing the uncoiling effect of a moth emerging from its pupa, their faces glistening with a sheen of slime in the steady light of his torch.

Their choreoathetotic movements abruptly ceased, and they wiped aside the clear sticky jelly from their pallid faces with their hands, and for the first time, they noticed him. Their new demonic eyes, burning like hot coals, latched avidly onto him.

"We've been expecting you..." the male in the driver's seat, probably the father, uttered ominously.

~ 114 ~

Brent's intestines instantly twisted into knots, and his testicles formed metaphorical icicles. He knew he was done for—there would be no escape from these dreaded, Undead things, once human but no more.

As he backed away, they crept out of the car and crowded round him, including the little children, until all he could see were their death-white, alabaster faces, their glowing-ember eyes and their unnaturally sharp and vicious canines.

"*We were blind, but now we see...*" the vampire family chimed in harmony.

They fed ravenously on the RAC man, who held up no fight.

Stanley Henslow was pleased with the absolute purity of their predicament, greatly edified by their acquisition of evil. He could now relate to his wife, Belinda, as an equal and actually be proud of his children, Adam and Becky.

They were a family again, and as a family, they would do things together forever.

MERRY CHRISTMAS, ONE AND ALL!

March 2012-April 2012

Healing the Sick

"It's no good saying one thing and doing another!"

Catherine Cookson

"You're *not* ill," Patricia told her mother for the umpteenth time. "You think you're ill, but you're not."

"I am so," Dorothy Unsworth insisted indignantly. "Anyway the doctor will confirm my suspicions."

Patricia, who never married, sighed in exasperation. It was always the same with her mother as with any hypochondriac. Indigestion denoted a heart-attack, a headache was the first sign of a brain tumour and the only cure for flatulence was an exploratory operation. This time the complaint was tiredness and lethargy. *Anaemia*, Dorothy assumed. *Old age*, Patricia argued. Her mother was a ripe old seventy-three years of age and still going strong, particularly when it came to self-diagnosing her countless ailments or fussing over her stash of medication of which she had so many she could have opened a chemist's shop right there at home.

Patricia put up with her mother's needless demands more out of understanding than pity. She had always been the youngest child and her mother's favourite and now it was her turn to show her mother the same kind of doting affection she had been privileged to all her life. Although she loved her mother dearly, lately—call it the onset of senility—Dorothy had become more of a nuisance than ever with her list of grumbling complaints. And Patricia had to oblige her as the dutiful daughter. No help from her brothers and sisters, mind you, who left the responsibility of looking after their mother solely in her hands.

Dorothy always took advantage of the good doctor's kindness, for only in his presence would she be at her most theatrical, bewailing her own helpless condition to the point of ear-bursting tedium. And Patricia wondered whether his pandering sympathy did more harm than good in resolving her mother's anxieties. There were other times, however, when Patricia suspected that part of the reason her mother called him so often was as an excuse to flaunt her daughter. *He's marrying stock*, she would sometimes comment, or *Don't you think it's about time you found yourself a decent man and settled down?* Together, she and her mother resembled a couple of love-starved spinsters ogling a hunky handyman.

True, Dr. Heckman was an exceedingly handsome man, the type of doctor who could make nurses swoon and patients blush, and, yes, Patricia was single again and unattached, but she could never envisage the good doctor looking at her twice. *I mean what would we talk about?* Was there any common ground between them, except perhaps her mother's health? And what would Dr. Heckman ever want with a struggling single mum?

Don't be so negative, she told herself. *You're not doing so bad for a late thirtysomething. Okay, you're not exactly model-material and you've got a few more greys in your hair and some extra worry-lines on your face and you've gained a few more pounds around your waist, but you're still basically the same old desirable brunette that you once were in night-school.*

Presently, her mother lay in bed moaning about how grotty she felt, her head propped up on a pillow. "What time is the doctor coming round?" she asked expectantly.

"The receptionist said he'll be down after he finishes surgery."

Dorothy checked the carriage-clock on the cabinet next to the Catherine Cookson novel she had not yet finished reading. The hands pointed to a quarter-past-six.

Outside, the town of Netherton was bathed in an ashen twilight, as cold as winter frost. The wind gusted fiercely, whistling through the eaves of the house, blowing maple leaves in swirling, skittering patterns along the pavement. A man with a scarf walked his Alsatian. A kid on a bicycle passed by, his paper-sack empty. Patricia closed the window, feeling the chill, and went over to the radiator, turning up the heat. "Now you just rest yourself and wait for the doctor."

She climbed down the stairs to attend to supper. Bryan was probably in his room doing his homework. A good boy, conscientious and hardworking, unlike his father who had drank heavily and lived off welfare, paying little attention to his family's needs, eventually abandoning Patricia when he learned she was pregnant. Fifteen years she had raised Bryan on her own, always afraid he would grow up to be just like his old man.

She looked in on Bryan. He was busy scribbling strange chemical symbols in his notebook. The radio played unobtrusively in the background, Blind Guardian's rocky, increasingly-menacing version of *Mr Sandman*.

"Dinner's at seven," she informed Bryan. "Beef stroganoff."

"That's great, Mom," he replied without looking up, buried in the magical world of the Hexagonal Aromatics.

Yes, Bryan was a good boy. Maybe he could make it to medical school. God knows he always applied himself.

Patricia left his door ajar as she made her way down to the kitchen.

She jumped as the doorbell rang. Putting aside the dishcloth, she walked down the hallway and opened the door, not before straightening her hair. *Here at last…*

Netherton's finest family practitioner stood outside, looking dapper in a blue suit and grey raincoat, carrying his little medical bag. "Good evening, Miss Unsworth."

As usual, Patricia resisted the urge to kiss him wantonly on the lips. "Dr. Heckman, come in, please."

He wiped his feet on the doormat and stepped inside, shivering slightly. "Chilly night," he said casually. "Looks like winter's just around the corner."

"Would you like some tea or coffee?"

"No thanks, I've got a few more house calls to make," he said, immediately getting down to business. "How's our patient?"

"Not as sick as she claims to be," she replied, noticing the gold-rimmed spectacles he sported which clearly showed off his yummy blue eyes and enhanced his rugged, athletic looks. His dark hair was somewhat tousled and wind-blown. *Roll over Dr. Ross and kneel down Dr. Kildare because Dr. Heckman's in town and dishier than ever!*

"Let's see what we can do for your mother, shall we?"

Patricia led him upstairs, catching a whiff of his cologne, as cool and refreshing as his demeanour, and fantasized about him spending a weekend with her at a hotel spa, where he proceeded to propose to her over champagne and candlelight. She quickly dismissed this image from her mind, concentrating on the matter at hand.

They entered Dorothy's warm, well-lit bedroom, the patient in question looking expectantly at the door.

"Ah, Mrs. Unsworth," Dr. Heckman said, "how are we today?"

"Not too good," Dorothy declared with a frail voice. "I feel weak and constantly tired. I think I've got anaemia."

"Oh dear," said Dr. Heckman, digging out his stethoscope from his jacket pocket. "We'll soon know what's wrong with you."

He went about ascertaining the cause of her tiredness, asking questions pertinent to blood loss, about her appetite, the span of her daily activity, the consistency of her weight, her waterworks and her bowel movements, whether she recorded any blood in her motions. Dorothy was extremely sprightly when discussing her ailments, enjoying the manner in which he fretted over her as though she were a poorly child. She described a recurring dream, more out of passing than anything else, of a dark stranger who visited her every night and made her feel as frisky as a spring lamb. Dr. Heckman, a busy man that he was, listened to her idle chatter with polite nods, focusing mostly on her physical condition. He examined her then: checked her pulse, measured her blood pressure, assessed for pallor around her eyelids, used a tongue-depressor to look into her mouth, auscultated her chest and laid his hands on her tummy. He spotted the barely-visible bruise on her neck. When he'd finished, he snicked open his kitbag and fished out a syringe.

"I need to take a sample of blood," he said, tying a tourniquet around her arm. "We'll see if you really are anaemic. I'm not totally convinced, although I admit you do look pale."

"This is the part I really hate," Dorothy remarked, grimacing.

"I think everybody does," agreed Dr. Heckman, understanding the universal fear of needles.

"I can't bear to look," she added, somewhat dramatically turning her head away for a moment, clasping her daughter's hand.

The needle pierced the bulging tributary of veins in her forearm, and Dr. Heckman carefully drew back on the plunger, blood flowing into the syringe. He released the tourniquet and applied a cotton ball to the puncture-wound. The blood he transferred into a small, vacuum-sealed test-tube with a rubber stopper and disposed of the syringe in a mini-sharps'-bin in his bag. He shook the specimen thoroughly and held it aloft, the blood within the bottle ruby-red and as thick as treacle.

"I suggest you take some iron supplements," he said, handing her a vial of tablets. "They should keep you in good stead. I'll get back to you once your blood results come through."

"Thank you, doctor. I'm sorry to be a bother."

"Not at all, my dear," said Dr. Heckman with a soft smile. "What would I possibly do without you? These house calls I make to you form the cornerstone of my medical practice."

They laughed at his comment before Dr. Heckman finally announced his farewell, packing up his medical bag. Patricia saw him off.

"Sure you won't stay for dinner?" she asked hopefully.

"I can't, I'm afraid," Dr. Heckman said on the doorstep. "I really have to get going, but thank you anyway. Have a pleasant evening."

"You too," Patricia answered cheerily.

She watched him disappear into the night before closing the door. He had impressed her again with his smart looks and medical know-how. *Definitely made my day!* she supposed, happy, and again imagined the good, caring doctor whisking her away to a spa resort where they would laugh and talk and declare their affection for one another. Silly, sentimental thinking, accepted, but certainly a comforting image in her barren loveless world. *What's a woman to do?*

Then she went into the kitchen, still beaming, and set down supper on the dining table.

Outside the gate, Dr. Heckman paused, looking up at the yellowish light cast down from Mrs. Unsworth's bedroom window. Heavy gusts fumbled at his hair, and he pulled up the lapels of his raincoat to ward off the bitter cold.

Anaemia, he thought. The signs were obvious, but did they know?

He walked down the street towards his Jaguar, passing the rows of terraced houses. There were still other house calls to make, still more samples of blood to take, all the findings consistent with anaemia.

His car was parked opposite a dark alley. He paused outside his car, strangely preoccupied. The arc-sodium lamp threw a weak, wan light down there, and for a moment, Dr. Heckman heard the distant rattling of a dustbin-lid. He located the sound and saw two sets of tiny, luminous eyes peering at him from the darkness. Dr. Heckman realized his presence had disturbed a couple of cats making strange love. There followed a loud hiss from the stray tom and a high yowl from the fluffy tabby, completing the primal act of coupling, and the pair jumped off the dustbin and slunk away, merging with the shadows.

Did the people know? Did they know what was happening here?

An outbreak of anaemia…

He would have to tread more carefully from now on and limit his activities to one household at a time. The last thing he wanted was the rate of anaemia to spiral out of control and attract undue attention. Attract the Department of Public Health.

Dr. Heckman uncorked the rubber stopper of the blood-bottle and gulped down the scarlet liquid, licking his lips greedily when he was done. An appetizer, he thought. The main course would surely follow when he returned at midnight. Mrs. Unsworth — that randy old granny — would, no doubt, leave her window open. Even though she was easy pickings, he didn't know how much more strain her heart could handle.

Never fear, he could always charm her daughter as a willing blood donor if the need arose. Hardly a challenge, she was smitten by him. She could easily satisfy the apocalyptic hunger that existed inside him.

The children's hospice could be another feasible option, at least as an emergency measure, but it was never a good idea to sustain oneself on old or diseased blood. Anyway, he still sadly had much to learn adjusting to his new life, having been unwillingly dumped on the doorstep of Damnation Inn and left there to burn.

He sat in his car, ditching his medical bag in the back seat. And promptly drove off to call on his next patient.

Spare a little blood, miss? You won't feel a thing, promise!

Just what the doctor ordered.

November 2009

The Haunting of Herman Hinkle

"A husband who submits to his wife's yoke is justly held an object of ridicule."

Honore de Balzac

Herman Hinkle hated his wife. It had taken ten years of marriage — ten dreadful years that had grown to feel like an eternity in hell — for him to come to this terrible conclusion.

Their relationship hadn't always been bad. It had actually been quite sweet in the beginning. They had met back at Chertsford University where Herman had gone to read English Lit and Faye Darnell had taken on the challenge of Media Studies. He had bumped into her at the Student Union and asked her out immediately, Faye subsequently accepting his offer of a date. He wooed her with the passion of a poet and they were soon seen as an item. After graduating, Herman went about setting himself up as a playwright of some distinction, obsessed with the Common Man to the same degree as his childhood heroes, Bennett and Bleasdale. He could always quote J.B. Priestley, who became the Radio Voice of the Common Man during the war, as an early inspiration for his choice of subject: *I can't help feeling wary when I hear anything said about the masses. First you take their faces from 'em by calling 'em the masses and then you accuse 'em of not having any faces.*

Faye took a job in a small advertising firm and quickly rose to the position of Marketing Assistant. Things were going swimmingly between them at this stage, a young couple trying to make a success of their demanding jobs and their seemingly-stable marriage. Then, Faye became pregnant.

Her miscarriage soured matters. It was a horrible and traumatic ordeal for both of them: Faye bled profusely down below and, in the middle of the night and in exquisite agony, had to be rushed into hospital to be operated upon. The couple were devastated, changed by the experience. A child would surely have solidified their relationship, kept them together for the rest of their married lives. However, with both rendered psychologically fragile by the loss of their unborn child, Herman withdrew into himself and Faye began externalizing her anger, quarrelling with him whenever she saw fit and blaming him for everything under the sun. Their dead baby became a taboo subject and was never mentioned again. Disliking rows altogether, Herman listened passively and pensively to his wife rant and rave at him, feeling the life he once knew was over. His work grew darker in tone and his productivity suffered, and Faye started smoking and drinking and window-shopping for newer models.

Cursed with male pattern baldness and sporting black, Peter Sellers spectacles, Herman was a meek, timid, unassuming man. Faye, on the other hand, was a vibrant, blue-eyed blonde, who could hold an audience in thrall in spite of the way she constantly humiliated her husband in public. *Politics don't make strange bedfellows – marriage does*, according to Groucho Marx, and indeed Herman and Faye made a peculiar couple, just as Arthur Miller and Marilyn Monroe might have done once. Yet, neither seemed disposed to leave the other. Having resigned her commission at work, Faye freeloaded on his still-better-than-modest salary derived from writing stage-plays, using him as a safe base to explore other men.

'Nookie Monsters' was her pet name for these amoral, marvellously-hung sleazebags. It was no secret what she got up to, but Herman put up with her sexual indiscretions with extraordinary patience, dependent on his wife's trophy looks as she depended on his money. He tried to turn a blind eye to these so-called 'romantic' liaisons, but it was becoming more difficult with each wanton fling. She took great pleasure in 'FuMBO', a not-so-secret abbreviation she devised which stood conveniently for 'Fuck My Brains Out'. Her put-downs, too, grew more cruel and bitter and harder to tolerate. There was only so much he could take and, like any passive-aggressive, he knew that one day he would explode.

He didn't expect it to be at the party his wife organized and hosted to see in the new millennium.

Herman reluctantly accepted his wife's decree of a garden party to celebrate the coming of the Millennium. Their five-bedroom house in the green belt of Oaks Fold was large enough to accommodate at least thirty people, and its secluded nature meant they would receive no complaints from the neighbours. Faye invited a sum total of twenty guests, consisting largely of her close personal friends and male cronies, only later adding a small number of Herman's work colleagues to the list as a grudging afterthought.

Festivities began at seven in the evening. The guests were shepherded onto the large garden lawn at the back of the house where there were lashings of punch and a barbecue fit for a king. Faye bossed around the three staff from the catering firm she'd hired and didn't waste time flirting with her 'men-friends' in full view of her husband and the other guests. The men in question did not protest, eager as they were to outperform the competition and prove their own manliness to their gorgeous hostess. Neither did her indiscreet attitude embarrass the majority of the guests who were busy gorging themselves on the free food and alcohol available in plentiful supply. Herman, however, took great offence to his wife's unabashed overfamiliarity with some of the male visitors, but such was his inherent passive nature, and subdued and demoralized by her repeated emotional blows, he could only grin and bear it. It amazed him how she had made him impotent, incapable of expressing his rage, except in the stage-characters he created. There was something to be said for sublimation, for in literary circles, Herman Hinkle was regarded as a very angry writer.

Only Nicola Strand, PA to the Assistant Editor, raised any objections over his wife's openly flirtatious behaviour towards the narcissistic hunks at the party. "How can you stand it? It's disgusting!"

"Please don't start…" replied Herman wearily. He waved away the member of the catering staff carrying a tray of canapés.

"She treats you abominably."

"I'm fully aware of that fact, thank you. But Faye has other, nicer qualities."

"Like what?" challenged Nicola, infuriated. "How can you be defending her? She smokes like a chimney, drinks like a lush, spends all your money and sleeps with other men right under your nose."

Herman dropped his gaze, took a small sip from his plastic cup of punch. He didn't know how to respond.

"Doesn't it make you jealous?" Nicola demanded. "Don't you have any self-respect?"

Herman's continued silence suggested to Nicola she might have hurt his feelings. It wasn't his fault, after all. His wife had dumped on him so many times she'd probably emasculated him. Nicola's grievance was with Faye, not Herman. Faye needed to change or go. "I'm sorry, Herman. I didn't mean to upset you."

Herman accepted her apology. "I know you mean well, Nicola. You're right, I should man-up, grow a spine. But you have no idea how much I hate confrontation."

"Someone needs to speak to her, put her in her position."

"I'll try," Herman assured Nicola. "Let me figure it out on my own."

The evening passed by as smoothly as the Hundred Years' War. Herman endeavoured to mingle with the guests, but found it hard-going since most of them hailed from Faye's personal address-book and came across as vain and obnoxious. He therefore decided to stick with Nicola and a couple of her colleagues, good literary folk, but despite their varied, interesting discourse, his heart just wasn't in it. He felt increasingly sick as he watched his wife flit between different men, smoking and drinking and laughing without a damned care in the world, unable to keep her hands to herself. As she moved on to the next man, he thought she might as well be wearing a sign across her forehead, declaring her intentions. He could imagine her whispering into their ears: *I'm extremely fuckable, you know! I can almost guarantee you'll get some later!*

With the selection of entrées and the barbecued steaks, hamburgers and sausages a digesting memory, now it was time to celebrate the dawn of the new millennium.

Winters in this part of England had grown fairly mild in recent decades (with no sign of a White Christmas), and this very special New Year's Eve was no mean exception. Still, the guests needed to be wrapped up warm to counter the chilly easterly wind which tugged at their coats and scarves. The night sky was clear and starless, the earth-lights of Chertsford twinkling in the distance.

The catering staff brought out a crate of expensive champagne as the clock ticked by and the designated hour approached. Fireworks were set up in eager anticipation of zero hour.

The countdown had already begun. "Ten... nine... eight..." cheered the guests in rowdy, convention-observing unison, as the old century drew to a close. "Seven... six... five... four... three... two... *one!*"

Jubilation, wild and rampant, broke out. The men grabbed the nearest girl and kissed them, according to tradition. Corks popped and the champagne flowed. The fireworks lit up the dark sky in explosive blooming constellations of reds and blues and greens and yellows, as the visitors at the Hinkle residence synchronized a drunken rendition of *Auld Lang Syne*.

An auspicious moment, thought Herman, giving any roving lips a wide berth. *Exactly two thousand years since the birth of Christ. Where will civilization be in another two thousand years? Colonizing deep space or...* extinct?

Wondering if the global computer systems had failed or the world's stock markets had crashed, as predicted by the prophets of doom, he decided he should find his wife. He searched the garden and spotted her leaning against the gazebo, in a passionate clinch with one of the male guests.

A pang of sadness stabbed his heart. The festivities around him seemed to fade. He took no notice of the loud, scintillating firework display.

He approached the smooching couple and tapped the man debauching his wife on the shoulder. "Excuse me," Herman interrupted.

The man ignored him and continued kissing.

Herman repeated his request, louder and more emphatically.

This time, it worked. The couple stopped snogging and looked in his direction.

"Mind if I speak with my wife?" Herman asked calmly.

The man, whom Herman recognized as an out-of-work actor named Eric Turnbull, stepped aside.

"What is it?" demanded Faye, appearing aroused and flustered and annoyed all at the same time.

"Happy New Year, light-of-my-life!" he said, kissing her perfunctorily on the lips. "Hope you have a fantastic year!"

Faye thawed a little, and for a moment she sounded like the loving wife he had married. "Happy New Year, Herman. Hope you achieve all that you set out to achieve in the next twelve months."

Herman glanced at Eric Turnbull, addressed Faye again. "Couldn't you have waited until the guests were gone?"

"I do as I please," Faye reminded him, shattering the illusion of marriage. "We're not exclusive."

"Is he next in line?"

"That's none of your damned business!" snapped Faye. "If you must know, he's my new love!"

Herman felt nothing but pity for her. *Love? The woman doesn't know the meaning of the word! You should tell it like it is and stick with the term 'Nookie Monster'!* Aloud, he said: "Well, I hope he makes you very happy."

"I'm sure he will," she said with a suggestive smile, openly stroking the actor's crotch. Eric grinned conceitedly back at her. "FuMBO?"

Suddenly, pity wasn't all he was experiencing. Herman could not prevent his gall from rising at the downright shamelessness of this vulgar mating display. "What the hell do think you're doing?"

"What does it look like?" she remarked provocatively. "Copping a feel, of course!"

"Don't you know how inappropriate that is, considering the number of people in attendance?"

"I know," she imparted with deliberate spitefulness, "but Eric's more of a man than you ever were."

Her inflammatory comment produced a furious response. "That was uncalled-for! Don't dare disrespect me, you — *you* — !" Fuming, Herman glared at her, clenched and unclenched his fists.

Partly fuelled by drink, partly down to her personality, Faye poured vitriol over his distress. "Or what, you pathetic little man? At least Eric's prepared to furnish me with a healthy baby. Makes a change from the unviable vegetable *you* sired!"

Herman crashed and burned.

The derisory eyes of Faye's crony friends turned towards him, apparently approving of the cutting reprimand. *You asked for it, buster!*

their collective gazes seemed to mock. The silence seemed to spin out for a brief eternity. Herman felt nauseous and small, wishing he could become invisible and disappear altogether.

Shaking, humiliated beyond compare, Herman decided not to intrude any further in case he said something he might regret and get an earful from his wife later. He left Faye standing at the gazebo as she made a fuss over her new Nookie Monster.

Just as he tried to find a quiet spot in the garden where he would not be noticed, Nicola caught him unawares, pecking him cordially on the cheek. "Happy New Year, Herman!"

"Right back *atcha*, kid!" he said, flashing a fake smile. "Still enjoying the proceedings?"

"What is there not to enjoy?" she stated, sounding quite tipsy. "Champagne, fireworks, a magnificent barbecue, your gentle presence and gracious manner. Thank you, Herman, for a lovely evening!"

"*No*, thank *you* for coming!" he replied humbly. "I couldn't have done it without you!"

Nicola smacked another kiss on his cheek and uttered her farewells. Before departing she reassured Herman with a concerned, conspiratorial whisper, "Don't let that hateful bitch get to you. She isn't worth it."

Nicola's workmates left with her, but not after expressing their gratitude for inviting them and offering him some small words of comfort. The rest of the guests carried on their noisy celebrations for a further two hours until the champagne ran dry. Then, they too departed, after thanking their hostess. No kind words were volunteered to the actual host who had splashed out on their merriment.

The catering staff began clearing up the rubbish at three in the morning and were done by four.

Exhausted, Herman retired for the night, relegated to the guest bedroom, trying to estimate the degree by which his wife's scathing words had dented his dignity and how far the extravagance of the party had drained his bank account. In the dead of night, he could hear Faye in the master bedroom, fucking her latest fancy man while her poor, beleaguered, brow-beaten husband tried to sleep in the other room.

Herman could not sleep, his wife's carnal moans keeping him awake. The bitch sounded as drunk as the bastard in bed with her.

Her cruel, hurtful words whirled around in his head: *Makes a change from the unviable vegetable you sired!*

How dare she throw that in his face, in front of everyone? Over the years, he had learned to accept her host of lovers, the way she frittered away his money or treated him with contempt. But *this* was too much! Faye had broken a powerful taboo, an emotive subject they had steered clear of all these years, something they had chosen never to talk about again. *She had crossed the line.*

Herman realized he'd reached breaking-point. He suddenly knew what he must do—there were no two ways about it. He decided to kill her and the horse she rode in on.

Some men break down and cry, others grab an Uzi and climb the clock-tower. Finding a suitable weapon wasn't a problem. Herman had inherited an antique pocket pistol from his late father. The gun, an authentic, nineteenth-century, double-action Remington Derringer, he kept locked in a rosewood trinket box on the uppermost shelf of his study.

Turning the key and opening the lid of the keepsake box, Herman gently lifted the gun and felt its shape in the palm of his hand. It weighed almost nothing and reminded Herman of the kind of small firearm preferred by petty thieves and riverboat gamblers or carried by ladies hidden in their purse or stockings. He checked whether it was loaded, which it was with two small-calibre bullets. Herman had never fired a gun in his life, but desperate times called for drastic measures. He clicked the barrel shut and strode determinedly out of the study, preparing himself for the task ahead.

He began climbing the stairs, the uncontrollable rage boiling inside him keeping him moving. Arriving on the landing, Herman tramped towards the master bedroom.

If he had harboured even the slightest misgiving over what he was planning to do, the ecstatic scream from behind the door, the sound of his wife at the height of arousal, crushed any doubts. He stormed into the bedroom, pistol raised.

The dimmer provided a low, muted light in the shadow-congested bedroom. On one of the bedside cabinets, an open bottle of champagne poked out of a bucket of ice. Faye had lit up a cigarette which she was puffing away with a dreamy look of fulfilment on the four-poster. Equally slicked with sweat, Eric Turnbull, her latest Nookie Monster, lay beside her, arm round her shoulder, sipping from his champagne flute.

"The sex was so great that even the neighbours smoked a cigarette," Eric was joking, causing Faye to laugh.

It was a laugh Herman had come to loath, the Laugh of an Interminable Bitch, as he called it. It got to him each time, and he wondered what he hated the most about her: her heavy smoking and constant drinking, her habit of squandering his funds, her gaudy make-up and awful taste in slutty, mutton-dressed-as-lamb designer-wear, her roll-call of lovers and countless infidelities, her hideous ill-treatment of him, or that detestable, braying laugh. *Too close to call.*

Her laugh lasted a little longer than her lover's and only ceased when she followed his startled eyes to the bedroom door.

She blinked, surprised, at the balding, bespectacled, pyjama-clad man standing in the doorway. For a moment she didn't recognize him or notice the handgun he brandished, trained on her. Then, realization struck and sheer irritation darkened her features as she spoke to him like a mother scolding her child. "What's the matter with you? Don't you know I detest being disturbed when I have company?"

Herman waved his Derringer at her. "You've gone too far," he stated with a wavering voice. "You can't exploit or bully me anymore."

"So you think you can shoot me with that stupid little pop-gun?" she spat out, contemptuously, "With a weapon as intimidating as your willy?"

"Come on, Mr. Hinkle," Eric intervened in the manner of a negotiator, preparing to get up, raising a hand in appeasement. "Let's talk it over like civilized men."

"*Stay back!*" Herman warned, trembling.

"You don't have the guts!" challenged Faye, consciously goading him.

"That's where you're wrong, *you cheating bitch!*" roared Herman madly, "I should have done this a long time ago!"

It was at that moment that Faye discovered her husband wasn't kidding. She saw that he was extremely worked-up, shaking all over, a quivering mess. She saw the tears rolling down his cheeks. She saw the tormented, agonized expression on his face as though in conflict with himself, wrestling with emotions he was not accustomed to. Faye had never seen him in this highly agitated state before and realized she had finally, unintentionally, broken him. Sent him down this murderous path, led him to this particular disturbing moment in time.

The look of wild confusion cleared from his features, as Herman relived the humiliation, replayed the cruel, unrepeatable insult [*makes a change from the unviable vegetable you sired*] in the moviedrome of his mind. It banished every reservation, hardened his resolve, granted him the strength of will he needed to make her pay for the years of hurt, to deal with her the way he saw fit.

Hand steadier and taking careful aim, he squeezed the trigger of a weapon supposedly as intimidating as his willy. "Goodbye, my dear..." Herman muttered calmly, gladdened by his wife's aghast, mortified expression and a desire to end her sleazy, selfish existence.

[*vegetable unviable vegetable*]

The shot reverberated around the bedroom with exceptional loudness, like a cannon-blast. A lingering look of astonishment appeared on Faye's face as the bullet lodged in her brain, a tiny, black, smoking, fatal hole, evident on her forehead like an ornamental bindi. Then she fell backwards, expressionless, still and very dead.

"Faye! *Faye!*" wailed Eric Turnbull, shocked and appalled, repeatedly calling her name. He shook her body, desperately trying to revive her, but he must have known she would never move or speak again. Finally conceding defeat, he turned his attention to her executioner. "You killed her!" he uttered incredulously. "You fucking *killed* her!"

Suddenly, Herman was filled with remorse. He had assassinated his wife in cold blood. That just wasn't code. "What have I done?" he murmured, dropping the gun.

Eric took his chance. Grabbing a handful of duvet, he leapt at Herman. "*You killed her, you homicidal MANIAC!*" he raged, enveloping Herman with the duvet while revealing the dead, naked woman in the bed. Naked himself, he began punching and kicking the smothered figure.

Completely covered by the duvet, Herman lost his balance under the weight of the blows and collapsed to the floor, helpless, unable to offer any resistance. But the punishment continued. Eric lashed out with his bare feet with growing savagery, each kick producing a muffled moan from beneath the duvet. "*How does that feel, you fucking Woody Allen lookalike?*" he bellowed. He decided to go one step further, picking up the beckoning Derringer pistol from the floor. He fired it point-blank into the duvet, the concatenation of the shot echoing around the bedroom. "*TAKE THAT, YOU MURDERING SONOFABITCH!*" He pulled the trigger again and again, but the barrel clicked empty.

Tiredness began to set in. As his rage dissipated and the adrenaline drained from his muscles and rationality began to return, Eric stared wild-eyed at the curled-up mass under the duvet. The figure had stopped moaning and moving since Eric had unleashed the second and final bullet of the gun. Horrified, he released the pistol and it clattered on the hardwood floor.

This didn't look good. Eric realized he might actually be in trouble. He had killed a man!

[*Oh, shit, oh, fuck!*]

Hastily putting on his clothes, he did a runner.

For Herman, the year 2000 began with him murdering his wife and getting beaten up for his efforts and surviving being shot. His injuries weren't as bad as one might have expected since the duvet had fortunately cushioned the force of the blows and ultimately slowed down the impact of the bullet. He had sustained a couple of cracked ribs and a few generalized bruises, and the bullet managed only to graze his left arm, a mere flesh-wound.

Herman lied at the inquest. He had never lied before in his life, but being a playwright of some note, the story Herman cleverly concocted—and which made the most sense—was that Eric Turnbull had shot Faye in a fit of jealousy and tried to kill him when he came in to investigate. Jealousy was considered a powerful motive as evidenced by a post-mortem that revealed Mrs. Hinkle had been eight-weeks' pregnant with another man's child. *Le crime passionnel*, as the Gallic-speaking world called it. The fact that Eric had fled the scene confirmed his guilt. It was also assumed he'd taken the murder weapon, which was nowhere to be found. The police launched a nationwide manhunt, but the search proved fruitless. They suspected he'd skipped the country. Interpol was contacted.

With suspicion resting firmly on Eric Turnbull, the notion that Mrs. Hinkle's actual killer might be her husband did not even enter, for a second, the minds of the investigation team. Summing up, Judge Gravestock expressed no sympathy for Mrs. Hinkle, whose promiscuity had let her would-be murderer into the marriage bed. She had been a sphinx without a secret, he remarked, quoting Oscar Wilde. More importantly, Judge Gravestock apologized to Herman for his wife's unforgivable wickedness and eventual murder and offered condolences for his loss.

Herman escaped justice, fooled the courts, the media and the public with his cunning piece of fiction. He became a free man. He celebrated his new lease of freedom with champagne and a cigar while digging out one of Gary Moore's timeless LPs, *Cold Day in Hell*, a cautionary tale he could easily relate to. Herman could identify with the protagonist of the tale who has been burnt once too often that it might even be considered justifiable homicide from someone who had been turned into a wretched cuckold. His slate and conscience were clean.

The funeral was a cursory affair on his part. He fumbled his way through the eulogy, struggling to find any kind words to say about his departed wife. Still, he did enough to satisfy the attendees, uninspiring though he was. They mistook his bumbling solemnity for grief.

What he wanted to say, jumping up and down in triumph, was: *How do you know when your wife's dead?* The sex remains the same but the dishes start piling up! But Herman doubted the mourners would appreciate the humour or accept him waving both hands wildly in true vaudeville style at the point of the punchline.

Still, he was comforted by the wisdom of H.L. Mencken: *Bachelors know more about women than married men. If they didn't, they'd be married too.* Maybe Mencken was also right when he claimed that adultery was the application of democracy to love.

Oscar Wilde, too, dreamed up insightful witticisms, one such being: *Bigamy is having one partner too many. Monogamy is the same.*

In the year 2000, Herman found freedom and a brand new beginning with a brand new love.

All his friends felt that Herman was a happier man. The change in him was refreshing. His meekness was gone. He came out of his shell and, with a confidence unseen in many years, began socializing with people he thought deserved his attention.

Detective fever gripped him. He went about developing a semi-autobiographical play using his supposedly traumatic experiences on Millennium night to draw upon, with a cheekiness he never thought he had. His interpretation was true to life, different from the events accepted by the police and publicized in the papers, with the husband shooting the wife and the wife's lover fleeing into the night after believing he'd killed the husband. Although he paraded his fact-based play in front of the public, no-one suspected anything out of the ordinary and considered the climactic scuffle as simply artistic license.

No Good Deed Goes Unpunished opened in Chertsford to a sell-out audience and mostly positive reviews. It generated interest in his body of work and Herman became a darling among the critics, who ranked his current effort up there with his previous best, *The Rules of Man*.

Not only had he got away with it a second time, with a play depicting the actual events of that terrible night, he received praise for his 'inventive' imagination.

The best, however, was yet to come.

Nicola Strand, PA to the Assistant Editor, caught his eye. He hadn't taken much notice of her at the Millennium garden party or at the publishing house, but now with no harridan of a wife to stifle his self-confidence, creativity or manliness, he thought he should make a try for Nicola, who had always come across as sweet-tempered and caring and supportive and understanding of his needs and worthy of his affections.

True, she would never make Model of the Year (unlike his erstwhile wife), but at least Nicola was pretty, with the loveliest hazel eyes, a radiant smile and a stylish brunette bobtail. Her most desirable trait, though, was her natural optimism. She normally saw the best in all situations and people, except in the case of Mrs. Hinkle; even then Nicola could not bring herself to despising the woman.

Herman asked Nicola out and she accepted, thrilled, overjoyed. Their first date took them to the lagoons of Venice and all the wonderful sights and sounds the Sinking City had to offer: punting on the canals, sampling the exquisite cuisine and fine wine, appreciating the gilded Byzantine mosaics of St. Mark's Basilica, wearing the latest in designer Italian fashions, but, most of all, making slow, sweet, sensuous love in the luxurious Hotel Danieli.

Herman hadn't had sex in almost seven years, but he managed to perform without impediment or hang-up. Nicola admitted she had long developed a secret yearning for him, but had been resigned to the fact the feeling would never be reciprocated. She had always loved his mind and imagined she would surely learn to love the rest of him if given the opportunity. She could not stomach seeing him suffer at the hands of his scathing wife. His misery had saddened her. So many times she had stopped herself from publicly humiliating Mrs. Hinkle lest Herman should feel the full ferocity of his wife's wrath. Herman found her concern for him touching.

Herman promised to dedicate his next play to Nicola. Nicola promised never to be disrespectful or unfaithful.

His stage-show travelling to the London West End and pots of money pouring in, and with a good woman by his side, Herman couldn't have seemed happier.

As their romance blossomed, Nicola eventually agreed to move in with him at his invitation.

Then, things started getting spooky, and Herman thought he might be cracking up.

It came on slow and insidious. It was almost imperceptible at first, but Herman Hinkle soon began to notice things. *Little* things. When two people spend so much time together, those small, subtle things can become magnified, significant and curiously out of place.

He first noticed something was strange when Nicola came home from work, one sultry August evening.

Herman had experienced a productive day, working on his new play, *Nicolette in a Dream*, while his latest play, currently showing in the West End, conquered the box-office. Nicola arrived in an uncharacteristic huff and he led her into the kitchen where he was preparing dinner.

"Tell me what's up?" Herman asked her, trying to appear like the considerate boyfriend.

"I can't stand this anymore," Nicola said, sounding distinctly hacked-off. She seated herself at the kitchen island.

"What can't you stand, darling?"

"Tony Stark, my boss, was acting like a complete doofus," Nicola explained. "He kept finding faults in the letters I typed. He called me incompetent just because I mixed up his schedule and a couple of appointments I'd arranged clashed… So I resigned."

"*Resigned*?" Herman said, nonplussed by the unwelcome news she had delivered. "But you've been doing that job for years and you've never complained before. Maybe you were just having an off-day."

"Too much of a high-pressured job for me, I'm afraid," she replied without regret. "Just not my thing." Nicola continued with a loving smile. "But at least we still have each other. I don't have much in the way of savings but I'm sure you can support me."

For a moment, Herman didn't know how to respond to this troubling turn of events. Eventually, he said: "Yes, I suppose you've still got me. I won't let you starve."

"I could use a fag," Nicola announced abruptly. She began rummaging through her handbag.

"But you've never smoked before in your life!" exclaimed Herman, astonished.

"That's why now's a good time to start," answered Nicola, bringing out a crumpled pack of Silk Cut she had purchased earlier. It was the same brand favoured by his dead wife, the same brand he had secretly called 'Slick Cunt', in keeping with his wife's practices. Nicola lit up and took a deep drag. "Hmm, that feels good…" She gazed at Herman through a haze of smoke. "Would you be kind enough to make me a screwdriver?"

"But dinner's almost ready," he said, wondering what the hell was going on with her.

Nicola was insistent, though. "Come on, one small drink won't hurt me. Then we can eat our feast."

Herman realized he had no choice but to pour her the drink. Silent, thoughtful, feeling a sense of disconcertion, he went back to tossing the salad.

"What's on the menu?" Nicola asked, sipping her drink and taking a puff of her cigarette.

"Don't you think you might have been a little rash ditching your job like that?" he asked, placing her meal in front of her.

"Hey, buster, what's with the third-degree?" Nicola demanded with unusual prickliness, her voice rising a pitch. "*How dare you question my motives!*"

"Calm down, Nicki," he uttered, not comprehending her sudden outburst, her unreasonable behaviour. "I-I didn't mean to upset-"

"*Well, you just did, you flaming asshole!*" she screamed back at him, getting up. "*I'll talk to you when you grow up!*"

Herman watched, bewildered, as she slipped her handbag over her shoulder, snatched her glass, and lifting the bottle of vodka and carton of OJ from the fridge, stormed out of the kitchen without touching her steak-tartare-and-garden-salad.

They had never argued before, but these days they seemed to be fighting with growing frequency. Herman loathed any form of confrontation so accepted her unpredictable hissy-fits in stunned silence. He loved Nicola with every beat of his heart, but her volatility was becoming increasingly difficult to handle. She would act unreasonably without warning, and he could find no clear solution to his problems.

He looked into himself initially to find the answer. Was there something inherently wrong with him? Was this the effect he had on women? Did his own cowardly personality bring out the worst in anyone he loved?

Or was there something fundamentally wrong with Nicola?

Herman could not escape her growing idleness or the fact that she was smoking like a chimney, drinking like a lush and spending his money for her sole pleasure. The day she came home in September with her hair dyed blond alarmed him.

"What's with the new look?" he inquired, staring at her hair, confounded.

"Don't you just love it?" Nicola said, playing around with her hair, showcasing it for him with her hands.

"What's the occasion?"

"No occasion. Blondes have more fun. And you know gentlemen prefer blondes."

"I don't think it suits you," he stated, and instantly regretted the comment.

Nicola turned on him in an instant. "The hell it doesn't!" she snapped viciously. "*Keep your damned opinions to yourself!*" And off she went after her scary emotional flare-up, stomping out of the house, leaving Herman strangely frightened.

The ultimate revelation came to him during a trip to Chertsford Victoria Theatre in November.

They had gone to see a contemporary re-imagining of the Scottish play set in the modern world of investment bankers and corporate raiders. Herman had always been a traditionalist when it came to Shakespeare, believing his plays should not be taken out of their original period-setting (i.e. more Franco Zeffirelli, less Baz Luhrmann), but Nicola insisted they see this particular version with its cast of unknowns.

Seated in the shadowy VIP box, sipping champagne, they were warming to the evil machinations of Lady Macbeth when Nicola spotted someone in the lower gallery. She threw one of her roses down at the figure playfully, catching him squarely on the back of the head. He looked up and saw Nicola waving down at him. With a wan, guilty smile, he waved back. He returned his attention back to the show.

"Who's that?" Herman asked quietly.

"Daniel Mayhew," Nicola whispered back.

The name didn't mean anything to Herman. He inquired further: "And who in particular is this guy?"

"He's the director of the play," she informed him with a low whisper.

"How do you know him?" Nicola didn't reply, and Herman was gripped by a horrible feeling. "You're sleeping with him?"

Nicola didn't protest against the accusation. She didn't even lie, either. "Yes, I *am* sleeping with him, to put it succinctly!" she burst out, irately.

The actors on stage stopped performing, their eyes like the audience's drawn in the direction of the interruption, straight up to the

VIP box. To Herman, the spotlights suddenly seemed brighter and the eyes of both actors and audience alike seemed to mock, to laugh at his misfortune. The embarrassment of the situation caused his stomach to turn. "How could you do this to me?"

"Don't act so ignorant!" Nicola stung out with pure venom. "You *know* why! You're not particularly exciting in bed! Daniel is a million times' better fuck than you ever were! He's a *real* man! He appreciates me for what I am, worships me from head to toe! He can do things with his tongue you could never do! He knows how to FuMBO!"

She motioned to Daniel Mayhew with a phone-me gesture and left the theatre box.

Realizing the embarrassing distraction was over, Daniel gestured to the actors to resume the play, and the theatre-goers went back to watching what they had paid for.

Herman should have slipped out, also. To end his shame and humiliation. Except he was rooted to his seat, unable to move, drowning.

He sat through the rest of the play, cowering cravenly, trying to hide himself in the shadows of the booth.

He was *haunted*.

[FuMBO]

Haunted by his dead wife, Faye. Could the dead possess the living? Nicola was exhibiting the worst traits of his dead wife. Somehow, Faye had taken control of Nicola, the girl Herman loved, and was using Nicola to wreak her revenge.

Because Faye Hinkle had been a vindictive woman, a fishwife as poisonous as Lady Macbeth.

In his mind Herman surveyed an open grave in a misty cemetery. He could see the lid of the exposed coffin creak open to reveal his wife's face, as grey as any corpse. He could not miss the bullet-hole in her forehead, like the dot of an exclamation mark. He could imagine her cataract eyes flick open and her withered lips mouth the words: *I'm coming to get you...*

Madness, unconditional madness, Herman thought, filled with despair. *Even in death she can't leave me alone!*

But WAIT!

An idea. A twinkle of hope. A potential way-out of his current run of bad luck. A promising last recourse to get himself out of his crazy predicament, defy this malice of circumstance.

Inside, Herman recognized there could only be one course of action to be absolutely certain. He realized how this would end, how to thwart her evil plans.

He suddenly stood up from his balcony seat, without thinking and without any attempt to address the audience, and yelled triumphantly: *"I'll show you, you dead, scheming bitch! I'll show you I'm not the gutless, spineless goon that you assume!"*

All things move towards their end.

Nicola had invited two dozen people for the private New Year's Eve garden party at the Hinkle residence. It was meant to be a double celebration since Herman had recently sold the film rights for *No Good Deed Goes Unpunished*. Some of those attending were Faye's old friends, whom Herman hadn't seen in several months, and Nicola, seemed to be getting on with them like a house on fire. She had hired the same catering service from Millennium night. Her hair dyed unnaturally blond, her face lacquered with gauche make-up, Nicola caroused unashamedly with Daniel Mayhew, the stage director, while her suffering boyfriend, Herman, kept a safe distance, his thoughts elsewhere.

This wasn't Nicola he was watching, Herman convinced himself. This was Faye using her as a vessel for her own bitter ends. No-one else could see it, but he could. Oh, yes, he could!

She didn't suspect a thing, but he would soon be free of her.

Wrapped in their woollies to stave off the chilly night, which threatened snow, the guests went through the motions of rejoicing the coming of another year. Food and punch pacified them, the company of others pleasant enough.

Then came the countdown to which everyone contributed in cheery waves... And suddenly it was midnight and a brand new year. Celebratory kisses and well wishes. Fireworks exploding in the night sky in dazzling colours.

Herman chose his moment carefully.

As Nicola kissed Daniel against the gazebo, Herman approached them, tapping the director on the shoulder. "Excuse me, do you mind if I speak with my girlfriend?"

Herman was suddenly filled with an eerie sensation, that phrase you could only say in French.

Daniel stepped aside, commenting, "She can't exactly be your girlfriend if you're letting me hump her."

Herman ignored the remark and kissed Nicola gently on the lips. "Happy New Year, light-of-my-life."

Nicola's irritation at the interruption softened. "Happy New Year, Herman. Hope you achieve what you set out to achieve in the next twelve months."

Nodding towards Daniel, he asked: "Is he your new lover?"

"Yes, he's my new Nookie Monster," she replied, nuzzling her head against Daniel's arm. Her hand slipped down to his crotch in a sordid stroking gesture. "FuMBO later?"

[*Nookie Monster? FuMBO?*]

"Once this party is over, I'm going to insist you collect all your belongings and leave my house," Herman ordered.

Nicola's initial surprise turned into a vitriolic glare. "You bastard! How dare you kick me out! I live here!"

Herman said it straight. "No longer! You're nothing more than a parasite feeding off my soul!"

Their raised voices caused the rest of the guests to stop what they were doing and look in their direction. A hushed silence ensued, save for the intermittent ignition and explosion of the fireworks.

Nicola glanced at Daniel for support, but he backed away. "Hey, this is between you guys. It's got nothing to do with me."

Raging, Nicola screamed at Herman with open hostility, "*You pathetic little man! You're not worth your weight in salt! At least the others were better men than you ever were! They were prepared to furnish me with a healthy baby, not the unviable vegetable YOU sired!*"

Herman pulled out the missing Derringer from his pocket. He had buried it under the patio before the police arrived at the scene of the crime nearly twelve months ago, but had specifically dug it out for tonight.

An apprehensive murmur ran through the guests. Nobody came to challenge him. Their host had obviously gone insane from years of victimization. Their faces resembled those of people watching a car-crash in slow-mo.

"Locked and loaded, my dear," Herman informed her.

Nicola was dismissive. "You think you can threaten me with that stupid pop-gun?" she ridiculed, derision glittering in her blue-contact-lensed eyes. "With a weapon as intimidating as your willy?" She laughed that interminable braying laugh of the harpy who had hijacked her body.

"Nicola, if you're still in there, I'm sorry I have to do this!" Herman declared sadly. "This is the only way I can exorcize you of the vengeful creature I once called my wife."

"You don't have the *guts*!" she contested defiantly.

But the fearful look in her eyes told him otherwise. It was the same look he remembered when he had confronted his wife not so long ago in the master bedroom. A panicky look suggesting she realized he was deadly serious, prepared to carry out the courage of his convictions.

"I got away with it once," Herman intimated, hurtling towards the inevitability of the situation. "Not this time, though." He loosed his final pronouncement with a small, sad shake of his head. "Goodbye forever, my dear."

Exactly one year since he'd resorted to murdering his wife, Herman Hinkle the Most Put-upon Husband in the World was compelled to kill her again. Kill her where she stood as she occupied the body of his girlfriend. Both bullets slammed Nicola hard in the chest and, with an expression of stunned disbelief, she collapsed to the ground, unmoving.

People screamed. Daniel Mayhew rushed forward and grappled the pistol away from Herman. He managed to bring Herman thudding to the ground, twisting his arm into the small of his back and thrusting a knee securely on his neck. "You're in for it now, matey! Someone call the police!"

Hours after Eric Turnbull had been caught seducing rich middle-aged women in the Côte d'Azur and fleecing them of their wealth and now faced extradition to the UK, Herman too was incapacitated in the midst of his own garden party. Rendered immobile, Herman gazed, half-dazed, at the lifeless face of his now-deceased girlfriend, Nicola. Eyes closed, her countenance bore a gentle and peaceful expression as though sleeping, full of innocence, her delicate features as pretty as a summer meadow, completely purged of the corrupting influence of his late wife's dark spirit. Even her hair, artificially blond, lacked any connotations of the sinister.

Realizing Faye had got her own back in the end and that he would never be able to bring Nicola back either, Herman burst into a flood of tears, mourning his life and a perfect love lost.

Yet, his ordeal would never be over.

If he thought his dead wife would now leave him in peace, then he was seriously mistaken. He was wrong to underestimate the extent of her control over his life, because unbeknownst to him, her spirit would continue to haunt him from beyond the grave, following him into prison where he would soon find himself gibbering on about ghosts in the psychiatric wing, suddenly very afraid of the nurse with the dyed-blond hair and deep blue eyes and her deliberately vindictive, almost contemptuous bedside manner, a little too spookily reminiscent of his dead-and-buried wife.

In sickness and in health, as the marriage vow goes.

[*Until even in death* cannot *do us part*]

Herman would learn to his dismay that sometimes not even death could contain a wife who was forever destined to be with her husband, dutifully as his sentinel and his tormentor.

They would always be inseparable, from here till eternity.

January 2011-February 2011

Harbinger

"Absolute truth does not exist. It is best to turn life into an exploratory game in the face of something so unknown and fascinating as our own existence."

César Manrique (1919-1992)

When Hilary Staples suggested a winter sun holiday for the New Year, Nicholas Haures thought it might just work. Each time Nicholas—or Nick, as he preferred to be called—rattled off various destinations, she dismissed them straight-off. She dismissed Nassau because she'd been to the Bahamas before. Not Turkey, Morocco, Egypt as she didn't trust the local water or cuisine, and besides she could still vividly remember her last case of 'Delhi Belly'. Australia, South Africa, Hawaii, Miami—too far to travel, and she didn't want to get into her Valium habit again. No, it had to be local, European. Why not the archipelago of volcanic islands just off the North African coast? The Canaries?

Nick pretended to go along with her. How about Lanzarote? he suggested. *Sounds doable. Should definitely be a damn sight posher than chavvy Ibiza,* Hilary hoped, who'd done the club scene in her teenage heyday and absolutely hated it. Nick knew something she didn't. The national emblem of the island was *El Diablo*—'the Devil'—because the early Iberian settlers had interpreted the volcanic eruptions of the eighteenth century as his demonic handiwork. Nick liked that. Nick liked that a lot.

On the plane over from Gatwick, sitting in business class, casually glancing through the in-flight magazine, Hilary asked him conspiratorially if he had ever heard that Arabs generally *washed* their arses instead of wiping them — *how scuzzy is that?* Nick pointed out that washing your backside was actually one of the highest signs of cleanliness, and not the opposite, since it meant you would not be wandering around with a sticky, stinky, itchy bumhole, and Nick bet the luxury hotel they'd be staying in had a bidet; but Hilary would have none of it, stubbornly deciding not to accept the rationale behind Muslims and their bum jugs, once again proving she lacked the necessary negotiation skills to hold a cogent argument. *When God was giving out brains, Hilary thought he said trains and asked for a slow one*, Nick readily thought of her. Hilary remained rather vocal, inappropriately so, talking of 'spics' and 'wogs', whom she claimed were unable to speak a single word of English and yet were sponging off the British welfare system, propped up by, dare she say, the plebby British Taxpayer. It never occurred to her that the country she was flying over to was run by these same 'spics' and 'wogs', and Nick knew she could not communicate in Spanish either, not that she made any effort to learn the local lingo, nor did she tone down her racist comments as though believing herself to be immune from any international backlash.

It might have been an uncomfortable journey until Nick decided to remind her of a loophole in the security checks at the airport: you could not pass greater than one-hundred-millilitre bottles through the gates in your hand luggage for risk of them being tampered with, but the stupidity of the authorities was such that they had overlooked the real possibility that you could technically put all manner and size of bottle in your suitcase, as long as it did not exceed your allocated weight allowance. It therefore stood to reason that any crazy Islamic terrorist with half-a-brain-cell could set off a liquid explosive device directly from the cargo hold.

That was enough to panic her. She began looking nervously around, pointing and staring at certain ethnic-looking passengers, mostly rich businessmen, who caught her accusing look and glared straight back.

Amused, Nick calmed her down and suggested she take a Valium.

She did, and it zonked her out. Thankfully, Nick got some peace for the rest of their four-hour flight to Lanzarote.

*****

Herodotus had already spoken of the mythical 'Orchard of Hesperides' in the far western limits of the known Ancient World as the remains of the lost continent of Atlantis where mighty Hercules supposedly completed the eleventh of his Twelve Labours by retrieving a prize of golden apples. Later, Roman galleons set up trading links with the aboriginal inhabitants, called Gaunches, without even considering settling on the island. The Gaunches were cave-dwellers with a Neolithic culture of cultivating the land and shepherding. An expedition led by a Genoese sailor called Lancelotto Malocello landed here in 1312, purportedly giving his name to the island. But it was Jean de Bethancourt, a French nobleman acting on behalf of the Spanish King, Enrique III of Castile, who is reported to have really put Lanzarote on the map in 1402, as well as using it as a springboard for his conquest of the Canaries. The story historians like to tell is that the Spanish colonists lived peacefully with the native Gaunches and even helped defend the island against repeated pirate raiding parties, but the truth Nick suspected was far from romantic as the small native population was decimated by the diseases introduced by the Europeans and further dwindled when Lanzarote became a port for slave-trading. The Spanish Conquistador, Hernando Cortes, himself would later admit that his fellow countrymen suffered a sickness of the heart that could only be cured by the acquisition of gold. The Canaries formed an important bridge between the Old World and New World, with Christopher Columbus himself stopping off there in his final push for the East Indies. The Ottomans briefly seized Lanzarote in 1585 before being vanquished by the Spanish Armada. Admiral Nelson famously tried to secure Lanzarote and its proximate islands for the British Empire but failed abysmally. Republican fugitives fled here during the Spanish Civil War.

Crime was almost unheard-of in Lanzarote, or the rest of the Canary Islands for that matter. There were the occasional unusual stories that made the newspapers, such as the eighty-nine-year-old gentleman who trashed his hotel room in one of the island resorts following a drunken row with his forty-nine-year-old ladyfriend, or the crafty bird-fancier who painstakingly trained a charm of magpies to steal silver from other people's bedrooms. However, a more international story that hit the headlines, Nick remembered, was a recent news article about an insane, homeless Bulgarian man who ran down the streets of Tenerife during a festival, carrying the decapitated head of a British woman he had stabbed to death and beheaded, which the public at first thought was merely a prop. Of further significant historical note, a prominent scandal from 2009 involved police arresting more than twenty politicians and businessmen, together with the former President of Lanzarote and the former Mayor of Arrecife, in connection with matters relating to accepting bribes for the distribution of illegal building permits along the coastline. Not that it bothered the islanders—they were as interested in the affairs of their *Cabildo* (government) heads or of Mother Spain for that matter, as the Channel Islands cared about events on the British Mainland. These days, Lanzarote was more cosmopolitan than most tourists gave it credit for. Approximately three-quarters of the population were Spanish-speaking, the rest Colombians, Italians, Germans, French, Irish, Asians. The British ex-pats made up around four-percent of the locals, and the natives were accommodating enough to speak English if required. The Spanish vernacular of Lanzarote was similar to the Spanish heard in Latin America, an articulate, more refined version of the language spoken in Spain. Interestingly, San Antonio on the Tex-Mex border was the only place in North America, even to this day, populated largely by ex-Lanzaroteans. Furthermore, the prehistoric whistling language of the Gaunches, their very peculiar way of communicating, still survived in the more remote parts, regarded nowadays as more of a curiosity than an endangered tongue that needed rescuing from extinction.

They did a round trip of the island, cramming in as much sight-seeing as they could in a matter of days. In Nick's esteemed opinion, Lanzarote was a very dry place, where it apparently only rained thirty days a year, as well as rather gusty, assailed by trade winds from the north. It boasted a relatively constant temperature (twenty-plus degrees Centigrade,) all year round, making it perfect as a popular holiday destination. The domiciles of the typical Canarian villages were flat-roofed and colour-coordinated, painted white to reflect the glare of the sun, rounded off by green doors and shutters. The sheer, almost heavenly whiteness of the buildings contrasted sharply with the semiarid, lava-black ground and made him think of those Sergio Leone Westerns he used to watch as a kid. There was neither billboard advertising nor high-rise buildings in evidence. The quietness of the roads, even during rush hour, reminded him of taking a casual Sunday drive in the British countryside. Many of the roads were lined by jacaranda trees and Canarian palms, which curiously enough resembled giant pineapples, as well as serving as a training ground for the professional cyclist over the winter months.

Following the rugged south-western coastline of Los Hervideros, with its cleverly-crafted balconies and the arabesque fountains of white foam shooting up against the stratified cliff-face with each surging crash of the waves, took them to the salt flats of Janubio and its now-redundant salt extraction/processing plant. At the bay of El Golfo lay an isolated emerald-green lagoon, in which was found the interesting, semi-precious green stone, olivin, a source of highly-original decorative jewellery. Rising up from the heart of Timanfaya National Park were the Fire Mountains, with their extensive dark lava fields and twisted sierras formed during the cataclysmic, continuous, six-year volcanic eruptions from 1730, dramatically changing the landscape, and the less devastating event of 1824. Nick and Hilary followed the winding crater route, which had been widely compared to the lunar landscape with a hint of Martian rust thrown in, and got a demonstration of some geothermal experiments, including the production of geysers of steam and the use of volcanic heat to grill meat, proving that the region was still very much active. Sensors at the resident laboratory monitored seismic activity, constantly registering gas and thermal emissions. Yet, even in this apparently dead, inhospitable environment of unusual black, towering rocky formations, jagged ridges and steep ravines, life clung on obstinately: white colonies of lichen, sporadic patches of hardy shrubs, crawling, slithering lizards and the occasional scampering rabbit. The further north they went, the greener it got. Lanzarote abandoned agriculture in favour of tourism in the 1960s when the tourist boom began. Thorn-bushes and scrubland gave way to increasing fields of corn, barley, potatoes, spinach and lentils. Journeying through the renowned vineyards of La Geria, they stopped to see the old grape presses and learned about the process of wine-making while taking the opportunity to do a little wine-tasting of their own in one of the *bodegas* (wine cellars). The black volcanic particles called 'picons' perhaps did the vineyards a favour in that they absorbed the dew, thereby preventing the moisture from being soaked down into the soil and eliminating the need to water the crops. The wine extracted from the Malvasia grape was purportedly once praised by Shakespeare. Northbound, they arrived in Arrecife, the island's commercial and administrative centre, with its only airport. Arrecife alone accommodated 60,000 of the island's 150,000 population. Here stood the Castillo de San Jose, the old fortress now operating as the Museum of Contemporary Art, and the Church of San Gines, dating back to 1574. At Mancha Blanca was the Los Dolores Church, named after the sainted patroness of Lanzarote and seen as a sacred place of annual pilgrimage and thanksgiving. The sculpted-white, monolithic Monumento al Campesino, designed by the prodigal son of Lanzarote, César Manrique, in honour of the hardworking farmer, marked the centremost point of the island. They haggled at the Sunday market stalls of Teguise, the ancient capital of Lanzarote, the vendors selling clothes, shoes, handbags, paintings, ceramics, and other homemade local handicrafts and souvenirs, traditional panpipe and folk music pumped out into the town square, a short ride to the island's highest recorded peak, Penas del Chache, measuring 671 metres, which had a panoramic viewpoint of Haria, home of the Valley of the Thousand Palm Trees and the burial place of Manrique, who died in a car accident in 1992. Their travels took them off the beaten track up to Guinate Tropical Park, which boasted a paradise of diverse birdlife, particularly parrots and penguins and pink flamingos, ostriches and owls, falcons and the mighty Canarian Egyptian vulture, as well as a fair mix of animal species, including the ever-popular otters and turtles and meerkats and capybaras. The Cactus Garden, designed on the site of ancient lava ash, had concentric terraces of cacti from Africa, America and the Canary Islands. They visited the wondrous, six-kilometre Tunnel of Atlantis, a naturally-occurring laval tube in the north, where the creative genius of Manrique was once again apparent, albeit with a discerning subtleness that maintained harmony with Nature, moulding the system of natural staircases and labyrinthine passageways into a fascinating attraction. Las Cuevas de los Verdes, or the Green Caves, where the inhabitants used to hide from marauding Berber pirates and

Turkish corsairs, now had beautiful artificial lighting, creating an extraordinary optical illusion. The Jameos del Agua, home to the blind albino crab and the enchanting subterranean grotto, with its transparent blue lagoon and walkways, led to a museum of volcanology studies and a magnificent auditorium, providing acoustics of outstanding clarity, a perfect venue for concerts and conferences. The non-profit César Manrique Foundation also displayed his artistic talents in the shape of a gallery of his most notable abstract paintings and blueprints of his Cubist architectural influences in addition to his own personal collection of original sketches by Picasso and Miro. Nick believed the Spanish made great artists, and considered Manrique to be up there with the likes of Goya and his impossible monsters born of fantasy or Dali's personal claim that his work functioned as a mind-altering drug. Manrique's art reflected his belief in the simplicity of things.

Whether they chose to bask in the sun or swim in the warm, turquoise waters, paraglide or mountain-bike or ride a camel down Timanfaya, enlist in a crash course in one of the harbour sailing schools, gain a personalized certificate for a forty-five-minute dive in a real yellow submarine to the shipwreck resting at the bottom of the Atlantic Ocean, or even ferry across to Fuerteventura island to commune with the chipmunks, sample the wild profusion of aloe vera, roam the golden sand dunes of Corralejo, and feel privileged to explore the exquisite beauty of Pajara, regarded as the richest village on Spanish soil, the surf-and-turf Lanzaroteno lifestyle supposedly provided a perfect antidote to the high octane pace of the twenty-first century. Except none of the aforementioned places of interest mattered to Nick more than the Castillo de Las Coloradas...

They were staying in Room 412 of the plush, five-star PRINCESS YAIZA HOTEL at the southern holiday resort of Playa Blanca. Nick would have preferred a simple self-catering villa apartment, but Hilary's father was a wealthy CEO of a finance company and he would not have accepted anything less for his only daughter than genuine first-class accommodation. While the UK was snowed under, once again bringing the transport system to a halt, they walked leisurely along the seafront promenade which stretched the entire south coast of the beautiful Rubicon Marina, admiring the yachts and designer boutiques. They took a stroll on the white sands of Playa Dorada Beach, lazed in the glorious sunshine, drank coffee straight from Gran Canaria's Valle de Agaete, and wined and dined in the upmarket restaurants, once Hilary had got past the mental obstacle that the salad might actually be safe to eat here.

Will you stop going on about chips? Nick scolded her on more than one occasion. *People will think we're uncultured, chavvy. And you wouldn't want that now, would you?* She continued to test his patience. *I didn't fly all the way to Lanzarote to have a full English breakfast!* he reminded her another time.

The majority of the restaurants dished out Spanish and Italian cuisine, with numerous steakhouse and kebab grill establishments also dotted along the marina; fish and seafood understandably figured greatly on the menu. The tapas, and in particular the paella, although slightly pricey, were a million times better, authentic, *proper*, than the supermarket imitation crap back home. Bacon here had a stronger, fuller flavour. Cigarettes were ridiculously cheap. Even the designer perfumes were half-price than those in the UK. The Hollywood films were dubbed in Spanish and nearly every television commercial advertised one pharmaceutical product or another.

The many public footpaths along the seaside promenade, a veritable haven for trekkers, artists and romantics, were spruced up by modern signposts. They stopped off at various coastal beauty spots, sitting on the benches to admire the picturesque view of the ocean. He must have walked approximately three kilometres east of the beaches of Playa Blanca when he spotted the lonely, weathered edifice standing on a promontory at the rocky headland of Punta del Aquila. It was an old Spanish fort, reminiscent of the Mortello Towers found around the British coastline. Consulting his guidebook, he learned it was called the Castillo de Las Coloradas, a watchtower originally built in the mid-eighteenth century, the tolls of the bell meant to warn the coastal fishing village of approaching pirates and slave hunters, providing a fortified sanctuary for the local folk, a place of refuge.

Everything that had come before suddenly meant nothing to him. He was drawn to the windswept mystery of this circular, old building; it seemed to be calling to him. He climbed the stone steps and crossed the short drawbridge to the single heavy, wooden door and realized it was locked, rendering the place only visible from the outside. He wanted to know what lay within its walls but managed to contain his disappointment that it wasn't ready to reveal its secrets to him. There was a reason why it was locked up, he was to learn much later, and how the fate of the islanders rested in his hands.

And why it somehow reminded him of Maxwell's demon, a thought experiment by the physicist James Clerk Maxwell who imagined a container full of gas molecules at equilibrium, divided into two parts by a cleverly-operated partition. When the so-called 'demon' opens this trapdoor, he allows only the faster-than-average molecules to flow through while the slower molecules remain on the other side, causing the favoured side of the chamber to gradually heat up and its counter-side to cool down, decreasing entropy and thus violating the Second Law of Thermodynamics.

Nick would find out soon enough.

Nick didn't know how he could have stuck with Hilary for so long, even if he was tapping her. She was considered by others as a 'thick, rich bitch', and her elitist, racist, constant talking-down to others and her belief that she was superior to everyone else and therefore above any form of recrimination grated on his nerves. But he would also say now, just like back then when they first met in a Chelsea flower-shop six months ago, that she was a proper babe: blond, tanned golden, boasting a body any men would covet, as well as hailing from a wealthy background, her Media, Art and Design studentship funded by the National Bank of Dad. Despite her opinionated aloofness, condescending attitude and intolerance of other people, she was a bit flaky, something of an airhead, in keeping with her hot babe status. Likewise, he could not fathom why someone as intellectually-challenged as her stayed with him, a bestselling author specializing in horror fiction. Physically, she was a beautiful work of art, all perfect curves, but in terms of her personality, she was a selfish, spoiled, empty, materialistic, image-conscious bitch who loved no-one else but herself. Maybe she liked his winsome, pretty-boy looks or enjoyed having sex with him. It wouldn't surprise him if she only went out with him for his cock. Perhaps, without blowing his own trumpet, he was a good fuck. She certainly was a sexy piece of ass and a really satisfying lay, one of the hottest bitches Nick ever had the privilege of fucking.

A case in point—or possibly not—would be their preamble down to a small, deserted cove, free of any passersby, a short walk from the Castillo de Las Coloradas, where they paused to watch the setting sun bleeding into the horizon and open an expensive bottle of Masdache. Their romantic stroll along the shore had wound down to an altogether agreeable hiatus, Hilary dancing barefoot, provocatively, on the beach against the lustrous pastel-red layers of the sky, Nick sat on a boulder, eyes closed, savouring the bouquet and palatableness of the wine. He suddenly felt her arms close around his waist, one of her hands rubbing down his crotch, and, well, one thing led to another. Hilary may lack intellectual depth, emotional warmth or any romantic ideals outside her self-centredness, but Nick knew immediately what she was after and could not turn down such an offer, particularly when she was initiating it since, in his view, she had a body made for sin. He got to his feet, opening his eyes, grabbed the prying hand and spun her round. "I need a good servicing-to, the mistress instructs her manservant," she giggled, tipsy, her eyes reflecting animal lust. She began to pluck open the buttons of his black shirt, hands sliding across his man's chest, stroking his washboard stomach. He smelled the salt tang of the ocean air, heard the tide ebb and flow against this spit of sand. The prevailing warmth together with the idyllic location and carmine sunset had obvious aphrodisiacal properties, conducive to love and romance. He leaned forward and they kissed, their mouths merging in a long, sensuous embrace, his tongue chasing hers, entwining. In the meantime, he began to expertly untie the straps of her white bikini bra, exposing her firm, luscious cleavage, which he viewed with desire, admiration and appetite, an epicurean's delight to fondle and squeeze. His lips detached themselves from hers and ran down the elegant curve of her neck, along the nub of her shoulder, arriving on the heaving mounds of her breasts. He nuzzled her gorgeous tits, knowing how wild that made her, biting her areolae playfully, hardening those nipples. Hilary shifted gears: her fingers delved inside his black combat shorts while dropping to her knees. Crouched down, she unfastened the cords of his pants and pulled them down, stretching the elasticated waistline. She did not waste time. Her mouth enclosed around his gradually enlarging member, got a grip and tugged. He held his breath, a wondrous heat spreading over his body, his skin tingling with a zillion pinpoints of desire. Hilary had shown so many times before she was one lady to give good head, and today proved to be no exception. The all-encompassing, rhythmic sliding motions of her mouth and the hungry licks of her tongue over his penis allowed the shaft and circumcised helmet to swell, attain full erection. Now fully-aroused, he reciprocated the gesture, his turn to move things on. He silently removed her exotic-blue sarong and lay her gently back down on the sand, exposing more of her nubile, sun-kissed flesh. His mouth travelled softly up her thigh, exciting her aching, sweaty skin, slipped his fingers under the fabric of her white G-string, discarding it without further delay. He caught the exquisite, enticing scent of her pussy, already gorged and moist. Cupping her butt, he pushed her legs wide open and dipped his face in there. His tongue explored between her shaven lips, and her head fell back in a sharp gasp of sexual pleasure. "Those juices run for you," she encouraged him on with an impassioned whisper, craving a repeat of past performances his mouth had proven more than capable of. He ate her out in the same proficient manner in which she had taken the time to worship his cock. Yet, all of this was meant to be a prelude to something more, something primal, something universal and inevitable: the actual act of coupling. They both knew it, they both expected it and they both relished the anticipation of flesh entering flesh, their bodies vibrating with warm sexuality, and the ineluctable rewarding outcome it would entail. They were experienced lovers, adequately skilled in satisfying their partner while gratifying their own carnal needs. Together, they were accomplished enough in the sack to figuratively rock the house and keep the party going. Their physical intimacy was genuine poetry in motion in an otherwise yet-to-be-discovered erotic home-movie.

Breathing hard, grinning, horny as hell, Nick shuffled out of his combat shorts, and grasping his well-endowed rod, carefully manoeuvred himself into her. The moment he entered, he came.

She hadn't been impressed at all. "Is that all you got?"

In retrospect, his farcical performance in this evening's sexcapade on the beach should have embarrassed him; instead he viewed it with a degree of indifference. Writers made great lovers, unlike soldiers or priests. Nick had always taken pride in and had been regularly complimented by so many girls on his enormity, his extraordinary staying power and his sublime style of lovemaking. Time and again, he and Hilary had achieved complement and harmony with one another's bodies. However, on this single occasion, rather than catapulting Hilary through the Gates of Seventh Heaven, he had dumped his load in her with as much grace as a teenage boy's first sexual encounter. No wonder Hilary had looked pissed. "Afraid so, babe," he had told her, withdrawing from her, without so much as a word of apology, going tactlessly on to suggest a rematch: "Maybe again later?"

"We'll see…" she muttered, grabbing her garments and attending to her personal dignity, but from the attitude and manner of her response, he heard: *If what I ought to expect next time is more of the same, then I really don't think so…*

Their previous Sexual Olympics were what had kept them afloat. No longer, though. Nick sensed, from Hilary's understandable disappointment, that their relationship might have reached its turning-point, that this love affair of theirs—if you could call it *love*—might be heading towards its conclusion. And, without sounding insensitive, Nick couldn't have cared less. "I'm going for a walk. Clear my head. Don't know what time I'll be back at the hotel."

The sun had completely sunk by now, the cochineal light ceded by the deepening damson of dusk. It remained pleasantly warm, despite the moderate sea breeze. Leaving a dissatisfied, half-dressed Hilary behind on the secluded cove, Nick found the steps back up to the promenade walk, joining the other tourists on this well-travelled route. Taking slow, leisurely steps, he soon came to a small rest stop, bordered by a low stone wall, arising off the main esplanade. All three wooden benches were empty and Nick crossed the flagged terrace and plunked himself down on the seat directly overlooking the wine-dark sea. He pulled out a crumpled pack of Marlboros from one of the side-pockets of his combat shorts, extracted a cigarette and lit up. He appreciated the light-headedness the first few drags produced and the subsequent sense of relaxation. Beneath a periwinkle sky with its myriad of winking stars, he sat alone on the bench and smoked, and took a measure of the seascape before him, as stunning as the contemporary realist paintings of Alex Perez, who sometimes employed a meta-quality to his work. Yet, Nick's eyes were quickly drawn eastwards to the edifice that had enchanted him the day before. From his viewpoint, he could see the Castillo de Las Coloradas in obsidian silhouette above the clifftop, its robust circular design a fine example of Canarian military architecture. Along the strand immediately beneath the sheer, bare cliff-face, Nick saw a tiny figure indulging in a spot of night-fishing. Nick perceived the charcoal-sketched vista he beheld to be oddly romantic, almost quixotic, not out of place for a writer who could hold dreamy, utopian ideas outside his horror leanings.

Regardless of the sound of surf crashing against the rocks below, Nick heard movement behind him, the distinct sound of two separate people settling down on another bench. Nick puffed away on his cigarette contentedly, without turning to look, his thoughts carried away by the sheer beauty and mystery of the overall scene to his left, the dark, inscrutable fortress on top of the isolated headland and the shadowy speck of a carefree individual blissfully fly-casting at the actual base of the cliff under a starkly-resplendent, starlit sky.

"*Encantador aquí, Rodrigo,*" Nick overheard a youngish female voice comment in right earshot, close-by. Which Nick thought roughly translated as: *Lovely up here.*

"*Estoy de acuerdo, Carmen. Es tan bonito como usted, mi querida,*" Rodrigo's voice responded with some affection. *I agree. As lovely as you, my dear.*

"*Usted nunca me dejan por otra mujer, ¿te?*" Carmen asked anxiously. *You will never leave me for another woman, would you?*

"*No seas estúpido. Te adoro demasiado,*" Rodrigo said in a soft, reassuring tone. *Don't be silly. I adore you too much.*

"*Pero él no le deja nuestro amor sobrevivir,*" Carmen said with regret, but Nick also detected fear. *But he will not let our love survive.*

"*Mi cariño, por favor, si de mí dependiera, nuestro amor duraría para siempre, incluso más allá de la muerte,*" Rodrigo told her sadly. *My darling, please, if it were up to me, our love would last forever, even beyond death.*

Nice, thought Nick, crushing out his cigarette on the ground with the heel of his shoe. *How gloriously romantic, yet so wonderfully macabre at the same time. Well, my good man, heed my lesson on love: no dame is worth going to jail for or dying over.*

The man continued, changing languages briefly. "Yes, just look at him, sitting there all alone... with all the power of the dark in his hands."

It was an accusation. But not against some unmentioned father or husband impeding their young love. It suddenly occurred to Nick that this couple might actually be referring to him. Why else would they unexpectedly switch from Spanish to English? They wanted Nick to hear what they had to say.

"*No se puede satisfacer su mujer. Ahora el asesino tiene la intención de acabar con nosotros de. ¿Cómo se atreve?*" Carmen spat in disgust. *Can't satisfy his woman? Now the murderer is intent on finishing us off. How dare he?*

Rodrigo was equally livid. "*Hijo de puta! Mamon! CABRON! Me gustaría arrancarle los testículos fuera si pudiera!*"

What the hell...? Nick couldn't believe the outburst. *You would CUT MY TESTICLES OFF if you could!?* Paranoia aside, there was no longer doubt in his mind that the insults were deliberately directed at him. Their fury was indeed meant for him. *But why?* What on earth had he ever done to these people? He had tried to ignore their conversation as best he could, but it was getting too personal. He could not possibly accept this volley of abuse lying down. He felt the need to turn round and challenge them.

Nick stood up and swung round, preparing to be as polite as he could, his most diplomatic... and stopped dead.

The other two benches were unoccupied. *Apart from him, the terrace was completely deserted.*

What the hell...?

Tourists passed by on the main pavilion walk, but there was no-one within his immediate vicinity. He might be a fiction writer, a person equipped with an enviable imagination, but in the real world he was a rationalist and pragmatist. He considered the options. Maybe the sound of the couple's conversation had travelled up from below him, carried on by the ocean breeze. He leaned over the stone wall, and looked down, but it was a precipitous drop to the rocks below. Warm gusts of wind tugged gently at his shirt collar, white foam lashed at the craggy shore. There was no sign of anyone down there.

As Nick pulled himself back to take his seat again, perplexed, unable to identify the origin of those earlier ghost voices, he was beset by another shock.

There was a man sitting on the bench next to him, causing Nick to start. "What the hell — ?"

"¡Hola, Señor Haures!" the man said in greeting.

"Where the hell did you come from?" Nick demanded. "Do you know me?"

"Sí, Señor," the man replied. "I have always known who you are. So has everyone on this island."

Nick studied the man seated beside him closely. He was dressed like a gypsy, adorned in a black T-shirt bearing the slogan LEGALIZE CRIME, a red bandana and necktie with a glittering skull earring dangling from his left lobe. He looked old with his deeply wrinkled face and long wispy-white hair, tied into a ponytail. He was missing several teeth, the remainder of them eroded stumps and discoloured brown from years of heavy smoking. But his eyes — yes, his irises — were milky-white with cataracts, seemingly unseeing. "What do you mean? How could everyone know me? I am not that famous a writer for my word to have spread as far and wide as this island. "

The blind old man, who had appeared from nowhere, answered. "You are integral to the past, present and future events of this island."

Nick frowned. "Except I've forgotten?"

Despite their lack of focus, Nick felt those eyes bore into him. "If you want to put it that way. You are a wolf in sheep's clothing, a haunting echo from a bygone era. You have forgotten who you are, and you have been forgotten by the descendants of the island. But your presence here can mean only one thing: that you shall come to learn who you are and the people will remember and fear you soon, and how your destinies are inextricably linked."

Nick tried to decipher the enigmatic comments of the blind gypsy, couldn't. "I don't understand what you mean."

"Nothing shall be what it used to be." The blind old man pointed across to the dark, lonely stone relic standing on the rugged promontory. "The secret lies within. It shall be revealed to you at the dawn of the New Year."

Nick could not hide his puzzlement. "I still don't fully get you."

But the gypsy continued to speak in riddles. "You will. Everything will come together in time. We all have a purpose. My purpose is to warn you of the *signs*. The signs will awaken your memory and direct you to your purpose, your calling. Whatever happens you cannot stop it. Nothing can ever be as it used to be. Your legend will live on for a very long time."

Nick looked away, taking in the soothing, relative calm of the ocean. Was the old man suggesting that the Castillo de Las Coloradas was the key to something not yet transpired? That he, Nick Haures, might be instrumental... to *what* precisely? "Who are you?"

"Alfonso Almeida..."

"The name doesn't ring a bell." But when Nick glanced to his left again, the old man was gone... as though he'd never existed at all.

In those halcyon days and sultry nights Nick became preoccupied by the blind gypsy's words. The old man had delivered a message, spoken of signs portending a terrible event. True, death had followed Nick throughout his life, but he had thought nothing of it before, putting it down to chance. The neighbour's baby had suffered a cot death, leading to the subsequent suicide of the grieving mother. The agonizing death of the local minister's terrier, Bracken, following a prolonged epileptic seizure, mouth foaming, eyes rolling up, limbs jerking violently, doubly incontinent, severely traumatized the priest's son. One of Nick's fellow mature students on his English course at University had passed away unexpectedly in his sleep, asphyxiating on his own vomitus after a night of heavy drinking with the boys. Nick's editor's wife, whom he had been banging, had drowned whilst taking a bath, high on heroin. And so the catalogue of tragedies continued. When he thought about it now, maybe there was meaning to be sought in all those sudden, unforeseen deaths, as they seemed to hint towards something much more dreadful in the here-and-now at Lanzarote, a dress rehearsal to the greatest nightmare of all. Some people had passed secret comments in the past suggesting he possessed a 'knack for disaster', but Nick had ignored them. What if, after all these years, there was a genuine truth to their fearful claims that he was a jinx of some kind?

Nick could not escape the extreme possibility and tried to find the meaning in the blind gypsy's sinister warning.

Was Hilary doomed? Should Nick keep her in his sights? Stay by her side? Have her checked out at the nearest British-German medical centre? He had returned to the hotel in the small hours of the morning and had slipped into bed without rousing Hilary, compartmentalizing the duvet to contain his farts which she would otherwise detect from a mile off.

She looked utterly gorgeous lying beside him asleep, and Nick wouldn't have minded waking her and convincing her of one more fuck and ravishing her, a festive shag in honour of Jesus, but he knew she might not appreciate it, particularly after his dire performance earlier in the evening. He lay awake for most of the night, thinking, while Hilary snored and ignored him.

Or was Nick himself destined to die?

Why am I panicking? What if the old man was crazy?

Nick would find out soon enough, either way. The old gypsy had mentioned 'signs'.

When the signs came, they were extremely subtle at first, but grew increasingly more pronounced as time drew closer to the advent of another year.

Nick almost missed the signs at first. Not because he wasn't looking, but he didn't know what to expect. Sitting on the dock at the marina the following sunshiny day, naked feet dangling over the sides, leisurely watching the yachts sailing out to sea, Nick was in the process of lighting up a cigarette—a joint would have been much nicer—when he saw something move in the water below. He looked down at the exact spot that had initially attracted his attention. The sun glaring off the crystal-blue waters, and minnows hunting for scraps of food. But Nick was sure he'd seen—*an object*?

There, again. From the corner of his eye. Other side, this time. Quick, darting movements under the waves.

He focused on the alleged spot. Nothing unusual there, only fish innocently in search of sustenance.

And so it went on, for a few brief minutes, picking up movement always outside his range of vision, but when his eyes travelled there, there was nothing of note.

Until he managed to actually glimpse something. For a split second, yes, but still enough time for him to give it shape and definition.

When his eyes fixed on the elusive dark object beneath the waves, no matter how ephemeral, Nick saw it was almost like a small cloud of ink radiating through the beautiful turquoise waters. Except there were things, tiny creatures living in that stygian ink-burst, that had nothing to do with the evolution of the piscine life of the sea.

He blinked, and the image was gone.

What had he witnessed? he wondered, intrigued.

Nick would subsequently spend the rest of the day haunted by the disturbing vision from somewhere else. He got a sense that he had woken something up. These eerie repeated sightings followed him around — at the shopping mall, on the beach, along the promenade, at the hotel when he woke up from afternoon siesta — always on the periphery of his vision, a vague, spreading ink-cloud in the actual fabric of reality which, when his eyes were drawn towards it, vanished in an instant. And always a sense of unnatural living things — or reanimated dead things — like an infestation of roundworms in a dog's guts, writhing within that small window of another world, maybe trying to crawl into ours.

Nick remained oblivious of Hilary's whereabouts that day, preoccupied by what he was seeing — or *nearly* seeing. As the day progressed, he realized with a disquiet mind that the manifestations, so far only in their infancy, were getting stronger, and bigger, but they still always remained relatively elusive to the eye, such as those shadow people he had heard about, always glimpsed on the peripheral aspect of the vision like a trick of the eye. By the close of play that day, Nick was still unsure what he had witnessed — Something? *Nothing?* — but felt certain that all would be revealed tomorrow, the eve of a brand new year, as prophesized by the blind old gypsy-man, that he might actually get to fully visualize the strange, unexplained phenomenon encroaching on our reality.

Hours before the advent of the New Year, Nick and Hilary were seated in the restaurant of the Princess Yaiza Hotel, probably together for the final time. They had ordered *ropa vieja*, a Canarian-spiced stew of chicken and beef mixed with chickpeas, with an accompaniment of *papas arrugadas*, washed down with a nice Rioja. Not quite outstanding fine dining, but good, hearty traditional fare, nevertheless. Soft, ambient strains of Caballe, Carreras and Domingo enriched the atmosphere.

Conversation was minimal, polite and superficial, not the intimate hand-holding of lovers by candlelight. It seemed they both knew that it was the end of the road for their relationship, but neither seemed willing to part without seeking some degree of closure. From the curtain blind of the hotel room, Nick had inadvertently seen Hilary arm-in-arm with another man, a local man, who had dropped her off at the hotel that evening for her dinner date with Nick. However, Nick suspected that Hilary expected one last tango across the dance-floor before calling it a day and moving on to her Spanish gentleman. After all, before even landing on Lanzarote, their lovemaking had been intense and satisfying, yet leaving Hilary wanting more, Nick always forced to oblige. He wouldn't have minded fucking her one last time, like the good old days, except he had more pressing issues to contend with.

"Have you enjoyed your time here?" asked Nick amicably, taking a sip of the excellent vino.

"Yes, some of it," replied Hilary. "Didn't think much of the meal though, or the service."

"What was wrong with it?"

"Food was way too spicy, and the Maitre D's an obsequious dick, as my Dad might say."

Even by her standards, that was low. If she was going to be so judgemental, why did she choose this place? Nick was glad to be out of the game for sure, a free man. "I'm sorry to hear that…"

"Talking of dicks, I didn't think much of our sex session on the beach, either." There it was; the elephant had been let out of the room. "You looked gormless. I felt humiliated."

"I think I'm man enough to sincerely apologize for letting you down," Nick said perfunctorily. "Can happen to any man."

Hilary accepted the apology without bearing a grudge, any antipathy — which might be a first for her. "I'm staying another week," she informed him, looked hopefully into his eyes. "What about you? Will you hang around with me for a little longer?"

The Spaniard can't be that great a lover, Nick sniggered inside, *if she's still coming back to me.* "I ought to fly out tomorrow, if the island will let me, or I may never leave."

"Where does that leave us?" said Hilary, sounding disappointed.

But Nick wasn't listening, having caught movement over Hilary's shoulder. Startled, he watched the nebulous cloud-like rift, gilded with fire, forming in the corner of the restaurant. There were multiple shadowy shapes trying to claw and crawl out of this alarming interdimensional fissure, grotesque, Cimmerian creatures with gnarled flesh and lantern-flame eyes. A low, inhuman screeching came from their lipless, razor-toothed mouths, growing gradually nearer. Nick felt the heat emanating faintly from the ashy, mirage-like rip. He was mesmerized.

Where do they come from?

He wondered how no-one else could be seeing this right now. Everyone in the restaurant seemed to be carrying on as per usual. It occurred to Nick that maybe the others could see what he was presently witnessing, but pretended not to notice. It would freak anyone out, but perhaps they had their reasons. Madness might be one eventuality they wished to avoid.

Nick imagined our world existing within different layers of reality. Perhaps these were the terrible creatures that schizophrenics and religious nuts and mad people could see under certain circumstances. A liberal-minded chap, Nick wrote about this kind of crap all the time, but he had never seen anything as 'loco' as this before. This was the very definition of 'supernatural'.

You've been reading too many books on the occult, my good fellow, Nick told himself. *I guess you should lay off the liquor, too.*

The dreadful abominations, frenziedly vying to break loose of the fire-streaked, impossible gulf of the unknown, fascinated Nick enormously, the strangeness, uniqueness and fearsomeness of their shapes could have easily sprung from the dark minds of Guillermo del Toro or Alex de la Iglesia, as wild and fantastic as the *Caballucos del Diablu* myth of Northern Spain, the herd of Devil's Horses stampeding across the sky, sent out to purify the souls of sinners on St. John's Eve. Yet, they existed always slightly out of focus, which was probably not a bad thing, particularly in respect to one's sanity. Their loudening, execrable screeching did not disturb the restaurant's clientele, who remained curiously oblivious of the unexpected rupture in reality, this dimensional leak, only metres away.

As Nick remained firmly transfixed on the yawning, otherworldly spectacle and its hair-raising, monstrous inhabitants outside of Hilary's range of vision, she continued nattering on about nothing in particular until she noticed he wasn't paying any attention, his eyes drawn beyond her, spellbound. "What? What is it?" she said, glancing back over her shoulder to where he seemed to be staring.

"The jury's still out on that one, I'm afraid," replied Nick, emerging from his silent daze. "Nothing to trouble your delicate little head."

When he looked again, the fracture between worlds had closed, but the vicious howls of the host of repulsive Lovecraftian beings floated back: dim, echoey, fading...

They might have missed the Pascalle de Papa Noel celebrations at Costa Teguise, but there would be no dodging the New Year's Eve parties all around them. They stayed local, at the JUNGLE BAR DISCOTECA in Playa Blanca to call in the New Year.

They sat, seats apart, in the packed beer garden, *al fresco*. Seats apart, since they had gone their separate ways following the dinner date. His name was Eduardo Garbiras, and he was a wealthy art collector from Barcelona. Hilary sat several rows ahead with her new man, head resting on his left shoulder. Nick didn't think she ever realized he was sitting right behind her.

Beware, my fine fellow, a high-maintenance bitch like Hilary cannot function without her boyfriend feeding off the palm of her hand. Nothing good can come of it. Not to over-generalize, women like her use their whole bodies, and the product of their bodies, i.e. their children, to manipulate, control and poison the opposite sex, he thought, agreeing to disagree with Pedro Almodovar's gender-reassigning worship of women. *God spare us from the Delilahs of Yesteryear to the Hilary Stapleses of Today, Amen!*

Regardless of this cynical observation, he wished her all the best, even though he knew this would be nothing more than a one-week dalliance, at her new man's expense. Nick remembered an amusing universal truth he had once heard and smiled: *Did you know twenty-five percent of women are treated for some form of mental illness during their lifetime? The remaining seventy-five percent are left untreated!*

Sitting on his high-backed chair, the singer on the stage was as good-looking as Hilary's new beau, if not a little grizzled, something of a rocker. He accompanied the music pumping out of the karaoke machine with his semi-acoustic guitar and vocals, what amounted to almost a cabaret act... or maybe a mini-concert, if Nick wanted to be kind. He sang fluently and effectively and played his guitar with the verve of a rock veteran. The relatively-diverse selection of tracks he'd chosen ranged from Enrique Iglesias (Julio's trumped-up son and all-round talentless shit but the same lucky fucker who managed to tap the gorgeous Miss Kournikova,) through the poetic musings of Red Banner and their punk version of Vangelis's *1492: Conquest of Paradise*, to Jeff Wayne's Blast-from-the-Past, Flamenco-tinged instrumental, *Matador*.

Still, Nick supposed it was a decent effort, and a good performance, and one that went well with a pint of Estrella or a jug of real Sangria. He drank and smoked like there was no tomorrow.

The singer — *Vespo? Crespo?* the name eluded Nick — had just dispensed with *La Bamba*, starting up a live cover of *Paint It, Black* by England's Rock Royalty, the Rolling Stones, when his face changed. When Nick meant 'changed', the man's face seemed to deform, distort, warp, *demonify* (if there were such a word), picking Nick out from the crowd and latching his glowering, igneous-red eyes onto Nick's, whispering into his head: *Hurry now. The hour approaches. You know where to go and what to do. Your path shall be clear to you...*

The illusion was only momentary, and when Nick blinked, it was just the plain old singer again, his face unmarked by the Devil, concentrating on his routine and crooning through his songs, behaving as though he was unaware of any psychic communication.

Nick looked around the crowded, candlelit beer garden and from their general demeanour, none of the gathered partygoers had borne witness to anything unusual, *surprise, surprise*.

The guitar act maintained his showmanship, and the congregation of people watched on, drinking, smoking, chatting, laughing, canoodling, boisterously awaiting the appointed hour when the firework displays around the island would kick start the many street fiestas and the true celebrations could begin.

A warm breath of air touched Nick's face as he got up and departed the Jungle Bar. It would be the last time he would ever see Hilary again, at least in this world.

I see the signs. How many unexpected deaths have there been recently? Should I worry about any new, inexplicable cases of demonic possession on the island?

As midnight approached, he hurriedly excused his way through the lively throngs of people to the place he was destined to find... or which had already found him.

There it stood. The Castillo de Las Coloradas. Deliberately built on the edge of a cliff, its circular stone walls dominated this lonely headland, silhouetted against the benighted sky, a sky that would minutes from now be lit up by fireworks. A building that had once offered sanctuary and hope for the former people of this island against the Berber marauders, but had piqued Nick's interest on first sight to the point of absolute obsession.

And now here he was. Where he was supposed to be.

As though struck by an epiphany, Nick knew what he must do. Almeida's words came to his mind, the blind old gypsy-man who seemed to be able to see into him, his message spoken with unusual deference. *You are a haunting echo from a bygone era, a wolf in sheep's clothing. Whatever happens, you cannot stop it. Nothing can ever be as it used to be. Your legend will live on till the end.*

Nick remembered the disembodied voices of Rodrigo and Carmen accusing him of ruining their lives, and the signs, not quite the wonderful and miraculous signs he'd expected, but a presentiment to something grim and foreboding and terrible. *It is an island in flux. The closer it gets to the New Year, the stronger the power of the other universe trying to spill through.*

Do not answer the call. Nick's better half warned him, stopping him in his tracks. The old fort loomed over him, brooding and forbidding.

Do not think like a man, a creature of dust, Almeida spoke to him in his head. *There's a part in you that's so dark, that when you find it, you will revel in its inglorious wickedness and never look back.*

But I was born in Chelsea.

Is that what you think?

I am a writer — that's all I got — with the power of words and a sound knowledge of the world.

Not only this world but other worlds, Nick heard the old Romani say. *But look at your progression as a bestselling horror writer. You always write about good versus evil, seeing life with dark glasses instead of rose-tinted lenses. But as your writing career has advanced, your work has grown more bitter and twisted with each book until good no longer triumphs and there is no upbeat resolution, reflecting your disillusionment and moral ambiguity. There is a reason for everything, a purpose for all. You have touched the dark hearts of many a living being with your novels, converted those undecided into believers.*

Who or what am I? Nick demanded to know. *Name it, for Chrissakes!*

Promise. *You have gone by so many old names. 'Haures', though, remains a consistent title.*

Nick tried to digest the small bite-size chunks the old gypsy messenger was feeding him. These little teasers were only making him more impatient, frustrated. He felt close to blowing a gasket. This was all getting too much for him — so much left unexplained. *And who the hell are you supposed to be and what is your damned relationship to me?*

The part of you that is missing. Eagerly awaiting your return so we can be reunited. Whole again. Blind no more.

Yet more cryptic nonsense, an ongoing insult to his intellect. Nick composed himself. There was always something to be got from keeping a cool head.

Almeida reminded him: *You have forgotten who you are and where you come from. But now you have returned, as foretold by the texts of Antiquity. Go. They fervently wait for their centurion to lead them into the battle ahead.*

Nick began moving again. He was still uncertain what to expect, what it all meant. Should he anticipate some kind of profound religious experience? He supposed it may have been only simple curiosity, a desire to know what was inside, which got him going again.

He climbed the steps, each step a tense, wearying effort. He tramped across the drawbridge, boots clacking on the wood, apprehension continuing to rise. Gentle gusts of wind picked at his clothes. He became oblivious to everything else, standing there at the oak door. Taking a deep breath, he clasped the wrought-iron ring handle and tested the door.

Unlike before, it opened without resistance.

And that was when he saw it and felt it, smelled the acrid sulphurous fumes. The impossible conflagration beyond the threshold engulfed him.

Clothes disintegrated, skin melted, tongue split, revealing the blackened, smouldering demon-flesh beneath, as Nick reverted back to his inherent state.

He surveyed the grotesqueries of the damned inside the infernal furnace and felt a belonging. *He was home.* Nick was one of them, had always been one of them.

It came to him suddenly — call it flashbacks, dreams, memories, intuitions, a spiritual re-awakening. He remembered why a fiery demon symbolized the island. Lanzarote was constructed over Hell. The people of this world had ignored the boiling, bubbling brimstone below, dismissing it from their collective memories as an archaic fable, a metaphor. Nick [*I have awoken, as augured by my djangoistic counterpart*] understood the unspeakableness of his nature. He arose from the Inferno, and he indeed had a purpose, even a special mention in the *Pseudomonarchia Daemonum*, a sixteenth-century grimoire proposing that even Hell had an order, a hierarchy. Before him were the legions he commanded. Out there, in the mortal world, were the apostles he had unwittingly created through his books. Demon or disciple, he knew unequivocally how to lead them, remembered his corrupt cause… and he *welcomed* it. He was a past master entrusted with the responsibility of exploring the spiritual dimension beyond the Self, deviously trying to ensnare that ever-replenishing source of inner energy, that deepest, essential part of Man, the eternal consciousness: the Soul.

Hilary Staples would finally show him the fear, courtesy and respect she owed him and everyone else after the things he would do to her and make her do in this unhallowed place. *TTFN, baby!* Her father would be arrested for millions in tax evasion and stealing pension funds, getting caught shredding documents and trying to liquidate his assets, planning a runner. Like with most rich people who took their greed above the law and got thrown into the slammer, he would tie a noose around his neck and finish the deed. *See you shortly, old chap! Not even your spectacles-testicles-wallet-and-watch nonsense can save you now. We've been waiting for you and have a spot especially reserved for you right here! A crooked fellow like you might even begin to appreciate the exquisite tortures we deliver!*

There was an unknown cosmic force guiding us all... or maybe not so unknown. Cervantes once wrote that God put up with the wicked, but never forever. Haures supposed that the Fallen Angels did God's dirty work, because He couldn't be bothered to or felt it too beneath Him to do it Himself.

It was Father Andres-Lorenzo Curbelo, the parish priest of Yaiza, who secured the survival of the people last time round by purging the land, exorcizing and banishing the demons, trapping them in... *where else?* ... A place that had previously served as a brave sanctuary, able to withstand assault, impenetrable to the outside world: the Castillo de Las Coloradas. Haures, the Malefic Prince, had since wandered the earth through the ages like a nomad, his powers weakening, memories fragmenting until he lost sight of his origins, believing himself to be nothing more than a pathetic human. Yet, all that time, he had been haunted by the sound of devils, as he unconsciously yet instinctively quested to learn his real identity, the why and wherefore, oft-expressed in his horror literature. He now recalled the relevance of Maxwell's demon and how he had, all those years ago, proposed the theory to the highly-regarded mathematician, *proven* the damned thing.

Fate certainly weaved a twisted tapestry, had brought him back here to the Hell-mouth after all those elapsed centuries. To impel him to be what he was meant to be: a Horseman, a Reaper, a harbinger of doom, the crucial catalyst spurring on events to their one and only inevitable conclusion.

In 1736, a padre had cast out the rampaging demons back to Hell in true Scriptural fashion to save his flock and help restore faith and order on a post-apocalyptic wasteland.

Now Haures had opened Pandora's Box.

What is horror? Horror can be a subjective experience. Something perceived as terrible, like a spider, by one person may be scoffed at by another. Horror can also be a universal experience, such as for most women walking down a dark alley at night, it might be the genuine fear of being raped. Every person or family or community or country had its own dread thing to fear. Take modern horror films, there was a common thread of nightmares that ran through certain parts of the world. The English remained spooked by the Victorian ghost story, while the Spanish took the old-fashioned ghost story to more surreal, fantastical heights. The Welsh fictionalized the footage discovered of a documentary film crew that disappeared while investigating a doomsday cult conducting ritualized human sacrifices to resurrect an ancient deity. In atheist Eastern Europe, sadistic pain inflicted by man upon man had crept into the mainstream. Far Eastern culture had for a long time survived on 'famine food' so, lo-and-behold, they developed movies advocating cannibalism, alongside their more traditional tales of vengeful spirits. Then there was the golem and dybbuk of Hebrew lore, the Beowulf-themed monsters of Scandinavian cinema, and the ongoing American idiotic obsession with psycho-slashers slicing and dicing their way through the teenage market. Whether it was a fear of the dark, or the closet monster in childhood, or the risk of thermonuclear war during the Cold War, Horror would always exist in the social spotlight, changing tropes and altering its anatomy with each passing generation, bucking trends and shifting patterns, mutable but forever present.

At the stroke of midnight, as New Year dawned on Lanzarote, the Timanfayan volcanic field erupted, obscuring the stars and smothering the island in a dense, fast-spreading, ground-hugging pyroclastic cloud. The suddenness of the explosions took the scientists by surprise, only becoming aware of this untameable force of nature when the recording equipment abruptly went off the charts, giving them no time to warn the public. As the lofty cinder cones around the Island of Three Hundred Volcanoes flowed with rivers of flaming magma, the volcanic upheaval and intense darkness was felt everywhere. The cherufes, once consigned to the fires of the Pit, were released in winged flight across the island, an island that now lay outside the reach of God's protection, and Hell reigned down, the foul, pressurized gases expelled from the bowels of the earth poisoning the air, the hot, molten lavamen burying and incinerating whole villages in minutes. This unforeseen catastrophe constituted a horror unique to the people of the island, as they were consumed in a sweeping, unimaginable holocaust, infinitely more devastating than Pompeii or Vesuvius, which surely would have made Haures's old chum, Malcolm Lowry, chuckle in his grave.

Almost three hundred years after he last brought destruction to the world of Man, Haures set another apocalypse on the people, the annihilation of all life on Lanzarote heralding the coming of THE END.

January 2013-March 2013

Invention of the Devil

"Television is an invention that permits you to be entertained in your living room by people you wouldn't have in your home."

Sir David Frost
Radio and Television Broadcaster

Prologue

The shift at the foundry has drained him. Shaun Hitchens arrives at his studio apartment in Netherton around midnight, exhausted, prepared to sleep for a thousand years. He needs to get enough kip as he is due to work the same shift pattern tomorrow, and for the rest of the week, long thirteen-hour days. No chance of a lie-in this week, he supposes.

As is his usual custom, he intends to physically unwind first, relax, before retiring to bed. He makes himself a quick snack, a Ploughman's sandwich, washed down with a Bud and flops on the sofa in front of the TV, turning off the lights, which normally proves conducive to sleep.

The glow from the television fills the room in an eerie ghost-light.

There is nothing worth watching on terrestrial television, which is fine by him; he will be sleeping soon. But as he scans the small selection of pretty lame cable channels, most of them scrambled, he lingers on one particular channel he has never noticed before. The screen shows an operating theatre, with white-tiled walls and in serious need of a lick of paint, dimly-lit by a single, flickering emergency-light overhead, and a metal chair on which is seated a man, dressed only in dirty underwear, gagged by duct tape and bound to the arm-rests by leather straps, unconscious.

Shaun stops eating. He recognizes the man immediately – there can be no *mistake – and a cold tingling courses its way up his spine. Despite all the decades that have passed between them, he is looking at his father, with whom age has caught up. Definitely him, not someone who looks like him.*

But what the hell is his old man doing here on late-night television?

A figure slowly emerges from the darkness behind the chair, and Shaun stares harder at the screen. The figure – it is a man, Shaun is sure – is dressed in scrubs and galoshes and a rubber apron, all black. He wears standard surgical gloves. But the most disconcerting aspect about this figure is his face. It is fire-apple red and grotesque and pulled back into a fixed, malevolent grin. The crooked nose is as pointy as the two horns on either side of the scalp. Then Shaun realizes it is a mask – the man is wearing a devil mask. And for the first time, Shaun notices the dentist's trolley beside the chair, professionally laid out with an eclectic array of sharp, deadly instruments, and gets a strong sense that something bad is about to happen...

1
The Father

Syracuse Hitchens had been a hard man to live with. Hard-drinking as well as a hard disciplinarian. Ever since he could remember, Shaun had been afraid of his father's temper, volatile and easily aggravated, and not helped by the old man's daily bouts of drinking. Shaun ran errands for him, including buying his daily ration of cigarettes and two packs of Special Brew after school, petrified to be in his presence on return to the Seven Sisters estate in Netherton, doing his best to make himself scarce for the rest of the evening, which was not always possible, particularly at bedtime. The number of occasions his father had physically dragged him out of bed and beat the living hell out of him because of something paltry and meaningless Shaun could not count. Sometimes he'd receive beatings for no apparent reason. Shaun learned to assume that angry dads were a normal part of growing up until he turned sixteen and ran away from home. He was glad he was a singleton as he did not wish his father's wrath to be inflicted on any siblings. Syracuse was prone to remind his son of the beatings he received from his own father, but any sympathy Shaun had originally harboured soon wore thin once his father slapped him awake in his bed and confronted him with the sickening reek of alcohol and tobacco on his breath and the dark promise of what was to come on his empurpled face when he produced his belt and whacked him repeatedly on his palm, if he was lucky, or more often flogged his back until the skin was frayed and peeling and bleeding and hurt so horribly as to make Shaun wish he'd never been born. The physical chastisement his father meted out went under the excuse of 'making a man' out him, and the old man would apply raw salt to the wounds soon after to complete the ritual punishment, causing the flesh to sting infinitely worse than the beating itself. Shaun still carried the scars from those lashings to this day, a solemn memorial to his pain as a child. He was amazed he'd suffered in silence for so long, kept his frequent punishments quiet, even from his teachers, since his father had made him believe he deserved the beating because he'd done something wrong and needed 'correcting'.

Shaun's mother, Ariel, had probably done the right thing and long-since jumped ship when her son was only six, abandoning the family for the gas man after it eventually dawned on her that her husband might actually kill her. The damage had been done, however. Her own alcoholic depression, brought on by years of mindless beatings from her husband, had spiralled into despair and suicide, only six years ago. Shaun had gone to the funeral, which had been poorly attended and thankfully without his father anywhere in sight, who had always blamed him for his mother leaving, as well as reminding him he'd been an 'accident'.

Shaun wondered why his hateful old man had not given him up for adoption, but it turned out Syracuse relied on the regular child benefit payments to fund his drinking habit. It was only when Shaun challenged his father for the first time on turning sixteen, bravely suggesting the old man get help for his drinking, that Syracuse beat him up for the last time, and Shaun left home for good and never looked back. A short spell at his father's sister, a practising Christian and nowhere near as punitive as her brother, and Shaun went his separate way on the very day he turned eighteen. He kept in touch with his aunt thereafter, but never spoke to his father again.

So seeing his drunken, mean-tempered, good-for-nothing father now, somehow on the television screen, appearing old and frail and helpless, after so many decades apart and remembering all the blind fury and domestic violence and the physical abuse he had suffered at his hands, Shaun Hitchens could not help but smile.

Shaun watches the man in the Satan mask approach Syracuse Hitchens and grab a handful of his hair and rip off the duct tape covering his mouth.

The old man flinches, opens his eyes blearily and instantly fixes his gaze on the devil-masked figure towering over him. Blind panic grips him. "Who-who are you?" he asks, stumbling his words. "Wh-wh-what do you want with me?"

"Your life!" his captor puts simply. Except his voice sounds distorted and mechanical as though being processed through an electronic speech synthesizer.

He gets the desired reaction from the open threat spoken with the scary artificial voice coupled with the demonic mask he wears in deliberate intimidatory fashion as Syracuse cowers further, frightened, while his bladder lets go. A damp patch forms across his groin, dribbling down his leg to collect as a yellow puddle on the floor.

"That's rather infantile *of you..." he responds in his modulated voice, slapping his prisoner across the forehead. Devil Mask – as Shaun names him – curls the fingers of his right hand into a tight, meaty fist and starts laying into the old man's face, chest and stomach with the power of a champion pugilist.* Smack! Whack! Smack! *"How does that feel, old man?" Devil Mask chuckles as he abruptly stops his five-second pummelling. The knuckle sandwich the old man has tasted has left him with a series of unsightly bruises. The assault on the left cheek is already starting to redden and swell up. Shaun suspects some broken ribs; he is sure he has heard the crack of bone.*

Syracuse is stunned for a matter of seconds, then as awareness returns, he starts to whimper in fear and pain. "Help me... please don't do this to me!"

"How do you think your son felt, then just a child, when you used to hit him in one of your drunken rages?" Devil Mask demands in those dark, electronic tones.

Shaun is taken dumb. How can this stranger in a mask know about his father's regular beatings of him when he was still a child? Had someone been investigating his past and set this up? And how can they actually broadcast this on television?

"I'm sorry... please no more!" Syracuse – this violent drunk who had frequently accused his son of being an agent of his own abuse – implores desperately.

"Too late for penance now, old man," Devil Mask replies ominously, going

on to quote Scripture. "Your sin shall find you out."

The old man is a quivering, broken wreck. "I'm so, so sorry... if only you give me a chance, I can change..."

"That won't be necessary," *Devil Mask responds without any compassion. Devil Mask reaches towards the surgical trolley. Shaun takes note of the implements laid out on it. Aside from a scalpel or two, they are hardly what he'd call surgical instruments: scissors, pliers, bolt-cutters, screwdrivers, hammer, hatchet, even a pair of garden shears. He gets a nasty sense he is looking not at a run-down operating room but some kind of a torture chamber.* "I've especially prepared a little something for this special occasion to help slake your thirst. I know you like a drink..." *Devil Mask lifts up a whisky jar from beneath the trolley. He pops off the cork.*

Is the guy intending to get my old man drunk? *Shaun wonders, perplexed.* Where's the punishment in that?

"A drink would be nice..." *Syracuse murmurs, relaxing a tad, despite his obvious injuries.* "I'm parched..."

Then, even under the low-intensity lighting, Shaun sees the wisp of fumes rising from the lip of the open jar, suggesting something either hot or pungent. He realizes something terrible is about to go down.

Sure enough, Devil Mask shoves a glass funnel forcefully down the startled old man's uptilted mouth and starts pouring.

Syracuse glugs down the contents like any veteran alcoholic but immediately starts coughing, unable to swallow further, choking against the inrush of liquid flooding his throat. His eyes roll up and fresh blood begins bubbling up from the corner of his mouth, trilling down his chin.

Devil Mask removes the funnel and puts the whisky jar back on the floor before stepping back cautiously.

Shaun soon recognizes what Devil Mask has fed his father.

While the blood continues to gush out of the mouth, corroding away the chin, Syracuse's stomach ruptures outwards in the form of several random explosive jets of blood, like a barrelful of water that has been fired at repeatedly, the punctures quickly enlarging and merging with one another as the corrosive liquid eats away at him from the inside out.

The walls of the abdomen lose their integrity, unable to contain his insides any further, and gravity pulls his organs — liver, kidneys, coils of bowel — down to earth. His innards splatter repulsively to the floor in a sizzling pile of red gore. Only the spine is apparent, left intact, around where the victim's abdomen ought to be.

The flesh on his chin dissolves and his jaw detaches itself and hangs off to one side by a thread of gristle.

The concentrated sulphuric acid has done its job, cleaned him out. Shaun stares at the fragile, gruesome remains of his father, the clearly visible spine from his empty abdominal cavity reluctantly attaching the chest to the legs, jaw swinging loose, and keeps down a strong wave of nausea. His old man may have been a horrible person in life, but did he deserve such a horrible death?

Devil Mask suddenly punches the ON button of the ghetto-blaster and closes in on the camera and, to the accompaniment of Hellraiser by Motörhead, speaks directly to the viewer with the cruel, booming voice of a demigod. "Join us again tomorrow for another edition of It's Your Funeral..."

The television screen fills with the crackle-pop of static as he abruptly cuts transmission.

2
The Landlord

Shaun finished his shift at midnight and returned home, hungry and tired, and in the dark of his studio apartment, went straight to his TV. Expectantly, he surfed the channels to find the station that had gripped him the night before. He located it without much difficulty even though it was tucked away in the pay-for-view adult channels and unmentioned in any TV guide.

Shaun could not get the grisly death of the father he hadn't seen in decades out of his mind, the dangling jaw, the gory dissolution of flesh as a result of forced consumption of concentrated acid, the old man's remains comfortably mopped up from the floor. A part of him had thought he had dreamed the entire episode, but presently his television screen received the view from the camera in the corner of the same basement room, set up like an operating theatre, the spilled blood from the previous night scrubbed completely clean, and sure enough, there was another person, stripped naked and tied to the metal chair.

Shaun hadn't imagined it, it seemed, and, yes, he recognized the latest victim. It was Luther Critchley, Shaun's current landlord.

Luther Critchley wasn't a nice man, though he clung to the pretence that he was. He would offer his tenants a cut-price rate of rent, even a rent-free stay, but it would only be in exchange for their services in the enterprise he allegedly ran. Rumour had it that Luther ran a child exploitation ring. It was only a rumour, Shaun couldn't be sure as to its validity, but Luther had already approached him and asked him whether he would be interested in doing some work for him. When Shaun had inquired as to its nature, Luther refused to disclose what it would entail, hinting only that he would be well-paid and that Shaun would be signing a contract of non-disclosure, just like many others in the building had done. To breach the contract would mean... *well... just think about it*, Luther had suggested, *and let me know*. Whatever work Luther had arranged for him couldn't be of the wholesome variety, and taking into account the need for such confidentiality and keeping in mind the rumour, Shaun decided on the spot, politely declined the offer to be in the man's payee. Only for Luther to instantly inform him that he would be increasing the rent and taking away the luxury of free cable TV. Shaun could have complained to the Ombudsman but his credit was bad and where would he live? Hostels weren't great places, full of drug addicts and chronic mentally-unwell men. He could inform the police, but where was the evidence, and Luther might pin something on him.

In a world where the likes of Jimmy Savile, Stuart Hall and Rolf Harris, former darlings of the Beeb, had their squeaky-clean, avuncular reputations turned on their heads, their vile exploits spanning decades finally coming to light, it seemed only fitting that a suspected pederast like Luther Critchley should serve his sentence in that metal chair, a more radical, and some might say *apt* form of punishment than that meted out to those child-molesting, sick, old fucks, who'd got away with it for so long. Perhaps it had been the culture of the BBC at the time but how could Savile's crimes have remained hidden for half-a-century unless they had been consciously brushed under the carpet? Even in his heyday the eccentricities Savile showed the world at large stretched beyond that of any fun, cuddly clown. Yet nobody would ever dare believe that Santa Claus was abusing the kids. Luther Critchley would take it on behalf of Savile, someone he claimed rather boastfully he admired. Maybe both men were in business together once. And what about all those disgraced priests the public was hearing about, accused of the systematic abuse of altar boys in their dioceses decades ago, subsequently forced to give up the frock and disappear off the scene, these embarrassing scandals quickly brushed under the carpet by their superiors in the Roman Catholic Church, just as the BBC had deliberately overlooked the allegations against Savile back then?

The soon-to-be torturer approached the condemned man from behind, the novelty Halloween mask taking on more sinister Satanic overtones.

Shaun remembered what Devil Mask had said yesterday when torturing his father. *Your sin shall find you out.*

There was a kind of perverse pleasure to be got from seeing this dirty old pervert's eyes widen in unutterable alarm as Devil Mask made his presence known. *This couldn't have happened to a nicer person,* thought Shaun, grateful to bear witness to the impending interrogation.

And, from all indications, execution.

Devil Mask does not waste any time. He removes the gag and slaps Luther Critchley in the face, stunning him for an instant. "Do you know why you're here, Mr. Critchley?" comes the synthesized, almost demonic voice.

"No!" protests the naked man, mustering some indignation above his fear, struggling against his restraints. "What do you want with me?"

"Your sin shall seek you out," Devil Mask informs him darkly. "You are charged with the abuse and rape of minors."

"I don't know what you mean," Luther remarks, suddenly defensive.

Devil Mask is slightly more specific. "Like little boys, do you?"

There is no mistaking the face of the sleaze merchant, middle-aged, grease-slicked, salt-and-pepper hair and cruel sneer. "I don't like what you're implying..."

Devil Mask decides not to beat around the bush any longer. "Quite the backdoor operation you've got! Taking pictures of little boys and posting them on the Internet!"

"How dare you accuse me of — !"

"Why should I believe you, a man of bullshit?" Devil Mask lifts a pair of garden shears from the instrument table. "Maybe this'll remind you..." And in one swift, lightning move, he clips off the man's dormant private parts from the root. The lopped stem of the penis still attached to the sac of testicles tumbles to the floor, and the open crotch gushes blood, spilling off the chair in red waves.

Luther screams upon realizing what has transpired, struck full force by exquisite pain. "WHAT HAVE YOU DONE? WHAT HAVE YOU DONE? OH MY GOD, OH MY GOD!" And passes out.

"There is no god here," chuckles Devil Mask, "only me." He gives Luther another vicious slap, bringing him back to wakefulness.

Luther feels the intensity and nature of his injury and starts shrieking again and again and again, hideous, shrill circles of sound.

Devil Mask appears to have no choice but to stuff Luther's dismembered organ into his mouth, dampening the wordless howls, causing the castrated man to nearly choke on his own manhood. "Quiet, please! I'm trying to think here... !"

Shaun's landlord, now rendered a eunuch, makes a concerted effort to control his panicking, and therefore his breathing. For one obscene moment, the manner in which that thing is shoved into his mouth reminds Shaun of a self-fellating contortionist if it were not for the fact that the guy is bolted upright, genitals fully severed from the groin and the testicle pouch with its dangling gonads giving the vague semblance of a second set of puppy jowls. Then the impression is gone. Just a guy chewing on his own dick, *thinks Shaun.* No hope of being taken to hospital and having it sewn back on.

"Now that we have some peace and quiet, would you like to know what I'm going to do to you next?"

Luther continues to moan.

"I would very much like to remove your gag, so to speak, but you might find your next forfeit unpleasanter still." Devil Mask picks up the duckbilled tinner snip from the instrument trolley and brings it close to the landlord's face to intimidate and terrify. Luther's eyes remain wide and bulging and petrified. "You see I'm very methodical in what I do, how I take someone down. I cut your nadgers off because you jerk off to porn that should never be porn, and you will never have that experience again." He pats the duckbill snipper fondly and grabs hold of one of the unfortunate man's pinkies within the jaws of the device. "This here tool should render you incapable of physically uploading and accessing inappropriate shit on any computer ever again." And as Luther realizes what Devil Mask intends to do to him next, his eyes protrude even more turgidly until they're at risk of bursting and his moans become more urgent, desperate, imploring, face pouring sweat. There is no indecisiveness on the part of Devil Mask for, without undue pause, he snips off all the fingers and thumbs, one by one, as far up as the knuckles, in quick succession, as smoothly

as a cigar cutter, with the incisive snap of bone. Each amputated digit drops to the floor soundlessly to join its companions, blood now seeping out more freely from the exposed knuckle-joints, painting the arm-rests in scarlet to drip off the ends.

The gradual mutilation of his body is too much for Luther to bear and his high, pain-stricken moans descend to dull, abject groans, as he teeters on the edge of unconsciousness.

Devil Mask is forced to slap him awake once more. He allows the endorphins in his torture victim time to kick in, numb some of that excruciating pain and bring some modicum of awareness of the surroundings, before proceeding. And all along the guy's mouth remains crammed in degraded fashion. "But I've saved the best for last."

As Luther's eyes adjust to the low lighting once again, tears streaming down his cheeks to mingle with the sweat and grime, Devil Mask reaches for his next instrument of torture, an ice-pick, and slowly, oh so slowly, brings the pointed tip closer, and closer, to the left eye. Luther panics further, trying to move his head away from the approaching spike, but Devil Mask holds the head steady with an almost vicelike grip using his other hand. Luther continues to struggle, reduced to rolling his eyeballs in his sockets in a futile attempt to avoid the inevitable.

Devil Mask puts the inevitable into words. "Poke your eyes out so you never see any kids again!"

He hovers the deadly tip of the ice-pick less than a millimetre from the man's cornea, largely for effect and his own amusement. When he realizes there is only so much terror a man can sustain, he punctures the iris with expert precision, producing a soft, moist **pop!**, like a pea squeezed out of a pod, blinding Luther instantly. Devil Mask drills the needle deeper still, but careful enough not to push it in too deep so as to pierce the brain. The injury takes Luther beyond the next threshold of pain. He cannot yelp with his cock in his mouth. Devil Mask pulls out the ice-pick in a dribbling trail of milky-pink ooze, and with a hearty but scary voice-synthed, "Now you see me, now you **don't**!" inserts likewise into the remaining eye, yet untouched. Another subtle popping noise as the point of the ice-pick enters the eye, and a faint squelchy sound when it is withdrawn.

There is only so much pain a man can endure, *thinks Shaun, stomach-turning disgust mixed in with fascination.*

Devil Mask is aware, just like the viewer, his victim is shutting down. How much more can he realistically do to this man? "I suppose you'll never have to see my ugly mug ever again. Or anybody else's in this life..." He pulls the damned thing out of the man's mouth. "Any last words before I close this meeting?"

Luther utters nothing intelligible, greatly confused and mindless, his feeble moans nowhere near offering any defence.

Time to wrap up business, *muses Shaun.*

Devil Mask is of the same opinion, it seems. "Lend me your ears, Mr. Critchley, because I never want you to hear the endless screams of all the children stripped of all their innocence and traumatized for life, defiled by your grubby hands, again." *He decides to put Luther out of his misery. He swings the ice-pick in an arc and skewers Luther straight through the left ear, the tip cleanly exiting through the right.*

The head lolls forward, motionless, unrousable.

Job done, Devil Mask looks straight into the camera. Motörhead's Hellraiser *fills the room as accompaniment.* "And here endeth another fine episode of It's Your Funeral. Nevermore shall Mr. Luther Critchley run his vile little racket again. Join us again tomorrow when our next guest for the chop will be Cyrus Fitch."

Cyrus Fitch? *thinks Shaun, startled. Devil Mask is full of surprises.* Is there something Devil Mask knows that I don't?

The TV screen goes blank, resting for another night.

3

The Boss

The following night Shaun picked out his usual midnight spot in front of the television set. Sure enough, there was Devil Mask creeping up behind his victim, and there was Cyrus Fitch the said-victim fastened to that metal chair.

Shaun absolutely loathed his job, making nuts and bolts at the foundry. He hated the tedium of his work, its directionless nature with no opportunities for promotion. He wished he had paid more attention in school, not that his old man had ever encouraged him to study. He still dearly desired to gain some basic qualifications, perhaps get onto one of those Direct Learning courses and get a GCSE equivalent in

Literacy and Numeracy and use it for a more worthwhile occupation. Pride meant he would rather be a simple working joe than become redundant and survive on welfare. But he couldn't fund the course yet, and it also explained why he was still living in this shithole (*chez* Critchley), let alone afford to divorce his wife.

More than his job, Shaun hated his boss, Cyrus Fitch. Despite the smart suits and big talk and cheesy grin, the guy was one seriously crooked fuck. There was a rumour that Cyrus had poisoned his uncle in order to inherit the foundry. Cyrus employed cheap labour, a migrant workforce, predominantly East European, who were resident in the country illegally and most of whom could not speak a word of English. The immigration authorities might have busted his ass if someone decided to blow the whistle on his racket, but no-one dared. They were all afraid of him and the risk of being deported. He paid less than the minimum wage and provided them with a place to stay, comfortably recouping his losses with the extortionate rent he demanded for the accommodation's overcrowded, squalid conditions, leaving them trapped and broke, below the poverty line and financially at his mercy. They did not know their rights—it would have been utterly pointless of them to investigate their rights— because of their illegal alien status. There was no doubt he fiddled his accounts, declared only the bare minimum to the Taxman as well as received further payment from his employees for the fake work visa and other documents he supplied his labour force. It was rumoured that he was turning his hand to nursing homes for the elderly with the same crooked working practices.

Cyrus also believed he was God's gift to women. He had a prodigious appetite. Not only had he gone through most of the single overseas women on the shopfloor, he had also slept with the wives, girlfriends and daughters (of consenting age, of course) of the men who worked for him. If any of those men were ever to find out what he had been up to between the bedsheets and dare confront him, Cyrus would readily inform the authorities of the person's fraudulent presence in the UK and let the Home Office deal with it. Hence, his turnover of personnel was quite high, but it didn't bother him. He was making tonnes of money, forever cutting corners and unscrupulously swindling the authorities as well as screwing over his own employees, channelling his substantial profits into various shady investments, his fat fingers allegedly in a lot of dodgy pies.

Shaun utterly despised Cyrus for another, more personal reason besides being Grade-A scum. His boss was gleefully fucking his wife.

The focus is on the room on screen. As with his previous victims, Devil Mask slaps Cyrus awake.

Cyrus takes in his dingy surroundings and his eyes widen, more out of bewilderment than fear, at the sight of the man in the sinister Satan mask. He realizes he is strapped to a chair, naked. He struggles against the restraints without success. "What the fuck?"

"Good evening, Mr Fitch," Devil Mask says by way of greeting, the synthesized voice in full, demoniacal mode. "Do you understand why I brought you here?"

"Who the fuck are you supposed to be?" Cyrus demands to know, getting impatient, irate.

"Your Judge, Jury and Executioner," Devil Mask replies, simply and to the point, instantly shutting Cyrus up. Shaun suspects that Cyrus must know things can only go downhill for him from here on out. "Anything to say before I begin?"

Cyrus tries to reason with his captor. "Whatever I've done doesn't deserve whatever you're about to do to me."

"You think you can treat your largely Romanian workforce like shit, either take them to the cleaners or enjoy their women against their wishes?"

"Why not?" says Cyrus arrogantly. "I do what I do because it's a sink-or-swim world. What's it to you?"

"Your sin shall find you out, and your punishment must justify and be proportionate to your crimes."

"What the hell gives you the right?"

"Because I am the Devil!"

"Bullshit! You're just a man, a fucking crazyman who thinks he's the Devil!"

"No need for name-calling. I do not care for your attitude. I do not get any sense of remorse or reflection or responsibility on your part. It's your funeral, pal." Devil Mask grabs a carpet staple-gun and in one neat, slick gesture bolts Cyrus's penis to his belly, with minimal blood loss.

Perfect insult to the man's masculinity, *thinks Shaun.* I guess you won't be using *that* in a hurry!

Cyrus the Stud screams in unmanly, high-pitched agony. As he gradually gains control of himself, he directs his anger back at Devil Mask. But he's also sporting his usual gleaming, self-conceited grin, the same grin he uses when he's handing over his employees, once he has no further use for them, to the UK Immigration Services. "Fight me mano-a-mano, you fucking coward! Let me whip your fucking arse!"

Devil Mask lifts a small set of pliers, brings it close to his captive's sweaty, ruddy face. "Do you know what I'm going to do with these?"

Cyrus doesn't reply, just stares, boggle-eyed, at the device.

The lamp-fixture on the ceiling buzzes, flickers.

"Dental extraction surgery," *Devil Mask finishes.* "Let's wipe that smug grin off your face, Mr. Fitch!"

Devil Mask prises open Cyrus's jaw with his fingers, and before Cyrus can protest or bite down, begins systematically pulling out his teeth, one-by-one, like the medieval barbers used to remove the rotten teeth of their clients before the scientific advent of dentistry.

Shaun hears the sound of each tooth being forcibly wrenched from its socket, the sound reminiscent of a nutcracker cracking open a walnut, and he winces, grossed-out. God, *that* must really hurt! You can never go wrong with tooth extraction even at the best of times. Has to be up there with the other notorious torture techniques, like the German chair or Strappado or just being drawn and quartered in the good, old-fashioned sense, the body tugged-of-war and torn apart, limb from limb.

Cyrus is shrieking like mad now, nerve roots on fire, as Devil Mask without respite yanks out the last of his molars, dropping it with a soft click to the floor amongst the rest of the teeth. "There, there, shush now. It'll soon be over!"

Cyrus doesn't like the sound of that remark. He suddenly stops screaming. His mouth is puckered like a toothless old crone's and stained bright crimson. "Everyone has a right to live," *he pleads in muffled, gummy mumbles,* "from the slums of India to the truffle-pig CEOs."

"Not in my book! Beggars and bankers? All shall answer before me!"

"Why must they? How could you possibly know any banker?"

"I knew a banker once, safe in his ivory tower. He loved money so much, and since he wasn't prepared to part with it, I stuffed rolls and rolls of banknotes up his arse and lit them. Lit up as brightly as a Guy Fawkes effigy he did and burned as rapidly as a case of spontaneous human combustion. Not much remained of him afterwards."

Cyrus continues crumple-mouthed and frightened, no longer the vaguely good-looking (if not slightly chubby,) fellow Shaun is accustomed to. "Please let me go! I'll forget this ever happened! I can pay you whatever you want!"

"I thought you were a man of much more spunk than that! No matter how much your offer tempts me, there is nothing you can bribe me with that will change my mind, back, sack and crack."

Devil Mask has picked up the cheesewire from the surgical trolley, and standing behind Cyrus and as far apart as the wooden handles will allow, stretches it out tautly in front of him.

"Oh, no... Please, no!" Cyrus begs him in stark desperation, mortally afraid. "I'll do anything you ask! Just please don't use that thing on me!"

"How many times have I and every torturer throughout the whole of history heard those words spoken?" Devil Mask wraps the cheesewire tightly around Cyrus's neck and pulls on the handles. "This might just hurt a tad."

The cheesewire pierces the skin and immediately severs the arteries which spray spasmodic fountains of blood in keeping with each beat of the heart, painting Devil Mask's apron. Cyrus squirms in his chair, moaning incomprehensibly, but his frantic efforts weaken as the cheesewire cuts through the muscles of the neck as smoothly as if they were nothing more than cheddar. Devil Mask continues to strenuously tighten the cheesewire which now stresses the cervical spine until it manages to slice through even bone and cartilage, separating the head as cleanly as any guillotine. Cyrus's head rolls forward and drops into his lap.

The face on the decapitated head wears a perplexed expression, and Shaun jumps, genuinely startled, when those eyes blink a couple of times. Then, after a few seconds, the eyes glaze over and stay open and fixed as all life slips away.

How could this station have ever got past the censors? Shaun wonders. Probably didn't, and airs illegally as a pirate station, specializing in snuff films.

Devil Mask, whose apron is covered in blood, talks to the camera with the rocky strains of Hellraiser playing in the background, which is fast becoming his chosen theme song. "Thanks again for keeping me company this evening. There is an old Machiavellian motto I live by: The end justifies the means. I hope you agree. Tune in again tomorrow, same time, same place, when we will be joined by a very special guest."

Shaun is intrigued. Surprise me…

4
The Wife

Shaun had once loved Lori, maiden name Gaffney. Otherwise, he would never have gone out with her, let alone married the woman. They had met down the pub, and Lori had become instantly attracted to the handsome but quiet man drinking alone in the corner booth. Lori was a dreamer, and she imagined that Shaun was on the fast track, some big-shot writer who was working on a new book. She also believed she'd be the envy of her girlfriends, having hooked such a hunk. Her friends were indeed impressed by her new catch, dictating the pace of her relationship with Shaun. She was understandably disappointed that he wasn't educated or rich, but at least she had her own diamond-in-the-rough, like Lady Chatterley's gardener. At least their babies would be gorgeous.

And Tammi was indeed a beautiful baby, all smiles and curls. Shaun and Lori got hitched at the Registry Office when Lori was almost eight months' pregnant. And for a while they were focused on raising their sweet little girl in a rented one-bedroom flat. Shaun did a number of menial odd jobs just to make ends meet, and Lori gave up her part-time work at the hairdresser's to look after little Tammi and play house.

Except as the months and years rolled by, boredom began to set in. Motherhood, it seemed, wasn't everything it was cracked up to be. What precisely were the joys of being stuck with a husband who didn't seem bothered with either bettering himself academically/vocationally or saving up so he could spend lavishly on her which she believed she deserved… and what had become of their daughter, who had somehow transformed from one of those quiet and contented babies into a loud, wild toddler, all needy and faddy and tantrummy, subsequently growing up into a foul-mouthed, precocious teen, hell-bent on joining the bad elements of the neighbourhood? Lori noticed that her own looks, too, were beginning to suffer; she was looking frumpy and feeling constantly tired. She continued to grow more and more disillusioned and unhappy with her lot. She was meant for more than this. As a self-styled Queen of Leopard Print, she had always considered herself desirable to any man. As sex with Shaun became stale, then non-existent, her eyes wandered and caught on Shaun's boss at the new foundry he'd found work.

Cyrus Fitch was just the man Tammi had dreamed of. He was full management material instead of an expendable blue-collar worker, loaded and reasonably-hung, but most of all he found her exciting, *desirable*. She didn't care whether he derived his source of revenue through legitimate means or otherwise, she just fantasized about being some gangster's moll. They fucked like rabbits in his office at the foundry while her husband toiled away on the factory floor and her daughter played truant with her friends.

When Lori eventually came clean to Shaun of her infidelity, not just her affair with the foundry boss but her lifetime of sixty-odd men she'd slept with, well before she'd met him, of which he had no previous knowledge since she had lied to him, to even after they'd wed when the Seven Year Itch had beckoned to be scratched, she was surprised how well he took it. He did not shout at her or hit her. He just told her to pack all her things and leave. He didn't mind if she took their daughter with her — she was a dead loss anyway, nothing good could ever come of her life. He couldn't divorce Lori just yet because he couldn't afford it. He would, however, be willing to pay whatever child maintenance Tammi was entitled to until she turned sixteen.

Lori couldn't believe how lightly she'd got off. She packed all her belongings, and with a spaced-out Tammi in tow, went straight to Cyrus's upmarket house in Outer Bridge and informed him of what she'd done, how she was ready to start a new life with him. To reiterate, Lori was a dreamer, wholly unrealistic, and she was convinced that Cyrus would drop everything and take her in. But it turned out Cyrus was going to do no such thing. He did not take it like a man. The moment he saw Lori and her brat-of-a-daughter, he freaked out and told her of all the women he was seeing on the side, weaselling his way out of any commitment. And in that moment, standing in the rain, the door slammed shut in her face after her lover had threatened to call the police if she didn't leave, Lori came to realize she had met someone a million times more self-centred and ruthless than her, bringing her crashing down to earth. After hurling a rock at the bastard's window she decided that Shaun wasn't all that bad, and she tried to win him back that same night.

It didn't work. Shaun didn't take her back and pledged never to clap eyes on her again.

She returned to her ailing mother, from whom she had been estranged since walking out of the family home at twenty-one years of age because her mother had worked as a mere domestic at the time. Less than a week after coming back, Lori would inherit the Council flat at the Seven Sisters in Netherton when her mother, crippled by emphysema, took an overdose of sleeping tablets. Many people believed that Lori had had a hand in her mother's apparent suicide, but it was never substantiated. Lori was now forced to start a new chapter in her life without carrying the perceived shame of her mother's former humble occupation. Rather than return to the trade of hairdressing because people should have a Right Not to Work, she lived off the earnings of a Pakistani taxi driver she'd seduced whose only condition was she get rid of her wayward daughter. So, without much ado, she placed her daughter into the care of the Local Authority, consciously choosing to ignore the catalogue of concerns Social Services disclosed around her daughter's risky behaviour in the succession of community placements they provided her. Lori just didn't want the hassle and lost touch with her only flesh-and-blood.

She thoroughly enjoyed sex with her much younger coolie, who was dirtier than Cyrus and even Big Cock Jock (her first love at 14) while promising to make enough money to whisk her away to the Sindh Province where she might live the rest of her days as a queen with as many house-servants as she desired. That still didn't stop her from playing the field, just as long as he didn't know. As Queen of the Leopard Print, she was living proof that a leopard never changes its spots.

The last Shaun heard from the rumour-mill was that his wife had been dumped by her Asian lad, rendering him heartbroken on accidentally catching her in bed with another man, and was now allegedly shacked-up with a proper Rasta, having sold her flat and invested the cash in helping him maintain his illegal but very profitable 'Skunk' farm while fermenting cannabis juice into alcohol as a sideline, real potent, crazy-making stuff. At least she could now finally live in luxury as the White Queen she had dreamed of and once been promised not so long ago. Who cared if it was with a crazy Jamaican who looked permanently stoned, grinned a constant, lickerish grin and took great pleasure in degrading her, like no-one before, every time he felt horny as fuck?

So Shaun was genuinely surprised to see his wife on the TV the next night. Devil Mask had kept his word about the special guest. He certainly did not disappoint.

But Shaun does not know what to make of his wife who is secured firmly to the notorious metal chair. He feels a sense of ambivalence. She is still his wife, the woman he once cherished and intended to spend the rest of his life with and who bore him a child, yet he hates her immeasurably for cheating on him with impunity and abandoning him for his boss. Maybe the police might bust her and her black man's ass for their illegal production of cannabis, but what is that Devil Mask said: The end justifies the means?

Let's roll with it, Shaun finally decides.

Presently, Lori is jerked awake by a vicious slap to the face. She looks around, notices her own nakedness, the straps tying down her wrists and the man looming above her, wearing the grotesque mask. Her fear rises to the surface. "What is this? What do you want with me?"

"Your sin shall find you out, Mrs Hitchens," Devil Mask informs her in that dark, electronic voice.

Lori doesn't know what to make of that spiel. "I don't get it. What do you want with me?" she repeats, afraid. "Where am I?"

"In Hell," Devil Mask says, and Shaun guesses that beneath that mask, the man is grinning, loving every minute of it.

"In Hell?" Lori does not understand.

"Your own personal hell."

"Why? What have I done?"

"What **haven't** *you done?"*

Despite her obvious fear, Lori frowns, puzzled, bemused.

"I think you know. You are being judged. This is your punishment for the things you have done, the people you have hurt. Do you want me to remind you?"

Lori shakes her head. She knows.

Devil Mask decides not to elaborate. Instead, he picks up a scalpel, and gets to work without further delay. If you can call it work. "The things I would like to do to a woman's body..."

"Wh-wh-what do you mean?"

"You are a dreamer. You shall now experience your worst nightmare. Your first sin is Vanity."

Shaun stares with mixed feelings as Devil Mask slashes her face multiple times, some of the random cuts superficial, others deeper, requiring stitches. Soon her once-attractive face is a snarl of bleeding gashes.

Lori screams. Devil Mask raises a mirror to her face to show her his handiwork. She screams again, and starts to struggle against the bonds fastening her to the arm-rests. Devil Mask continues, holding her head still and cuts upwards from each corner of her mouth through her cheeks. She sees the hideous Chelsea grin he has created, teeth exposed Reaper-like through the flayed cheeks, in the reflection in the mirror he brings up to her face. Lori screams more out of the disfigured horror she has become than from any genuine physical pain she might be experiencing. "Kill me, please kill me!"

"In time, my fugly thing..." Devil Mask responds ominously, and grabbing a handful of her hair, begins to carefully cut through the top of her forehead. Within seconds, while she shrieks in horrendous agony, he rips back the skin and underlying fascia from her skull until it is completely detached like a wig. Once again, he allows her to survey his effort. She sees those long golden locks she has tended to so lovingly lopped off so unmercifully, soon discarded to the floor. She goes into another volley of deafening shrieks, and Devil Mask delivers a vicious blow to her face to shut her up, knocking her out momentarily. "Don't you know I can't stand crying women?"

Holding each ample breast – those voluptuous breasts once admired and enjoyed by her husband and many other men, besides – Devil Mask proceeds to slice through their margins with surgical precision, removing them from her chest. The accompanying pain awakens her with a jolt, and she sees her breasts, her pride and joy, in his hands, nothing more than miserable, excised sacs of flesh. She resumes her screaming, and Devil Mask punches her again, instantly silencing her shrieks. She moans somewhere between life and death. Her face is hardly recognizable, a battleground of unsightly cuts and now beginning to visibly swell.

Devil Mask casually drops her mammaries in a floppy, deflated heap and grabs her by the ear, crouching down and whispering into it, wanting her to hear. "Your second and final sin if we don't count your dope-manufacturing business, fucking up the kids on the street, is Lust!"

Lori moans in vague acknowledgement.

Devil Mask presses a button on the side of the chair, and Shaun picks out a whirring sound and realizes the metal chair is one of those recliners, as it transforms itself and becomes close to horizontal. An expensive piece of hardware, *Shaun considers.*

His train of thought stops abruptly when Devil Mask spreads the woman's legs without receiving any noticeable resistance, revealing her neatly-trimmed Venus mound, and his fingers carefully open up the lips like a gynaecologist in the process of performing an examination, stretching them wide. In a shot, however, Devil Mask shoves a very non-medical, transparent plastic tube into her vagina, causing Lori to start with another unintelligible moan. It seems her lips now meet and encompass the much-wider diameter of the plastic pipe, holding it tightly in place. "What is happening to me?" she murmurs, sensing her private parts being manipulated, violated.

Devil Mask gives his opinion of her as a person. "You see you are a cunt *who'd fuck a nigger as much as a dirty Paki!" he barks down at her. "And don't say this is your contribution to Civil Rights and Equality!" He lifts a small animal cage from behind the metal chair, containing a couple of furry animals. Shaun has a horrible suspicion what is about to transpire, cannot come round to saying it. "Ah, now for my* pièce de résistance..." *Devil Mask shows her the pair of grey rats he is carrying, trapped in the cage. "Starved for a good three whole days," he informs her, gleefully. Lori has little time to protest at the sight of the vermin. Slashed and scalped and beaten up and her prized tits chopped off, she is already in a bad way. But Devil Mask wants Lori to hear and fully understand what he intends to do to her next, penetrate the tiredness and pain. No point using hints or pussyfooting around since it is so obvious. "As you are such an accommodating lady, I shall allow them to enjoy the moist pleasures of your cunt!"*

Instead of raping her – which it wouldn't surprise Shaun she might actually enjoy since during their break-up she confessed to having once survived a 'roasting' from half a professional football team, but, alas, never graduated to a WAG – Devil Mask lifts the door of the cage and introduces the severely-hungered rodents to the end of the pipe. Shaun cringes, nauseated, as the two rats, one after the other, going crazy upon catching the strong smell of tuna-fish pussy, scamper up the clear hollow tube and disappear into the vaginal canal, tails and all.

Devil Mask whips out the plastic tube that has been dilating her groin, as he might a tablecloth while leaving all the crockery untouched and standing, trapping the hungry rats inside. "Boy and girl," he chuckles, "Wellington and Millington. A fun time is to be had by all! A banquet fit for a king!"

Shaun imagines he can hear the rodents gnawing and nibbling, nibbling and gnawing... burrowing through the walls of her vagina, feeding on her sexual organs. He imagines them mating inside her pelvis among all the blood and delicate, ravaged tissue, having a field day in her body, a very ratty celebration. My God, he can see the rats as two lumps bulging up from beneath her lower abdomen, moving around independent of each other...

Will this sexual torture never end? Shaun demands to know desperately, as he tries to keep down his supper.

And all the while Lori is still conscious, probably feeling the slow death inflicted on her by the rats as they inhabit and explore her inner regions and eat her from within and her lifeblood gushes out of her private place. Or perhaps her shock and confusion renders her immune to any more suffering and from the full terrible knowledge of what is happening to her. Soon she has haemorrhaged so much blood, she becomes forever still.

Devil Mask suddenly loses interest in his deceased victim, covered in her blood, and is addressing the camera. The ghetto-blaster is playing that all-too-familiar rock track again. "Be grateful I have felled the Tree of Temptation," he announces, laughing loudly like some demented game-show host. "Hahaha... join us again tomorrow on It's Your Funeral when we meet a truly forgotten princess..." He cuts broadcast and static fills the room.

Shaun has seen his wife wasted tonight, and what disturbs him is not the horrific manner in which she has died but how a part of him has actually relished every minute of her humiliation and torture and execution. The question that lingers so contentiously in his mind: Should we fight evil with evil?

5
The Daughter

Another day, another dollar. As with the previous few nights, Shaun had factored in the time and cable station he would watch upon returning home into his figurative diary.

The foundry owner had gone missing. Shaun had been interviewed at work by the police but he had given very little away. The police seemed especially interested in Cyrus Fitch's unscrupulous employment practices, in particular his largely overseas workforce. Then, later that day, Shaun had been questioned again by a different set of police officers regarding the disappearance of his landlord, after apparently receiving a tip-off about the man's child pornography racket. The apartment block was now crawling with cops. Some of Shaun's fellow tenants had been arrested and taken down to the police station for further questioning. Shaun knew at some point the police would come knocking on his door because they could not find his wife. They might click that he had already been interviewed twice before... *I mean, coincidence?* Suspicions aroused, they might easily connect two and two.

He felt the net tighten around him until there might be no possible way out...

Devil Mask was somehow selecting victims whom Shaun knew and, disturbingly, the deranged murderer was getting closer and closer to home. Devil Mask had dispatched Lori, Shaun's wife, last night.

Shaun had already guessed who the next torture victim [*truly forgotten princess*] would be.

Shaun had not seen his daughter in a very long time, since she was an early teenager, in fact. But he kept tabs on her from behind the scenes. After all, she was his daughter.

By eight years of age, Tammi Hitchens was swearing like a real trooper. At age ten, she was excluded from primary school for punching a teacher and breaking his nose and glasses while alleging he had tried to strangle her in detention, later proven a lie. Just joining secondary school, she was openly truanting and smoking pot and drinking White Lightning and burglarizing the houses in the neighbourhood with her teenage friends who were several years older than her. When her mother could take no more of her antisocial behaviour, Tammi Hitchens was accommodated by Social Services. Each placement broke down very quickly because the care staff could not contain her frequent outbursts and conduct difficulties, physically lashing out at them or completely trashing her room, or manage her risks, primarily running away and meeting up with much older men, wholly at their mercy, a ring of unsavoury characters who groomed her for their own deviant ends. By fourteen years of age, the criminal ring put her to work, attending to a nightly succession of men in more ways than one, very popular with her depraved clientele, and Social Services seemed unable to get a handle on her, and she simply vanished off the map. Before turning sweet sixteen, she got hooked on 'Crack' cocaine, upping her game to fund her habit. By seventeen, she had contracted HIV. At eighteen, she was pregnant.

All she needed was guidance, Shaun supposed, racked by guilt. He had never been there for his daughter, focused only with putting food on the table, relying on his wife to set the boundaries and administer the discipline. Shaun had seen Tammi, a vulnerable child like any other, go off the rails, not unusual in many respects when all the kids in their housing estate grew up to be unmitigated fuckups. Then Lori, not content with neglecting their daughter during those good times, had decided when they separated to abandon her and forget about her entirely.

Every so often, intelligence, whether true or otherwise, reached Shaun's ears that his daughter had been spotted, working the streets, but he never made any attempt to find her and reunite with her, the opportunity to start over and play the loving father he should always have been, always looking out for his baby. He feared that one day he would receive news that his daughter's long-dead corpse had been discovered by chance in the gutter, the victim of a drug overdose or brutally murdered by her pimp or by one of the many perverts she serviced.

Shaun did not want to believe he was seeing his eighteen-year-old daughter, barely an adult, on *It's Your Funeral*. He could not believe what had become of her, lying there on the flat metal recliner, hands held in restraints, naked as the day she was born, looking so skanky and pale and diseased, all skin and bone, except for the prominent bulge she carried... *That bulge.*

Heavy with child.

His unborn grandchild.

Shaun looks on, appalled, as Devil Mask approaches the bound, recumbent girl in the Kill Room. Everyone is answerable to their conscience, Shaun tells himself. It is what defines our humanity.

But what if you *kill* your conscience, or your conscience lets you down in some other form, what then? *his other self counters.*

Then, you *cannot* call yourself 'human'. You are de-humanized, soul-less, empty. *And there certainly has been a de-humanizing process to what Shaun has witnessed in the last four days on this impossible channel — he has felt his own conscience fall back further and further with each atrocity committed. Okay, he has seen butchery at work in that bogus operating theatre, but, regardless, the people who probably deserved to suffer and die —* I damn the following people — *his violent drunk-of-a-father, the pederast landlord, his lecherous, exceptionally-immoral boss and his own narcissistic, oversexed wife — suffered and died.*

For your sin shall catch you out. And the end must justify the means.

Sometimes our conscience may betray us at the most critical moment. But what remains relevant to this day and to every human being on this planet is that the quiet conscience is the invention of the Devil, *according to one, Albert Schweitzer.*

And Shaun admits his own conscience has appeared very much asleep of late. No matter what kind of girl Tammi has turned out to be, what she has done with her life, she does not warrant Devil Mask's particular brand of attention. Shaun has to stop this.

Showtime!

Devil Mask delivers a hard, echoing slap to Tammi's cheek. "Wake up, hoe!"

Tammi's eyes flicker open and focus, wide-eyed, on the scary-masked figure looking down at her. "What's going on? Who are you?" *She sounds irritable, jittery, which may have nothing to do with fear but, rather, withdrawal from stimulants.*

"You are being tried and sentenced," *Devil Mask informs her in that electro-modulated voice.* "Your sins shall seek you out. Let any who dare dwell in my unhallowed pit be damned beyond exorcism."

"I don't know what I'm supposed to have done wrong."

"Really?" *asks Devil Mask, feigning surprise.* "Does 'Crack' cocaine ring any bells? How about prostitution and infecting your clients with a deadly virus?"

"Isn't a girl allowed to earn a living?" *Tammi demands to know, initial alarm replaced by anger at her current captivity.* "Don't those kerb-crawling fucks deserve it more? What they did to me, taking away my innocence so young? They are the ones who should stand trial, not me!"

Shaun is moved by the words his daughter has uttered, the undaunted manner she has uttered them. There is a simple honesty about them as well as a strangely balanced point of view. She has always been a feisty creature, even as a child, and despite all the shit she must have gone through, here is her feistiness on display, causing him, absent for so long, to swell up with paternal pride.

But Devil Mask is in wicked form. "True, you sucked a lot of cocks as a teenager and I'm sure you can give good head and, yes, those men deserve to die from the disease you spread, but you yourself made no concerted effort to change. You did not even listen to your social worker or seek sanctuary in a refuge for women or accept help from the police. Like mother, like daughter. Keeping it in the family: tart-of-a-mother, slag-of-a-daughter. You deserve everything that's coming to you." *He picks up a large, wooden mallet from the instrument tray, feels its weight in his hand.*

Tammi remains sullen and unafraid, prepared to face the music. "I don't really care whatever vigilante shit you inflict on me."

Devil Mask hesitates at the open challenge, suggesting that he might actually be doing something wrong. But he is having none of it and recovers his resolve. "It's an unjust world we live in, babe," *he remarks, full of mischief, bringing the mallet down hard on her right knee.* "What exactly do you think is the shelf-life of a whore?"

Tammi shrieks in outright agony as her right kneecap shatters with an ungainly crunch. Devil Mask does likewise to the other knee, delivering another unpleasant THWACK!, *the sound of willow on leather, causing the knee-joint to cave inwardly. Tammi screams hideously again.* "OH GOD! THAT FUCKING HURTS SO MUCH, YOU CRAZY SONOFABITCH!"

"I don't think you'll be going anywhere in a hurry!" *Devil Mask chortles cruelly.*

This is not on! *Shaun reiterates.* She's still only a child! I must stop this! *But he has no idea how. He despairs as her infinite distress reverberates through his absolute core. Shaun can only watch on helplessly as Devil Mask continues to sadistically torture his poor, estranged daughter.*

"I want to show you how it's done properly," *Devil Mask tells her when she quietens down as though he were a teacher speaking to a pupil. He uses the mallet to smash her arms in, pulverizing each elbow. More fevered, God-awful screams.*

Devil Mask examines the bones of her face, putting his gloved fingers in her mouth. "It's like looking into the face of your mother… except you're like a fucked-up version of her. You could have turned into a truly beautiful young lady if you'd made a real effort to change your life instead of looking like this dirty, strung-out, prematurely-aged hag." His other hand has lifted an ordinary kitchen kettle, and he empties its steaming-hot contents all over her face. The boiling water scalds, reddens and blisters her moribund-grey skin in a matter of seconds. Permanently scarred, perhaps, but somehow she is not permanently blinded, her eyes protected by her closed eyelids. She lets loose more shrieks, high-pitched and deafening and unsustainable. "So unless your client is a blind fuck, you will never be able to ply your trade anywhere again since nobody will ever find you vaguely attractive."

Shaun cannot stand much more of this horrendous punishment. He doesn't want to see his only daughter get tortured by this evil man or hear any more of her tortured screams without eventually going insane. But what can he do to save her? What can he do?

Despite her terrible ordeal, Tammi remains chock full of defiance. "I've experienced a lot worse, the things I've been asked to do. So do your damnedest, you fucking lunatic!"

"I doubt you have," Devil Mask warns darkly. "You will be eating those seemingly-gutsy words by the time I'm through with you."

"And besides I've got nothing to lose," adds Tammi jubilantly.

"You forgot about your baby…" So far no-one has mentioned the elephant in the room until Devil Mask raises the issue just now, gently patting her pregnant belly. "Thirty-two weeks by my estimation."

Shaun holds his breath in uncontainable apprehension and the utmost dread.

"None of your business," Tammi tells Devil Mask obstinately.

"We will see…" Devil Mask grabs the blowtorch, switches it on. The nozzle splutters to life.

Shaun tightens up. He cannot forget the beheading of his boss or the genital mutilation of his wife. What has Devil Mask in store for his pregnant daughter?

Tammi stares at the blue hissing flame, eyes suddenly round and bugged and fearful on the raw, weal-marked face. "What are you going to do with that?"

Devil Mask applies the flame of the blowtorch to her vaginal opening, cauterizing the lips, pink flesh sizzling, melting, smoking, blackening, sealing shut. "So that you can never receive any more cocks!"

Tammi is screaming beyond anything humanly possible. Shaun is shocked and angry, wanting to block out the unendurable sounds of his daughter's suffering. Fists clenched, he is close to throwing the television-set against the wall.

There is no respite. Devil Mask turns off the blowtorch and picks up a scalpel. "You see, I cannot allow this baby to come into this world," he explains when her screams have begun to abate. "Not with a mother like you, cunting yourself for money and due to die from AIDS soon. It would be an uphill struggle for the poor blighter, a matter of survival, the moment it is born. The end justifies the means."

And while Tammi is recovering from her burnt, messy, now very dead vagina, heaving massive sobs, and her father watches with growing horror, revulsion and dismay, Devil Mask makes a long incision down the midline of her swollen belly. No anaesthetic at hand, either. Tammi's lungs are producing an almost banshee-like clarion of noise. Blood spouts out from the edges of the wound like the parting of the Red Sea. Devil Mask explores deeper and hacks clumsily through the distended, muscular wall of the uterus with a grisly sound of meat ripped off bone. Thick, clear amniotic fluid pours out, mixing with the already evacuating blood. Devil Mask conducts the Caesarian section like some blundering backstreet abortionist, and the extensive blood-letting leaves the whole room resembling an abattoir.

"You beat me to it!" he suddenly exclaims, triumphant. He rummages through the wet, sticky contents of the womb and removes the baby, still attached to its umbilical cord, cradling it in his arms before placing it face-down on the chest of its mother. It is a boy, grey as though made of rubber, very small-for-dates, floppy. There is no first breath and it does not move. "You did the job for me! The thing's probably been dead for quite some time! I guess the smoking, malnutrition and hard drugs must have done the trick!"

Tammi is stroking out, a consequence of the blood loss and psychological trauma. Her eyes roll up in her head, and her wasted body twitches and shakes all over. Her tiny, dead progeny tumbles off her chest, ripping the placenta away with it, and splatters to the floor, gracelessly, shabbily, woefully. Then, Tammi utters a last, protracted breath and is still. Shaun is beside himself with shock and grief.

Once Devil Mask has finished with Tammi, he homes in on the camera with the same throwaway rock theme blasting in the background. "Thank you again *for joining us on* It's Your Funeral…"

"YOU FUCKER, I'M GOING TO TRACK YOU DOWN AND KILL YOU, YOU HEAR ME? I'LL FUCKING KILL YOU!" *Shaun is yelling at the television set, insane with rage, sobbing inconsolably, lamenting the senseless murder of his pregnant daughter.*

"Not if I find you first…" replies Devil Mask, as though he has heard him, looking straight at and speaking directly to his single audience. In the best Irish-inflected, Eamonn Andrews impression, albeit in electronically-synthesized tones, he announces, somewhat amused: "Shaun Hitchens, welcome to This Is Your Life…"

Blind with madness, Shaun hurls the TV against the wall.

6

666

Shaun didn't know how long he'd been out. He woke up and for a moment he thought he'd gone blind. But his eyes adjusted to the dark and he realized he was in the sitting room of his studio apartment. He checked his watch. He could not believe the date or the time. It was eleven-fifty-eight the next evening. A whole day had come and gone. How was that even vaguely possible? He must have blacked-out or something. But what could have caused such a shock to his system?

It soon all came flooding back.

Shaun had watched his daughter get slaughtered by that masked killer purportedly in the name of justice, and he felt that bitterness and anger flare up from the pit of his stomach. Devil Mask had removed various people from Shaun's life who had wronged him over the years, yet he didn't know why Devil Mask should be so interested in him. Their final executions had taken place on this pirate cable station that specialized in torture porn. Was the whole world watching? *Or was it all for his benefit only?*

And for the first time since the station had begun transmitting its daily string of live murder parading as extreme vigilante justice, Shaun genuinely shuddered at the latter [*for my eyes only*] thought, feeling irrevocably trapped between the Devil and the deep blue sea.

True, there had been a quiet contentment to their suffering and their deaths.

But his daughter had been an entirely different kettle of fish. She had been the vulnerable one, ironically innocent in so many ways, neglected and groomed and prostituted and mortally-infected and made pregnant before being savagely tortured to death.

Devil Mask had stepped over the line, gone rogue, out of control — call it what you will. Shaun pledged to hunt him down and make him pay for what he had done. Make the fucker suffer like he had made his victims suffer.

Suddenly, at the stroke of midnight, the television, lying on its side, screen cracked, cord ripped from the wall-socket, sprang to life, startling Shaun, turned on by impossible hands. Moving in a slow daze, he replaced the unplugged television set on the TV cabinet and sat. His eyes accommodated to the steady glow from the television screen.

No guessing which station it was tuned to.

Devil Mask stood in the same operating theatre, carrying a parody pitchfork, standing beside his next victim. "Do I have your attention?" he asked the camera in that mechanized, demonic voice.

When the victim raised his head and looked up at the camera, Shaun gasped to discover it was actually *him*.

Shaun doesn't understand what is going on. How can he be in two places at once?

He stares, disbelievingly, at the man, a duplicate of him, stripped naked and handcuffed to the arm-rests of the recliner, set at forty-five degrees.

"Do I have your attention?" Devil Mask reiterates in that dark, artificial voice.

The Shaun in the studio apartment nods his head.

"Good," Devil Mask responds, satisfied. "We must complete the cycle."

Now I'm having a conversation with the TV set, *thinks Apartment Shaun.* Television really is the Devil's invention.

Devil Mask is concentrating back on the other Shaun in the metal recliner. "Your sin shall find you out."

Recliner Shaun responds wearily, despairingly, hopelessly: "What sin, you crazy fuck? What the hell am I have supposed to have done?"

"You summoned me to attend to your business you didn't have the guts to carry out yourself. You are equally culpable in these crimes. Now you must pay

the Piper."

"That's shit! I didn't summon anyone! I didn't touch any of them! You did it all!"

"Is that what you think?" Devil Mask asks enigmatically, cackling. And Devil Mask pulls off his mask. Beneath that creepy, devilish disguise, all along, is the face of Shaun Hitchens. "Human beings are basically flawed, and it is my humble duty to exploit those flaws."

How the fuck can I possibly be in three places all at once? Apartment Shaun screams inside, mind spinning, staring, bug-eyed, at the incomprehensible picture in front of him. How can he possibly be seated in his flat watching an evil version of himself about to torture a second lookalike? This is insane!

This can only end badly for me, another part of him predicts.

"You murdered them all with your two bare hands," Devil Mask tries to remind him.

But Apartment Shaun has no recollection of doing any such thing. "I am not a killer."

"Oh, yes, you are!" exclaims Devil Mask, Punchinello-style. "Very metaphysical, don't you think? Your psyche fractured into three personalities, three distinct entities, which is why you see another two of you on screen. You are seeing you do to yourself what you did to your enemies. We three are the unholy trinity and the ultimate sixth sacrifice to the Dark Lord..."

And, suddenly, behind the identically-faced torturer and the captive on the screen, a shadow materializes on the back wall of the execution chamber. It is ten-feet-tall and winged and horned and hoofed and radiating an illusion of fire. The fiery, nightmare-shaped silhouette bellows in loud, maleficent laughter. "It will end badly ever after for you, mortal! The end must justify the means! You paid with your soul!"

Shaun understands his punishment, gears up for the inevitable, finally accepting that, yes, it can only end badly hereafter.

Epilogue

Eustace Wainwright has just arrived home. Another long and stressful — and yet rewarding — day at The Chertsford Echo, wrapping up his work well after midnight. The story he has been covering recently echoes around in his mind, like a ghost refusing to be laid to rest. Some fellow called Shaun Hitchens has been found dead in his bathtub in nearby Netherton, having mutilated various parts of his body and cut himself open from groin to sternum and removed a number of his own organs before he died. In other words, the wounds were self-inflicted – the guy actually tortured himself to death. Furthermore, the police have implicated him in the disappearances of five people relatively close to him. Charred remains, suspected to be those of the missing people, have been discovered in the basement furnace of the block of flats he inhabited. Macabre stuff, indeed.

Eustace needs to unwind, detach himself from the gruesome events of the day, before he can find solace in sleep. Nothing remotely interesting on TV, as usual, but... what is this?

It looks curiously like an operating theatre. Except there is a man, stripped naked and strapped to a metal chair. There is something strangely sinister about the whole set-up, judging by the haggard state of this fellow and the mean-looking implements on the surgical tray.

But that isn't the worst of it. Eustace recognizes the man in the chair. It is the notorious banker and hedge fund investor, Piers Heymans, who missold thousands of mortgages and PPIs, leaving his clients on the breadline while making himself disgustingly wealthy, whom Eustace, then a young news reporter straight off the blocks, had investigated and exposed. He remembers the trial and how Heymans escaped a conviction on a technicality. Getting off scot-free and deciding to take early retirement and make himself scarce, Heymans went off to the Cayman Islands to live out the rest of his life. It pissed off the public and, in particular, Eustace's sense of justice no end.

But what is he doing here on this television channel Eustace cannot locate in the TV guide?

A figure approaches from behind the metal chair, picks up a transparent, plastic tube of rolled-up banknotes and gazes directly at the single camera, a figure wearing a grotesque Satan mask and black surgical scrubs. He speaks with an electronically-modified voice directly to the viewer, breaking down the fourth wall: "Are you sitting comfortably? Good, then let's begin..."

September 2013-November 2013

Birdwatching

"A bird in the hand is worth what it will bring."

The Devil's Dictionary (1911)

Ambrose Bierce

When boarding school closed for the summer break, Oliver Hurrell half-expected to receive an eager, loving welcome from his parents. After all, he had turned thirteen during the course of the academic year, was now classified officially a teenager, and he hadn't seen his family since the Christmas/New Year period. The reality, though, came as a huge disappointment.

Oliver's father, Stewart, picked him up directly from his dorm room, and the drive back to Oaks Fold, was a dull, dour affair. After a brief, initial unenthusiastic exchange of greetings and forced pleasantries between father and son and queries on how the end-of-year exams had gone, they shared a dragging silence for the rest of the journey home, broken only by the low drone of BBC Radio 4. Oliver had grown accustomed to his father's cold, distant manner a long time ago, the aloofness and that general brooding lack of involvement when it came to family matters. As far back as he could remember, Oliver had never heard his father express any kind words of affection towards him, even when Oliver had been a toddler.

During the long drive home, Oliver wondered as to whom his father was currently fucking. Stewart Hurrell, a senior investment analyst for a large firm in the City, liked to fuck. His affairs were common knowledge, and Stewart did little to hide them from Oliver's mother, Stephanie. Stephanie, in contrast to her husband, was a ridiculous optimist, who in her infuriating short-sightedness believed that the Hurrell household conformed to some kind of Norman Rockwell family ideal and pretended not to notice her husband's constant infidelities. A successful interior designer, she cheated on Stewart with equal vigour, possessing a sexual appetite almost as voracious as her husband's. Yet, Oliver's parents never contemplated divorce and stayed together, eschewing countless invitations to swingers' parties, keeping the illusion of a blissful marriage alive, while in many respects leading completely separate lives.

And neither seemed able to spare any time for their only child, Oliver.

All Oliver had craved growing up was for his parents to spend some quality time with him, eventually becoming resigned to the fact he might never receive it. Only his mother came anywhere near in making a fuss over him, but even then it was a kind of superficial affection she offered, concealing a detachment almost as profound as the emotional rift between Oliver and his father. With little time for their growing son but in a perfunctory attempt to fulfil their responsibilities towards him, his parents had hired a succession of nannies to mind him, all of whom Stewart openly seduced and slept with. Once he'd hit his teens and now considered old enough, Oliver's parents had abandoned him at boarding school and let him get on with his life.

Heralding from a rich background provided little consolation for Oliver because, as any normal child sought, it was the simple love and attention of a mother and a father he had yearned and subsequently given up on. Thrust into the presence of parents who were for all practical purposes emotionally unavailable, as good as absent, obsessed as they seemed with material wealth and satisfying their own carnal desires, he had been brought up understanding next-to-nothing about friendships or human feelings, learning only to look out for Number One, bearing a huge, festering resentment towards his unreceptive parents.

And a slow-burning, bitter hatred…

EDGERTON GRANGE, the Hurrell family home in Oaks Fold, was a secluded, six-bedroom house from the Queen Anne period with small-paned windows, decorative gables, half-timbering and fancy red-brick work.

Stewart Hurrell parked the black BMW X5 SUV in the circular, flagstoned forecourt, bordered by a league of sycamores, horse chestnuts and common alders. Both father and son emerged from the vehicle, Oliver carrying his rather bulky suitcase. The burnished summer sky was alive with swallows, sparrows and starlings, the chaffinches, thrushes and treecreepers nestling in the branches contributing further to the diverse birdsong.

Stewart jiggled the house keys in the lock, and as Oliver stepped into the house for the first time in over six months, he was set upon by a greeting of "*SURPRISE!*" in the lobby from a small gathering of grown-ups, led by his mother.

Stephanie wrapped her arms around her son, drew him into an embrace and kissed him fiercely on the cheek. "Welcome home, Ollie!"

Oliver feigned enthusiasm, hugging his mother back without feeling.

The same spoken sentiment was plastered across the banner in the spacious drawing room: WELCOME HOME OLLIE! Party balloons of various colours, along with bunting, were fixed around the walls. The French doors were open, leading to the huge garden, letting in a warm summer breeze. The sun had started to set, producing a rich auburn glow just above the tree-line.

The handful of attendees, largely friends of the family, sipped their glasses of champagne and tucked into their nibbles.

"It's a time for celebration," Stephanie announced to the guests. "Our prodigal son has returned."

Oliver settled into the atmosphere of the occasion, the only kid at his own party, and went through the motions in order to satisfy his parents and their friends.

"How was your year?" Stephanie asked routinely.

To sum up, Oliver had kept himself to himself, awkward in the presence of his peers. With an interest in the Sciences and IT, one could have called him a 'loner', an 'outcast'… or a 'loser', if one were being particularly malicious. He had been bullied because the other kids at Stowebridge School had thought of him as '*strange*'. Without any friends or social life, this had given him plenty of time to study and kill his exams. Oliver did not volunteer this information. Instead he replied:

"Fine."

"You never wrote to us or rang us," his mother said, sounding concerned.

Neither did you, he thought of saying. "I was busy."

"Any girls catch your fancy?" inquired their perpetually-tipsy neighbour and possible poofter, George Grayson, grinning.

It's an all-boys' boarding school, moron! The teenage girls from the prestigious neighbouring Wimple Hill Ladies' College, who visit some of the boys at Stowebridge, are total dogs! Besides, Oliver had no interest in girls. Yes, he had experienced a sexual awakening this year, but his heart belonged to Jason Bateman. He had first discovered this gorgeous comic actor in the hilarious comedy series, *Arrested Development*, and had gone on to worship his subsequent movie appearances. Jason Bateman was the man of his [*wet*] dreams, his first-ever adolescent crush. Again, Oliver did not mention this particular nugget of information, even though he accepted no-one should go through life ashamed of who they are and whom they love. "I've got my eye on someone."

Soon, a large birthday cake made an entrance, and as Oliver blew out the thirteen candles to a round of applause, he secretly wished to emancipate himself from his parents. After the birthday cake was cut and consumed, Stephanie Hurrell brought in a covered birdcage. "This is from us."

Oliver lifted the blanket. He was expecting a talking mynah bird or a pair of cooing white doves. He was disappointed.

"What are they?"

"Lovebirds," Stephanie explained. "Hand-reared. Only three months old."

Perched in the cage were two birds, no more than six inches long, from the tops of their heads to the tips of their tails. Each had a peach-coloured face, neck and throat. Their wings and bodies were a pastel-green and their upper tail coverts and rumps a lovely cobalt-blue. Their flight feathers possessed a black trim. Their beaks were horn-coloured and hooked, their eyes white-ringed with dark irises and their legs and feet plain grey. From first appearances they looked practically identical with it being difficult to ascertain their genders, something experts called 'sexual non-dimorphism'. Except, if you looked closely enough you could notice subtle differences: one appeared slightly stockier in build than the other and its greenness was more olive-hued.

"The larger one is apparently the hen," Stephanie informed her son as though reading his mind.

The lovebirds sat side-by-side on the perch, unmoving, undauntedly observing the observers, as though revelling in the limelight.

Oliver tried to sound excited. "Thank you, Mom, Dad…"

"You're welcome, my darling."

Oliver held up the cage, peered in.

"Do you want to name the birds?" encouraged his mother. "Christen them, I mean?"

Her son was at a loss for ideas.

"How about Adam and Eve?" proposed Stephanie.

"Too Biblical," objected Stewart Hurrell, the first thing in relation to Oliver he'd uttered all evening.

"Mork and Mindy?" suggested Stephanie again.

"Who's ever going to remember that show?" derided her husband.

"Or Pom-pom and Tum-tum?" she said, trying to be cute.

"With names like that, they'll certainly lose the will to live. I know I would."

"Maybe we should ask the Birthday boy. What do you think, Ollie?"

Oliver experienced a brainwave. "Steffie and Stewie."

"Oh, how sweet and, oh, so clever!" piped Stephanie brightly. "He's naming them after his Mom and Dad!" She patted him on the head, pleased. "Steffie and Stewie it is, then!" She produced an absurdly-sweet smile. "Look after them. They will keep you company for many years to come. Care for them like you would your own Mom and Dad."

"I will, Mom, I'll look after them."

The remainder of the joint Welcome Home/ [much-belated] Birthday Party went without a hitch. Everyone moved into the garden, got drunk in the last rays of a fading sun, once Oliver had unwrapped the rest of the Birthday presents piled up beneath the grand piano. Embarrassing though this ritual proved to be, he fooled the assembled guests by pretending to like the gifts he'd received, just as he supposed his parents had pretended to be happy to see him again and had organized this dumb, celebratory event, for the purpose of assuaging their guilt.

He promised never to go through the spanking machine again.

*****

In the days that followed, his parents left him pretty much alone at home, except for the part-time Hispanic housekeeper, Mrs. Teresa Covas Alvarez, coming in for a few hours to do the cooking, dusting and cleaning. Maybe not entirely alone.

There were also the lovebirds.

Oliver felt his parents had dumped these lovebirds on him, just as they had dumped him in boarding school. The lovebirds were yet another infuriating example of his parents showering him with gifts instead of genuine affection.

He kept the lovebirds in his bedroom, caged. With all the time in the world and nothing better to do than study, Oliver decided to read up on these tiny parrots, considering he was stuck with them. His online research yielded a lot of useful information, nothing too complicated for a grade-A scholar and aspiring scientist.

It seemed they were 'lovebirds' literally by genus: *Agapornis* = *agapein* ('love') + *ornis* ('bird'). These particular birds in his possession were of the Peach-faced variety, the commonest species of lovebird, native to the dry, arid regions and scrublands of Angola, Botswana, the Namib Desert and the Orange River valley of South Africa, congregating close to lakes, wells and boreholes. Oliver would have preferred the sleeker Black-masked lovebirds or even the top-of-the-range Fischer's lovebirds, but he supposed his parents had bought him these Peach-faced lovies because they must have come cheap and were purportedly ideal for the first-time owner.

Nevertheless, Oliver took it upon himself to learn all he could about these exotic birds, which he discovered were not just lovebirds for taxonomic reasons but also lovebirds by their very nature. Even these three-month-olds, still only babies, seemed to have formed a deep, monogamous bond and would spend long periods sitting together like young lovers, billing and petting and preening each other, and making cute, little kissy-peeps.

Oliver read somewhere that it was a common myth that all lovebirds must be kept in pairs. They were easily capable of bonding with their owner as much as with their mate, so long as they got adequate social contact, attention and affection. Unless you were short on time to spend with your lovebird, then it was always best to get them a companion.

The cage Oliver's mother had provided was a good size (1m x 1m x 1m) and equipped with three wooden perches, a swing and a ladder and a variety of toys which hung down from the roof of the cage: toys with interlinked rubber hoops, toys with plastic keys, toys with bells and toys with mirrors. These kept the lovebirds entertained and busy.

Active, playful, curious and cheeky, Steffie and Stewie packed big, engaging personalities in their brilliant, pint-sized bodies, with the intelligence of a large macaw. Steffie, the darker and heavier and female of the lovebirds, turned out to be the more active and agile of the two. Whereas Stewie, the cock, just sat idly around, looking anxious, Steffie made the most of her new environment, monopolizing the toys. She would inquisitively try out each individual toy on offer, climb up and down the ladder, perform aerial acrobatics, twirl upside down from the roof of the cage, bob her head around, squeeze through the hoops, stare at her image in the mirrors, launch herself at the swing, swaying back and forth, and ring bells. Bells were a particular favourite of hers. Steffie would grasp the toy with her beak, shake it vigorously and ring the tiny bell, maybe to prove she could do it or perhaps to gain the approval of her new master. She would flit to the food container, grab a beakful of Trill seed mix and dried fruit, skim across to the water container, take a few sips of the vitamin-fortified water, and either fly back to the perch or go back to playing with the toys, a swift, fluid movement achieved within the space of a couple of seconds. Steffie was a proper busybody, an unstoppable dynamo... also, a beautiful little lady, full of grace, elegance and poise. Stewie could be lively if called upon, but he was still the more passive and reserved. He was still a handsome fellow, with a clown's charm to his character. It amused Oliver how he would stand on his tippy-toes, stretch his neck way up and waddle around jauntily, like a penguin.

Both birds loved millet and, of course, the honeyed bird-stick. They took time out daily to trim their beaks on the cuttlebone. Oliver installed a plastic bird-bath (with a waterwheel at one end), they could enter at will, to keep their colourful plumage in good condition.

Oliver was fascinated by their poo. He was astonished how small, inoffensive and chalky it was. He found out that the general white portion was their dried urine (since lovebirds do not pee), consisting of urate salts, and the dark thread within was the bird's actual (but modest) faeces. He let the pine shavings on the tray at the bottom of the cage collect the droppings, rendering the entire thing easy to clean.

The thing Oliver hadn't been told about was how vocal lovebirds were… and, boy, were they vocal! Their voice apparatus allowed a wide range of articulations. They chirped, twittered, clucked and chattered endlessly to each other nearly all day long. They squawked when raising the alarm and produced a loud, ear-piercing *ACK!* when looking for Oliver's attention. Give it another eight months and they'd be moulting to showcase more flamboyant colours, calling to copulate and engaging in nesting behaviour. Their little bodies jerked each time they chirped. They enjoyed the relaxing rainforest sounds Oliver played for them, chattering animatedly. But, most of all, they proved partial to Blur, in particular to the Britpop classic, *There's No Other Way*. They hopped and shuffled sideways on the perch, tweeting and cheeping tunefully, making fluttering little note-calls, each time Oliver repeated the song. If not spending hours swinging or hanging from their toys or staring curiously at their reflection or ringing the bell, they maintained their energetic chattering, confirming what he'd read about a lovebird's talkative nature.

Oliver had heard of the voluntary animal rescue services, where people in the street fostered and cared for an injured bird or animal, and once it was fully restored to health, they would return it back to the wild or even adopt it. He wondered if veterinary medicine might be a career option for him.

And, as the evening rolled in, the lovebirds would yawn, stretch their wings and legs and start beak-grinding, which although sounded like they were preparing for battle, apparently indicated that the lovebirds were happy, content and ready to sleep. Blinking, as opposed to the unrelenting stare, was another special signal, similar to that seen in cats, usually communicating: *I trust you, my surroundings are safe, etc.…*

The lovebirds would then snuggle up to one another while still sitting on the perch, turning their faces in towards each other, almost one-hundred-and-eighty degrees, and fall asleep. So drew to a close an average day in the life of a baby lovebird.

Playing and feeding and shitting and sleeping.

Two key pointers which Oliver didn't abide by, and a few others besides: firstly, lovebirds need at least ten hours' sleep or they wake up cranky, and, secondly, you're supposed to ignore them for one week to let them acclimatize to their new home. Then you introduce your hand into the cage in graded fashion until they eventually learn to perch on your finger. Once totally comfortable in your presence and consenting to being handled, they will happily perch on your shoulder (making you feel like a pirate!), climb down your shirt and explore your pockets.

But Oliver, who'd never kept a pet in his life, grew restless very quickly. He felt he'd been patient enough and he'd had enough of just watching them. Time, he felt, to interact with them, physically.

He went in when the birds were at their most vulnerable: at night, having fallen asleep. Oliver inserted his hand in the cage and started stroking them while they were sleeping. The birds instinctively woke up, spooked, sensing a threat. They flew around the cage in a flapping frenzy, squawking abruptly, panicking, unable to see in the dark. Eventually, worn out, knowing they could not escape their pursuer, they lined up in the upper corner of the cage and let Oliver stroke their silhouetted forms. After a couple of nights of doing this, the birds learned to gather in the corner sooner, realizing their tormentor would leave them alone once he'd stroked them. Oliver almost felt he was violating them every time they assumed the position.

Then it wasn't enough just to stroke them. He wanted to take them out of the cage.

This time, with the desk-lamp trained on the birdcage like a spotlight, he reached in again. For several minutes, he would chase the birds around the cage, with them shrieking in alarm, baby 'fluff' feathers floating down, until they were exhausted. He snatched them from the cage, one by one, palm enclosed around the wings, and spoke sweet nothings into their faces, kissing their beak and crown, forcing them to get used to his voice and grasp. The cock just looked startled and bemused, amusingly so, but the hen was considerably more feisty. She didn't like being handled one bit and had a tendency to bite his fingers. The literature claimed that lovebirds were the 'pitbulls of the parrot world' with a predisposition to nip those they loved and bite hard those they didn't trust or those who were not sensitive to their mood. Hens were apparently more aggressive and territorial than cocks. Introduce a canary or a budgie into their cage and Oliver had read that the lovebirds would peck at their feet until the visiting bird bled and died.

With tiny, stinging nicks on his fingers and worried he might catch polyomavirus, parrot fever or tetanus if he wasn't careful, Oliver deemed it necessary to condition the lovebirds, train them while they were still young, give them a crash course in acknowledging his dominance, like a rodeo artist taming a wild stallion. He predicted it would be a steep learning curve for them.

Once he held them in his hand and they attempted to bite him, he sprayed their face with water from the mist bottle. It made little difference to their behaviour and they continued to nip him. So he moved on to flicking their face sharply with his finger, the bird equivalent to being punched, stunning them for an instant. Still they would persist in biting him wilfully, particularly the hen. So Oliver, in his misguided way, went one step further and plucked off a tuft of blood feathers on her head. Steffie nearly fainted, eyes glazing over briefly, head falling back. When he released her and she regained her senses, she looked as though she had undergone some sort of brain surgery. The denuded squiggle on the back of her head looked vaguely like a craniotomy scar.

Yet, they squirmed and twisted in his hand and went for his fingers. Growing bored, irritated and frustrated, the novelty value of these birds gradually wearing off, he proceeded to discipline them by dunking their heads in the bird-bath, hoping they would associate this with 'naughty' behaviour. Any affection he felt for them disappeared with the dreaming spires. What had started out as punishment, with good intentions, soon turned into straight torture. Even though they were now less inclined to bite him, he was soon shoving their heads in the water just for the sake of it, exerting and relishing his superiority over them. As the old saying goes: *The Devil always finds work for idle hands.*

Oliver explored the hinterlands of his own cruel mind, thought of new inventive ways to hurt them. For him, it was also a way of avoiding getting attached to them. Teflon poisoning was not a viable option, as they would just drop dead — what would be the fun in that? He might prick their eyes with a drawing pin, blind them, but he didn't want to be lumbered with a disabled bird. He thought of literally snipping (not clipping) off their wings with a pair of scissors, but unfamiliar with avian anatomy, he did not want them to bleed to death. He greatly enjoyed squeezing their feet, with their sensitive nerve-endings and major blood vessels, hearing them shriek shrilly in pain, or partially-drowning them, watching them recover slowly from the shock, leaving them confused and wet and shivering on the perch.

Forensic psychologists will tell you that a strong predictor of psychopathy in adulthood is the presence of Hellman's 'ego triad', evidence of bedwetting, fire-setting and the torture of small animals from a young age. When employing Freudian psychoanalytic thinking, animal cruelty symbolized a marked regression to a primitive desire to demonstrate power over Nature.

One evening, just days after acquiring the birds, Oliver sat down to dinner with his family, an almost unique and inconceivable occurrence. Mrs. Alvarez had prepared mussels in Galician sauce with crusty bread for starters and paella as a main, a Spanish dish traditionally comprising rabbit, chicken, chorizo and king prawns in saffron rice, with Arbequina olive oil ice-cream for dessert, before heading out into the night.

"How are the lovely little darlings?" asked Stephanie, referring to the lovebirds.

"The birds are fine," Oliver lied.

"They make wonderful Valentine gifts, of course... for future reference," Stephanie said, tapping her nose knowingly.

Oliver didn't much care for Valentine's Day unless he could spend it with Jason Bateman and offer him the lovebirds as a gesture of his undying love. Starry-eyed, he wondered if Jason Bateman would accept. "Interesting..." he replied. Which, in his opinion, it wasn't.

Stephanie sipped from her glass of Rioja. "Isn't this nice? The three of us having dinner together."

Oliver hesitated to ask: "I was hoping I could spend the evening with you. Do something, anything..." *Watch TV, play Monopoly, pretend to be a Wii Guitar Hero.* "We haven't talked in a while."

"I'm afraid I can't, Ollie," imparted Stephanie, a dreamy, faraway look floating into her eyes, "I'm seeing a major client this evening... [*code for* I'm getting laid...] But I appreciate the suggestion. [*I bet you do*] I'm sure your Dad's also busy."

Stewart Hurrell did not speak, just sat and drank, probably also contemplating whom he would be fucking tonight. His disinterested, reticent expression suggested he regarded this little family get-together a terrible inconvenience.

"We could make time next week," Stephanie finished, ruffling Oliver's hair.

"Look forward to it," was all a deflated Oliver could safely muster without giving his parents a piece of his mind. They barely understood his needs, seemed completely oblivious, while putting their own needs before his, consistently shirking their responsibility. Oliver came second place to his mother's lovers and his father's mistresses, yet they deluded themselves into believing everything was hunky-dory. He thought he could achieve real, more meaningful family relations with the *Sims*.

Oliver spent the rest of dinner like a swan, serene on the surface, but paddling furiously beneath the water.

When dinner was eventually done and dusted, his parents went their separate ways.

Once more, they left their son alone, unsupervised, to his own devices.

Maddening for Oliver was how his parents (even his vacuous, interminably optimistic mother,) had conveyed the impression — tactlessly, and in not so many words — that they had considered dinner tonight and time with their son as something of a chore. Understandably, they left him feeling horribly neglected, both emotionally and socially, unvalued and seething.

Consumed by rage, Oliver took it out on the birds.

Where once the lovebirds had been cute and cuddly and round and proud, small bundles of energy, Oliver had reduced them to timid, cowering wrecks, their vitality sapped, in a matter of days. Their once-beautiful plumage had grown dull and matted — Steffie's sparkle had faded significantly and Stewie had lost his natural shine. They stopped chirping. They now huddled together nervously every time Oliver came within close proximity of the cage. Previous winsome eyes were now melancholic and imploring. Their unceasing playfulness had given way to wariness and suspicion until they now simply regarded him with outright fear. He had broken their spirits and doubted they would ever trust him again. It didn't bother him, though, because he knew they didn't have long left.

Having already severely traumatized them, Oliver resorted to actual violence. He put his hand in the cage and gave chase, the birds flapping around madly, emitting high-pitched shrieks of protestation and panic. He tired them out and grabbed them, one at a time, and hurled them against the inside of the cage, taking immense pleasure from the spray of feathers and the rattling sound the impact made. The lovebirds proved hardier than the delicate creatures he'd assumed. He only terminated each abuse when he was sure the stunned bird had endured enough punishment and might be at imminent risk of blacking-out. It took them longer to recover, and Oliver was certain they had sustained a few serious injuries, definitely some smashed bones.

Such had been her original vivacious and enterprising temperament, the hen tried her best to carry on as normal. Although she continued to play with the toys, she appeared slower in flight and movement, less nimble and daring, wobbly on her feet, unsteady and unsure of herself. Banging her head against the cage repeatedly, Oliver thought, may have affected her balance. He watched her crawl up the metal rungs of the cage, shake the toy with her beak and ring the bell for the last time. It was a sad, poignant moment, of a poor thing only seeking her guardian's approval. She must have still respected Oliver enough — her only natural expectation of him being to keep her safe and happy — and probably couldn't understand why he was treating her in the undignified way he was. Maybe she believed she had done something wrong and could rectify the relationship between them with this single, intelligent, hopeful gesture. Oliver heard the silvery tinkle of the bell and almost cried. But he pushed back the swelling tears that threatened to spill over, anger recurring with a formidable vengeance.

FU, mommy dearest!

His hand shot into the cage and eventually managed to catch the fleeing, squawking hen.

"Why must you always fight me?" he sighed wearily, feeling her struggle in his hand.

As she went to bite him, he grabbed his staple-gun and crunched a staple directly into her skull, across her counterfeit craniotomy scar. Dark blood oozed out of the minute entry wound and bubbled up from the nares above her beak. He threw the hen back into the cage, her body smacking against the wire mesh and dropping to the floor, face-up. He watched, awe-struck, as she suffered a massive seizure at the bottom of the cage. Her body and wings thrashed around mindlessly, skirling the pine shavings with soft, scratchy noises, head arched back, eyes staring out sightlessly. He thought of filming the whole dreadful scene and posting it on *YouTube*. The hen convulsed violently for perhaps ten minutes before her toes curled up and her fluttering body became limp, eyelids closing over, staying closed.

Oliver took a minute to reflect on what he'd done before continuing. He marvelled at the fragility of lower life.

His conscience tried asserting itself. *Hope it's all been worth it, Ollie.*

Indeed, it's been an absolute hoot! came Oliver's prompt, inward confession, the actual tone, however, implacable and pitiless. He was buzzing, and he wasn't entirely finished yet. There was still the small, nagging matter of the other bird, and Oliver was keen to maintain the momentum.

He realized the cock had witnessed the demise of his mate in trembling silence.

Oliver held up the dead lovebird by her wings, spread out like those of an angel, and taunted the cock by crushing her body against his for several seconds in a seeming forced act of obscene frottage, the remaining bird shrieking, shrinking away, terrified. The cock did not try to shrug off the dead body smothered over him, instead continued to generate a squall of piercing shrieks, obviously overcome by grief. He appeared to collapse for a moment before painfully picking himself up and leaning against the side of the cage for support. He gently tugged the feet of his deceased mate with his beak in a futile attempt to wake her.

"I know exactly what I'm going to do to you, you pathetic, little shit...!" Oliver sneered into his face, throwing the dead hen aside. No point in leaving the cock to pine over the loss of his partner.

By now, the cock was growing visibly drowsy, zoning out, eyes slowly blinking closed.

Oliver snatched him up in his palm and assessed his condition. It occurred to him that, in this particular case, the blinking had nothing to do with trust or affection, but was a prelude to the loss of consciousness, of approaching death, perhaps.

Oliver thumped the cock's face with a finger-flick.

Eyes opened only briefly.

Oliver flicked the face, again.

And again it produced an unsatisfactory response.

Oliver gave a vicious squeeze of his toes.

The cock jerked momentarily awake with a feeble squeak, then drifted off again. He wasn't just dying, but seemed to be relinquishing life of his own inconsolable free will. Perhaps, he hoped to join his erstwhile partner in the Great Bird Sanctuary in the Sky.

Oliver clutched him in his hand, making various attempts to revive him by stimulating the pain reflex, but the cock continued to slip away.

The eyelids closed halfway, and the cock — a symbolic representation of Oliver's father — slumped forward, became permanently still.

The cock had apparently died from shock.

The horrible deaths of the birds, their short life in this world, did not resonate with him on any humane level. He felt no sympathy, no compassion, no regrets. All he had experienced was a kind of morbid, addictive rush, just short of exhilaration, and a sense of liberation.

What did they ever do to me?

He didn't care. He had undone all the work the previous owner had put in hand-raising them from birth. These lovebirds should have lived for ten years, thrived with the right care and nurturing, made perfect companion parrots, but in Oliver's custody they had lasted only ten days. They had been infants, young and innocent, when they had died, dependent on him to protect them from harm, keep them safe and happy.

Maybe they would get their own back on him some day, if there was any truth to the concept of karma.

"*Madre de Dios!*" exclaimed a middle-aged woman's voice from behind him.

Mrs. Alvarez stood in the doorway, staring at him, shocked and aghast, a hand over her mouth. Oliver hadn't heard her approach.

"What is it?" he demanded, looking up from where he was otherwise engaged.

"*El Diablo…*" she murmured, pointing an accusing finger at him and crossing herself. "*Hijo del mal…* !" *Evil child!* She summarily turned and fled down the stairs, screaming of demons and curses, and uttering wild litanies in Spanish he failed to translate.

It didn't take long for his parents [*both of them, twice in two nights, I must be privileged!*] to come racing up the stairs to his bedroom.

"You caused Teresa quite a fright," Stephanie said, with a quick apprehensive survey of the bedroom, the shelves of books and ornaments, the clothes on the bed, the silent TV and music centre, the posters of Jason Bateman hanging from the wall. "We thought something had happened to you."

"I'm okay," replied Oliver. "There's no need to worry."

"What happened to the sweet, little tum-tum things?" his mother said, as if she couldn't guess. She, like her husband, could clearly see the bloody scalpel in Oliver's hand.

"They're dead," he stated, without mincing words. "I killed them."

His parents approached, crowded curiously around the desk, over which Oliver was hunched. They saw both lovebirds splayed out in a pool of dark blood, slit open from beak to pelvis, explicitly revealing their glistening internal organs, their feathered hides stretched out tautly and pinned to the wooden chopping board on which their bodies rested. The top of their skulls had been surgically removed, exposing the brains which resembled diminutive, pale-pink walnuts, the soft, buttery texture of scrambled eggs. Oliver had been in the process of slicing around their hooked beaks to examine their miniscule, vermiform tongues. Oliver had received a pleasant and unexpected surprise when he began to dissect the cock. He had mistakenly assumed the lovebird was dead. The moment he made the first incision into his chest, fresh blood had welled up in the wound and the bird had awoken, his eyes springing wide open, letting off an urgent, ear-piercing squawk, starting to struggle against the pins fixing him to the board. Therefore, on a purely educational note, a golden opportunity had presented itself with Oliver now gifted the luxury of being able to perform an actual vivisection, cutting open a live animal instead of a dead one, allowing him to observe the exact point in the procedure the tiny heart stopped beating and the panicking, shrieking creature expired.

Well, I hope this is the first of many, doc!

Stewart hesitated for a moment, unsure what to make of it all. Then, he cleared his throat and a nonsensical smirk touched his lips. "Animal cruelty is alive and well and being practised by a disenfranchised teenage boy!" he remarked, unsuitably amused. "How original!"

"I think someone's got anger issues," added Stephanie, making light of the gruesome necroscopies her son was conducting.

"Teenagers, hey, what can you do?"

"Boys will be boys!"

It wasn't the reaction Oliver had expected... or perhaps it was, so out of tune were his parents to his needs. The birds had evidently died on his watch, under suspicious circumstances. But did they notice? Look what they'd reduced him to! He had deliberately mistreated and murdered the birds his parents had given him. Didn't that mean anything? Here he was desecrating the dead bodies, and they dismissed the whole incident as typical teenage angst, tying it to growing up, becoming a young man. They'd never pegged him for a sociopath, and even now the thought didn't cross their ignorant minds. They should report him to the RSPCB, at the very least.

Why won't they hear me?

He felt a powerful rekindling of that festering grudge, that unimaginable hatred for his parents, and a callous, overwhelming disregard for life — *all* life.

"Ignore me at your peril," he delivered his doomful warning, and when his parents exchanged quizzical glances, without catching his meaning, Oliver knew they, like Icarus flying towards the Sun, had sealed their own fate.

The headline in the evening edition of the *Chertsford Echo*, twenty-four hours later:

BOY, AGED 13, SLAUGHTERS HIS PARENTS:
POLICE DISCOVER DEPRAVED HORRORS COMMITTED BY SON OF CITY MILLIONAIRE

A 13-year-old boy, who cannot be named for legal reasons, was arrested last night in the sleepy village of Oaks Fold for the double murder of his mother and father. Jehovah's Witnesses visiting the Hurrell property called the police after they heard screams emanating from within the £1.5million private residence. Police arrived at the scene to find both parents butchered in the manner of a torture porn-style execution.

During his interrogation in police custody, the public school-educated teenager, a singleton, confessed to the murders. He admitted he had knocked out his father, Mr. Stewart Hurrell, who is in a senior analyst position in the corporate hierarchy, tied him to a chair and made him watch, dismayed and sickened, as he proceeded to rape his own mother, Mrs. Stephanie Hurrell, before cutting both of them open, while they still breathed, and removing their internal organs. The police were contacted and arrived on the scene minutes later to find the kitchen splashed with gore and the boy apparently sitting, calm and smiling, on the floor, in a pool of his parents' blood, clutching a scalpel, with a distant look in his eyes. His mouth was stained with blood since he had allegedly been eating his father's brains. The teenager did not resist arrest.

The motive for the crimes is unclear, but the teenager, who is cooperating fully with the police investigation, claimed the murders were definitely premeditated and he was only simply trying to make his parents take notice of him. He is yet to express any remorse for the double act of parenticide, a crime that is regarded as the manifestation of a seriously disturbed young mind and extremely rare, with only a handful of cases occurring every year in the UK. The boy is due to be examined by a forensic psychiatrist when his relationship with his parents will be thoroughly scrutinized.

The locals were shocked by the killings and wondered how anything like this could ever happen in Middle England. The Spanish hired-help for the Hurrells, Mrs. Teresa Alvarez, 43, called the boy the "Anti-Christ", having observed him conducting a trial run on a pair of lovebirds he had received on his return from boarding school.

As crime scene investigators examine the evidence, the Crown Prosecution Service is aiming to prosecute the teenager for Rape and First-Degree Murder, whereas the Defence counsel is citing Manslaughter by way of Insanity. The teenager could face life in prison if convicted or life in a maximum-security psychiatric facility if deemed insane.

The trial is set at the Old Bailey for three weeks' time and is likely to cause a nationwide sensation and raise questions in Parliament over appropriate methods of parenting.

In an official statement made by DI Irwin Guilfoyle of the Chertsford Homicide Unit, he declared that he had never in all his twenty years of service investigated "a crime of such chilling intensity, of such heinous evil perpetrated by anyone so young..." adding, "I suppose that's what you get when you put money before family..."

November 2011

Margin of Deceit

"The important thing was to love rather than be loved."

Of Human Bondage (1915)

W. Somerset Maugham

1

They met at work and fell in love.

Nothing uncommon in that, one might argue, why should it be? Lots of people enter into an office romance, whatever race, creed or colour.

But what if they came from a profession where the divorce rate was greater than fifty percent and the break-up estimate as high as two-thirds? And what if both parties were in their mid-to-late thirties and had never actually fallen so head-over-heels in love before?

So, the odds increase, and one is suddenly dealing with something exceptional.

Doctors make notorious bedfellows, second only to the successful movie star and third to those who work in the sex industry. Even the Rock god is more faithful to his one, true muse, despite a constant gaggle of groupies, than the poor old doc. Maybe it's the pressure of the job—not an easy thing to save lives while working exhausting hours. Or could it be that doctors know more about the mechanics of sex and arousal and understand the neurochemical, physiological and psychological processes inherent to Love better than any great poet, living or dead, that they are eager to impart some of their scientific wisdom in the forum of the bedroom to another of the same professional background, like a pair of vampire lovers trying to impress each other with their erotic know-how?

Work hard and play hard, as the legend goes.

The perfect release from the pain and suffering of other people.

2

Dr. James Hennessey worked in Anaesthetics. He told his colleagues he spent his childhood and much of his teenage years in Londonderry, Northern Ireland, the son of a bank clerk and a seamstress, before graduating as a doctor from Liverpool University. He eventually found a suitable rotation at Fairview General in the Home Counties, where he decided to settle. The remarkable thing about James was that he was bereft of an Irish accent, the upshot of twelve months of elocution lessons, paid for by his parents who wanted their only child to choose a profession they considered worthwhile. Neither a drinker nor a smoker, James's only poison was nitrous oxide – or laughing gas – which he would sometimes sniff in a dark, quiet theatre suite at the end of a particularly gruelling shift.

Dr. Maeve Strauss had built up a reputable private practice back in South Africa. Except, she had grown restless with treating the Walking Worried and dreamed of seeing Western Europe. Maeve supposedly came from Old Money, from a long line of property developers. Independent-minded with a formidable business acumen of her own, she leased out properties she had bought with her personal funds along the beachfronts of Cape Town. She had a weakness for horse-riding, fine art and champagne. She arrived in England to explore its quaint history and experience working in its world-famous NHS, a change from the African veldt, although the exchange rate might have had a little something to do with it. Most of her earnings she converted to Rand and sent back home. She opted for Obs & Gyn, once her favourite specialty, at Fairview General.

As James pointed out, following the well-publicized tale of Hitcham Gale: "All roads lead to Fairview."

3

They didn't hit it off at once, at least not in James's opinion. He first saw

Maeve at the Medics' Disco, held at the Doctors' Mess bi-annually, normally prior to changeover. "Out with the old blood, in with the new!" as Mr. Mintz, the Chair for Surgery, described this time of the year. Ironic turn-of-phrase for someone who had been at his post for almost three decades and had no intention as yet of stepping down. Asked when he would retire, Mr. Mintz would always reply: "Never… since I am forever young!"

Maeve liked Mr. Mintz. Here was a person after her own heart. James didn't think much of Mr. Mintz. The man was eccentric, too laid-back and blind to the point of incompetent. And it was on the subject of Mr. Mintz when James and Maeve first got talking while the gentleman-in-question stood in the corner of the mess, busy chatting away to two pretty nurses.

Maeve was struck by how damned good-looking James was, yet he did not even try to cop off with the nearest lush. Maybe he was married or seeing someone. No, she thought instinctively, he wasn't wearing a ring, nor had he brought a special someone to the do, unlike some of his colleagues, who had brought along their wives or girlfriends (or both!). Anyone who wore black so comfortably must have some unresolved personal issues. She detected an unhappiness about him, a sense that he had lost someone close to him and was trying to compensate for his loss by burying himself in his work and his studies. She believed if one stripped away his insecurities and his deliberately regimental attitude, it would bring the untapped party-animal to the fore, ready for the taking.

Being of a serious ilk, James didn't go for Maeve in the beginning. He thought she was loud, absurdly friendly and far too liberal for his liking. And what was it with her dress sense? She was wearing a short green-and-orange striped dress with pink stockings and purple platform boots and looked like she had dropped straight out of *That '70s Show*. After introducing herself, Maeve hit the dance-floor where she insisted he join her. James refused point-blank and watched her boogie-on-down, drunk to the gills on punch. She kept dragging men from the sidelines to dance with her, but they soon excused themselves, finding her a proficient dancer but very intimidating. *Certainly not my type,* James decided, *I prefer my women to be reserved and demure. Give me a brunette any day and, please God, save me from the redhead. They're fiery and crazy!*

James thought nothing more of Maeve until he met her in theatre that same week. She was assisting her senior in the excision of a massive ovarian tumour. As the abdomen was opened and the teratoma, weighing eight kilograms and containing all hair and teeth, was removed, she asked him what he was doing after work.

Not much, he told her.

Would he like to join her for a coffee? she asked him.

Why not? he replied, thinking what harm would there be in drinking one cup of coffee with a colleague? It had been a taxing operation and he could use a pick-me-up.

At the hospital coffee-shop, later that afternoon, as Maeve told him about her life in South Africa and how homesick she felt, James realized he was dealing with a unique individual. Here sat a sweet, gentle, girlish creature, who had sacrificed a lot just to travel overseas and work in a strange land with strange people when she should be living the high life back home. In many respects, she was all alone here and he wouldn't be doing the decent thing if he didn't offer his hand in friendship and provide her with some emotional support.

Then, at the end of their little encounter, Maeve asked him something he wasn't expecting. Would she be wrong in asking him to be her Valentine?

James went silent, not knowing what to say.

"All innocent and above-board," she explained. "Like a pseudo-romantic date. You know, could be kind of fun."

And the more he thought about it, the more he warmed to the idea. Yes, it could be fun, celebrating Valentine's Day just for the hell of it! After all, it was better than doing what he had done every year: watching the same two Meg Ryan films back-to-back. It was a deal, he eventually decided, agreeing to her proposal, and banked on having a real swell time!

4

James lived by the notion that if you needed to do something, you did it properly or not at all. All or nothing, so to speak. Valentine's Day was no exception.

James did everything by the book. He bought Maeve a dozen red roses and a heart-shaped box of Belgian chocolates. Then, he took her to the most expensive French restaurant in the centre of Fairview, LA VIE EN ROSE.

There, under the soft candlelight, they enjoyed a three-course dinner of chilled oysters, duck confit with pan-fried aubergine-and-asparagus and crème brûlée for dessert, rounded off by Irish coffee. Together, during the course of their meal, they managed to polish off two whole bottles of Dom Perignon.

Too drunk to catch a movie at the local cinema, they returned back to the Doctors' Residence and talked. *Really talked.*

They discussed their likes and hates, hopes and dreams, old flames and past conquests, their most embarrassing sexual encounters and the most exciting moment of their lives, the qualities they looked for in their ideal partner, and so forth.

Maeve learned that James had gotten married during the second year of medical school and his wife, Amy, had died in childbirth a year later. He had never truly recovered from his loss and had avoided dating since her death, because no woman seemingly matched up to her high standards. In short, he had idealized Amy.

James felt Maeve's company made a refreshing change from his constant preoccupations and it was nice to let one's hair down once in a while. Maeve had been involved with someone for almost eighteen years, an architect going by the name of Austin Taylor. Their relationship had gone stale years ago, and Austin now took her for granted. They met every so often and continued as a couple, despite no longer sleeping together. They promised never to get married or have children. These days, Maeve saw Austin and herself more like business partners, both successful and wealthy and jointly owning numerous houses, flats and paintings. It came as no surprise that, back home, she would go to work in a Lamborghini Diablo and Austin likewise in a Porsche 911.

"You do realize," James said, taking off the bow-tie to his rented tuxedo, "that I am not by nature an unsociable person."

"I understand you a lot better now," replied Maeve, pitying him for the burden he had carried with him for so long. *So much sadness for one soul to bear.* "Circumstances turned you into someone you're not."

"I guess I'm too conservative for your tastes."

"No, you're not," she responded with a gentle smile. "I think you make a great friend."

"Music?" he asked brightly.

"No fear," Maeve said. "Back in a tick."

She disappeared to her own room and came back with a CD. She insisted he play Nightwish's *Wish I Had An Angel*. He obliged, putting the disc into his hi-fi. It was a heavy gothic track about yearning for an angel to satisfy one moment of lust at the expense of everything else. It surprised James that someone so refined could have a taste for symphonic metal. "The British don't care much for such noisy, dark rock. As I'm Irish, I'll let it pass."

"Afrikaans is not much different from the Dutch language," Maeve informed him, over the pounding music. "This kind of song is in the blood of the Dutchman as in the soul of the Scandinavian. The Scandinavian people are keen to reclaim their pagan heritage once stolen from them by a middle-eastern cult." She suddenly got up again and started dancing, interspersed with spells of head-banging.

"You're a very graceful dancer," observed James, also having to raise his voice. "Don't tell me... you took dance lessons."

"Ballet, actually," Maeve shouted back. "Till the age of fifteen."

"Why'd you stop? You could have gone professional."

"Then I wouldn't have become a doctor... or met you." Maeve lowered the volume to the speakers and came and sat on the bed next to James. "I want to be near you."

James nodded meekly, not hiding his wonderment at her close quarters. "Nice," he commented politely.

"What if you were to follow my lead," murmured Maeve softly, "follow my feeling?"

It dawned on James where this was heading. "You're drunk. You don't know what you're saying."

"I know how I feel."

"What about Austin?"

"Austin doesn't own me. I'm a big girl. I can make my own decisions."

"I couldn't do this to my wife."

Maeve had an answer for everything. "Your wife isn't here. She would want you to move on, be happy."

"But I'm Dracula, I'm Hamlet, I'm Heathcliff, I'm no good for you."

"Let me be the judge of that."

Still James stalled, even though he knew full well he was losing the battle. "Let's not do something that we might regret in the morning. It's way past midnight and I think we should get some rest."

"Please…" she whispered, hushing his lips with her index finger and pulling him towards her. She looked so ravishing in that silky black number that he did not resist or try to move away. Besides, there was love in those enchanting green eyes of hers. Their lips touched, pressed harder. Their tongues joined the chase, seeking the warmth of the other's mouth. Although Maeve had initiated it, it felt right and a part of James cried out for more.

Hands groped sensitive flesh, to tingle, tantalize, tease. They slipped out of their clothes and soon were crawling over each other's body with an overwhelming passion.

Sat up, back against the wall, James entered Maeve effortlessly, feeling the full length of her smooth, moist hollow with his firm, throbbing member. Legs astride, Maeve rode him vigorously as she might ride a steed and they peaked at exactly the same moment.

Twice more they made love that night, and by daybreak they were desperately in love.

"So what are you doing for the rest of your life?" James asked, holding her in his arms.

"Loving you," she whispered back.

5

Maeve had found her angel and James had found release.

Their sexual awakening had come as a revelation to both of them as neither thought they would be capable of love again. There is something to be said about the excitement of fresh love because it is like drinking deep from the fountain of eternal youth — one feels like a child of Dionysus, whose only purpose in life is to satisfy every primitive desire. James and Maeve were hooked on one another like heroin, for they would work during the day, experiencing butterflies in anticipation of when they would meet again, and retire early to bed each evening, going at it like a couple of college kids under the bleachers. They experimented with as many positions as possible and none disappointed. They tried different locations—including Mr. Mintz's office after hours while still clad in their surgical scrubs—and never once got caught.

Soon they were announcing themselves as a couple to their colleagues, and speculation spread amongst the staff as to who seduced whom. James was already thought of as moody whereas Maeve was considered too much of a rich bitch. Regardless of the grapevine, the change in their manner at work could not be denied—both were content with their middle-grade lots and there was a noticeable sparkle in their eyes.

As a couple, they spent a weekend away in Paris, where they climbed the bell-tower of Notre Dame Cathedral—a childhood dream of James—and explored the many exquisite treasures of the Louvre— always a popular choice with the ladies, and particularly so for Maeve. They went clubbing at night, picking out the goth scene of downtown Paris, where Maeve taught James how to head-bang to dark metal. Then, as the city wound down, they snuck back to their hotel room and made sweet love until they were completely exhausted.

They had just made love and, as usual, it had been an intense, intoxicating experience. However, thoughts were now turning to their flight back to the cold, damp climes of Old Blighty later that morning. Catching his breath, James poured Maeve and himself each another flute of champagne.

"You know scientists define three stages of Romantic Love," James said thoughtfully.

"Really?" said Maeve, lying beside him on the bed, her body like her lover's glistening with a thin sheen of sweat. "Tell me more."

"It begins with Lust. Overrides everything."

"Sounds like where we're at," Maeve remarked, laughing.

"Can last up to eighteen months."

"Hope it does."

"Attraction is the second stage," James went on.

"Shouldn't that count as the first stage?" asked Maeve, puzzled.

"Lust is governed by primal instincts as opposed to real attraction which is something much deeper and more meaningful," explained James. "It's where you see your partner for who they really are. You are no longer concerned with having sex all the time, but keeping your partner happy and healthy. Your functioning returns to its original factory setting whilst still maintaining that emotional connection."

Maeve took a sip of her champagne. "For how long does this stage last?"

"Rarely longer than three years," James informed her.

"That's not much time," mused Maeve. "And the final stage—?"

"—Is Attachment. It's a case of putting up with your partner and cementing your relationship by having children and leaving a legacy for your future generations. Some people never reach this stage."

"Children?" Maeve exclaimed, feigning horror. "God forbid!"

"I know," James humoured, "we are not going to go there."

"Or wedlock, for that matter," Maeve reminded him. "Let's just enjoy ourselves whilst we can. Who knows where it'll take us? We might still be together when we're old and grey."

"I never thought of Love as the Great Addiction," James said with a faraway expression, "only as the Great Affliction... Was I ever so naive?"

"I think we've already laid the foundations of our relationship, wouldn't you say?" piped Maeve, cute as a button.

"I think so, too," agreed James, and kissed her.

6

Zurich was the crowning piece of their relationship.

Maeve insisted on holidaying in Switzerland as the place appealed to her sharp business sense. Why not instead, as James pointed out, go to Geneva where the rich lived as opposed to Zurich where the rich worked? Because, as Maeve told him, she wanted to walk the land of the corporate lawyer and investment banker.

Maeve was completely overwhelmed by the staggering abundance of multi-national banks in the financial district. She had never imagined there could be so many, and felt like opening a Swiss account of her own.

They came across boulevards populated almost exclusively by jewellery stores. James bought Maeve a pair of diamond earrings which cost in excess of one-and-a-half thousand Euros. Returning the compliment, Maeve gave James a black designer velvet jacket, purchased at a comparable price.

In the older sector of the city, the streets were cobbled and winding, with cafés and delicatessens and cheese-shops and confectioners aplenty and overflowing with tourists. Maeve and James ate a lot of chocolate and drank a lot of wine. They visited St. Peter, boasting the largest clock-face in all of Europe, and the Kunsthaus Museum, which housed originals of Maeve's favourite painter, Marc Chagall. They went boating on the crystal waters of Lake Zurich and could not escape the Romanche charm of this world.

They stayed briefly at a ski-resort up in the mountains and took skiing lessons, but soon gave up as they just about survived breaking their necks on the icy slopes. Still, the scenery was breathtaking and the evenings pleasant enough. They threw themselves into the regular beer-fest, drinking and dancing and yodelling until their bodies ached and their throats were sore. Then, as the snow fell in powdery clumps and the night grew long, they retreated to their chalet in the woods and physically declared their love for one another. Handcuffing Maeve to the bedposts while teasing her to the point of ecstasy proved particularly satisfying.

One such evening, they were lying on the fur-skin rug next to the roaring fire when James said unexpectedly: "I think you should tell Austin about us."

Maeve immediately put aside her champagne glass and didn't answer for a moment. "Shouldn't we wait?" she finally responded. "We've only been going out for four months."

"I want us to be exclusive," James continued, brooding. "I hate the idea of sharing you with another man."

"We are exclusive. I haven't slept with Austin for years. I see him as nothing more than a friend and a business partner."

"Be as it may, Austin has a right to know."

"I will tell him when the time is right."

"And when will that be exactly?" James demanded. "I mean, look at yourself, woman, you're the one having an affair!"

Maeve sounded hurt. "Please don't spoil this…"

"I can't go on like this," James said, impassioned. "I want you all to myself."

Maeve closed her eyes, reflecting. "Do you really love me, James? Sometimes, I think you only like the idea of us."

James countered. "I could equally say you only like the emotions associated with us."

"Is that why you're afraid of telling your parents?" Maeve asked quietly.

"That's a different matter entirely," James argued heatedly. "I haven't told them because they wouldn't understand. They're devout Catholics and you're Calvinist. My family is lower middle class and you come from good stock, not to mention I'm four years your junior. Your family won't exactly be over the moon, either."

"I thought love conquered everything, transcended age, class, religion."

James paused, realizing he had no reason to feel indignant. He glanced at the crackling flames in the hearth. Then, he looked deep into Maeve's eyes. "I love you, Maeve, I really do... if there ever was a way for you to believe me—"

"I believe you," replied Maeve, tenderness in her voice. "I've decided you're right. I'll tell Austin when we get back."

They hugged and kissed.

"I'm glad we had this talk," James said, nodding.

"Me too."

"I love you so much that if I ever died, I'd come back as a ghost and haunt you."

Maeve's eyes widened in mock horror. "I hope for my sake you're only joking."

"Indeed I am, Dr. Strauss," James said in a half-sensuous, half-professional tone. "Now where were we...?"

"Right about here..." Maeve directed her colleague and lover to her secret meadow, and his mouth carried on from where it had left off. "Ooh, Dr. Hennessey," she moaned, arching her back as he pleasured her, "you're such a cunning linguist... !"

The souvenir they took with them from Switzerland as the perfect reminder of their mad time together was a Brienz chalet cuckoo-clock.

But little did they suspect that their happiness was about to be shattered.

7

Fate shot three spiteful arrows in quick succession in the general direction of their relationship.

The first of these to strike home was a series of long-distance phone-calls.

When Maeve told Austin that she had found someone else, he was furious. He threatened to fly over. "I suppose this is my reward for sending you abroad!" he shouted at her down the line. "Who is the bastard?"

"A colleague at work," she answered calmly.

"'Figures… Must be someone quite desperate. You're not exactly a spring chicken."

It was a cruel and hurtful remark, but Maeve did not let it faze her. "I love him and I still love you, Austin, but not in the same way."

The thought that Maeve still felt some modicum of love for him placated Austin a little. "So where does this leave us?"

"I don't want to lose you as a friend," she admitted truthfully. "We have a long history together. And we're business partners. Our shared ownership of our properties and possessions could cause a serious legal wrangle."

Austin was now calm enough to see reason. "I never saw this coming. I was so absorbed in my work, I neglected our relationship. I could try and win you back, but I think your mind is made up. Instead, I'll think about what you've suggested about us remaining as friends, and if I decide to accept your betrayal, you owe me, Maeve, you owe me *big time!*"

Not soon after, Maeve received an angry phone-call from her parents, who were concerned for her well-being and insisted she come home, pointing out that her private consulting room was going to waste and suspected she had started drinking and got herself involved with a complete stranger. Even her eldest brother got in on the act, stating that her playtime was over and her real life with her real family and friends waited patiently for her back in Cape Town.

Never before had her family been so demanding—obviously Austin had spoken to them—and Maeve drank and cried on James's shoulder. She felt homesick, missed her family immensely, and didn't know who else to turn to.

James explained that she was juggling a lot of balls at once, including her family, her ex-partner, her current, very hectic job and the emotional dependence she had developed on him. Her parents were right to be upset since they wanted their youngest daughter to be with them in their golden years. Austin, presently, had the upper hand, and if he wasn't cool about it, could cause a lot of trouble – she really *did* owe him. But she should assess her life and figure out what she wanted and maybe even visit her family to tide things over. If she wanted some breathing space from their relationship to consolidate her thoughts, he would happily step back.

The second missile to rock the boat occurred several days later.

James was knocking on for Maeve after work when he discovered her door slightly ajar. "Hello…" he said and entered.

Maeve sat hunched on the bed, head in her hands.

James was immediately concerned and knelt down beside her. "Maeve, what's wrong? What's happened?"

She looked up. She had been crying. "I'm pregnant…"

A look of momentary disbelief crossed his brow, replaced by a wide boyish grin. "Congratulations…!"

"I don't think so," said Maeve, turning away.

James sensed her shame and inner turmoil and tried to speak to her at her wavelength. "How did this happen?"

"We had sex."

"But you have an intra-uterine device in place. Your womb ought to be a hostile environment for conception."

"There is a one-percent failure rate."

James kicked himself. "I knew I should have used a condom."

"No, don't blame yourself," Maeve said generously. "I wanted to feel you inside me."

"You sure you're pregnant?"

"I didn't want to believe it at first. But my period was two weeks overdue when I've always been regular as clockwork. And I checked and re-checked the pregnancy test."

James gathered her up in his arms. "Don't worry, we'll get through this." He asked a pertinent question. "Are you going to keep the baby?"

"What would you do?" she inquired tentatively.

"This is your show, sweetheart. I will respect your decision either way."

"In that case, I want an abortion," Maeve said adamantly. "I can't be having children at my age."

"Whatever you choose, that's okay with me," James told her. "Besides, if we're ready to have children in the future, we can always adopt an African baby like Madonna or Angelina Jolie."

She laughed, somewhat reassured. "Thank you for being so understanding."

"Hey, that's what I'm here for," James added, lightening the mood further. "You're the little Afrikaans princess to my lowly warrior and I would do anything to keep my Royal Highness in the luxury she is accustomed to!"

Maeve did as she promised. She underwent a termination of pregnancy at a private clinic. James was there for her throughout her stay. Except the pregnancy itself and the procedure which followed had already tainted their relationship. It put a strain on their feelings for each other and their lovemaking lessened considerably, as though they were afraid they might be doing something irresponsible and taboo.

The straw that broke the camel's back was a piece of correspondence from the Home Office. Apparently, renewal of Maeve's Work Permit had been rejected by the reviled pen-pushers down at Whitehall.

"On what grounds?" James asked incredulously.

"They didn't give a reason on paper, but the authorities told me it had something to do with employing doctors primarily from the EU, blah, blah, blah... !"

"That's ridiculous!" exclaimed James, getting worked up. "You're as good a doctor as any foreigner, possibly even better!"

"It makes no difference now!" Maeve uttered in despair. "It's final! I have to leave the country at the end of my six-month block!"

"Not necessarily." James dispensed with his anger and had a huge grin on his face. "There are ways of keeping you here. I could marry you if you were willing."

Maeve looked at him strangely.

"Okay, not the greatest solution, but, hey, worth a try!" He went on, enthusiastically: "I've been doing some digging and it's possible for you to work officially as a GP, here in the UK, being a trained family doctor yourself and there existing such a shortage of GPs anyway. All you have to do is pass a couple of exams, which is nothing you haven't done before."

"I don't know if I can," Maeve said. "This Work Permit thing seems non-negotiable."

James was running out of contingency plans. "Then, I could emigrate to South Africa and work in one of your private hospitals." Except, he knew outright he couldn't make the move. Unless one had full College membership (which James didn't), one could only work in a government hospital. Horror stories (all true) had been told of stepping through the entrance of these godforsaken places and finding the walls stained with blood, and one knew straight away that the blood would be HIV-positive. South Africa, despite its pockets of prosperity and the end of Apartheid, was still a Third World country. No, the idea didn't much appeal to James. "So this is it, then?"

"I've thought about what you said and I think it best that I return home. It's where I belong."

"But you belong with me," James said, panicking. "We're good together."

Maeve kissed him on the cheek. "I love you so much and I'm going to miss you."

"You don't have to do this…"

"You *know* I do."

She was right, of course, James was loth to admit. He could see no clear alternative. There was nothing left for her here, except him. And he wasn't worth the heartache she would suffer if she stuck by him and abandoned her family. She needed them and they needed her. He would have to be the bigger person and let her go, do the honourable thing, like Rick Blaine telling Ilsa she needed to be with her husband, Victor Laszlo. They would always have Zurich. Maybe Maeve's relationship with him might even strengthen her friendship with Austin—they could start afresh without fear of consequences. "Will I ever see you again?"

Maeve spoke with great affection. "I look after all my close friends… and you, James, have a special place in my heart. I will ring you often and visit you once in a while, and I will want to make love to you when I see you."

"What if I find someone?"

"Then the decision to see me would be entirely yours."

James sounded despondent. "You do realize I'm not going to meet anyone like you ever again."

"Don't sell yourself short. You are one of the smartest, sexiest, most romantic men I know, and you don't even know it. That's why I fell in love with you."

"And there was me getting all mystified by your sudden interest in me," remarked James, forcing a smile. "You're not bad yourself."

"We should make the most of whatever time we have left."

"I concur, Dr. Strauss," James replied, brightening up a tad. "Shall we dance?"

In his room at the Doctors' Residence, they danced to Nightwish, for old times' sake.

8

Maeve left at the beginning of August. They had spent a few quality weeks together, including visiting a health spa and taking a trip up to the Scottish Highlands.

After one last night of passion, she boarded the plane and went home.

At Heathrow Airport, Maeve told James how much she loved him and how much she would always love him.

James reciprocated the sentiment, adding: "Even though what goes up must always come down, I want my little daisy girl to leave on a high."

"I imagine you'll meet someone and forget all about me," Maeve mentioned out of passing.

"Never!" intimated James. "You've unlocked my potential, brought joy to my life. I will always be grateful. And, as a lifelong friend, I will make myself available to you 24/7."

"If only we met in another place at another time, things might have been different. I feel I've known you all my life. Knowing me, I'll probably be so alone years from now that I'll wish I'd stayed with you. But I'll cross that bridge when I get to it."

"I wouldn't mind if you hooked up with Austin again," he said unexpectedly, "or another fella from one of your High Society bashes. It would be such a waste if you spent the rest of your days without a gentleman to care for you."

"Don't put ideas in my head!" Maeve joked. "Just because I'm high maintenance doesn't mean I'm going to hop right into someone else's bed so I can be tended on hand and foot!" On a more serious, personal note, she asked: "Will you be okay?"

"I'll be fine," James reassured her. "You mustn't worry about me."

Maeve took a deep breath. "I guess this is it..."

"*Ma chérie*, it was not to be," James said sadly. "I was never one for goodbyes."

"Be strong for your little Afrikaans princess, my brave warrior," declared Maeve. "Remember, this is not goodbye. It's a case of 'I'll see you when I see you'."

"*And parting is such sweet sorrow...*"

"*Sien jou wanneer ek jou sien.*"

Then, Maeve was gone, embarking on her nine-hour flight home. From the observation deck, James watched her plane take off and wept.

When Maeve arrived back in Cape Town, she tried to ring James, but he did not pick up the phone. She was overjoyed to see her family and friends and, in the weeks that followed, re-integrated into her old life with relative ease. She re-claimed her medical practice and worked twelve hours a day. During the weekends, she lazed on the beach or went on Safari. Her relationship with Austin never recovered, but at least he was agreeable for them to remain just good friends. Everything was back as it should be, except one trifling detail.

Despite embracing the normality in her life, her love for James did not fade. In fact, it grew stronger with each passing day, proving the old adage about absence making the heart grow fonder. She yearned to speak to him again, to see him... yet he would not answer her calls. She texted him, but he would not respond. Perhaps, he needed some personal space or no longer wanted to continue their friendship and decided to lose touch with her for good.

A month or two later, she tried his number again, and discovered it had been disconnected. Quite concerned, Maeve rang Fairview General and spoke with Mr. Mintz, who informed her that James had got drunk one evening and shot himself during a game of Russian roulette.

However, rumour had it he had committed suicide.

Maeve was devastated, inconsolable. There had been no indication he had been vulnerable enough to do something so drastic. Her initial shock turned quickly to self-condemnation. She blamed herself for his death. Why would such a handsome, dynamic man in the prime of his life kill himself if it wasn't because of her selfishness? The time they had spent together had meant so much to her that she should never have left him.

What are you doing for the rest of your life? he had once asked her. *Loving you,* she had replied. He had been the best friend she had ever had, something of a soulmate... and a lover of astounding versatility. He had meant the world to her, and she had deserted him. Now he was gone. Forever.

She had even missed his funeral.

9

A letter arrived with the morning mail the day she was due to travel to England to visit his grave. It was addressed to her and she knew immediately from the handwriting that it was from James. His solicitor had evidently sent it. The words *'To be opened in the event of my death'* brought the full impetus of her grief home.

She opened the envelope and unfolded the letter.

It read:

My Dearest Maeve,

If you're reading this, then it means I am dead.

Take this letter as you will: as a suicide note or as the guilty confession of a man who fell in love when he never intended to. I feel I need to set the record straight and I beg of you not to think less of me.

You see, I am not who you think I am. I am nothing more than a FRAUD. I am not Irish, I'm not even British. I am an unknown actor from Romania. I was born Gheorghe Babescu. I came to the UK ten years ago to find my fame and fortune but instead worked briefly as a rent-boy before I realized I had a talent as a con-artist. I took elocution lessons and waited for the right moment to swoop. Then, as luck would have it, along it came. I stole the identity of one Dr. James Hennessey, who suddenly dropped dead of a cerebral haemorrhage, right in front of me in a bar, one dark winter's night. I leapt at the opportunity to masquerade as a doctor: I passed off Dr. Hennessey's credentials as my own, assumed his name and took over his life. It was difficult at first, but I read textbook after textbook and learned the fundaments of medicine. I am an actor, after all, a memorizer of lines. Moving from Liverpool to Fairview also made things easier. I forged everything: the passport, the driving licence, even the GMC certificate. I could now live out the rest of my life – the life stolen off a deceased doctor – in peace with nobody none the wiser.

Then, YOU happened.

I was not attracted to you in the beginning. I thought of you as a business venture, someone so financially-orientated and gullible she could be easily swindled, relieved of her crown jewels. It was not you who pursued me, but I who seduced you. I said everything you wanted to hear, preyed on your sympathy. I played the grieving widower with gusto. As you now know, I never had a wife who died in childbirth, but it sounded pretty damned impressive at the time.

Then, the predator fell in love with its prey.

You were so different from the other doctors. Without a doubt, you were the single-most sweetest, kindest, happiest person I had the good fortune to meet, and I felt terrible cheating you. You were the life and soul of the party. I fell for you in a big way. Someone said that love waits for no man – and I was THAT man. There were times when I wanted to come clean, but I felt it might still be too early, and possessing a moral compass, you might report me to the authorities. I hated lying to you when you were so honest with me. I enjoyed every moment we spent together and I really valued our friendship. I thought our love would last a lifetime.

But fate intervened and you had to fly back home.

I was lost without you, as fragile as crystal, knowing that I would only see you once in a blue moon. I drank because I could no longer live with my feelings or my conscience. You cannot imagine what it must feel like losing someone like you when you're someone like me. Even though our love was never set in stone, your face was etched permanently in my mind. I couldn't allow our friendship to become tame, stagnant, pedestrian.

Love can do strange things to a person. It can strip you of your dignity or instil a new-found sense of responsibility. It has a habit of changing someone decent into a jealous, violent obsessive or turning a bad man into an honest one. Such is the dual, humbling nature of love.

As you can now see, my whole life has been based on one big lie. Except how I actually feel about you. I can't live without you, Maeve, so I have no other option but to do what I am about to do. I care for you and, I pray, some day, you will find it in your heart to forgive me.

Yours Truthfully,

James

Maeve read the letter again, [*if I ever died, I'd come back to haunt you*] moved, but without shedding a tear.

In many ways, James—was she still right in calling him by that name?—had taken her for a ride, and one could argue that she should close the chapter and turn the page... but Maeve couldn't. Even if he had woven a tangled web of deceit from the outset, James had progressed, evolved, eventually matured to a point where he could see right from wrong. The letter confirmed this and it was his undying love for her that had transformed him into a better person, open and caring with a full matching set of scruples.

And she had taken it all away, been instrumental in his downfall, when she herself harboured a wicked secret of her own. Being the only legitimate, working daughter of the high baron of a South African crime syndicate who was also founding member of the far right Afrikaner Weerstandsbeweging political organization—a fact she was afraid that might catch up with her—ought to have made her resilient against all forms of sentimentality, but Maeve could not escape her feelings. This new knowledge of James's deviousness meant without a doubt he had been her ideal partner, as written in the stars, and she would probably not encounter his like again.

She did not wish to undo everything they had done together. She still loved and respected him and a large part of her wanted him to be with her. They had spent a magical time together, and such was the intensity of their relationship, it could not be easily forgotten. She would treasure it for the rest of her natural life.

Could she forgive him?

She would try... for circumstances had changed him into someone he wasn't.

Such was the power of love, compelling yet humbling.

10

"*Sien jou wanneer ek jou sien, my liefling,*" Maeve said as she placed a floral wreath against his tombstone. "See you when I see you, my love."

February 2008-May 2008

Shetani

"He declared he would shoot me unless I gave him the ivory and then cleared out of the country, because he could do so, and had a fancy for it, and there was nothing on earth to prevent him killing whom he jolly well pleased."

Heart of Darkness (1902): Part 3

Joseph Conrad

1st May 20-

Dear British Prime Minister,

I shall begin with an anecdote. I remember walking into a pottery shop in Lagos recently once. I hear the native shopkeeper squabbling with a black customer over a jug. I can tell from where I stand that this piece of negotiation has gone on for quite a while by the look of frustration on the shopkeeper's face, and by the sounds of it, the customer has managed to drop the price of the jug to nearly half of what it's worth. And the customer isn't finished, animated in bringing down the sale-price even further, while the shopkeeper is growing more and more ticked-off.

Twenty-two Nairas? the customer is asking, not noticing — or, perhaps, deliberately *ignoring* — the shopkeeper's exasperation.

Finally, the shopkeeper has had enough. *Stop it! You want to ruin me?* He pulls out the trump card. *Pay me* white!

But this directive does not shift the customer's desire to bargain further. He tentatively inquires: *Twenty Nairas?*

Can you get out of my shop please?

I can't help but crack up laughing. Both shopkeeper and customer

~ 244 ~

stare at me and exchange bewildered glances, which makes me laugh even harder…

'Pay me white', you see? I speak of two completely different styles of shopping and paying for goods. Whites just get on with it and pay the damned man. Blacks are prone to gabbling and haggling, enjoying the thrill of the chase.

Pay me white… geddit?

O Africa, Brave Africa, why do you suffer so?

I think you are the most exciting place on Earth, a land of great adventure, but we must help you lessen your pain and regain your confidence. You have a troubled history. You know tragedy and the darkness of human souls.

Some would argue that it all started when the colonial powers of the West invaded the Dark Continent with their subsequent ruthless exploitation of the land and subjugation of its natives. If you know any history you might agree. The big-game hunters and ivory traders were small potatoes compared to the overall rampant greed, decadence and crimes of the colonists. You only have to think of the segregational mentality of the Apartheid era, the international scandal around the exploitative practices of Leopold II of Belgium and the human rights abuses his Force Publique visited upon the Congolese people. Even the British are far from innocent: the mass slaughter of the Zulus in the name of the Empire, and the concentration camps during the Mau Mau Uprisings to cite but a few of the atrocities committed.

In the succinct words of the Nobel Prize-winning Bishop Desmond Tutu: *When the missionaries came to Africa, they had the Bible and we had the land. Then they said: "Let us pray." We closed our eyes and prayed. When we opened them, we had the Bible and they had the land.*

But has the situation improved since decolonialization in the 1950s? Much of the world would disagree. Today we constantly hear of famine and droughts, poverty, disease and mass starvation, the rising AIDS epidemic, the high infant mortality rate and low life expectancy, the Brain Drain, the brutal suppression of simple human liberties, civil wars and child soldiers, and the horrors of genocide frequently perpetrated by countless dictators and tyrants, of which Africa has its highest share. Africa seems to be a magnet for attracting evil men.

I think it only right that I should follow with a shortlist of Africa's most notorious men who have attained power and decided to capitalize on a bad situation.

Sekou Toure was celebrated as a hero in Guinea for defying French colonial rule. Becoming Guinea's first-ever president in 1958, Toure set up Gulag-style death camps in which he imprisoned, tortured and executed the elite classes, such was his constant paranoia of the wealthy and educated, whom he feared would oust him from power someday. His regime conducted half-a-million extrajudicial killings and over one million of his people fled the country during his twenty-year rule.

Francisco Macias Nguema declared himself President for Life in 1972. During his ascendancy, Equatorial Guinea became known as the 'Auschwitz of Africa' after he focused entirely on internal security and sanctioned the execution of all pro-independence political rivals, with himself acting as head of the judicial system. A third of the population was either killed or fled his regime. Targeting intellectualism, he killed everyone who wore spectacles and ordered all schools closed in 1975. Skilled citizens and foreigners left, and the economy went bankrupt. He was eventually overthrown by his nephew in 1979, tried for genocide and executed forthwith, but not after Francisco Franco declared Equatorial Guinea, a former Spanish colony, an 'atheist state'.

In the politically-unstable climate of Zaire, once the Congo Free State in which Leopold II caused fifteen million deaths as King of Belgium in his pursuit of personal enrichment, a certain Joseph Mobutu would achieve power in 1965. Mobutu immediately cancelled all future elections and set up the Popular Movement for Revolution as the only legitimate political party in the country, the membership to which was mandatory for all citizens on pain of death. During his lengthy tenure in office, he gifted his people with the public hanging of government rivals, secessionists and suspected coup plotters and managed to hoard an incredible $4 billion in numerous bank accounts around the world. He was finally deposed in 1997 during the First Congolese War by Laurent Kabila. As Mobutu's successor Kabila was no better. Political oppression and personal gain remained the order of the day, and Kabila oversaw a second civil war. What makes the atrocities in the Democratic Republic of Congo rather unique was the ongoing persecution of pygmies, who were deemed subhuman and hunted down and cannibalized by both sides of the war.

Despite his previous history as a known warlord and illegal arms trader, Charles Taylor was elected president by the people of Liberia in 1997 through actual legitimate democratic means. His military forces, however, didn't waste time in raping, torturing and maiming innocent civilians and using much of the population as virtual slave labour. Plundering the country's vast natural resources of gold and diamonds, Taylor quickly amassed a personal fortune greater than Liberia's entire Gross National Product. Taylor actively helped rebel forces in neighbouring Sierra Leone by smuggling 'blood diamonds' in order to finance their ongoing war against the Sierra Leone government.

When Mengistu Haile Mariam took over as President of Ethiopia in 1974 after ousting Haile Selassie (not exactly an angel himself, no matter what the Rastafarians claim) during a bloody military coup, he soon earned the nickname the "Red Terror". Within four years his regime had executed almost two million of his fellow countrymen, considered as one of the worst mass genocides of the twentieth century, and during the Ethiopian famine of the mid-1980s, stole international food and financial aid and distributed it amongst his cronies whilst the majority of the population starved. It was not an uncommon sight to see university students and intellectuals, political opponents and government critics hanging from lamp-posts every morning. Eventually ousted in 1991, he fled to Zimbabwe where he remains today as Robert Mugabe's house guest, despite unsuccessful attempts by successive Ethiopian governments to extradite him. Tried and sentenced in absentia by his own people in 2007, Mengistu's rap sheet apparently measured 8000 pages long. Deliberately excluded from the international news coverage was how only a small percentage of the estimated £150 million raised by Live Aid in the 1980s went to famine relief while a significant proportion of the funds were siphoned off by Mengistu.

Since seizing power in Sudan, the largest country in Africa, during a military coup in 1989 against a democratically-elected government, Omar Al-Bashir immediately dissolved parliament, abolished all political parties and closed down the international media outlets. The ensuing complex twenty-year civil war has claimed the lives of over two million people and uprooted eight million others. Al-Bashir imposed and used a bastardized version of Sharia law to enslave, torture and massacre the predominantly non-Muslim people of the oil-producing regions of the south and engineered famines in rebel areas that opposed him, killing livestock and poisoning the water supplies. Al-Bashir provided sanctuary for known terrorists only to turn against them, one prime example being Carlos the Jackal whom Al-Bashir handed over to France in exchange for financial and military aid. The situation in Darfur is regarded as one of the worst humanitarian disasters in African history. Even the oil-rich Arab sheikhs can't be bothered to financially help out their fellow Muslims of Sudan or Ethiopia, preferring to blow millions every night in the London and Monte Carlo casinos and on high-class hookers instead.

Jean-Bedel Bokassa had served as a soldier in the colonial French army and, gradually rising through the ranks, helped establish the new army of the Central African Republic during its independence in 1960. After overthrowing President David Dracko in a coup d'état in 1966, Bokassa immediately abolished the constitution and began to rule by decree. Obsessed with pomp and pageantry and the heroic achievements of France's finest military leader, Napoleon Bonaparte, Bokassa, wearing crown, robes and sceptre, adopted the title of 'Emperor' after an egomaniacal US $30 million coronation ceremony which roughly translated to about one-third of the country's entire budget. Very few of the world's political leaders accepted the invitation. The British Foreign Office, outraged, declined brusquely. The US President at the time, Jimmy Carter, appalled by Bokassa's apparent delusions of grandeur, cut off all financial aid to the country. The few foreign diplomats and businessmen who did manage to attend were treated to a lavish banquet of the finest meats, which unbeknownst to them consisted of the choicest cuts of actual prisoners, carefully butchered, delicately seasoned and expertly roasted. Whilst enriching himself to the tune of US $125 million from the country's limited precious resources of diamonds, oil reserves and uranium deposits, Bokassa brutalized, tortured and executed those he considered did not live up to his own personal mad ideal of a Central African 'Empire'. In keeping with his desire to transform the capital city into a semblance of fashionable Paris, Bokassa insisted that all schoolchildren buy individually-tailored school uniforms. Their parents, who couldn't even afford the expense of a textbook, were forcibly coerced into doing so; of those who did not comply with his new edict, their frightened, barefoot children were rounded up in Bangui Prison and their heads smashed in with rifle-butts. Removed from office in a French-backed coup in 1979, the French Foreign Legionnaires undertook the gruesome task of unearthing the mass graves of hundreds of schoolchildren on the grounds of the prison. The half-eaten remains of another hundred children were found in the swimming pool at Bokassa's palace. David Dracko resumed his presidency at the request of the French government. Bokassa returned in 1986, mistakenly believing his former people still loved him, only to be arrested, convicted and sentenced to death for crimes against humanity. His sentence was later commuted to life imprisonment. Bokassa died of a heart attack in 1996, leaving behind seventeen wives and over fifty children.

Milton Obote triumphed in Uganda's first presidential elections in 1962. Four years later, he had promoted Idi Amin, a former heavyweight boxing champion and great admirer of Hitler's political vision, to army chief and his trusted strong-arm man. However, Milton Obote had no inkling of what lay ahead. In 1971, when he was due to fly home from a Commonwealth Conference in Singapore, he learned that Idi Amin had assumed control of Uganda in a military coup, forcing him into exile. Idi Amin was mad to begin with, but once he assumed power, he graduated into a monster. Idi Amin's subsequent reign of terror was marked by brutal repression, torture and mass murder. His first act as president was to deal with the imagined threat to his new power, the senior staff of the Ugandan Army, whose arrest and bayoneting he sanctioned. The severed head of the former army chief-of-staff he preserved in the freezer compartment of his refrigerator at his palace in Entebbe. He butchered anyone who spoke out against him: journalists (including *foreign* journalists), students, teachers and judges alike. Their dead bodies were promptly tossed into Lake Victoria (the source of the River Nile), and the sheer number of rotting corpses floating downstream proceeded to clog up the Owens Fall Hydroelectric Dam. Bodies were found dismembered, with genitals, hearts, livers, brains and eyes missing. His State Research Bureau organized prison camps where incarcerated citizens were forced to bludgeon each other to death with sledgehammers, gladiatorial-style, for sheer entertainment. When one of his wives, Kay Amin, died following a botched abortion, Idi Amin demanded that her head and limbs be amputated, with her head sewn back face-down, in reverse, onto her torso, her legs sutured to her shoulders and her arms attached to her pelvis so he could teach their six-year-old son a lesson in the wickedness of women. He announced on state radio that he had received a vision from God who had told him that Uganda's 50,000 Asians, for generations the backbone of Uganda's commerce, were the cause of all the country's economic problems, promptly ordering them to leave. They left in a mass exodus, and Amin proceeded to hand over their pharmacies and surgeries and warehouses and businesses over to his inept goons in his State Research Bureau. Within weeks the shops were completely deserted, all stocks appropriated by the new owners and their families and the shelves never filled again. To deflect worldwide media attention away from Uganda's dreadful economic collapse, Amin invaded Tanzania in 1979. The Tanzanian President, Julius Nyrere, fed up with Amin's moronic antics, sent in his troops who advanced towards Kampala to the welcome cheers of the broken Ugandan people, crushing Amin's military forces in their wake and forcing Amin himself to flee to Saudi Arabia. Milton Obote was reinstated as president to a nation where, in all, Amin had presided over the death of almost 300,000 of his fellow countrymen and left it an estimated US $250 million in debt.

Robert Mugabe had always championed majority rule in Rhodesia. His vision finally realized, he became Zimbabwe's first president in 1980 following independence from Britain, with widespread domestic and international support. For almost two decades he was revered as an honourable man, winning the hearts and minds of his fellow countrymen, in some circles compared favourably to Nelson Mandela. However, as time progressed, he gradually began to lose popularity due to the increasingly draconian manner in which he exercised his authority to stay in power. From 1999 onwards, he has encouraged nepotism and cronyism and has used the police and militant groups like the War Veterans Association to enforce ZANU-PF policies, prevent opponents from voting and silence dissident voices. Mugabe's government has tortured and killed opponents and human rights activists. He has displaced more than one-third of the population. While allowing elections, he has restricted outright all his opponents' ability to campaign. When Morgan Tsvangirai, leader of the main opposition party, the *Movement for Democratic Change*, won 42% of the vote, Mugabe had him arrested and charged with treason. As he has seen his support dwindling, Mugabe has played the race card, confiscating farms owned by whites and giving them to his supporters in his so-called Land Redistribution Programme. Understandably, these whites have been forced to emigrate back to Britain. Foreign journalists, if caught, face life imprisonment. Homosexuals have also been discriminated against and targeted by Mugabe's repressive regime. British authorities believe Mugabe has stashed large amounts of money in foreign bank accounts. He has faced international condemnation, with Bishop Desmond Tutu and the British government as Mugabe's fiercest critics. He was stripped of his honorary Knight Grand Cross of the Order of the Bath by Queen Elizabeth II in 2008 for *"the abuse of human rights and abject disregard for the democratic process in Zimbabwe"*. The situation is worse than it has ever been. Hyperinflation with the Zimbabwe dollar deemed worthless, having lost its value, the exchange rate continuously widening with Z$1million currently equivalent to US$1. Thousands of acres of farmland, once rippling with maize and wheat and sorghum, now lie abandoned, reverting back to nature. Factories lie silent, the reservoirs empty. Daily power cuts in Harare. The scarcity of cars and countless deserted petrol stations. There are frenzied, angry queues outside banks and supermarkets. While Mugabe jets his wife off to a private clinic in Paris for treatment of a simple headache, cash-strapped banks restrict withdrawals to Z$5million per person since there is no paper left to print more money. Supermarket shelves lie almost empty, offering plenty of seasonings but no meat, jams but no bread, cereals but no milk, strengthening the grip of the Black Market. Those who decide to remain in Zimbabwe drive to Botswana and South Africa and bring back a carful of provisions. Boys living alone in the brutal, overcrowded slums play football, barefoot, dressed in rags, dangerously malnourished, with a ball made of rolled-up plastic bags. Destitute women forced into prostitution know AIDS will kill them. They dredge muddy water from the bottom of deep holes because their taps have run dry. Dysentery is soaring. No point in sending patients to government hospitals because there are no doctors or drugs to treat them. In secondary schools, no staff can afford to work. One-third of the students are orphans and one-sixth HIV-positive.

Despite the risks, most of the schoolgirls, including those who still have parents, are advised to sell their bodies to get food. How could this happen to a country once praised as the 'Breadbasket of Africa'? No longer does the grass sing but wails a lament, a funeral dirge.

Ethnic tensions between the Bantu-speaking Hutu and Tutsi tribes have existed for centuries. Burundi experienced two acts of genocide in living history, the 1972 mass-killing of Hutus by the Tutsi army and the 1993 killing of Tutsi by the Hutu population. Hostilities in Rwanda with the displacement of large numbers of Hutu in the north by the rebels and periodic localized extermination of Tutsi to the south, culminated in the assassination of its Hutu President Juvenal Habyarimana. His death was followed by the internationally-denounced Rwandan Genocide of 1994, the extermination of over 800,000 Tutsis and pro-peace Hutus by government-led Hutu militia and the systematic rape of between 250,000 and 500,000 women and girls. Military leaders ordered the Hutu men to rape the Tutsi, condoning the acts taking place, making no efforts to stop them. Compared to other conflicts the sexual violence in Rwanda stands out in terms of the organized nature of the propaganda and the intensity of the brutality towards the Tutsi women. Rape was used as a weapon by the perpetrators of the Rwandan massacre in order to weaken, humiliate, and ultimately destroy the morale of Tutsi men. Sexual violence against Rwandese women during the Rwandan genocide included individual rape, gang rape, sexual slavery, raping with objects such as sticks and weapons, mutilation of breasts, vaginas or buttocks, the rape and often subsequent killing of pregnant women, the deliberate transmission of HIV by HIV-positive Hutu men to Tutsi women and their families. War rape occurred all over the country and frequently in public, at sites such as schools, churches, checkpoints and government buildings. The long-term effects of war rape in Rwanda for the survivors included long-lasting psychological damage (post-traumatic stress disorder), social isolation (social stigma attached to rape meant some husbands left their wives who had become victims of war rape, or that the victim became unmarriable), unwanted pregnancies and babies (some women resorted to self-induced abortions), sexually-transmitted diseases, including syphilis, gonorrhoea and HIV/AIDS (with no access to anti-retroviral drugs).

I could go on…

Grim reading, I'm sure. *The horror! The horror!* as is Joseph Conrad's oft-recited quote.

Please, this is not an excuse for me to dredge up and sensationalize the worst, cruellest acts of human savagery in living African memory. I do not intend to lecture or preach. I would not dare overstep my bounds. I know my station. I am merely putting everything into perspective.

We in the West worry about the FA Cup Final, what we're going to give our girlfriend for Valentine's Day, the state of our Pop Charts, whereas in Africa most people worry about where they're going to get their next meal.

Rock star and philanthropist, Bono, once stated in heartfelt despair: *Africa makes a fool of our idea of justice, a farce of our idea of equality. It mocks our pieties, doubts our concerns, questions our commitment. Because there is no way we can look at what's happening in Africa and if we're honest conclude that it would be allowed to happen anywhere else.*

Eloquently-put, meant to grab us and shake us from our blissful slumber. Wake up, people! Why invade Iraq on the strength of a lie when the whole world could see that Zimbabwe, a former British colony, needed our help?

Yet, there is hope. Africa is a beautiful place with so much to offer, its poignant dark light of which Toto famously sang about. I should know. I have lived and worked here, experienced all that is good. The good, may I add, far outweighs the bad a millionfold. The Serengeti, going on Safari, the diverse and majestic wildlife iconicized by Disney, Mount Kilimanjaro, Victoria Falls, Mombasa, Cape Town. A magnificent landscape and colourful tribes celebrated in the exciting exploits of the fictional Victorian adventurer, Allan Quatermain. Chinua Achebe, who spearheaded the African Writers' Series by writing the archetypal African novel and setting the bar for other outstanding authors, like Peter Abrahams and Ben Okri. Generations of people of hardy stock as evidenced by the Olympic-winning long-distance runners. What could be cuter than a black baby with its gentle, quiet nature and big, round adorable eyes?

I am pleased that the leading politicians of the world banded together, and under pressure from the international community, requested the IMF write off the debt of Africa's poorest nations. A fresh start, perhaps, for the people from which they can build a brighter future. Most Africans are deeply-religious folk and decent, morally-upstanding citizens, full of dignity and compassion, far from ignorant or intolerant. All they ask for is to be able to feed themselves through the efforts of subsistence farming and the production of cash crops. It is their universal right to demand clean water and medicine, that their children have a basic school education, their genuine entitlement to free and fair elections in the country of their birth, things we here in the West take for granted. The mining and drilling and manufacturing industries continue to provide a substantial source of revenue as does the ever-expanding information networks and communication technologies. More investment by the world banks is still needed for the common people, instead of lining the pockets of greedy, grasping governments. The UN should be more proactive in stamping out dictatorships and preventing further barbarity and human abuses; after all, it is an international organization designed to police the world.

Nelson Mandela dreams of an Africa at peace with itself, in unity, whereby its leaders combine in their efforts to solve the problems of the great continent.

The Maasai Warriors of East Africa speak of supernatural entities called the 'Shetani'. Superstition dictates that the Shetani are malevolent spirits, allegedly capable of taking on many forms, but are depicted as essentially anthromorphic, distorted, exaggerated, grotesque manifestations of the animal shape. The Maasai believe the Shetani to be the root cause of all the injustices and evils in Africa, possessing and poisoning the minds and bodies of all those nefarious African leaders. We all agree power corrupts. Power particularly corrupts those who had very little to begin with. With power ought to come great responsibility and should be handled with intelligence and wisdom, ultimately serving the people you're supposed to represent and who've put their absolute trust in you. But why does power have the irrevocable tendency to corrupt? Is it something within the fundaments of human nature, or is there perhaps some truth in the popular myth of the Shetani?

What benefit a man if he gains the whole world but forfeits his soul?

As you are aware, I am a simple aid worker with the International

Red Cross, held hostage in a prison cell. It seems my figurative hourglass has now run out. I can hear the boots of my captors stomping down the corridor, getting louder, the clanking of keys. They have promised to rape me before they execute me. I can only guess the British government weren't able — or prepared — to raise the one million sterling ransom the military junta demanded. I hope my captors do me the small courtesy of sending this letter. The problem with civil wars: you lose track of the side fighting the moral high ground. Both sides become as evil as the other.

Do not weep for me. I have no regrets. I have lived (however short my life shall be) to the full. I have done my bit to alleviate some of the suffering of the African community. That should be reward enough.

Tell my boyfriend, Nate, that I love him and will miss him immensely. And my Mom and Dad for equipping me with and nurturing my moral centre and making me the honest woman that I am today. All I request is you say a small prayer for me, put in a good word to the Man Upstairs. I have resigned myself to the fate of unwilling martyr. Jesus will always be with me as God in Man.

These will be my final words. Let my death not be in vain. I don't really intend to be 'the Voice', John Farnham, that obscure one-hit wonder, spoke of, encouraging us to all rise up from our apathy and collectively change the world for the better. I don't claim to know how to solve all the problems of Africa. But with a little support and guidance from the West, we can transform Africa into the magnificent place it ought to be and help its proud people with their enduring spirit prosper.

Goodbye and God Bless,
Holly Tindle

April 2011-May 2011

Getting his Dues:
A Kashmiri Folktale

'Kashmir' (1975)
Title of Song
Led Zeppelin

Once there was a village on the fringes of the fabulous city of Srinagar. As with most folk who hailed from this region, its inhabitants were a hardy and beautiful people who paid alms to the poor and donated gifts every month to their kind and noble king in exchange for his everlasting protection from wandering thieves, cut-throats and bandits. The village was situated close to the banks of the mighty Jhelum River against a stunning backdrop of the beclouded, majestic peaks of the mountains in the north.

The people of the village lived peacefully and productively. Most worked on the land as farmers, labouring on the fields to collect grain, and as herdsmen, shepherding yaks and goats. The village was equipped both with its own physician, who was looked upon as an excellent healer of the sick, and an apothecary, who dispensed the necessary medicinal herbs. The people had also built a small house of worship where they offered their submission to Almighty Allah.

Our story concerns a priest (*or moulvi sahib*) who held high office in the royal court. He was a close friend of the wazir to the king and ranked junior only to the palace imam. Aside from preaching at the Grand Mosque of Srinagar, the priest performed many of the ecclesiastical duties in the surrounding villages. He was well-respected and feared and proud of his heritage; he came from a long line of Mughal warriors who had once led the mass conversion of Hindus to the Islamic faith. Armed with amulets, talismen and incantations and able to recite all the sacred verses of the Quran, he carried responsibilities beyond that of any physician, concentrating more on the spiritual health of the people rather than treating mortal diseases. He also served as the censor of births, deaths and marriages. His powerful prayers assisted the dying in their transition to Paradise as well as officiating over and therefore validating any nuptial union.

One day, during harvest time, the physician's son returned home from a trip to a neighbouring village. He had always hoped to follow in his father's footsteps and currently acted as his father's apprentice and was a keen student of science. Also a lover of *ghazals* and mystic poetry and a wild romantic at heart, he brought back a pretty young maiden from the other village. He told his father, the physician, that he had fallen in love with this gentle creature and wanted to marry her. His prospective bride was an orphan and had been raised by her cruel-hearted aunt, who was now only too pleased to see the back of her.

His parents were thrilled that their son had found someone to cherish and felt she would make a welcome addition to their family. They announced their son's engagement to the village community. They gave their future daughter-in-law some gold bangles and an expensive jade engagement ring. They invited the priest to their home in order to seek his approval for the forthcoming wedding. They valued his pious opinion and considered his blessing a simple but necessary formality.

On his arrival the next day, the priest was shown into their modest, rustic dwelling, where a small celebratory *wazwan* of roasted whole chakor and baked furrei fish, mutton in the form of fried ribs and spiced *kofta*, and heeng-and-saffron-flavoured chickpea *pilaf* rice awaited him.

When they had feasted on these delicious dishes and moved on to the *kahwah* (or green tea), the groom's mother presented the soon-to-be bride to the priest. She crossed the room and sat before him, lowering her eyes in a humble, respectful manner. He regarded her closely. She was tall, slim and fair with the complexion of a delicate lotus flower. Her eyes were the shape and colour of almonds with lusciously long eyelashes, her nose that of fine, polished china and her lips ruby-red and enticing. She possessed dark, flowing hair, as soft as silk, and scented with the sweet fragrance of jasmine oil. Her exquisite beauty would have captured the hearts and souls of most ordinary men.

But the priest requested the bride leave the room which she promptly did so he could discuss some matters of concern. He abruptly refused to give the impending matrimonial alliance his holy blessing. "This marriage must not go ahead!"

The physician's family were shocked by his unexpected pronouncement, more so the groom. "Why mustn't it?" the groom implored, aghast.

The priest elaborated. "The girl is *cursed*! As long as she stays under your roof, great tragedy will befall your family."

"How can this be?" said the groom's father, confounded. "She is only an innocent child."

"Child, yes, innocent, *no!*" the priest warned, his tone hard and severe. "It is a shame you do not sense her evil as I do. Her black heart speaks to me. She means to bring your family only mischief and misfortune, take you away from the grace of Allah. I believe she is either a daughter of *Shaitan* or quite possibly a djinn at the very least, intending to dazzle and deceive you with her apparent loveliness. It explains why she is an orphan and why her aunt was so desperate to get rid of her."

This was grave news. The groom was heartbroken, full of sorrow. His mother, who had grown increasingly fond of the girl in recent weeks, began to weep silently. However, her husband, the respected physician, struggled to accept the priest's words. Was this divine intervention or was the priest actually lying? But for what reason would the priest lie? And how could his family simply ignore the so-called sage advice delivered by this devout man of God?

"What do you suggest we do?" asked the physician, a part of him wishing he had never consulted the priest in the first place.

The priest considered carefully, offered his wisdom. "It is the will of Allah that we shut her up in a coffin and let it float on the surface of the Jhelum at midnight. The waters will either drown her and send her back to the Pit, or they will extinguish the animated fires composing her spirit, if she is indeed a djinn."

"But what if she is human?" challenged the physician.

"Then, Merciful Allah will grant her entrance into Paradise," replied the priest calmly. "But I can assure you she means you no good. Follow my instructions and only then can you exorcize your home of the malign influence of this wicked enchantress. Allah has spoken."

Suspicious though he was of the priest's ulterior motives, the physician was forced to consent to the priest's extreme proposal. After all, the priest carried greater authority than him and understood, practiced and enforced the sacred Islamic laws. The physician's family reluctantly agreed to the plan. After receiving his usual sizeable commission and saying a cursory *"Kudha hafiz"*, the priest took his leave.

Around midnight, the physician's family took the former bride-to-be to the river. Disgraced in the eyes of one of God's revered clerics, she did not speak, did not protest, only seemed to accept the inevitability of her fate. They gagged her mouth, tied her wrists and ankles, put her in a wooden coffin and floated it on the waters.

Once the grim business was done and dusted, the old physician addressed his profusely grieving son on the moonlit banks of the river. "Now, we bring this dreadful affair to a conclusion. Do not despair, son, for before the harvest season is over I will make sure you are wedded to the purest, virtuous bride."

Downstream, the priest waited expectantly. Above him, a slender crescent of moon crowned the starry night sky, keeping a cold, silent vigil over the deeds of Man. A forest of chinars and deodars stretched wildly behind him, possibly hiding predators unseen. Considering he never ventured into these lands at night, the journey to this spot had been somewhat anxiety-provoking. Yet, afraid though he might have been of being ambushed by a snow leopard or a black bear, fortunately all he had encountered was the rotting carcass of an ibex, a blind club-footed sadhu in deep meditation, and elsewhere the dying embers of a campfire, around which sat two emaciated-looking men in the process of smoking either opium or bhang (or perhaps both), and who failed to notice the priest sneak by, unaware as they were of their surroundings or their own individual states of self-neglect and absorbed only in chasing their all-encompassing narcotic bliss.

The priest waited patiently on the riverbank, greatly pleased with himself. He had concocted the perfect scheme. He had dreamed it up on the spur of the moment at the exact instant he'd clapped eyes on the bride. Endowed with the irresistible virginal beauty of a *houri* of Paradise, she had embellished his heart with desire and he had immediately craved her for his own harem. His advice that the bride be set adrift on the river had been a terrific piece of cunning as had been his dishonest performance in putting the fear of God into the gullible fools at the physician's house. Presently, he waited eagerly here for her to appear. Allah most Exalted had surely commanded him to take another wife for whatever purpose He had created him. Of course, if she failed to satisfy his enormous sexual appetite or refused to worship him like Allah Almighty he could always sell her off to some ruthless slave merchant.

Growing anxious again, wondering where she could be, he was on the verge of cursing the physician's family for not carrying out his instructions when he suddenly caught sight of the coffin in the distance as it glided towards him. "There is my sweet, wholesome angelic bride!" he exclaimed, delighted. "May I enjoy the pleasures of her heavenly body!"

He waded into the water, stopped the coffin, pulled it ashore and deposited it on the ground. By moonlight, he unfastened the chains and, in a state of high anticipation, raised the lid, ready to take the entombed girl to his bosom.

Except, his incarcerated fair bride was nowhere to be seen. Instead, the coffin accommodated a host of coiling, slithering vipers. Several sprang out and stung him. Excitement transforming into sublime horror, the priest shrieked in pain and cried for help. Then, when he looked again, he realized it wasn't a nest of vipers at all but a djinn, gimlet-eyed, charcoal-skinned and foul-smelling.

When it spoke in a dry, raspy voice, it breathed sulphurous smoke into his face. "Do you remember me, priest?"

The priest did indeed recognize this hideous creature born of fire, for only three seasons ago he had helped the imam expel its unclean presence from the Grand Mosque. "But we banished you!"

"Yes, you did, priest, but I am now back here to seek vengeance." The djinn chuckled sickly. "I plan to take your crooked soul and dirty heart to where I belong, and none of your fraudulent prayers will be able to save you now!"

"What have you done with my bride?" the priest uttered in the grip of sheer panic.

"I am the same bride you coveted so dearly!" the djinn bellowed in an avid declaration of companionship. "I promise I shall keep you company from now till eternity!"

As the djinn suddenly grabbed his wrist and he exploded into flames, the priest screamed a last, protracted, torture-stricken scream. Disintegrating into charred bones and ash, the priest realized he had met a creature more corrupt and unscrupulous than himself, and at that moment, learned that he had actually in his own deliberately misleading way been correct about the bride's supernatural origins.

As they say, there's always a first time for everything.

March 2011

An Act of Faith

"Soon shall We cast terror into the hearts of the Unbelievers, for that they joined companions with Allah, for which He had sent no authority: their abode will be the Fire: And evil is the home of the wrong-doers!"

The Holy Quran (Sura 3.151)

Since even before the genesis of the world, Gog and Magog, Cyclopean beings of immeasurable power and ancient evil, have dwelled outside of time and space, imprisoned beyond the Wall of Zulqarnian. Every day they claw and gnaw away at this impenetrable, extradimensional barrier, seeking to invade and reach the world of Man, and every night, just as they can glimpse the faintest traces of reality on the other side, they fall into a fitful slumber, worn out by their day's labours. Yet, by the next morning, the Wall has reverted to its original thickness, and Gog and Magog are compelled to start all over again, destined to repeat the action, trapped as they have been for untold aeons in a perpetual, immutable cycle of eating and sleeping. Until Doomsday, that is, for their escape, as it is prophesized, will signal the Beginning of the End...

The shrill ringing from the Rooster alarm-clock roused Hassan Omar from his deep sleep, and he reached out an unsteady hand to silence the din from the bell. His efforts were rewarded when he eventually found the blasted thing. He yawned loudly and opened his eyes, shaking away the cobwebs of half-remembered dreams from his mind. At seven in the morning, sunshine streamed into the master bedroom of the fifth-floor apartment through the narrow slit between the curtains and Hassan could hear the honking of gridlocked traffic in the street below.

Beside him, another figure, human-shaped and shrouded, stirred.

Rise and shine! he told himself. Today promised to be a special day. A monumental day. He had important business to attend to. Vitally-important business.

He pulled back the covers, swung his legs out of bed and sat up, gently massaging his temples.

The other person occupying the bed emerged from the covers and opened sleepy eyes. "Is it time to get up already?" she murmured, sounding slightly dazed.

"Only if you don't want to be late for work," replied Hassan. He twisted his torso round and planted a kiss on his girlfriend's forehead. "Morning, Serafine, my darling."

"Morning, Hass," she said softly.

"I'm going to shower. It would be nice if you could join me."

Hassan got to his feet and took his naked body into the bathroom, where he proceeded to turn on the power-shower. Serafine Gerber likewise dragged herself out of bed and padded to the bathroom, slipping out of her pink negligee before accompanying Hassan under the shower-head. Hot water cascading over their exposed flesh, they stood facing each other in silent anticipation. Then, Serafine's eyes met Hassan's gaze and she realized what he desired most of all.

He raised both his hands up to her ample breasts and started fondling, jiggling, squeezing them. He drew his mouth over each nipple, licking and sucking and nibbling them in turn, teasing them with his tongue. He felt her nipples harden against the palm of his hands. Serafine meanwhile gasped, relishing the wonderful sensation arising from his keen interest in her breasts. She reciprocated the sybaritic gesture by reaching down to his crotch and grasping his penis, stroking it, manipulating it, playing with it—stimulating it.

Hassan began to develop an erection. "Do what you do best, my darling," he expressed his edict.

Serafine understood what he meant, what she should do next. Not one of her favourite things, but what else could she do? She did not wish to offend him.

She knelt down in the mistiness of the domestic waterfall with her face at the same height as his growing appendage, and Hassan closed his eyes, preparing for the imminent act of phallic worship, letting

Serafine do her thing. As is the custom with most Muslim males, he was circumcised and cleanly shaven down below.

Serafine promptly guided his semi-flaccid member into her awaiting mouth, drawing it in and out, flicking her tongue across the dome, circling the ridge behind the swelling glans. The thick vein on the underside pulsed, inflating the length with more blood, raising the shaft towards the perpendicular. She continued with this morning ritual until Hassan's dilated penis was a thing of beauty, a magnificent virile phallus. Now her mouth encompassed most of the rigid, engorged shaft.

At this stage, she would have liked to take him between her parted labial lips, deep into the pink, moist valley of her being but she knew this wouldn't be happening. As usual, he would be expecting her to finish him off.

As she completed the pointed act, she withdrew her mouth at the moment of climax.

The grip of his hands maintaining her head at waist-level, his hips jerked involuntarily and his neck arched back, consumed by rapturous pleasure, as the tip of his penis erupted in a creamy gush of semen. He spatterhunded her: white streamers jetted forth in a rhythmic arc and squirted across her face and well-proportioned breasts.

Her tongue tentatively swept a globule of jism off her cheek— Serafine immediately grimaced at the bitter taste which went unnoticed by Hassan—before the downrush of misty torrents washed away the physical evidence.

Despite some of the disgusting things he made her do, Serafine felt lucky to have a man like Hassan. Not only was he as slim as an athlete and handsome-looking and worked as a scientific officer at a successful chemical engineering firm, he could sometimes be a really considerate, passionate lover. She didn't care he was of the Muslim faith or whether her parents frowned upon their relationship. She loved him. She would do anything for him.

"Did I do well?" she asked, sounding vulnerable, still crouched.

Spent but greatly contented, basking in the warm afterglow of a particularly strong orgasm, Hassan delivered his verdict: "You did exceptional, baby!"

He watched his girlfriend pick herself up and begin the actual task of showering. She was indeed a stunning girl: dark-haired and ivory-skinned, with a fabulous body God had designed for sin. His family would be horrified if they learned he was dating a Jewish girl, even if he thought about converting her to Islam, but none of that would matter soon. Through the rising vapour, he spied her ravishing nakedness, as she sensuously sudded her gorgeous breasts with a loofah, and he experienced a reprise of the sexual hunger he had experienced minutes earlier.

Having showered and breakfasted, Hassan made his way through the streets towards Edgware Road, heading for the local Underground station.

The June morning was bright and muggy, the temperatures expected to climb into the mid-nineties by midday.

Hassan and Serafine had often spoken about the increasing cosmopolitan nature of London. Where else in the world could you see Muslims and Jews living side by side, at peace with one another? Their relative harmony here certainly put the ongoing Israeli-Palestinian conflict to shame. Anyway, it was the Western powers following the Second World War who had stupidly placed the uprooted, persecuted Jews smack-bang in the Middle East, surrounded by resentful Arab nations, who weren't even consulted prior to making this political decision. Why should Jerusalem belong solely to the Jews when it was a city equally holy both to Christians and Muslims? Israel had quickly established itself as a superpower and proceeded to massacre anyone they considered a threat to their homeland. It was no secret that Mossad was a more ruthless and dangerous organization than MI6, and even the CIA, with the much-vilified Hamas nothing more than popgun-toting tin soldiers by comparison. The billions of dollars of financial aid the United States provided for Israel annually to murder innocent Palestinian men, women and children sickened Hassan. Jews might complain they had been persecuted for thousands of years and being given their own country was a blessing, but Hassan didn't see it that way. He believed that the Jews had deliberately exaggerated the numbers who had died during the Holocaust in order to gain the sympathy of the world and their own piece of land. Serafine, a second-grade teacher and always a gentle pacifist who saw the best in everyone, pointed out that we were all Children of Abraham, with the Jews tracing their roots back to his son Isaac and all Muslims descended from the other son Ishmael, but Hassan could only nod and pretend to agree with this simplistic view. There was no way he was prepared to accept that Muslims and Jews shared a common ancestry—this was nothing more than horseshit propaganda dreamed up by the West to appease the anger of the Muslim man.

There had been so many wars fought over the centuries in the name of God, claims that one's religion was superior to one's neighbour's. The subjugation of the early Christians by the Romans, the slaughter of opposing Moor and Christian soldiers during the Crusades, the Mogul conquest of the Indian sub-continent and conversion of Hindus to Islam, the rape, pillage and murder of Muslims and Hindus (and Sikhs) by either side during the Partition of India of 1947, the massacre of hundreds of thousands of Chinese citizens and the rape of tens of thousands of their women by Japanese troops at Nanking, the annexation of Tibet this time by the Chinese Army in the early 1950s against meagre passive-resistance from the Buddhist population, the Iran-Iraq War of the 1980s between the Sunnis and their Shia brothers and their longstanding dual persecution of the Kurds, even the ongoing sectarian violence between the Catholics and Protestants in Northern Ireland. These days, it was the Jihad imposed by the Muslim world over the supposed evils of Western society and the West's relentless, Right-wing scapegoating and demonization of Islam.

Hassan boarded the Circle Line, the passengers crammed in the train like sardines in a tin-can. As he stood, swaying to the rattling motion of the high-speed train, he put on his headphones, distracting himself with music from his iPod.

So why had religion come about?

Man was a Savage, aimless, lacking direction, bereft of laws governing his behaviour, far removed from the grace of God, concerned only with satisfying his own primitive desires and baser instincts. In a time of unconscionable murder, rampant lust, drunken orgies, frivolous greed and idol worship, God furnished Moses with the Ten

Commandments and consolidated the Hebrew faith. For a while things were fine and the people led a virtuous, moral life, devoutly worshipping their divine Creator. But soon Man was corrupt again, and God sent down his prophet Jesus to deal with the immoralities and iniquities of Man. So emerged Christianity, quickly growing into a dominant force and a positive influence on the masses. As the centuries passed, Man lost his way once more and God decided to intervene again, appointing another prophet — Prophet Muhammad, *peace be upon him* — to rein in the faithless. And Islam was born.

Hassan could confirm that all Muslims viewed Moses, Jesus and Muhammad as hallowed prophets of Islam, with the latter bestowed the highest praises and exaltations. If Islam was supposed to be impervious to criticism, since the Quran is the Last Word of God and its Prophet the Perfect Human Being, why did people dare trash, or even mock, the sanctity of Islam?

Ignorance, plain and simple.

Forget about the atheists who regarded God as a delusion and religion as the source of all evil — they were Hell-bound, anyway. No, the problem stemmed from the right to freedom of speech and self-expression. People could think what they liked, say what they liked, write what they liked as long as it did not involve hate-speech. Secular Islam has frequently been accused of preaching intolerance and violence towards critics and other religions.

The fatwa issued for the execution of author Salman Rushdie in 1989 by Ayatollah Khomeini, forcing him into hiding, Hassan considered just. The publication of his novel, *Satanic Verses*, was a direct insult to the Prophet Muhammad, *peace be upon him*. Rushdie more-than-implied that Islam was a man-made religion invented by an imperfect, disillusioned opportunist, alluding to the infamous incident when the Prophet Muhammad, *peace be upon him*, was allegedly tricked by Satan into including a few rather questionable verses in the Quran which he later retracted at the behest of the Archangel Gabriel, later to be known as the 'Satanic verses'. The blasphemous manner in which the characters staffing the brothel in the book were named after the Prophet's wives and Mahound stuffing his face with every pork product under the sun was just too much to bear. Rushdie would surely think again if he valued his life. Beware, too, V.S. Naipaul for that matter!

In November 2004, the Dutch film-maker, Theo van Gogh, was assassinated for producing a documentary, *Submission*, highlighting the plight and abuse of women in Muslim society. Dare he think he could interfere in Islamic politics, something he knew nothing about?

Then there was the case in September 2005 when the Danish newspaper, *Jyllands-Posten*, published inflammatory cartoons, caricaturing the Prophet Muhammad, depicting him as a suicide bomber. It caused worldwide protests from the Muslim community, culminating in the arson of the Danish embassy in Syria and the public burning of the Danish flag in Gaza City. The newspaper was eventually forced to apologize. Bad enough it compared the ordinary Muslim to a terrorist, but to claim to know the physical appearance of the Prophet Muhammad, *peace be upon him*, when in fact he had attained complete perfection and could never be rendered in any sketch, illustration or painting. Even the Hollywood producers of the much-loved movie, *The Message*, starring Anthony Quinn, were careful in not showing the Prophet's face.

Referring to the Prophet Muhammad, *peace be upon him*, as "a pitiless warlord, pillager, butcher of Jews and polygamous" could only sink you into cowardly anonymity, as one French editor would discover.

When you question the integrity of the Prophet Muhammad, *peace be upon him*, calling him a "paedophile" on the strength that at the age of fifty-two he wedded his most cherished wife, Aisha, who was only six at the time and with whom he consummated the marriage when she turned nine, despite keeping various other wives (including several war widows and his own adopted son's divorced wife, Zaynab) and countless concubines, was it any mystery why those middle-school kids in Melbourne, Australia, in December 2009 defaced a copy of the Bible, tearing pages, urinating on it and finally setting it on fire? Can you imagine anyone desecrating the Holy Quran in that way or burning effigies of the Prophet Muhammad, *peace be upon him*, in public and getting away with it?

There was a reason for the self-censorship around Islam. Hassan would reiterate that his so-called Holy Book is the perfect Word of Allah as revealed to Muhammad, His Final Prophet and Perfection Incarnate.

It was the sheer ignorance of the West that caused conflict with the Islamists.

Western scholars talked about the subordinate status of non-Muslims in Islamic countries (*Jizya* tax), the persecution of homosexuals, and execution as the only fair punishment for apostasy, but these same scholars did not realize that these are laws clearly set down in the Quranic text, and the Hadith (the Words and Deeds of the Prophet Muhammad, *peace be upon him*). Staunch feminists moaned about the subservient role of women in Muslim society. True, women had fewer rights than men, who could take up to four wives, without similar provisions made available to women. It was apparently totally acceptable to beat women if they talked back and stone them to death for the crime of adultery, because they were less intelligent, cursed by menses, and more women occupied Hell than their male counterparts. A woman's place was in the home, Hassan would gladly inform these impudent feminists, and not to be paraded around in public.

A common myth involved the prohibited use of alcohol. In fact, the Prophet had stated that a Muslim *can* drink alcohol, albeit responsibly, but they had to maintain sobriety for the mosque. *I bet you didn't know that!*

Perhaps, the Quran might seem full of contradictions, ambiguous explanations and cosmological inaccuracies, but these were deliberate and down to a matter of interpretation, in order to test the faith of the follower, separate the Believer from the Unbeliever.

Need the rousing lectures of the well-educated Dr. Naik remind everyone: why did Cassius Clay, Malcolm X and Cat Stevens turn humbly to the teachings of the Quran if no moral inspiration lay within? And please do not dare say that Islam only attracts malefactors and outcasts and losers?

Hassan continued to listen to the tunes on his iPod through his ear-buds, counting down the Underground stops, watching the commuters getting off and getting on.

The politicians tell us we live in enlightened times. But is this really the case?

Hassan believed the liberal ideas of the West had, instead of emancipating the individual, turned the people into selfish, decadent creatures, disconnected from their neighbour and in perpetual pursuit of material possessions. It was precisely this corrupt, hypocritical facade of democracy which Hassan could not accept. Neither could the Neo-conservatives bear presiding over this moral decay of society.

The struggle that had once begun in the 1950s with Sayyid Qutb, an Egyptian expert in Islamist theory, who dreamed of creating a humane society, capturing the meaningful technological and medical advances of the West but ideally within the ethical framework of Islam, regulated by Sharia law, had continued with Osama bin Laden, the acknowledged architect of 9/11 and 7/7, until his contemptible, Presidential-sanctioned slaughter in May 2011. A setback it may seem for Islamic fundamentalism, but the war was far from over.

The Neo-cons, full of hard-line Christians and complicit Jews, believed their own jingoistic, elitist thinking that they could change the world, obsessed with stirring up fear of invisible enemies, whether it be communist regimes, radical Islamism and other organized 'evils'. Except there was nothing revolutionary about the Neo-cons, no matter what they arrogantly claimed — they promoted conformity and corporate greed and had long since begun to believe the unscrupulous lies they circulated. Everyone knew they were the real masterminds behind the current multi-trillion-dollar global recession of 2008, fostering the moronic recklessness of the Wall Street gamblers, their mothers as utterly amoral as the high-class hookers their Wall Street sons fucked every night, no different.

FOX News was the legitimate mouthpiece of the Neo-cons, but its distorted, paranoid fear-mongering world view was more consistent with a comedy channel than a news corporation. *Keep the public afraid,* seemed its unspoken motto. Hassan remembered his father watching FOX News every night before he retired to bed, just to end the day with a laugh. One would be shocked to learn that Al-Jazeera, in stark contrast, read the news with complete, solid impartiality.

Nowadays, we witnessed the constant, needless interference of Western governments in the affairs of Muslim states. Hassan wanted to say it like it was. Former Prime Minister, Tony Blair, wishing to fulfil a vaguely noble desire to go down in history, would be remembered as Dubya's pet poodle during the 'Blairaq' War, pre-empted on deliberate misinformation and which would result in the 'suicide' of leading weapons expert for the MoD, David Kelly, under highly suspicious circumstances. Now the same, despicable, conniving man, who should have been tried for war crimes, was an ambassador of peace in the Middle East, which defeated the object of any sustainable peace in the region. The invasion of Taliban-controlled Afghanistan and later Iraq on spurious intelligence had achieved very little for the people they were supposed to be liberating from so-called dictatorships, just as they were now in the process of destabilizing the infrastructure of Syria and Libya in the name of democracy when in fact it was for their own business interests (oil), then complaining that the Jihadists had filled the power vacuum. People needed to be led, in Hassan's opinion, in the blessed ways of Allah, and empowering them, giving them autonomy, *democratizing* them, only caused more problems than it solved.

Maybe, as some political analysts suggested and Hassan ignored, the Neo-cons were no different from Al-Qaeda in terms of their ideology and guiding principles, with both organizations on opposite sides of the same coin, each fighting to cleanse the moral decay of liberalism.

Terror networks. Militant training camps. Enlistment and mobilization of the soldiers of Islamic Jihad in the shape of secret sleeper cells. Yes, the Holy War still raged on and would continue until Allah deemed otherwise.

Hassan was deeply saddened by the sorry state of Muslim families in this country. The parents, illiterate immigrants, would watch Bollywood films all day long on satellite television, neglecting the emotional well-being of their children. Their sons, completely Westernized, would be concerned only with shagging, Rap and Cannabis, and unlike Hindu teenagers, would flunk their GCSEs. The daughters, having led a sheltered life, would have married in their late teens and got pregnant soon after and would now be wrapped up in caring for their kids; granted a little freedom in their early twenties, they would surely realize there was more to life than their interminable domestic duties and would rebel against their factory-working husbands. And what about the media uproar against the Islamic Sharia Council, accusing it of frequently ruling that the wives of alleged rape and domestic abuse return to their husbands? How dare Fleet Street question the authority of this unique, judicial establishment when it had been entrusted to observe and uphold traditional family values according to Islamic law? Perhaps the Islamic Sharia Council wasn't doing enough, but a righteous Muslim woman should know her place when it came to matrimonial matters, and that other firmly-held Islamic belief: *Death before Dishonour*.

However, there was something that always made Hassan smile: a recent news report spoke of Pakistani men in Bradford scouting for and grooming disaffected British teenage girls from poor white trash backgrounds, whom they showered with expensive gifts and fed a cocktail of alcohol and drugs before putting them to good use as prostitutes.

Hassan secretly grinned at this encouraging thought, as he got off the train at High Street Kensington. Shabash!

Hassan remembered the imam at his local mosque during Friday prayers telling him about the Signs of the End. Fornication would become prevalent, producing misbegotten, disrespecting, foul-mouthed children. There would be no respect for the elders. The consumption of intoxicants would become widespread. Anti-religious art and literature would become rife, with a gradual, corresponding extinction in spiritual knowledge and prayer neglected in favour of worldly gain. Dishonesty would become a way of life, falsehood and bribery virtues, and Trust would become a means of making a profit. Singers would become common and idolized, with people dancing late into the night. Women would conspire, speak back and curse and appear naked in spite of being dressed, leading pious men astray with their feminine wiles. We would get smogs and acid rain and an increase in the frequency of and devastation caused by earthquakes. Men would lie with men and women would commit adultery with other women, and soon men would begin to look like women and women would begin to resemble men. More importantly, the nations of the earth would turn against the Muslims like a gathering of starving people sitting down to a table full of food.

These signs would be followed (in no particular order) by the accession of Masih ad-Dajjal, the Anti-Christ, in the Middle East in his evil quest to turn Mankind against the Second Coming of Jesus Christ and the appearance of the Mahdi (both of whom will attempt to restore the masses to the righteousness of Islam), the destruction of the Ka'aba in Mecca with the demolishment of its sacred black stone and the looting of its precious treasures by Unbelievers, the emergence of Gog and Magog causing fiery destruction to all the major cities across the globe, the rising of the sun in the west, the taking of the souls of the True Believers by the restless wind...

On *Qiyamah*, or the Day of Judgement, it is written that every person, Muslim and non-Muslim alike, will be resurrected by Allah and held accountable for their actions on earth in their own tailor-made Book of Deeds in which every small and great detail of their existence is supposedly recorded. Their lifetime of good deeds will be placed on their right hand and every bad deed on their left hand, like measuring scales. If their good deeds outweigh their bad deeds, then they will ascend to the graceful heights of *Jannah* (Paradise), and if the reverse is true, they will descend to the fiery torments of *Jahannam* (Hell). To secure Heaven, every Muslim will be assessed on the degree of their observance of the Five Pillars of Islam: basic creed of belief in Allah and His Messenger, prayer five times daily, fasting during the month of Ramadan, almsgiving and holy pilgrimage to Mecca (*Hajj*). Whoever fully accepted Allah as their Lord, Islam as their Religion and Muhammad as their Apostle was ultimately entitled to enter Paradise. All non-Muslims were destined for Hell.

Hassan walked with purposeful strides through the noisy, sunshiny streets, watching the people go about their daily business, each person unaware that today promised to be a special day for all, in particular the *Kuf'r* (Unbeliever) whether they be Jew or Christian.

O you who believe! Do not take the Jews and Christians for friends; they are friends of each other; and whoever amongst you takes them as a friend, then surely he is one of them (Sura 5:51), since Evil is the handiwork of rabbis and priests (5:63) and all Christians and Jews will surely suffer a painful doom (5:73), burn in the Fire (5:72). Let not the Believers take for friends or helpers Unbelievers rather than Believers: if any do that, in nothing will there be help from Allah: except by way of precaution, that ye may Guard yourselves from them (3:28), meaning Muslims were allowed to feign friendship with Unbelievers only if it was of benefit, but should never accept friendship inwardly.

Hassan made his way towards Palace Green and eventually arrived at his destination: the Israeli Embassy. He hoped Mr. Abel Kaplan, the Israeli Ambassador to the UK, would be within the walls of this elegant building to accept Hassan's urgent communiqué.

He crossed the threshold and entered the lobby. He joined a short queue of people who patiently proceeded in single file towards the tall Metor detector where a stocky security officer stood guard, making sure no-one brought in any contraband items, a straightforward precautionary measure. Every so often the metal detector would beep and the visitors would need to expose anything metallic on their person — coins, keys, fountain pens, etc. — before being directed to the reception desk on the other side of the lobby to go about their appointments.

Soon it was Hassan's turn to walk through the metal detector. As he stepped through the rectangular gantry, the system beeped.

The security guard, whose name-tag read LEVINE, requested as matter of routine: "Can you empty your pockets, please?"

"Is Mr. Abel Kaplan in his office at this present moment?" inquired Hassan.

"I did see him arrive, sir..."

"Good," said Hassan, satisfied. "I need to pass on an important message of peace."

"Are you unwell, sir?" Levine asked unexpectedly, noticing the exhaustion in those eyes, the heavy perspiration on the brow and how the man's skin appeared to be a funny shade of green. *As though the man's slowly dying from inside*, Levine thought curiously. It was just a thought, a gut feeling.

"What? ... *No!*" Hassan snapped back. "Like I was saying —"

"Sir, then, could I see what's in your pockets?" Levine repeated.

"I'm afraid I can't allow you to do that," Hassan told him calmly. "I'm still liable to set off your sensors..."

Levine, a normally suspicious person by nature, made more so by this sweaty, sickly-looking Arab wearing a long black coat out of keeping with the hot weather outdoors, grabbed Hassan's arm. "Then, I must insist you leave."

"Unhand me, you Infidel!" Hassan yelled, managing to shake off the grip. He ripped open his coat, buttons popping in all directions, to reveal an incendiary device strapped to his chest. He whipped out a small cylindrical gadget from his pocket. *"Back the fuck away!"* he roared, circling the floor like a cornered animal, gripping the activator in his right hand, his thumb poised over the red button.

The people in the lobby panicked. Some gasped, others screamed. One woman fainted. Most were simply rooted to the spot, genuinely frightened, silently praying for their lives. No-one dared approach this Jihadist, this real-life suicide bomber.

Levine the security officer stared at the bomb speechless, a stunned, idiotic expression frozen on his face. Working in security he knew a little something about bombs, and this was no ordinary bomb he could tell. The contraption appeared more hi-tech than what he remembered on those TV documentaries. The intricate machinery, the delicate wiring, the metal casing hiding the actual explosive... *Fuck, the crazy Arab was wearing some sort of complex nuclear device!* The radiation alone must already be killing this loon. Not that it mattered to this madman, Levine was sure. He could see no reason in those wild, fanatical eyes.

Hassan took no further notice of the security guard who seemed to be having some sort of spaz attack.

Jihad meant 'to strive for a particular cause', a course of action prescribed by Allah Himself. *O Messenger, rouse the Believers to the fight. If there are twenty amongst you, patient and persevering, they will vanquish two hundred: if a hundred, they will vanquish a thousand of the Unbelievers: for these are a people without understanding (8:65). Let those fight in the cause of Allah Who sells the life of this world for the Hereafter. To him who fighteth in the cause of Allah – whether he is slain or victorious – soon shall We give him a reward of great value (4:74).*

Hassan was definite that one of the staff must have tripped the silent alarm by now and sharp-shooters from the Met would shortly appear on the scene to bring him down, instead of even attempting to negotiate with him. Not that Hassan – on earth for the last time – would ever be open to any form of negotiation or surrender. "My devotion lies with Allah and his Holy Messenger and the 1.6 billion Followers of Islam in the world today!" he boomed his mad-eyed pronouncement. "Blood stains the hands of your fascist Jewish leaders! I vow to avenge all my Palestinian brothers and sisters whose indiscriminate slaughter your evil Heads of State have ordered for more than half-a-century! I convey a message from Allah proclaiming that the Righteous shall prosper and the Wicked shall perish!"

Recruited from University and radicalized very quickly, he and his Muslim brothers had been plotting the downfall of the Unbelievers for several years while carrying on their daily lives as usual, even drinking and fucking white bitches (just for show, of course, a necessity in the name of Allah, while considering himself more important than any active practising Muslim), the bumbling British government completely clueless of his clever deception. His Muslim brothers had broken into Sellafield and stolen a good stockpile of plutonium. He had considered doing a Goldfinger and sneaking a nuclear weapon into the Bank of England and irradiating its entire monetary supply and gold reserves. But smarter heads had prevailed, suggesting a different, more attainable target. Hassan had been silently biding his time, waiting patiently for the order to strike. The so-called mental health experts might want to commit him to the nuthouse, citing 'Folie à Plusieurs', a delusion shared by many, but what the hell did those mind-fuckers know about Islam, or spirituality for that matter, having discarded God for their own misguided version of the truth in the form of cheap, reductionist, atheistic science? What Hassan was about to do, he hoped, would be regarded as a pivotal moment in history, a call to arms in Allah's cause, the necessary catalyst enabling every practising Muslim to rise up and strike terror into the hearts and minds of the Unbelievers. For Allah is All-Knowledgeable, All-Wise, Most Merciful and Compassionate and Oft-Forgiving, and would reward their martyrdom, if slain in battle, [Faith, blind and enduring and pure.] with a jubilant bounty.

This was going to be unforgettable, sublime, epic.

Not even Serafine Gerber, the woman he had been living with for the past year, would be able to change his mind even if she could. She was in no position to now, anyway, since she had learned at her own expense that beneath his outward civilized veneer lurked the soul of a mercenary.

As with most Muslim males, his carnal desires had come before hers.

[Consider 1001 Arabian Nights or the sexual symbolism of the domes and minarets.]

Believing himself to be a better lover than most white fucks, Hassan had taken great pleasure in milking, capitalizing on her affections while degrading her at the same time—she had never liked going down on him—but she was in love with him and she had thought he loved her. Except the man who loved her existed only in her head. After he'd strangled her in the shower this morning, into her breasts Hassan had carved: KIKE WHORE SUCKS COCK.

A fitting end, he supposed, *to a worthless Jewish cunt.*

Besides, beautiful virgins awaited him in Paradise for his endless sexual gratification—*In them will be Maidens, chaste, restraining their glances, whom no man nor Djinn before them has touched (55:56). We have created their companions of special creation. And made them virgin, pure and undefiled... Beloved by nature... For the Companions of the Right Hand (56:35-38). Verily for the Righteous there will be fulfilment of the heart's desire; Gardens enclosed, and grapevines, and voluptuous women of equal age (78:31-33).*

Great shall be my reward in Paradise.

Like the clandestine Hassassins from centuries ago who binged on hashish before conducting their assassinations and the Thuggees' sacrificial offerings to *Kali Ma* (the 'Black Mother', otherwise known as Fatima, the very same Prophet's daughter), and with *Mass Destruction* by Faithless blasting into his ear from his iPod, Hassan the One-Man Doomsday Machine consciously and triumphantly decided it was time to complete the mission he was born for, make this quick and merciful for everyone concerned, as his thumb hovered a mere gnat's hair over the red button of the hand-held detonation device...

"Allahu Akbar!"

A police marksman's bullet suddenly pierced his brain, wherein that single split second, Hassan endeavoured with a determined, last-gasp mortal effort to press down on the activating mechanism...

As the nuclear bomb obliterates the Israeli Embassy and everyone and everything within a one-mile radius, sending a spectacular mushroom cloud blossoming high up over central London, poisoning the sky with atomic fall-out, the well-calculated suicide attack sets off an apocalyptic chain of world events in the days that follow. Israel retaliates by firing its arsenal of nuclear missiles at Iran, who send out crack troops to invade the Jewish homeland, turning the once-great sacred city of Jerusalem into a ground zero combat zone. Pakistan and India enter into a much-belated nuclear conflict, annihilating each other in the process. The West responds by carpet-bombing the Middle Eastern Arab states. Riots, led by prominent Muslim clerics, erupt all over the civilized world, depleting the resources of the police and military as chaos and anarchy reign and government breaks down.

The Last Hour will not come until the Christian hordes land in Dabiq, Northern Syria. An army consisting of the greatest Muslim warriors will travel from Medina to conquer these Roman Crusaders from Constantinople, and the true nature of the Islamic State caliph shall be revealed, not as the Mahdi but the Masih ad-Dajjal (the Anti-Christ), overseeing the burning-to-the-ground of the Ka'aba, followed by the descent of Jesus who will raise his sword against the Anti-Christ. Eschatological prediction dictates the cold wind shall sweep up all the righteous souls in a Rapture-style taking, leaving behind the wicked on earth to suffer the dark times ahead.

And, once represented as Guglana the lunar deity in the pre-Islamic, Sumerian Epic of Gilgamesh, *Gog and Magog once trapped within their unearthly prison for a near-eternity, finally rupture and breach the crumbling, once-impassable Wall of Zulqarnian and, Allah willing, in keeping with prophecy, cross over into reality itself, tearing cities asunder, plunging the world of Man in flames and slaughtering 999 out of every 1000 people as their presence on earth marks the Beginning of the End and the countdown to the Day of Reckoning (Qiyamat), begins when every human being will be killed, resurrected and judged.*

June 2011-July 2011

Contretemps, Paris

"Paris is like a whore. From a distance she seems ravishing, you can't wait until you have her in your arms. And five minutes later you feel empty, disgusted with yourself. You feel tricked."

Tropic of Cancer (1934)
Henry Miller

We arrived at Charles de Gaulle airport a good seven hours before we were due to fly back to London Heathrow. Dumping our luggage at our feet, we seated ourselves in a strategic position at Terminal 2A. Strategic, because we were directly opposite the toilets just in case we needed a comfort break, with a McD's located diagonally from us if we ever got peckish. Our flight was scheduled to depart at nine-twenty local evening time and we could collect our boarding pass an hour before flying.

"How're you feeling?" I, Dean Hayes, asked my girlfriend, Hermione Singer.

"Surviving," she replied, quietly, next to me.

"This could turn out to be the best part of our holiday," I ventured.

"It wouldn't surprise me, Dean," she remarked wearily. "I think I've lost the will to live."

"I don't blame you…"

"Maybe…" she began absently, but failed to complete the thought. I didn't press her. She, like me, had been through a lot. Morale was low. Despondency had long since set in.

We bided our time at this pit-stop. As I watched the comings-and-goings on the concourse, Hermione fitted the buds from her iPod into her ears and listened to her music, absorbed, detached from all subsequent conversation.

There was a Jamaican man just a few seats to our right, sporting impressive dreadlocks and reading a holiday magazine. On our left sat a multicultural middle-aged couple chattering away animatedly in French. The father was a balding white man, his wife darker-skinned, possibly Moroccan. Their son, of mixed heritage and in his early teens, was occupied with his Nintendo DS.

Around us, people went about their daily lives. Businessmen toting briefcases. College/university students, sounding Scandinavian, swapping anecdotes and laughing, discussing where they'd been or perhaps the adventure they were about to embark upon. Teachers leading a group of excited French schoolchildren towards the shuttle-bus service to Euro Disney. Whole families, whether American, Australasian or African, caught in the tourist trap. Dashing pilots, gorgeous air hostesses and attractive stewards, wearing the uniforms of their respective airlines. A twentysomething black girl with broad hips and an immense behind served as domestic, periodically checking the toilets.

Every so often, a gendarme clutching a machine-gun would walk by, obviously part of airport security, and, for some, probably an unnerving sight. I wondered what would happen if one of them went berserk and opened fire...

Checking my watch, I learned it had just gone three. I left Hermione beside me to while away the hours with her music. Tiredness creeping over me, I closed my eyes and reflected...

Don't be fooled by what you think you see...

Yes, we had got to the airport seven hours before our return flight. Now you may wonder why we could not have spent our remaining free time catching a few more Parisian sights and why we would be so keen to get back to Chertsford, England, considering we were in Gay Paree, historically a haven for writers and artists, and a place of fine dining and magnificent architecture, the so-called City of Lights and Lovers, but unfortunately I can only say our weekend away had turned out to be something of a catastrophe.

In fact it was the worst holiday I had ever been on. Hermione would probably agree in her own right.

I remember some of our previous, more recent, breaks together. I remember being sketchy in Amsterdam in February, probably on account of all the hash boxes we visited. I remember the incredibly maddening beauty of Florence in May, the history of Renaissance art encapsulated in one unique city. But Paris, our first time there together, by contrast, was a complete wash-out.

I was a published author, of flash fiction, and Hermione a struggling artist, specializing in sunflowers. Both of us were still relatively unknown, each trying to get our foot in the door, get noticed by the critics, but at least we were passionate about our separate crafts. The steady stream of minor works we sold put food on the table and paid the rent and left enough to go places. We thought we needed a weekend break. Why not visit Paris?

I suppose I could put it down to poor planning and a degree of naivety on our parts. We'd got up at five on the Friday morning in order to pack as much sight-seeing stuff as we could on that day. We should have taken the Eurostar to the Gare du Nord, but believing that flying would be a quicker, more convenient way of travelling, we jetted off from Heathrow. Not only was there a lot of stomach-turning turbulence, but halfway across the English Channel, the BA flight seemed suddenly, but briefly, to lurch violently and drop from the sky as though its engines had failed. I can tell it didn't go down well with us or the other passengers, half of whom started screaming and panicking. Nevertheless we managed to arrive safely at Charles de Gaulle, eventually, with half the passengers vowing never to fly again.

We got ripped off from the word 'go'. The cab driver, who took us from the airport to our hotel, swindled us, charging us a gob-smacking eighty-five euros when the journey should have cost no more than fifty. My fault, I suppose. I should have realized he was a crook and a cheat from the moment we sat in his cab, preying on the gullible, and was, in all likelihood, unlicensed. Not the absolute worst start to a holiday in another country, I suppose. When my best friend, Nate, arrived in Mumbai, he lost all his luggage and got his wallet pickpocketed before he'd even set foot outside the airport; the British Embassy paid for his flight back to the UK the same day.

The HOTEL MIDI turned out to be just south of the river in a relatively downmarket part of Paris. Checking in, we were charged four hundred euros for our two nights in the hotel, which was run by greedy, corner-cutting Arabs, and the place was in quite a drab, dilapidated state. The service was abysmal, the demeanour of the greasy-looking concierge generally rude and ill-disposed. However, his eyes lit up like diamonds when we paid for our room. The only reason I can think of why we didn't just check into another, more respectable hotel was that we'd booked this place online, a fortnight in advance and our reservations were non-refundable. Again, poor forward-planning.

I really should have bothered learning a little French or hired a personal translator because the first café we visited, the grouchy owner spoke no English, and I decided to ask him (rather inappropriately, mind) if he knew of any other cafés that spoke English. Insulted, he asked us to leave in a tirade of vulgar French. Radio 4 listeners once voted French the most poetic language in the world, with Urdu running a close second, and as Hermione and I vacated the place on account of my unintentional *faux pas*, I had to admit that even those splenetic obscenities hurled in our general direction possessed a certain *je ne sais quoi*. When we did find a café that spoke a modicum of English, I couldn't read the menu and hungrily but unknowingly tucked into a baguette filled with tomatoes, green pesto and goat's cheese. Allergic to goat's cheese, I promptly suffered an anaphylactic reaction, with my tongue swelling up, my airways narrowing and my breathing becoming increasingly laboured. If Hermione hadn't acted instantly and injected me with the Epipen I normally carry, I would have certainly passed out. I left the café worse for wear, the weary expression on the proprietor's face suggesting he was fed up of serving troublemaking English tourists.

I am sure you can see that already things weren't exactly going according to plan. I can assure you it gets worse.

Hermione suggested we climb the Eiffel Tower, which seemed like a good idea as any since it was, like the Arc de Triomphe or Place de la Concorde, one of the standard touristy things to do. Apparently there was a nice, classy restaurant up there. The Eiffel Tower turned out to be only half-an-hour's walk from the hotel. It should have been a pleasant stroll down the Boulevards of Paris, but it soon started to drizzle. In fact it rained throughout our entire stay in Paris, and this in the middle of July, while New York, of all places, was experiencing an astonishing forty-degrees-Celsius heatwave. How messed-up is that?

When we did get to the Eiffel Tower, we witnessed a mile-long queue of rain-soaked tourists utterly focused on venturing up the damned thing. We immediately abandoned the notion of joining this impatient mob, instead getting accosted by a throng of street merchants, who demanded we buy their over-priced miniature replicas of this famous landmark, cheap, mass-produced trinkets posing as souvenirs. We bought a two-euro key-ring of the Eiffel Tower from a particularly fanatical pedlar before retreating hurriedly down the steps to the cobblestoned banks of the River Seine. I could have serenaded my sweetheart romantically along these very banks or hopped onto one of the waiting tour boats and taken a trip down the river, but with the sky a murky grey and daylight fading fast, we planted ourselves on a bench, umbrella-less, sheltered beneath a flourishing maple, until the rain let up.

With the rain easing off, we retraced our steps back to the hotel, witnessing an aspect of Parisian society that existed just beneath the surface. Not the moveable feast immortalized by Ernest Hemingway, or the intelligence and good manners of a nation that had attracted F. Scott Fitzgerald, or the feeling of paradise a Parisian spring brings that humbled Henry Miller's ambivalence, or even the comparison of Paris to a vast University of Art, Literature and Music, a seminar, a postgraduate course in Everything, according to James Thurber. Paris might have deeply impressed the likes of Charles Dickens and James Joyce, and Mark Twain (maybe-not-so-much since he was more discerning), but in today's age of EU economic bail-outs and over-sexed prats like Sarkozy and Berlusconi constantly courting controversy while in power, I saw only eight-year-old Senegalese kids pushing crack cocaine, skanky, Albanian teenage girls angling for business, and a filthy homeless man, extraordinarily carrying a dog-eared copy of Jean Cocteau under his arm, rooting through the wheelie-bins and tucking into the decaying, half-eaten remains of a French baguette.

We dined out at a nearby McD's. Can you freakin' believe it? All this way to Paris and Hermione insists she's famished and we eat in McD's—just about summed up our first day and set the bar for the rest of the weekend. The image of the malodorous hobo had put paid to my appetite and I barely touched my Big Mac and fries.

That night at the hotel, we made love. Or more precisely went through the motions of lovemaking: the missionary position, quick and passionless, love without soul. Unimaginative, ironically so, considering our individual careers relied heavily on imagination.

I tried to sleep against the hunger and the heat and the humidity and the noise of honking traffic and screeching sirens and the brawling, drunken voices coming from outside the local bar. The hullabaloo died down around four in the morning and started up again an hour later, completely ruining my already-broken sleep.

Hermione, such was her temperament, slept like a log while I woke up unrefreshed and cranky. My mood improved a tad after we'd breakfasted on buttered croissants, café au lait and OJ in a traditional local café, but soon slipped back into a downer when Hermione insisted we visit the Musée d'Orsay.

I could not fault her reasoning, however. It would have been nice to have seen the enigmatic-smiling Mona Lisa, but the Louvre would have undoubtedly been a suffocating hive of activity. The Musée d'Orsay, on the other hand, might be slightly more accessible. The problem was Hermione declined the offer of a taxi and insisted we do the journey on foot. And as we walked, the rain resumed its relentless assault.

After a few geographical miscalculations and wrong turns, we eventually stumbled upon the Musée d'Orsay by pure chance. Drenched through and desperate to find dry land, we encountered the unexpected. More queues, more rain. The line crawled at a snail's pace, and together with the falling rain, really stretched my patience. There was yet one more thing we didn't bank on: we had to pay to get in. The National Gallery in London didn't ask for an admittance fee so why, for God's sake, should the Musée d'Orsay? The place had better be worth it! We got in eventually after an hour waiting in line, grateful to be out of the rain. I decided we should make the most of this place, get our money's worth, and hoped Hermione, a talented artist in the process of developing her own portfolio, would illuminate me with a critique on the intricacies and nuances of Monet, Cezanne, Degas, Gaughin and Van Gogh. Unfortunately, due to Hermione's anxiety around crowds, our tour turned into a half-assed effort with Hermione demanding we leave almost the moment we got in; we reached a compromise and just wandered round the galleries, glancing superficially at the works of the Old Masters rather than actually examining them. In fact, the only painting that truly stuck with me from our short spell at the Musée d'Orsay was an oil painting by William-Adolphe Bouguereau, depicting Dante biting an equally-unclothed Virgil on the neck like a vampire – or so I imagined. There was something hellish, strangely compelling and unconsciously homoerotic about this visually-stunning scene.

I retracted my own recommendation of visiting Notre Dame Cathedral, dissuaded by Hermione's mindless insistence we walk there. Notre Dame, as most people know, is famous for the heart-breaking tale of the disfigured bell-ringer in love with a beautiful gypsy girl, and I thought it might prove a suitable romantic venture. However, now, more than just a little disenchanted with the wet, cheerless weather and my general lack of motivation, I hailed a cab and journeyed back to the hotel, Hermione wondering what was wrong with me.

We luncheoned at a reasonably-priced restaurant, and while Hermione tucked ravenously into her chicken chasseur, I found my Barbary duck confit extremely oily, crispy and somewhat sickly – so much for sampling the finest cuisine in the world. Although I was incapable of finishing my meal, I managed a few morsels and had at least something in my stomach. From his expression, the Egyptian owner of the restaurant seemed offended by my lack of appetite and appeared only too glad to see the back of us foreigners.

We decided not to retreat to our cramped hotel room just yet since it would only deepen Hermione's sense of claustrophobia. We spotted a small park opposite where we were staying and opted to spend the afternoon there. It may not exactly be the Tuileries Garden, but it still gave us an opportunity to commune with nature. The rain had stopped and the summer sun had come out tentatively. Seated on a park bench, we fed the pigeons small chunks of crusty bread. We watched the birds flock around us, competing for the scraps – it was a gratifying sight and even managed to quell the taste of duck which kept repeating on me. For the first time since arriving in Paris I had gained some respite from the dreadfulness of our holiday. For the first time I was at peace.

That was until the Big, Fat Gay came mincing along the path towards us...

As the pigeons rested indolently on the grass, basking in the warm sunshine, we were approached by a Frenchman, shaven-head and bordering on the obese and dressed in a flamboyant, flowery shirt and pink chinos. I knew he was a flaming queen even before he opened his mouth.

He greeted us in French followed by something I didn't quite comprehend. I asked him whether he spoke English. Indeed he did.

"You touriths?" he asked with a strong lisp. *You tourists?*

"Yes, can we help you?" I said, not content with someone disturbing our peace.

"I thaw you, Monsieur, from far away and thought you looked like a model and would very much like to take you to bed…"

"Excuse me?" I replied, wondering if I'd misheard him.

"I would like to have great thex with you." *Thex = sex*

I couldn't believe my ears. I had never considered myself particularly physically attractive, let alone attractive to the homosexual male. "Look, I'm flattered, but I have a girlfriend if you hadn't noticed," I said, gesturing to Hermione who seemed to be smiling.

But the Big, Fat Gay was persistent: "Forget her. Come with me and I will thow you love."

"Yes, forget me," Hermione remarked, cracking up into laughter, "He really fancies you."

"I'm glad you find the situation highly amusing," I chastised Hermione, feeling betrayed. "Don't encourage him!" I addressed our interloper. "I'm sorry, but I must ask you to go away."

"We could do thome real botty-love together. I could thpank you, lick you out, thuck you off, and you could cum all over my mouth."

This was getting way too explicit for comfort. It occurred to me that the Big, Fat Gay must be on day release from a local psychiatric ward to be propositioning strangers in this indecent manner. I was growing mad at his inappropriate sexual advances in a different kind of way. "Listen, I'm not gay! Now leave before I call the police!"

But the Big, Fat Gay wasn't leaving. He leaned forward, whispering amorously into my ear and gently stroking my thigh, "There'th no need to play hard to get." I caught the overpowering whiff of Chanel No. 5.

My personal space invaded, my masculinity threatened, I pushed his chubby fingers away and, standing up abruptly, fists clenched, delivered a response that proved far from subtle and lacked any respect for the Napoleonic code straight into his admiring, perfume-scented face. "Will you please kindly *fuck* off?"

The message finally got through. With a look of hurt and rejection, the Big, Fat Gay murmured: "*Pardon moi, mon ami*, if I dithgusth you. I did not mean to disthurb you," and with his tail between his legs, grossly humiliated, he waddled off.

"You didn't have to be rude to him!" Hermione admonished, flushing with shame and embarrassment, largely at the angry frowns and stares from the other park-goers. "He might be unwell or one of those colourful, eccentric characters that frequent this park."

Before I could give her a piece of my mind, the heavens opened up again and rain pelted down in fat droplets.

Screw this! I don't need the aggro! I thought, sick and tired. I got up and walked away, Hermione following close behind me, demanding to know what the matter was.

I bought some Philip Morris cigarettes from a tobacconist [My last pack, *I promised Hermione.*] [It's always your last pack, *she remarked.*] and sat myself down in a wine bar, looking out of the window at the people in the street. The rain descended from the prematurely subfusc sky in brief showery bursts. I smoked and drank one glass of red wine after another. I began to understand what Hemingway meant when he spoke about the moveable feast. It was a completely different culture and lifestyle here, laid-back and languid. Even in this undesirable part of town, perfectly-groomed middle-aged men, cheating on their wives, went out with their young mistresses, who seemed perfectly-done-up and olive-skinned. The reverse, too, was true. I can't remember who philosophized that London was like a teenager, a street urchin, unchanged since the time of Dickens, whereas Paris reminded them of a man in his twenties in love with an older woman. I was suddenly wishing I was going out with one of these French birds, age no impediment. I could not imagine what the wealthy, high-class *Parisiennes* shopping in Champs-Élysées must look like, smell like, *feel like, what they must fuck like.* And all this time Hermione stayed with me. She kept harping in my ear, moaning about my smoking and drinking, but I ignored her, hoping she would return to the hotel and leave me in peace. However, she didn't leave my side, kept watch over me like some neurotic guardian.

While darkness fell, and the street-lamps came on, I knocked back the cheap plonk as if it was nothing more than mineral water. I grew increasingly intoxicated as the evening progressed, becoming less aware of my surroundings, my head swimming, my thoughts muddying up. I remember the succession of songs issuing from the speaker-system — Edith Piaf, Serge Gainsbourg, Les Negresses Vertes — until I lost track beyond the Beautiful South's cover of *Dream a Little Dream of Me*. It called to mind Victor Hugo: *Music is the vapours of art*. I think at one point I suggested we go to a club, arguing that it was a Saturday night, and vaguely remember Hermione gesticulating in sheer exasperation. I do not remember much else after that.

What happened that night I recalled not, except perhaps some words that seemed to bounce around the confines of my mind: *How can anyone ever trample a delicate crystal rose?*

With a snort I jerked awake. I checked my watch. Quarter-to-four in the afternoon. I glanced around me. I was still at the airport. I had caught myself napping, and presently woken up feeling more exhausted than ever. Not surprising considering the poor quality of sleep, or lack of, I had endured over the weekend period. At least this evening I'd be returning home and sleeping on par with Rip Van Winkle.

I turned to talk to Hermione, but she wasn't in her seat. Her bags were still there, however.

I wondered if Hermione might be taking a comfort break, and waited for her to come out from the little ladies' room opposite.

I had suggested we spend a peaceful Sunday afternoon at the ever-popular Père Lachais cemetery, where among the crows and tombs and floral wreaths we might raise the ghosts of Chopin, Bernhardt, Proust, Oscar Wilde and Jim Morrison before driving back to the airport, but Hermione declined the invitation without a second thought.

We could have taken in an afternoon matinée at the local cinema, *Les Diaboliques*, perhaps to while away the hours, a cult film which inspired Robert Bloch to pen *Psycho*, the source material for the subsequent Hitchcock adaptation, but again the idea was rejected off-hand. Nor did

Hermione seem interested in catching the latest Woody Allen flick, *Midnight in Paris*. The renowned French director, Jean-Jacques Annaud, once claimed that Hollywood shot movies for the benefit of audiences around the world whereas the French made films aimed solely at Paris.

Ironically, waiting to fly back from Charles de Gaulle airport promised to be the best part of our stay in Paris. We could maybe swing by Duty Free in Heathrow and purchase a bottle of Grey Goose.

The Afro-Caribbean man to my right was currently browsing through yesterday's edition of the *Le Monde* newspaper, engrossed. On my other side, the middle-aged couple with the mixed-race teenager continued to chat. The turnover of people along the concourse, both passengers and flight attendants, of all ages and different nationalities, was high.

I waited patiently for a good twenty minutes, but Hermione did not emerge from the rest-room. With a sense of foreboding, I decided I should go forth and investigate. Picking up the luggage, I wandered into the LADIES, unannounced, and checked the stalls. All were vacant. I spoke to the black, wide-hipped female toilet attendant but she spoke no English. I showed her the photograph of my girlfriend I carry in my wallet, but she didn't seem to recognize her.

The disquietude was swelling into a free-floating anxiety. Where had Hermione disappeared to?

Maybe she'd gone to get some food. That thought relaxed me a little and I went to check the diagonally-located McD's. No Hermione. I checked the café/restaurant next door. Again, no trace of her. Nothing.

And all the while, those words kept repeating in my head: *How can anyone ever trample a delicate crystal rose?*

The anxiety resurged in me with a vengeance. Heart lurching, I felt on the verge of panicking. I went back to the seat where we'd been sitting, hoping Hermione had returned, but to no avail. Hermione was nowhere to be seen.

I approached the Jamaican man reading the newspaper, but he just shrugged his shoulders, unable to assist. The mixed-race family were equally unhelpful, and seemed somewhat puzzled by my question. As far as the people in my vicinity were concerned, no-one had seen Hermione.

As if she'd never been there at all.

Then, an idea occurred. I could call her! Ring her on her mobile! I accessed her number on my mobile phone and rang her. Wherever she might have vanished to, she would surely answer. I heard the muffled sound of a ringing mobile, and it struck me that it was coming from her handbag. I opened the handbag, rummaged around and pulled out her mobile. I cut the connection, slipped my mobile back into my jacket pocket, alarmed. This looked bad. Hermione had never been out of easy reach of her mobile phone. Then why should she leave her phone and the rest of her belongings behind?

My imagination began to run riot. I remembered that Polanski film, Harrison Ford running around Paris in a desperate hunt for his kidnapped wife. Hermione's disappearance might have a perfectly innocent explanation, but I was envisaging the worst, growing more frantic, fearing for her safety.

Still lugging our bags, I stopped a passing police officer, a husky fellow, whose name-tag informed me he was called Martin Leclerc and who carried a real gun in his belt. *"Parlez vous anglais?"* I asked for the hundredth time since coming to Paris.

"Oui, Monsieur," Officer Leclerc replied, looking me once over, sizing me up: my black clothes despite the humid weather, my agitated state, the sweaty panic awash on my face. "What seems to be the problem?"

"My girlfriend... she's gone missing," I said, grappling with the enormity of my fears. I gave him a brief account.

"I see. I think I should take you to Airport Security. They might be able to assist you."

I thanked him profusely. He led me down the concourse in silence towards another sector of the airport, the short journey made oddly unsettling by the adrenaline pumping through my system. I tell a lie — it wasn't entirely in silence since he radioed-in a colleague and I managed to comprehend a fragment of the conversation, along the essence of *'cherchez la femme'*. Strange how those words uttered by every hot-blooded Frenchman, second only to the amorous *'Je t'aime'*, had taken on a whole new sinister meaning.

We arrived at the Airport Security block, a corridor of sterile, air-conditioned offices discreetly located in this sprawling terminal, rarely glimpsed by the average airline passenger unless in trouble.

Officer Leclerc took me directly to DIRECTEUR DES OPÉRATIONS, a large, sanitized, minimally-designed office. The Director sat behind his big rectangular desk in easy access to his computer equipment and an array of filing cabinets. There were already two other people gathered in the room, seated strategically around the table. All eyes turned in my direction, curious, unprejudiced. As introductions and handshakes were exchanged, I dropped my baggage in front of me and grabbed a chair. I declined the offer of coffee. The name of the Director of Operations was Emile Duprey and his Chief of Security, Sylvestre Reinier. The third man in the room, the person Officer Leclerc had contacted on the way here, was apparently a seasoned police detective called Gerard Arbogast.

The serious, almost un-Gallic manner in which they were treating my case as a prerogative, expediting my emergency to the highest authority, comforted me a little, gave me hope. Director Duprey promised to resolve this unfortunate situation as sensitively and efficiently as possible.

"How do you know your girlfriend is missing?" inquired Reinier, the Head of Security.

"I only shut my eyes for a few minutes and when I woke up she was gone," I explained, stating a simple fact. "She didn't return."

"Did anyone see her leave?" he followed-on.

"None of the people around us noticed."

Detective Arbogast entered into the dialogue with a searching question. "What do you think might have happened to Mademoiselle Singer?"

I don't claim to be a Professor of Logic, but I had considered various possible scenarios. Had Hermione taken an earlier flight to London? Except there were no earlier flights scheduled to London other than the one we were waiting for. Or had she maybe taken a flight elsewhere? Or could she at this very moment be wandering the streets of Paris, wondering what went wrong with the holiday, between *us*? Might she have met someone else without me knowing it? Yet, through all this speculating, there was no escaping the glaringly-obvious: she had left all her belongings behind, evidence enough to support my worst, dread fear. "I'm worried she might have been kidnapped."

"Let's not jump to conclusions just yet, Monsieur Hayes," cautioned Detective Arbogast, jotting down my response in a notebook. "Let's remain objective, stick to the facts for now." He probed further, continued scribbling. "How would you describe your relationship with Mademoiselle Singer?"

"We've been together for twelve months, and in recent weeks, it hasn't been going great," I disclosed, as truthfully as I could muster. "As far as I'm concerned, this holiday was supposed to be our last ditch attempt to patch things up." I related the disheartening events of the past two days, my frank disappointment, how we'd thought of going back to England within twenty-four hours of arriving here and how the whole thing had turned into an unproductive and unnecessarily expensive mess-of-a-holiday, a waste of time and money. "Bad planning and organization, I guess."

Detective Arbogast apologized for the unpleasantness of my time in Paris. "Did you fight?"

"I don't remember much of last night—I had the common decency to get drunk and introspect—but I know Hermione was upset."

"Do you have any enemies, anyone who might wish you harm?"

"Not really. Hermione and myself have always kept a low profile."

"Thank you for providing us with a preliminary statement," Detective Arbogast said, closing his notebook. "It's a start."

"What can you do?" I asked hopefully.

"We don't normally initiate an investigation unless the person's been missing for at least twenty-four hours," the detective advised me.

"However, we've taken the liberty of notifying the British Consulate," Director Duprey interjected. "A representative is on their way now."

"We could take a look at the security cameras, as a matter of routine," suggested Security Chief Reinier, just then.

"Excellent thinking," concurred Director Duprey. "It might prove a useful exercise."

The central security room, located a few doors down the corridor, past what seemed to be a number of empty interrogation rooms, was a glassine, hi-tech chamber, filled with computer workstations and data processors, as crucial, I suppose, as the Main Control Tower, one wall silently ablaze with a bank of digital security monitors, capturing every aspect of activity at the airport, forming a complete picture of the here-and-now. A pair of security officers, whom Security Chief Reinier introduced as Quintal and Seligny, manned one particular L-shaped station, keeping vigil over the screens, scanning for anything suspicious.

Reinier brought his men up to speed, explaining he was trying to identify a particular segment of CCTV footage. I informed him of our approximate time of arrival at the airport (about half-two) and where we'd been sitting (in a section of the terminal near the McD's outlet, the rest-rooms and the Euro Disney shuttle stop).

Expertly, conscientiously, Quintal (or it might have been Seligny) rewound the security feed on one of the wall-monitors until he pinpointed the exact time and location Hermione and myself had occupied, bringing the digital image to life on a computer screen on the console.

And let it run...

We crowded round the monitor, instantly gripped by the surveillance footage.

Something was already not quite right... a particular detail missing from the bigger picture.

I stared at the stream of footage in mounting bewilderment, utterly stumped, trying to understand what I was witnessing. There was the intermarried couple and their half-caste kid. There was the dreadlocked, Jamaican man, flicking through a magazine. And there was I with all our luggage dumped in front of me.

But there was no sign of Hermione...

There was I appearing to talk to an imaginary person on my left before closing my eyes. In other words, I was talking to no-one in particular.

Reinier speeded up the sequence of video footage a fraction, sharing my surprise. As I'm sure from their expressions did the others in the security operations' room. Nobody spoke.

There was I napping for about half-an-hour... waking up, looking around perturbed, getting up and collecting my bags, commencing my wild goose chase, starting to panic, approaching Officer Leclerc...

"Did someone tamper with the recording, erase my girlfriend?" I demanded to know, presently. But I knew deep inside it was a preposterous accusation.

I had come to the airport alone, and sat alone. *That* was the gospel truth of it.

Then, how could I have [*How can anyone ever willingly crush a delicate crystal rose underfoot?*] convinced myself otherwise? Could I be losing it?

A small part of me half-expected Hermione to make an appearance on the footage, but she remained shockingly absent throughout the given timeframe, refuting instead of corroborating my testimony.

Yet, the mystery had only deepened further, reinforcing my inner turmoil. The reality was I was still clueless as to Hermione's whereabouts.

I was suddenly experiencing a horrible feeling suggesting that Hermione might not have even accompanied me on my trip to Paris when Officer Leclerc entered the security room and communicated something into Detective Arbogast's ear.

A dark, steely look furrowed Arbogast's brow, as he gave a curt nod to Officer Leclerc. Unholstering his automatic, Officer Leclerc grabbed my shoulder roughly and spun me round, frisked, cuffed and apprehended me before I even knew what was happening.

"What is the meaning of this?" I protested, now very confused and frightened.

Arbogast addressed me directly, cross-examining me, judging me, condemning me, no longer my saviour: "If you claim that Mademoiselle Singer was with you at the airport until she vanished as you allege, what I don't understand is why her dead body was found in your hotel room by the maid this morning..."

I must be quick in my confession. On sleepless nights of which there are many, what happened on that last night in Paris plays over and over in my head like a film in slow motion, haunting and taunting me, threatening to destabilize my psyche, drive me insane.

The cataclysmic news Detective Arbogast revealed unleashed the full force of the jarring memories from last night which had eluded me for much of today, deliberately buried by my own mind to protect my sanity. The missing tract of memory came back to me in a rush, unbidden, like a repellent flashback. The blur was gone, the fragmentary pieces fitting together like a jigsaw puzzle. During those moments Arbogast and Leclerc arrested and led me away at gunpoint, I re-lived the unspeakable events of last night in Bright Glorious Technicolor. No-one was stitching me up or framing me for a crime I did not commit. Because what I'd conveniently brushed under the carpet was I'd actually *dunnit*. Dissociation explained my forgetfulness, but presently it all came flooding back to me.

Intelligence is the Wife, Imagination is the Mistress, Memory is the Servant, according to Victor Hugo, and *Conscience is God present in Man*.

Now replete in the details, I wanted to die — or at least throw-up.

How can anyone ever trample a delicate crystal rose?

Well past tipsy I certainly was, supremely plastered in fact. I must have consumed the equivalent to three or four bottles of wine that Saturday evening. Hermione wrapped an arm around my shoulders, curved her other hand under my armpit and hauled me swaying to my feet. The alcohol had severely dulled my coordination — I could hardly walk — and I must give Hermione credit for managing, moaning and complaining, to guide me, staggering and stumbling, back to our hotel room.

I immediately collapsed on the bed, kicking off my shoes, remotely switching on the wall-mounted fourteen-inch TV. The headlines on the BBC World News Channel announced there had been a massacre of nearly one hundred civilians in a Norwegian summer camp by an evil, Right Wing Extremist Cunt, that Amy Winehouse the Daft Cunt had been found dead from a suspected drug overdose in her Camden home, and Rupert Murdoch the Cunt of the Century was due to appear at a special committee hearing over the Phone Hacking Scandal. If the Leveson Inquiry did its job properly, walked the walk and refused to succumb to any backhanders, then father and son should rightfully go to jail since Mr. Murdoch did not make his billions with his old fuddy-duddy act and because the buck involving the unethical practices of his News Corporation stopped with him.

Hermione stood over me, arms akimbo. "I can't believe you got smashed!"

Even though I was far gone, I could tell she was in one of her moods. I could hear the reproach and disgust in her voice. "Had to..." I said, trying to justify my behaviour. Introverts derive their inspiration from within, extroverts from the outside world. We were both introverts. Alcohol was my poison, for Hermione it was hojicha, a type of Japanese tea. "I thought I'd make the most of our last night in Paris, have some fun."

"So it's no fun being with me?" she inferred somehow. "We should have stayed at home."

"No shit, Nancy Drew!"

"And you're ruining what little's left of it," complained Hermione. "I've given you enough latitude this evening so please show me some respect."

"Stop bringing me down," I replied, getting distinctly annoyed. "I want to revel in my exquisite inebriated state."

But Hermione kept on carping, affording me no peace. "This is so irresponsible of you!"

"I'm not hurting anyone…"

"You're hurting me!" she bemoaned, sitting down on the edge of the bed. "We can't live like this! Don't you care about us?"

There is another person in every man, a dark man with a cruel streak, who takes great pride in tormenting those who are unknowingly begging for it. The disinhibiting effect of the wine made the task all the more easier. "I don't think there is an 'us' anymore."

An expression of horror dawned on her face. "What's come over you?"

Either she hadn't heard me properly or she could not come round to believing what I had just uttered. I made it clear this time, gave Hermione no room for misinterpretation, followed by her marching orders. "I've had it to the skin of my teeth with you! I can't do this anymore! I'm calling it a day! I think we should break up!"

Her initial outrage was replaced by a nervous laugh. "You're kidding, right?"

"No pretence, no deceit!" I said, keeping my voice deliberately callous. "I hate the very sight of you! How could you have not suspected something was wrong by the way I've been avoiding you? The only reason you're going out with me is because I'm all you've got! When we get back to England, I'm going to insist you move out of my flat!"

Hermione tried to reason with me, appeal to my sensibilities, rather clumsily though due to the overwhelming panic. "How can you do this to me? I thought you loved me."

"That ship sailed a long time ago," I replied implacably, without any hint of melodrama.

"I was expecting you to propose to me in Paris."

"There's a Greek tragedian you might have heard of called Aeschylus who claimed that marriage was a three-ring circus: *engagement ring, wedding ring and suffer-ring...*" I paused for effect, for fictitious applause, before continuing: "I can't go through with that, risk it. Besides, I got a refund for the engagement ring."

"How could you...? How could anyone ever willingly trample a delicate crystal rose? Why are you being so nasty to me?"

I almost admitted to her I was actually thoroughly enjoying myself torturing her—the sadistic pleasure, the outward relief, the empowering sense of liberation from the shackles of a stale, interminable relationship—but instead I decided to keep it simple, to the point. "You're welcome, my dear."

"Please don't do this to me!" she pleaded, hoping I would change my mind. "We're just another couple having problems—we can sort it out. I can't possibly go back to living with my estranged parents at the age of thirty-one. The only life I want is with you, Dean! I don't know what I'm going to do without you!"

"Frankly, my dear, I don't give a damn! ... You're relatively young, you're okay-looking... you'll manage to find someone who actually gives a shit!"

She was emotional now, distraught, gushing tears, shaking all over.

"Just because it feels as if I've ripped out your heart and presented it to you on a silver platter doesn't mean you've got to fall apart. Consider it a blessing, a chance to turn the page, to move on with your life."

She wasn't listening. Her desolate sobs rose to shrill, hysterical wails. *"Please don't leave me!"*

I should have comforted her, held her tightly in my arms no matter how long it took, let her bawl her eyes out in a safe space until she could sufficiently manage her harrowing grief.

But I was past compassion or caring. *"Will you shut the fuck up?"* I barked pitilessly. *"Show some pride, woman! You know damn well how much crying girls infuriate me!"*

The combination of misery and panic was giving way to glowering anger again.

She began throwing wild punches at me, howling: "I hate you! I *fucking* hate you! How can you do this to me, you *bastard!*"

The ferocity of her blows nearly caused me to tumble off the bed. I pushed her away. *"You have to stop this madness, or I'll make you stop!"*

She came at me again with her fists, swearing and cursing, beating at my arms and chest.

Humans are savages by nature. No matter how much you dress it up, disguise it, the monster lies just below the civilized veneer, waiting for its cue to emerge into the open and wreak havoc. *Why won't the fucking bitch leave me alone?*

My judgement blinded by alcohol and rage, acting purely on impulse, I punched her viciously on the chin, my knuckles connecting sharply with her teeth, the iron-fisted strike breaking her jaw and silencing her shrieks instantly. Blood flew from her mouth, spattering the bedsheets, and in the subdued, ensconced lamp-light those multiple, ruddy spots reminded me of the colour of the wine I had drunk earlier.

I should have stopped there—Hermione looked dazed, didn't appear to know what had hit her—but I was livid, incensed, fired-up, wholly convinced that it was too late for remorse.

I was on a roll. *Locked, cocked and ready to rock…*

I could have battered her face with my fists until I completely pulverized her cheekbones and she lost consciousness… or unhooked one of the tasselled curtain-rope tiebacks, slung it round her neck and tightened it, strangling her… Or perhaps stabbed her in the throat with the Swiss Army knife I always carry, ripping out her windpipe in pulsing freshets of warm blood. Instead I chose the option immediate to me: I grabbed the pillow and smothered her face with it, forcing her down onto the bed, my knees astride her torso as though riding her—or raping her.

Mewling like a cat, panic-stricken, Hermione tried desperately to free her face. Her hands came up, grasping instinctively, but seemed unable to release the suffocating pillow from her face. She tried pushing me off, but I clutched both edges of the pillow and kept it firmly pressed over her face with the full weight of my body. Hermione was now making muffled, choking noises. As she writhed and scrabbled beneath me frantically, I bore down on her as strenuously as I could, allowing the whole process time, sensing her airways collapsing and her life ebbing away. Soon, her moans grew weaker and fainter as did her feeble, impossible effort to breathe. I maintained the pillow securely over her face, and her arms fell to her sides and she went limp, unresponsive.

The euphoric sensation associated with her demise, the rush I felt, quickly passed, and I removed the pillow from her face.

The sweat generated from her excessive struggles had caused the shape of her features to be imprinted on the pillowcase in the same manner as the Turin Shroud purportedly conveyed the face of Jesus.

Hermione had died an undignified, undeserving death from violent asphyxiation with a look of mortal, frenzied terror fixed on her face. Her eyes bugged outwards with a glazed-over appearance and significant haemorrhaging had occurred into the corneas. Her tongue protruded abjectly from her mouth, her lower lip split and bleeding, her jaw bruised and dislocated, tending to the right. Deprived of oxygen, her skin possessed the faint, bluish hue of clinical cyanosis. Her long, blond hair was in unlovely, sweaty clumps and tangles.

I became pensive, lost in a dark, disturbing place for how long I don't know.

I had done it. I had done the deed. I had wilfully stepped on my fragile, hand-blown crystal rose, hearing it crunch underfoot, crushing the remaining minute fragments of broken glass to fine powder... and, worse, relished every moment of it.

Listening to the sounds of Paris that exist in the small hours—the passage of traffic and police sirens, the unnecessary squabbling and mirthful laughter of sheer drunkenness, and, loudest of all, the disintegrating minds of human monsters silently pursuing their single, depraved purpose, committing crimes unconscionable and in cold blood—I lay beside the dead body of my girlfriend, and as if nothing happened, drifted off to sleep.

Here endeth my confession.

I will finish off with a quote from the former French writer, one Octave Mirbeau: *Murder is born of love, and love attains the greatest intensity in murder.*

It isn't that I created a lurid international incident and currently await extradition back to England to stand trial for murder and for possibly perverting the course of justice that haunts me every night I spend in my dingy prison cell, or the fact that I had, at my tether's end, snapped, and unleashing the wrath and violence all of us had the potential for, punished Hermione for a dismal failure of a holiday in Paris.

No, sadly, poignantly, it is the knowledge that I couldn't put a value on my love for her.

BONNE NUIT

August 2011-September 2011

Lonesome October

"It was night in the lonesome October
Of my most immemorial year"

Ulalume (1847)
Edgar Allan Poe

The ambiguous and unendurable month, as Doris Lessing described it, was drawing to a close, and with it another Halloween. A cold, inscrutable mist haunted the dark streets of Harkenville, occasional whoops of drunken mirth breaking the silence of the night. Doorstep after doorstep, jack-o'-lanterns grinned wickedly by the steady candle glow from within. Little witches, vampires and devils had long since turned in, having exchanged their ghoulish costumes for their jammies, their razorless swag of sugary treats for a peaceable call from Mr. Sandman.

And, as the witching hour approached, a group of friends gathered in the pool house round the back of a suburban house, telling tall tales and knocking back bottles of Bud.

"Urban legends refer to presumably real-life incidents which, when we come to verifying their authenticity, prove too good to be true," Richard Tustain was explaining. "The main defining characteristic of these stories is they're told by regular folk, much like you and me, frequently about a friend-of-a-friend, who for whatever reason winds up in a weird, chilling or compromising situation that, by the very nature of the punchline, defies credibility."

The party down at the Brandon residence, earlier in the evening, had rocked, but it had broken up before time, too prematurely for some. Still an hour or so remained for four constant friends to drink and chew the fat. Alas, college tomorrow.

"I don't think I know any urban legends," claimed Wendy Fallows, looking up from the mystery jigsaw she was calmly working on.

"You *must* do," Richard pointed out. "Everybody knows at least a handful without even knowing it. Alligators roaming the sewers of New York, mistaking your Mexican pet rat for a Chihuahua, or finding black widow spiders nesting in your unwashed, lacquered beehive hairdo... Ring any bells?"

"Vaguely..."

"These far-fetched but fascinating tales have become part of our modern folklore, passed down generations by word of mouth, and it takes no great stretch of the imagination to understand their popularity. Every culture in the world has its own unique variation. They may be apocryphal, of doubtful authenticity, but they must have sprung from some grain of truth long ago." He paused, taking a swig of beer. "Come on, Wendy, you're supposed to be my girl! It's not as if I'm hunting for any absolute truths, here! You *know* what melts my butter!"

"All too well..." she remarked in mock-exasperation, returning her focus back to her jigsaw puzzle.

"How about swapping stories?" Richard asked Zach Hauser and his girl, Astrid Lavelle.

"Why not?" Zach replied. "We could make a night of it."

"Okay, let's have some fun," Richard said excitedly.

"I'm expecting a visitor," Zach mentioned, out of passing, "an old friend of mine. You haven't met him yet, but I think you'll like him. He said he'd drop by after midnight. I know it's your father's place, Richie, I hope you don't mind."

"Why should I?" Richard permitted. "The more the merrier."

Ghost stories were out of the running, they decided, since they were mostly for kids and, besides, didn't you need to be around a campfire or something? Horror stories, although perfect Halloween fare, were even fewer in number, as terrifying as a black kitten with a ball of twine, and during bygone years, repeated *ad nauseam*. Conspiracy theories, another intriguing category, for the most part accommodated the nerd. Which left them with urban legends. Not that Richard minded — he intended to graduate as an American folklorist, inspired by his hero of a professor emeritus, Jan Harold Brunvand, some fine Midwestern day. *The man's a legend!* as Richard often declared.

"How we gonna do this?" mentioned Zach. "We don't want to be telling the same stories."

"Good point," Richard considered the problem, suggested, "Why don't I recall the ones which I think are amusing and you —"

" — I pick the ones that are downright creepy?" Zach finished the thought.

"Know any good, creepy urban legends?"

"Better than you think."

"This should be interesting," Richard said, grinning broadly. "I accept your challenge!"

Zach turned to Astrid. He shook her awake as she lay quietly snoring away on the other end of the couch. She moaned sluggishly, bloodshot eyes opening briefly. "You umpire."

"Get bent... !" she murmured absently and closed her eyes again. The single spliff they had been puffing on less than half-an-hour ago seemed to have overpowered her. Or maybe she was just plain beat from Brandon's Halloween do.

"See what I have to put up with?" Zach commented jokingly.

And so, in the best Halloween tradition, they began, facing each other on opposing couches, Richard Tustain on one side with his fair hair, pirate's swash, eye-patch and rapier wit, his equally-blond but clean-living sweetheart, Wendy Fallows, stretched out on the floor beside him in her white fairy costume, assembling a jigsaw, against the might of the two goths with their dark velvet clothes, spiky black hair, mascara and piercings, Zach Hauser eager to wage battle, his sluggish girlfriend, Astrid Lavelle, not so much. The swimming pool cast ripples upon the ceiling amidst an arena of flickering candles, the radio, a low hum in the background, lending its presence to the atmosphere. It promised to be a night dedicated to a turn-taking game of proverbial trick or treating, a contest between the dark elements of the macabre and the gentle absurdities of the funnies. The two, furthest extremes of human emotion: Fear and Laughter. In a piece titled: *Horror vs. Humour.*

Zach, the young aspiring horror writer, was first off the mark, commencing the contest with the macabre, his specialist subject. "I'll kick off with the old classic, *The Hook...*

"This guy and this girl are making out in a parked car, out in the country, late at night, headlights off, radio on. He's getting horny and she's getting all romantic when a newsflash comes in over the radio. A dangerous mental patient has just escaped from the state hospital and was last spotted in their neck of the woods. He is instantly recognizable since he has a hook for a hand. The public are advised not to approach him. Well, you can imagine, the girl gets upset and bursts into tears, fearing for her safety, but the guy, who is getting really hot under the collar, isn't prepared to leave. But she cries and cries and gets more and more worked up, so he finally consents to take her home. Furious because he had major plans for her, and now it seems he must postpone them for another night, he starts the engine, hits the gas and, in a cloud of burning rubber, they drive off. At her house, he clambers out and goes round to the passenger side to open the door for her when he receives the fright of his life. There, caught on the door handle, is a bloody hook!"

"You captured it perfectly," Richard said after a brief pause. "You couldn't do more eloquent than that. I'm *impressed*!"

"Thanks," said Zach, encouraged. "I've got something else along the same lines."

"Go right ahead. Don't let me stop you."

"In this story, a young couple on a date are parked out in the country, again, late at night. When it's time to drive home, the car won't start. So the guy asks the woman to lock the doors and stay put while he goes out for help. He walks off, leaving the woman alone in the car. Some time later, the woman hears rain falling on the car. As more time passes and her boyfriend doesn't return, the woman starts to panic. She decides to turn on the headlights to see if he is coming down the road. What she sees instead, in the full glare of the headlights, is her boyfriend's dead body hanging upside-down from a tree with his throat slit from ear to ear. What she thought was rain was actually his blood drip-drip-dripping onto the car..."

Richard gave a short, sporting round of applause.

"I'm not done yet."

Richard raised his hands in a rueful gesture, urging Zach to continue.

"A woman is driving home late at night when she realizes she needs to stop for gas. She gets to a gas station and the attendant fills up the tank and takes her credit card. A strange look appears on his face. He informs her there is a problem with her card and asks her whether she would be kind enough to step into the office. Puzzled, she follows him in. The moment she's inside, he locks the office door and tells her he must call the police immediately because he's just seen a stranger hiding in the back seat of her car with a *hatchet*."

"Three plays zero," Richard announced. "My turn to get on the score-sheet."

Zach listened.

"This car salesman," Richard began, "is perusing through the classified ads of a newspaper when he comes across something he didn't bargain for: *For Sale, brand-new Porsche 911 Cabriolet $100.* Thinking it's some kind of misprint, he dials the number listed. *No, there's no catch*, the woman answers. All he has to do is fork out $100 and he can drive it away today. So the salesman goes out to her house to take a look. Nice property, landscaped garden, swimming pool, tennis courts. Standing in the driveway is the car in question, and it is better than anything he could possibly have imagined: flash, shiny-red, plush leather interior, multi-CD changer, engine which runs zero to sixty in four-point-two seconds. Perfect, the deal of a lifetime! *The price is still $100?* he asks. *That's right*, the woman replies. His hand is shaking as he's writing the cheque. But he can't leave without asking why she's selling a spanking new car for only $100. She tells him. Ten years ago she married a rich, handsome lawyer. All went well until about a month ago when he suffered a midlife crisis and ran off with his hot, new secretary. He phoned last week, apologizing for his behaviour and requesting a small favour. He was short on cash so could she sell the sports car and send him half the money? She agreed."

Zach smiled, nodded his approval.

"In keeping with the theme of automania, I got one more," Richard said after a moment's breather. "A family sets off on their summer vacation, the car bouncing along with Mom, Dad, the twins and Grandma. Unfortunately, out in the middle of the desert, Grandma pops her clogs. Bewildered and distraught, and literally miles from nowhere, the family decide to wrap Grandma's body in a blanket and lash her to the luggage rack on the roof of the car. They drive off down the highway, frantically in search of the nearest police station to report her death. They get to a police station in due course and pile out of the car, leaving the keys in the ignition and the body still strapped to the roof rack. On returning with the desk sergeant, the car has been stolen. Grandma and their worldly possessions are never heard of or seen again."

Zach cracked open another bottle of beer, surveying Richard thoughtfully. "This guy is driving along the interstate one wet, fall evening when he happens to notice a hitchhiker. Feeling sorry for the poor soul, he pulls over and offers them a ride. The hitcher turns out to be a young woman, curiously attractive in a vague, pale kind of way. She gets in and tells him where she's heading. As she's soaked through, he gives her his coat to wrap herself with and keep her warm. He tries to make conversation with her along the way, but she says very little. So they make the rest of the journey in silence. He soon arrives at the stated destination, only to discover she's vanished from the passenger seat. Worried and frankly a little startled, he goes up to the address given and the door is opened by a frail, elderly lady. He is shown into the hallway and when he inquires whether the woman made it to the house safe and sound, he sees a portrait of the same young woman hanging from the wall. The elderly lady tells him that the young woman was her only daughter, killed in a car accident some thirty years ago at the exact same spot he picked her up from. And he should find the coat he borrowed her draped over her headstone down at the local cemetery."

"Speaking of hitchhiker stories," Richard said, not wishing to be outdone. "This travelling salesman picks up a hitchhiker for company. But this fella's rough, grizzled, intimidating appearance frightens him, so as a means of feeling less uneasy, he picks up a second hitchhiker, this time cleaner-cut and much younger-looking, who gets in the backseat. No sooner is the salesman back on the highway when the young man pulls out a gun and orders him to stop. When the car reaches a standstill on the shoulder, the holdup man gestures for the other two to get out of the car. But as the young car-jacker is motioning toward the door with his gun, the older hitchhiker dives into the backseat and, quick as lightning, disarms him, knocking him out cold with one hard elbow-blow to the jaw. He proceeds to relieve the would-be robber of his wallet and offers to split the takings with the salesman. Noticing the salesman's horrified expression, he adds as way of reassurance, *Just be thankful it's my day off!"*

Zach threw himself back into the breach. "This guy's driving home after dark when he sees an oncoming car with its headlights switched off. Doing the dutiful thing, he flashes his headlights at it. The other car promptly turns round and starts tail-gating and high-beaming. He's forced off the road, straight into a tree. The attackers drive off. It turns out they're frat boys and they have just completed their blood initiation."

"So I guess you've moved on to campus lore," observed Richard.

"Five plays three," Zach reminded him.

"My chance to race on ahead. Familiar with classroom Q-and-A legends? Here's some old chestnuts... In an end-of-term exam, a philosophy professor simply asks, *WHY?* One student's winning answer is *BECAUSE.*

"A student submits a term paper he has blatantly plagiarized from an upperclassman, who himself earned a passing grade. The professor awards it a higher grade with the comment, *I wrote this paper as an undergraduate, and I always felt it deserved a better grade.*

"In another Q-and-A classic, two students attend a party the night before an exam and sleep through the alarm-clock. They then make the excuse they were out of town and suffered a blowout on the way back to campus that prevented them from sitting the exam. Their professor agrees to give them a modified exam but puts the students in separate rooms. The first question, making up a whopping 90% of the test, is *WHICH TYRE?*

"Students are told that, as it is an open-book exam, they may use anything they can carry into the classroom. One particularly ingenious student carries in a 70kg grad student from the same department to write the examination for him.

"The final story is an essay in Chemistry 101: *Is Hell Exothermic (gives off heat) or Endothermic (absorbs heat)?* Most of the students ended up writing proofs of their religious beliefs using Boyle's Law (gas cools off when it expands and heats up when it is compressed), or some variation. However, one student wrote the following: *First, we need to know how the mass of Hell changes with time. So we need to know the rate at* which souls are travelling into Hell and the rate they are leaving. We can safely assume that once a soul enters Hell, it will not depart. Therefore, no souls are leaving Hell. As for how many souls are entering Hell, let's explore the different religions that exist in the world today. Some of these religions state that if you are not a member of their religion, you will go straight to Hell. Since there is more than one religion which gives the same spiel that other religions are false and their followers destined for Hell, and since people do not belong to more than one religion, we can safely project that all souls go to Hell. Looking at birth and death rates, we can expect the number of souls in Hell to increase exponentially. Now, we must look at the rate of change of the volume in Hell because Boyle's Law clearly states that in order for the temperature and pressure in Hell to remain the same, the volume of Hell has to expand as souls are exponentially added. This raises two possibilities: 1. If Hell is expanding at a slower rate than the rate at which souls enter Hell, then the temperature and pressure in Hell will increase until all Hell breaks loose; or 2. Of course, if Hell is expanding at a rate faster than the increase of souls in Hell, then the temperature and pressure will drop until Hell freezes over. So which is it? If we examine the postulate given to me by Alice Stedman during my Freshman year that, "It will be a cold day in Hell before I sleep with you", and take into account the fact that I did not succeed in having sex with her, then #2 cannot be true, and thus I am certain that Hell is exothermic and will not freeze over. The student who formulated this essay received a grade A, hands down!"

"Hellapalooza!" Zach exclaimed. "That's a bunch of corkers—I especially enjoyed the last entry, which should have been mine! You gained five points with that instalment of legends! It means you overtake me." He resolved to make up for lost ground. "There're these two female college roommates. One spends the evening at the pictures while the other stays behind expecting her boyfriend to call any minute. When the movie-goer gets back to her room, she tiptoes in without turning on the light, thinking her roommate's probably in bed with her boyfriend. Sure enough, from across the room comes the sound of rustling bedsheets, heavy breathing and muffled moaning. Tuning into her Walkman, the girl falls asleep. In the morning she wakes up to find her roommate strangled in her bed, sliced open and disembowelled, and scrawled in blood on the wall is the message, AREN'T YOU GLAD YOU DIDN'T TURN ON THE LIGHT?"

Richard: "One resident of an all-male college dorm goes down the hall to take a shower, leaving his two roommates chatting away in the room. Coming back, wearing only a towel around his waist, the freshly-showered man hears voices drifting out of the room and assumes it's his roommates still shooting the moon. He decides to stage a dramatic entrance. Whipping off the towel, kicking open the door and brandishing his penis like a tommy-gun, he yells, *Rat-a-tat-tat, DIE you dirty pig-dogs!* He is greeted by the stunned expressions of his parents, his fiancée and her Austrian parents, who have paid a surprise visit. His future in-laws call off the engagement."

Zach: "A cheerleader passes out during a Sunday game and is rushed straight to hospital. She reluctantly confesses she performed oral sex on all the members of the men's football team which would might explain the staggering amount of undigested semen pumped out of her stomach."

Richard: "Fed up of people stealing his milk from the communal kitchen, this pissed-off college student attaches a note to his milk carton, *LEAVE MY MILK ALONE. I SPAT IN IT.* When he comes back, someone else has written, *SO DID I.*"

Zach: "A male college student consults the campus doctor because of the severe headaches and wooziness he is experiencing first thing in the morning. A physical exam reveals nothing out of the ordinary, except for some rectal bleeding, which the physician puts down to excessive anal sex. Understandably shocked since he has never once practised homosexuality, and soon altogether suspicious, he searches his dorm room and uncovers a bottle of chloroform in his roommate's closet. It transpires his roommate has been sedating him at night and sodomizing him while he lay unconscious."

Richard: "A narcotics officer is conducting a lecture on drug awareness at a high school. His presentation includes passing around a plate bearing two joints so that the students can see for themselves what the genuine article looks and smells like should they encounter a drug-pusher in the street. He also warns the students that he expects there to be *two* marijuana cigarettes on the plate when it gets back. When the plate has gone round the class and comes back to him, resting on it are *three* joints."

Zach chuckled at the hilarious connotations, pressing onwards: "A

Sheriff and his deputy stop to check out a car parked in a cemetery. The deputy reports back to the Sheriff's car with the news that there's a young couple inside, making out. Crooked as a bent post, the Sheriff orders him to blackmail the couple by telling them they'll get their asses hauled into the clink unless the girl submits to sex with both cops. The couple, petrified by the enormity of the threat, accept the terms, and the deputy has his wicked way with her first. The Sheriff is unbuckling his belt and about to get into the car when he recognizes the terrified girl inside is his own teenage daughter."

"That's what I like to hear," Richard commented. "America's Finest upholding the law." Transferring his eye-patch from one peeper to the other, he forged ahead with another apocryphal treat. "A young man buying condoms brags to the pharmacist that he has a blind date with a hot chick that evening and he hopes to get lucky with her. The pharmacist humours him, despite his own conservative views on premarital sex. When the young man calls for the girl later in the day, the door is opened by the pharmacist, who is none too thrilled. The young man discovers to his embarrassment that the pharmacist is the girl's father."

"Know any baby/babysitter stories?" Zach inquired.

"You bet I do," Richard replied, relishing the role of raconteur. "Who doesn't? Regardless of what I know or don't know, the ball's in your court."

Shoehorned into the spotlight, Zach Hauser composed himself. "Right, dude, here goes." He summoned up his best narrative skills. "Picture a scene: a dark, stormy night, children tucked up in bed, the babysitter downstairs watching TV. Suddenly the phone rings. The babysitter runs to answer it. There's a man on the line who asks her disquietingly, *Have you checked on the children?* When she demands he identify himself, he growls, *I'm going to chop up the children, then I'm coming after you!* He hangs up. At first she thinks it's a crank call, but when he rings back half-an-hour later with the same sinister warning, she gets nervous. Deciding she shouldn't take the threat lightly, the babysitter dials the number for the police. They recommend she keep the man occupied when he phones again which ought to give them enough time to trace the call. Following the next menacing phone-call, the police contact her and urge her to get out of the house immediately.

They explain the calls were traced to the upstairs phone extension. As it happens, the caller had already butchered the children and she would have met a similar fate had she stayed in the house.

"In the next story, there's this couple planning to go to the theatre one night but their regular babysitter cancels at the last minute. So they make a few hurried phone-calls and hire a different girl to tend to their baby. They've never met her before, and find her a little strange when she arrives, since she's dressed like a hippie and looks a little spaced-out. Anyhow, they leave their baby in her charge — they're running late as it is — and, I mean, what could possibly go wrong looking after a sleeping baby? After the show is over, the mother calls home to check on things and the babysitter tells her not to worry. *I was feeling a bit peckish, so I basted the turkey and popped it in the oven at three-hundred-and-fifty degrees. Should be ready soon.* The couple have no idea what she's talking about — they certainly didn't buy a turkey — and rush home. Getting to their house, they sprint to the kitchen and peer into the oven. Their worst fears come to life when they realize what's cooking. Tripping-out on LSD, the babysitter has put the baby in the oven and roasted it.

"This other couple are packed and ready, waiting to jet off to some island in the sun. The nanny they employed while they're away on vacation phones up, telling them she's caught up in traffic and running late. They'll surely miss the flight if they don't leave right now, and she assures them she'll be at their house in less than an hour. So the wife straps the baby to the highchair, promises him nanny'll soon be here and kisses him goodbye. Weeks later, on returning home, summer-tanned and rejuvenated, they find their baby still strapped to the highchair, stiff and mummified, having died from starvation. It turns out that the nanny died in a car-crash on the way to the couple's house just as they were setting off for their vacation, the news of which ultimately failed to reach them in their tropical paradise.

"The last of my dead-baby legends concerns a young couple who happen to board a plane carrying a baby wrapped in a blanket. Throughout the flight the girl keeps the baby wrapped up and close to her. On several occasions the stewardess asks whether the baby would like a bottle of warm milk, but the girl declines. Gradually, the stewardess becomes suspicious because the baby doesn't feed or make a sound. She notifies the authorities, who detain the couple at the airport. You guessed it—the baby was dead and, what is more, had been gutted like a fish, stuffed with bags of cocaine and sewn back up."

"Well-played," indicated Richard. "The old dead baby/drug mule legend. That brings the score to—"

"—Thirteen-twelve, advantage Zach," came Astrid unexpectedly.

"I thought you were asleep," mentioned Zach.

"How can I sleep with you two churning out such crazy stories?" uttered Astrid.

"You're deliberately trying to gross us out," Wendy half-commended, half-complained to Zach. "God, those stories got gorier and gorier."

"Thanking you." Zach tipped an imaginary hat.

Astrid smacked her lips. "I'm dry," she croaked, sitting up.

Zach handed her a freshly-opened bottle of beer. "Guaranteed to whet your whistle."

Richard caught Zach checking his watch. "Your friend hasn't shown up yet."

"Don't worry, he'll be here—he said he would," maintained Zach. "I'm looking forward to you guys meeting him."

"That great, huh?" Astrid asked.

"*That* great!" affirmed Zach.

"Like you, crazy as a fox."

"Crazier!"

"Well, Fellow Urbanites," Richard announced, "let's see if I can rightfully restore the balance."

Zach awaited his turn. Astrid took up the position of chairperson and umpire. Wendy idled away her time on her jigsaw with one ear glued to the unfolding tales. The water rippled, the candles flickered and the mist swirled against the pool house window. The radio hummed to the sound of Bobby "Boris" Pickett, whose benign, avuncular manner fondly recalled everybody's earliest childhood memory of Halloween, as customary as pumpkin pie or bobbing for apples.

Richard strove to draw level. "This young Mexican guy travels up to the Tex-Mex border on his motorcycle. Before he is allowed to cross over to the States, the border patrol searches his possessions in case he is trying to smuggle drugs into the country. All he is carrying is a passport and a half-smoked packet of cigarettes. They let him through. That evening, he makes his way back down to the Mexican border on foot. He is searched again, but no contraband is found on his person. This goes on for several weeks: back and forth, back and forth he journeys, day after day, and always via the same route. Seeing a pattern emerge and baffled by these twice daily encounters at the border crossing, the senior guard stops him one day and asks: *Every morning you ride your motorbike across the border and every evening you walk back home. You must be smuggling something, but I can't for the life of me think what it could be.* With a cheeky wink, the Mexican lets him in on his little secret. *If you must know, old gringo, I was smuggling motorbikes!*"

"That one's a bit lame," Astrid said, disinterested.

"Lame but cute," Richard replied.

"Cute but funny," piped Wendy.

"How about rumours surrounding fast food franchises?" Zach continued. "There were those stories about a dead mouse which was supposedly discovered in a bottle of Coke, allegations that McDonald's once made burgers out of worms, and how some disgruntled employees masturbated over the pizzas to get back at the customers…"

"Oh, gross!" Wendy said, grimacing. "Remind me not to eat out again."

"But my favourite," Zach went on, undeterred, "is not about the claims that the Ku Klux Klan owned Church's Fried Chicken and had contaminated the recipe so that it would sterilize the black male population… no, it involves good Ole Colonel Sanders. Ever noticed how Kentucky Fried Chicken is no longer called Kentucky Fried Chicken? Rumour has it they no longer use real chickens, which is why they were forced to abbreviate their name to KFC. They use these genetically-altered chicken substitutes, with no eyes, beak, feet or brain. Nothing but lumps of living flesh. Cheaper to breed, fed by tubes, grow very quickly and produce greater quantities of meat. And the hell of it is *nobody can taste the difference!*"

"Hmmm, typical corporate mentality," Richard mused. "Who knows what lengths these companies go to maximize their profits and keep their shareholders happy? I doubt their CEOs would dare feed their own products to their own kids." He coughed, clearing his throat.

"Change of theme... This housewife is painting the bathroom. She disposes of the paint thinner in the toilet. She forgets to flush. Her husband uses the toilet while smoking a cigarette. He flips the butt into the bowl. The toilet explodes, propelling him through the shower door. EMTs carrying him to the ambulance, hearing how he got hurt, laugh so hard they drop the stretcher."

"Okay," went Zach. "This housewife — maybe it's the same housewife, maybe it's a completely different woman — goes shopping at the local department store. While using the rest-room, she has her purse snatched right from under the stall-door. Upset, she drives home after reporting the theft to store security. All she can do now is hope and pray that the thief was caught on camera. A couple of days later, she receives a phone-call from the store manager informing her that the security officer has found her purse. But her relief is short-lived because when she gets to the store, she is told nobody at the store made the call. Her confusion clears when she gets back home and finds the place burglarized in her absence. The robber had created a diversion and gained entry using the keys from her stolen purse."

"I'll match it and go one better," Richard declared, upping the ante. "Two more about the same hapless housewife.

"Coming back from shopping, she sees the legs of a man, whom she presumes to be her husband sticking out from under the car. Tiptoeing over, she playfully unzips his fly and reaches into his pants while he's busy fixing the car. Getting into the house, the wife finds her husband reading the newspaper at the kitchen table. He explains to her that it was necessary to call in a professional since he was making no clear headway with the repair job himself. Blushing, she gathers up enough courage to tell him the mistake she's just made, and both rush to the aid of the poor mechanic whom they discover has knocked himself out after banging his head against the chassis when his fly was unexpectedly unzipped.

"This married couple has rented costumes to wear at a masked Halloween party. The husband hasn't seen his wife's costume. The moment he is fully dressed in his gorilla costume and ready to go, the wife tells him she's got a terrible headache and can't make it, insisting he go to the party without her. Thinking nothing of it, he does. But the wife has an ulterior motive: she suspects he's cheating on her and wants to catch him in the act. Arriving late at the masquerade, she spies her husband in costume. But he's standing there all on his lonesome and, deciding to set a trap, she flirts with him. They dance and soon wind up having sex in the closet, still without identifying themselves. The wife slips away before the midnight unmasking and is back in bed by the time her husband returns home. Determined to test his honesty and whether he will mention his night of sex with an apparent stranger, she asks him how he enjoyed the party. *Some of us guys didn't feel much like dancing*, he tells her, *so we went upstairs and played poker all night. But the guy whom I loaned my gorilla costume to sure had one hell of a good time!*"

Zach burst out laughing. Richard joined him, loudly and proudly. Astrid remained at the pinnacle of nonchalance.

"She's got to be one stupid housewife," Wendy remarked, marginally offended. "You really know how to make women appear useless, you sexist pigs."

"That's why they call it *slapstick*, babe," Richard reassured her, "Any hoot, they're only stories. No need to get your knickers in a twist."

"Don't call me babe," Wendy warned, part-serious.

"I know, I know..." Richard conceded.

"Men are like toilets: occupied, out of order or full of shit!"

"One Halloween," related Zach, taking his turn, "this girl tells her mother she wants to go dancing at the local disco. Her mother absolutely forbids it, but the girl insists she's going. Just as she's stepping out of the house, her mother warns her that little girls who don't listen to their mothers always meet the Devil. Arriving at the disco, the girl is about to order a drink at the bar when a dark, handsome stranger strides in through the door. He is incredibly good-looking (much like myself) and extremely well-dressed (all in black, like you know who). The stranger asks the girl to dance, despite all the other women fawning over him. She can't refuse, smitten as she is, held captive by his charms. Once on the dance-floor, the girl notices how everyone is walking away and staring at them peculiarly, afraid. When she returns her loving gaze towards her partner, she notices he has horns on his head, cloven hoofs and something poking from the back of his coat—she realizes to her horror it is a tail and cries, *The Devil!* She tries to run away, but the stranger laughs a deep, infernal laugh and grabs her shoulder. When she manages to release herself from his grasp, he exits the disco in a lingering whiff of sulphur and screeches away in his Lamborghini Diablo. To this day, the shoulder where the stranger touched her, the flesh has never healed and still burns, burns, oh it burns..."

Richard went down a different track. "Imagine a big, lavish wedding. During the reception, the best man is getting up to make the toast, but the groom beats him to it, saying he'd like to say something first. He thanks everybody for coming, for their kindness and loyalty, and for all the generous gifts they brought with them to this happy occasion, but adds he will seek to get the marriage annulled. Gasps of shock and disbelief are uttered around the hall, more so from the bride and her family. He asks them to look under their tables to understand why he is making this astonishing decision. Under each table is attached a photo of the bride and best man, naked as sin, engaged in sexual congress in the chapel vestry."

Next up, Zach. "This couple spend their honeymoon at a reasonably-priced hotel in Las Vegas. Years later, flicking through cable, they are horrified to discover a movie of their honeymoon on the X-Rated Channel, evidently filmed with a hidden camera through a two-way mirror. Moral of the story: couples should be aware that the reason some honeymoon resorts rent out penthouse suites at cut-rate prices is outweighed by the considerable profits they make from selling homemade porn films to interested clients."

"These two friends are driving through wet, rural country when their car breaks down. Knocking on the door of a nearby mansion, they are pleasantly surprised to find themselves in the presence of an attractive, middle-aged widow. She welcomes them in and offers to provide them with shelter for the night. They can call Triple-A in the morning when the storm has cleared. Months later, one of the friends receives a mysterious package. Perusing through what amounts to legal documents, he calls up his buddy on the phone. *When we stayed over at that old widow's place that night*, he asks, *you didn't slip away to her bedroom, did you, by any chance?* Not akin to lying, his buddy acknowledges he did. *And did you use my name?* Again, his buddy confesses, but how could he possibly know? *Because she died and left her entire estate to me.*"

Richard's story produced a couple of good-natured guffaws from the gang. However, Zach was poised to attack. "This is a double feature. This businessman decides to go to a bar. He meets a beautiful woman and accepts the invitation to spend the night with her. The next morning he wakes up to find her gone. But she's left behind a message on the bathroom mirror with lipstick, reading, WELCOME TO THE WONDERFUL WORLD OF AIDS.

"Another businessman, attending a conference in a strange city, picks up a beautiful woman he meets in a bar and they check into a seedy motel. The next morning he wakes up with the mother of all hangovers, and there's some serious blood on the bedsheets. The woman, of course, is long gone. Reaching the local hospital, he is found to have a cleanly-stitched incision in his side, where one of his kidneys was removed. He had been duped by an international ring of organ traffickers who lure out-of-town businessmen to motel rooms with the promise of sex, where they are drugged, cut open and their organs harvested for sale on the black market."

"Talking of druggings," said Richard, "any weed left?"

"Fresh out," said Astrid, shaking her head.

"Shame," said Richard, trying not to sound too disappointed. "Still, never mind." He tackled the next comical tale. "One of my most favourite tales is of the man who buys a box of expensive cigars and insures them against fire. After smoking them all, he makes a claim with the insurance company stating they were destroyed *in a series of small fires*. The case goes to court. The presiding judge doesn't mess around and orders the company to pay out and, befitting the bizarre nature of the case, calls for the man to be arrested and charged with arson. The man is subsequently fined $1000 for each count of fire-setting."

He looked expectantly at Zach, who threw up his hands in defeat. "Cleaned out, I'm afraid."

"No more stories? You must have something? Score's level."

"You've bankrupted me."

"Close, but no cigar," Richard remarked, offering his commiserations. "I always took you for a slacker. But you've proved yourself a quick study. And there was me patronizing you! Given what you know, you're gonna make a damn fine horror writer some day." He reflected on the matter at hand and went in for the kill. "This man is driving around one night, lost in thought, after being ditched by his girlfriend. Instead of wallowing in despair, he's feeling horny as hell. He passes a pumpkin patch and the thought that a pumpkin is soft and squishy inside arouses him further. Seeing that there's no-one around, he pulls over to the side of the road, picks out a plump-looking pumpkin, cuts out a suitable hole and goes about satisfying his needs. Absorbed in this lewd act, he fails to notice a police car pull up. The cop walks over, not believing he's actually witnessing a man, pants down, porking away at a vegetable. As polite as can be, he taps the man on the shoulder and asks, *Excuse me, sir, but do you realize you're screwing a pumpkin?* The man, realizing he's been caught red-handed, feigns horror and quips: *A pumpkin? Damn... is it midnight already?*"

Groans of good humour.

"I'm pooped," yawned Astrid. "I've got class tomorrow."

"Game, set and match, I think," Richard trumpeted forth. "There's more where that came from, just a drop in the ocean, but I won't bore you with the details." He marvelled at the sheer volume of urban legends they had covered in one sitting. They had certainly battled it out like two Attorneys-at-Lore. In all honesty, it had pretty much been Even-Stevens most of the way with nothing really separating them. "I declare the games officially over."

Or were they? The curious expression on Zach's face contested otherwise. "I still have one last ace up my sleeve." He did not get a chance to elaborate for Wendy let out a small, startled cry. Richard and Astrid crowded round her. They realized instantly what had unsettled her. The mystery jigsaw she had been working on had formed a picture... a picture — still incomplete — of the exact same pool house they were in, with the four of them accurately depicted in their current poses. A portrait of them in real time. Incomplete, because a couple of pieces still needed to be slotted into place.

Only Zach remained unmoved. "Like I said, time to use my trump card—"

"I thought you said you were bankrupt," said Richard, mesmerized by the impossible, if not fascinating scene in the jigsaw. *Stone the crows, is it really us? How the hell is that possible?*

With trembling fingers, Wendy fitted in the final missing pieces to reveal the jigsaw puzzle in its full glory. The trio stared in horror at the image of the axe-wielding lunatic at the window.

Blood choked their hearts, sweat sheened their skin as cold as October frost.

Suddenly, the noise of a window shattering, the tinkling of glass…

Then came the ominous thump-thump-thump of heavy boots over the background drone of the radio broadcasting *This Ain't the Summer of Love* by the Blue Öyster Cult.

Footsteps drawing nearer, growing gradually louder…

Uncomprehending and open-mouthed, they looked towards Zach for answers.

"Meet Axel Hacker," introduced Zach, looking past them, somewhere beyond their range of vision, "your friendly neighbourhood axeman! HAPPY HELL-O-WE'EN, EVERYONE!"

Still crouched on the floor, Richard, Wendy and Astrid had no time to look up or scream as the fire-axe came swinging down, slicing their heads off in one fell swoop…

August 2006-October 2006

Black Lung

"No matter what Aristotle and the Philosophers say, nothing is equal to tobacco; it's the passion of the well-bred, and he who lives without tobacco lives a life not worth living."

Molière

Harold Hartman enjoyed smoking. Thoroughly loved this particular, solitary activity. He appreciated the pleasurable sensation of light-headedness it entailed, the feeling of quiet contentment and gentle relaxation. Like Oscar Wilde, he considered it a manly occupation, didn't much care for Freud's interpretation of it as being an oral fixation. Harold's father had smoked before him, and his grandfather before him. His great-grandmother had smoked like a chimney and lived to be one-hundred-and-seven, but it wasn't tobacco that killed her. Half-deaf, a little senile and wobbly on her legs, she tumbled down the stairs and broke her neck.

Harold had been smoking since his freshman days at Chertsford University where he had gone to study English Language. He took up the habit not for the purposes of staying slim or a desire to look 'cool' like the Marlon Brandos and James Deans of the world, but because each cigarette allowed him to bring the world to a standstill, letting him drift off into his own dreams and thoughts and imaginings for that brief, calm spell the cigarette burned. He noticed the evil weed greatly complimented the demon drink in the Student Union, although he seldom drank to the point of drunkenness and violent puking. His roommate, Tarquin Hugemot, smoked a lot of pot, but Harold decided to stay square, sticking with his Dunhill bogues since cannabis only made him paranoid. Friends forever, Harold and Tarquin acquired a reputation together: the Smoker and the Toker. Rocking a grit with his main, main man, Tarquin, at the Battle of the Bands showdown between the female-led Menstrual Jam and the blatantly homophobic Buggered Rectums, Harold remembered he smoked a good sixty ciggies that awesome night. *Live a little, love a lot and have a fag straight after,* as he often mentioned to his good friend. He kept in touch with Tarquin, who progressed on to creative director at MADAME TUSSAUDS.

Harold met his future wife, Laura Sudbury, at graduating class. She found him to be an intelligent individual, exiting the year as a straight Honours student, and a kindly, harmless soul, albeit a little shy, but his smoking quickly became her greatest bugbear, to put it mildly. She did not like to see him throwing money to kill himself slowly with the thousand-plus carcinogens within each drag. She hoped he would make it as a big-shot writer, but that would not be possible if he were dead. They married and had an adorable daughter, Libby, and while Laura used her business acumen to open a small café/restaurant, Harold obtained a well-paid job as a proof-reader for HAMBLEYS PUBLISHING, run by a gloriously eccentric lady, Marianne Keene, who maintained a strong family atmosphere at work, conducive to creativity and productivity.

Laura utterly despised smoking. She insisted Harold kick the habit, using the government anti-smoking campaign of horror television ads in her endless diatribes to make him quit, emotionally-blackmailing him by keeping her body off-bounds until he had. Harold tried various means to give up: nicotine gum, lozenge, patch, even self-help groups and government-sponsored programmes; he tried everything but nothing helped him quit. Even if there'd been an inhalator and spray in those days, or an e-cigarette, it would not have made a jot of difference. It's no joke when they say that nicotine is twelve times more addictive than heroin. Harold suffered all kinds of withdrawal symptoms: impaired concentration, difficulties getting off to sleep, feelings of panic, overeating. So he carried on smoking, trying his damnedest to make sure his wife didn't find out.

What she doesn't know can't hurt her, surely? You see, you can divide people into Smokers and Non-smokers, Harold philosophized. *A Non-smoker might smoke socially or occasionally but will be fine without a fag for days. A Smoker, who has supposedly quit, will be thinking of a cigarette at a set of traffic lights during rush hour. Some people possess the willpower to simply scrunch up and discard their packet of cigarettes and never smoke again, while others just go through the motions and try every device available, but can never quit. I'm that person locked in mental gridlock, dreaming of a cigarette, waiting for the damned lights to change. Besides, do I really want to wait thirteen years for my macrophages to mop up the soot particles and return my lungs to the healthy pinkness of those of a Non-smoker's?*

He would drive to the nearest Waitrose car-park, early in the morning, and smoke five cigarettes to get him into the mindset for work, put him in a good mood and allow him to tackle any challenges the day might bring. During his breaks at work, he smoked outside to prevent the odour of tobacco getting into his clothes. He knew it was deception, against his own moral ideals, but smoking was his only vice and he hoped it would count as nothing more than a simple white lie, that what his wife didn't know wouldn't hurt her. He disclosed his early-morning behaviour to Tarquin, who found his secret activity both amusing and a little sad, sitting there all alone in the supermarket car-park; Tarquin called it "the romance of smoking" and didn't even suggest he stop. Harold would finish his day eating a nice hot, spicy curry (or kebab) before coming home late in the evening, administering a few generous squirts of clinically-proven mouth freshener.

Yet, his wife could *still* smell tobacco on his breath. Harold accounted for his dragon's breath by theorizing that as his lungs tried to recover from his decade of smoking, they would periodically 'burp' up small pockets of tobacco-scented air, hence the whiff. But as anyone knows, the only way to explain how a non-smoker/ex-smoker can constantly reek of cigarettes is by using Occam's razor: no matter the amount of denial, the simplest explanation is that the person is probably still secretly smoking.

From Harold's late arrival home, his growing detachment from family life, Laura began to suspect he might be having an affair. Progressively more suspicious, but unable to prove anything, she hired a private detective to follow him. And soon the detective reported back, showing her photos of her husband lighting up in the deserted car-park. Instead of being glad that her husband hadn't been unfaithful to her, Laura was furious he had been covertly smoking and confronted him with the photographic evidence. He didn't deny it, apologized for lying to her, relieved that the cat was out of the bag. She remained hysterical, extremely irrational, perceived smoking to be the equivalent of adultery. In an uncharacteristic tirade of profanities, she gave him an ultimatum: it was either her or the cigarettes. He opted for the cigarettes. *It's what defines me*, he reminded Tarquin. Harold felt the late, great comic, Benny Hill, summed it up best: *I thought I couldn't afford to take her out and smoke as well. So I gave up cigarettes. Then I took her out and one day I looked at her and thought: "Oh well," and I went back to smoking again, and that was better.*

A classic of downright denial concerns the guy who swears on his heart that he's given up smoking until his wife calls the plumber one day to deal with a blocked toilet. When the plumber investigates, he finds the U-bend clogged up by an accumulation of cigarette-butts that the guy has flushed down the toilet each time he sneaks off into the bathroom for a puff. Unlike Laura, the wife in the story didn't need to pay a detective to uncover her husband's dishonesty.

As far as her unreasonableness went, comparing smoking to adultery, Laura remained uncompromising, maintaining her position that Harold had cheated on her. So Laura began openly cheating on him—*physically*. Harold accepted her many lovers and life at home completely disintegrated. His wife filed for divorce and left him for a rich Egyptian businessman who frequented the café/restaurant increasingly and grew ever-fixated on her. Kids need firm, consistent guidance, in order to learn our precious values and allow them to achieve independence and contribute as healthy, productive members of society, but with Harold having grown incredibly distant from his teenage daughter, neglectful of his fatherly duties, Libby made the mistake of associating with the wrong crowd and got hooked on heroin, prostituting herself to fund the habit, and when Harold last heard, she had gone into rehab.

But he never gave up his cigarettes, feeling he could smoke freely again.

Changes at work meant he could be employed as a writer in his own right. Harold found his own voice, and he tapped out essays, poems and stories on his typewriter with growing confidence under the gaze of a reproduction of Van Gogh's macabre oil canvas, *Skull with a*

Burning Cigarette on the wall, and a white marble ashtray by his side on the writing desk with the old legend: REST YOUR BUTT HERE. Smoking became his sole province. So knowledgeable was he on the subject, like some connoisseur, he could easily write a thesis, if he chose, on the characteristics, similarities and differences between fire-cured, bright-leafed, perique or Turkish tobacco. He even devised a formula to accurately measure the weight of smoke = weight of unlit cigarette − (weight of smoked cigarette + its ashes). Harold went through a phase of pipe-smoking, wearing a smoking jacket for the occasion, then cigars, but he never abandoned his Dunhills.

There followed a gradual shift in social attitudes away from those days when cigarettes were issued as standard during the war. With growing perception of smoking as an antisocial activity, smokers' numbers diminished over the years until they now formed the minority. Harold recalled how at weddings and social functions in the days of yore, nearly every gentleman would be seen smoking; nowadays, exemplified at Tarquin's son's wedding, Harold was the only one smoking in the freezing cold outside, shunned like some plague-carrying pariah. Even Tarquin had long-since given up weed. The smoker had become part of a select clique, a dying breed, and Harold had become their mouthpiece, through the articles he churned out on the subject. Despite his isolationist views, he even undertook a short lecture tour, a cosier, more personal platform from where he could continue to advocate the 'Romance of Smoking'.

It is a common misconception that smoking relieves stress. Nicotine is a stimulant; therefore it increases the heart rate and blood pressure. Its subtle gratifying effects are due to it stimulating the reward centres of the brain, tweaking our dopamine levels, as well as strengthening our synaptic connections, thereby increasing concentration and focus. But the problems begin with both its psychological and physical dependence, meaning all the smoker ends up doing is feeding the habit, chasing the addiction. Not to mention that physicians attribute smoking to every disease under the sun, except perhaps Parkinson's Disease, a deficit in dopaminergic transmission. As Harold discussed during one of his lectures, if either Muhammad Ali or Michael J. Fox had smoked cigarettes, they may not have gone on to develop Parkinson's Disease, which raised a minor chuckle with the conference-goers.

Harold did not question his devotion to his cigarettes until he woke up one morning, coughing blood, and went to see his doctor, who referred him on to a lung specialist at Chertsford Memorial Hospital. After undergoing a series of investigations, he was called into the outpatient clinic.

Dr Onslow didn't waste time in breaking the bad news. "I'm afraid you have lung cancer."

Harold went silent for a stunned moment, trying to digest the horrendous information. "Could there be some mistake?"

"No mistake. The biopsy and scan couldn't have been more conclusive."

Another long, fraught silence. "What does that mean?"

"You have a particularly aggressive type of cancer. It means that if we don't operate on you now, you will be dead in six months."

Harold was certain Dr Onslow knew of his fame. After all, Harold was the man who championed smoking, a celebrity of sorts, having made something of a name for himself in literary circles. Reading between the lines, he could sense nuanced satisfaction in Dr Onslow's smug tones and see undisclosed jubilation in his big, fat face: *serves you right, you faghead!* Why shouldn't there be? Harold sat on the opposite side of the fence and the War on Tobacco had claimed the scalp of its unofficial chief spokesperson. "How can this be?"

It was meant to be a metaphorical comment, but Dr Onslow answered it anyway. "Every time you smoke a cigarette, you switch on certain genes that cause cancer. Once you have smoked enough cigarettes and gone above a certain threshold of activated genes, you develop the cancer. Fortunately in this case, the tumour hasn't metastasized. I will make an immediate referral to a cancer specialist so we can start treatment as soon as possible..."

But Harold was no longer listening. Despite longevity in his family, the unthinkable had occurred: he had acquired the Big C. He decided to recharge and rally the troops. *Where do we go from here?* The medical profession might ramble on about excising the tumour, resecting part of the lung, poisoning his body with radiation or flooding his bloodstream with the best licensed carcinogens in the world, going by the benign name of chemotherapy, but Harold didn't really give a flying fuck, to use common parlance. *Most doctors enjoy* Slick Cunt, as one cuckold playwright whom Harold adored put it, *because of its low tar content…* [*code for* Silk Cut, *of course.*] He thought of those people who spend a lifetime mocking death, but lose their bravado and cry like a baby when they are diagnosed with cancer and told they have only three months to live. He thought of that TV drama about that chemistry teacher who starts manufacturing crystal meth after being diagnosed with terminal lung cancer. Spurred on by his own minor celebrity and Van Gogh's cigarette-smoking skull, Harold did not weep and politely declined the surgical interventions and nonsense therapies offered to him by the doctors and made a conscious decision not to quit his forty-a-day habit, instead increasing his literary output.

Put that in your pipe and smoke it!

His appetite went. He lost weight and grew rapidly scrawny, feeling constantly tired and finding it harder to breathe. He set his affairs in order and prepared to make peace with the Holy Fucker who had set this death sentence upon him, premature as it seemed punitive. Harold decided that before he shuffled off this mortal coil, he should do one last lecture circuit, his swansong.

The cancer continued to progress, to consume him, and he continued to smoke. By the time he arrived back in his home town of Chertsford at the POSTLANDS HOTEL, which would serve as the final venue of his tour, on the First of April, he was a very physically unwell man.

His popularity, and the sombre knowledge of his ill-health, had sold-out his final lecture, attended not only by the usual faithful and other smoking aficionados, but also by tobacco lobbyists and shareholders, an impressive overall turnout of two-hundred-strong. Harold even spotted Gary Chapman, one of the new generation of writers at *The Scribbler*. In his last address, Harold spoke about the impact smoking had and if it still had a place in today's society… *and, ladies and gentlemen, is it still good to smoke?* "I have received a lot of hate-mail in my time — by people who want my head on a silver platter — and been called all kinds of unflattering names, many of them unmentionable, but the one that has stuck with me is the 'Merchant of Death', having been constantly accused of exploiting people's personality weaknesses and encouraging them to smoke. But, believe me, when I say there is no profiteering in what I preach. The public has known that cigarettes kill since research on the subject was first published in the *British Medical Journal* in the early 1950s. Even today, the Surgeon-General claims that nearly three hundred smoking-related deaths occur each day, costing the NHS a pretty penny: five billion pounds to treat smoking-related diseases annually. The lure of the cigarette, the temptation to smoke, cannot be understated, despite being implicated as a health hazard. I myself have been a slave to nicotine all my life and you can see for yourselves that I have nearly smoked myself to death. However, unlike successive governments, I do not spin the truth or operate double standards. The politicians have condemned and pursued the tobacco companies for decades, practically done away with tobacco sponsorship and advertising, stamped warning labels on our cigarette packets, overhyped the dangers of second-hand smoke, even implemented the Smoking Ban across the UK, yet despite their penchant for witch-hunts and ever-increasing draconian measures, they do not make smoking illegal like street drugs. And why not, you may ask? I mean that ought to be the next logical step in the progression, shouldn't it? Except they believe that by making a packet of cigarettes more and more costly, it will prevent fewer people taking up the habit. They are mistaken, of course, because the forbidden has its own powerful lure. So I ask again, why don't they? They might if it weren't for the ridiculous twelve-billion-pound revenue generated from ruthlessly taxing and fleecing the average smoker, like you and me, that goes straight into their government coffers. But that's not the point I'm trying to make. I'm not here to attack our so-called leaders. In their defence—if you can call it a defence—most of them are lawyers by profession anyway, therefore lacking any scruples, convince you black is white, as crooked as Julian Clary is gay, and they will have to answer to somebody some day for their indiscretions. Humans are flawed beings, and we all make bad decisions in our lifetimes. I know I have. But smoking wasn't one of them. Life is made up of a series of moments. Cigarettes have constituted a lot of those little moments of calm; they have afforded me great pleasure throughout my life, and will continue to do so for whatever remaining time I have left on this earth. Ultimately, it's about freedom and responsibility and personal choice. I would encourage *not* people to smoke, but *rather* for them to think for themselves, challenge authority—even my authority on the merits of smoking for that matter—take ownership for their lives and make an informed decision with all the facts and education at their disposal about whether or not they take up smoking and indulge in the smoking lifestyle. Because it is a lifestyle choice, perhaps a selfish lifestyle choice, some might say. And, like any decision in life, accept the consequences without regret, whatever those consequences might be. If there's nothing else you take away with you from this little forum, it's my only dying wish you remember my concluding message about personal choice and taking responsibility for whatever decision you make – nothing wrong with making a bad decision as long as you accept any consequences that might arise. And there must be no regrets."

It was such an impassioned speech, delivered with a kind of brutal honesty and wisdom, that it brought a tear to many an eye. Harold Hartman held it together for a good forty-five minutes, added another nail to his coffin in the conference hall, and conducted a Q&A for a further half-hour that no-one would have suspected that the cancer had spread to his brain and liver. The audience, including the pro-smoking lobby, rose to its feet and exploded in a rousing, celebratory salvo of cheers and applause. Their deepest sympathies lay with this brave man, all skin and bones, his breathlessness giving him trouble talking, aided by a walking cane, who made no qualms that cigarettes had ruled his life and were soon to take that life away from him. He expressed no regrets over the illusion that he was in charge of his smoking habit, instead in fact the submissive partner in his relationship with the cigarette. Here was a man who believed sincerely in his cause, *their* cause.

And that was when he met Krista Avery.

As he was about to step off the lectern, a girl in her mid-twenties came up to him, "Hello, Mr Hartman."

"No more questions or autographs," Harold said, waving her away. "I'm very tired. Time to go home and die."

"Do you mind if I join you?"

He looked at her curiously. She did not seem fazed by his unusual, but truthful, comment. "You want to die?"

"No, of course not. You blew my mind out there. The least I can do is return the favour by taking you home and making the last few moments of your life special. I can drive you."

"Well, I think you ought to, young lady, since I can no longer drive my car on account of my left side being somewhat paralyzed not to mention the partial blindness. The joys of brain mets, I suppose."

His failing health did not appear to deter the woman who was at least forty years his junior, natural blond, blue-eyed and self-assured, and a damned sight more awesome than his own fake-blond, mistrustful ex-wife had ever been. Harold had to roundly admit Krista was *smoking* hot! *Pardon the blokishness of the pun!*

He accepted the lift, and she drove him home.

He showed her around the house, his study: the painting of the smoking skull, the famous shelf of his books and literature dealing with the whole art of smoking. "This is where the magic happens."

Krista seemed unduly fascinated by his nicotine-stained, clubbed fingers, the dreadful grottiness of his death-breath. Now why would a pretty little thing like her be interested in a pathetic old man like him, an old man on his deathbed, for that matter?

Krista told him she was a smoking fetishist. Harold knew a little on the deviant subject of capnolagnia: the peculiar worship of the burning cherry, the spiced blend, the loose ashes, the unique, nebulous patterns of smoke raftering up to the ceiling, an entire subculture based around the sexual connotations of smoking. She viewed him as a god, considered him the epitome of smoking glamour.

He was flattered by her praise and high estimation of him, so far removed from the Merchant of Death moniker, being accused of peddling misery.

Well, he guessed it took all sorts, whether it be whips and chains and handcuffs or those skinny, bespectacled weirdos who were strongly attracted to and fed vast quantities of food to enormous women or, perhaps, putting the sex back into smoking. *You have the sweet face of angelic innocence and purity, but the delightfully wicked mind of a little devil. Where have you been all my life?*

She took out a camera, and they fooled around. He remembered that detective, hired by his wife, snapping him in that car-park against his will all those years ago. On this occasion, however, he obliged to be photographed of his own free will.

Harold stripped off and agreed to model naked for her, and Krista caught various provocative poses of him, smoking. She captured tasteful shots of his withered, diseased frailty haloed in a mist of smoke, pouring concentrated funnels of smoke out of his nostrils, blowing perfect smoke rings, or fetchingly creating a noose of tobacco smoke around his neck. She hoped to interest the Turner Prize judges with these black-and-white images of smoking porn, and Harold suspected this elegantly-presented portrait of a genuinely-nude, terminally-ill and vaguely-famous old coot, wasting away to a near-skeleton while shamelessly, if not perversely, promoting the thing that was killing him, might just win them over.

She took off her clothes too, and he gasped at the beauty of her shape and contours. Except he noticed cigarette burns in different stages of healing all over her body, normally hidden by clothing. In keeping with her masochistic tendencies, she insisted he stub out the cigarettes on her body or flick the ash into her mouth. He decided against playing the misogynist and treating her body like an ashtray, and they explored each other's bodies, instead. With the eroticized expertise of a high-class call-girl, Krista touched him, shared a kiss which proceeded to her hand closing around his flaccid member, yanking it up-and-down rhythmically. Despite the cold bones of his cachexic body, the strong foetor of his laboured breathing, he surprised her by getting it up, maintaining a good, hard erection for a respectable timeframe, eventually erupting in a strong orgasm while gratifying her desperate yearning to be close to her legend and do something special for him when he needed it most.

He thanked her, for keeping him company, when there had been no-one else in that narrow window between the remnants of life and the approach of death.

Naked on the floor, he killed another cancer-stick and prepared to die, listening to *End of the Line* by the troupe of famous rockers, the Traveling Wilburys.

Harold took his last puff and, with his head cradled in the lap of his greatest, intimate admirer, expired. Harold had experienced his happiest moments in the last few hours of his life, on that April Fool's Day, and he gladly relinquished his life a contented man. Since Sir Walter Raleigh returned from the New World and introduced tobacco to the Europeans, popularizing its aromatic, halcyon pleasures, Harold would join the ranks of people, including the Marlboro Man, who had snuffed it in the name of the evil weed.

A sad day for the smokers of the world, mourned Krista. But what of his legacy?

Harold had stated his case clearly — there could be no confusion — imparted his message and hoped his insights and recommendations would reverberate with generations to come: freedom of choice and sensible or brave decision-making, and you mustn't harbour regrets in what you firmly and truly believe in.

Now doesn't that make you want to smoke?

March 2013

Deadliner

"*Blind with enchantment, he felt that life was just beginning.*"

The Curious Case of Benjamin Button (1921)

F. Scott Fitzgerald

1
The Proposition

I approached the girl sitting all alone and pretty in the mess hall during her lunch break at HAMBLEYS PUBLISHING. "Mind if I ask you something really creepy?"

"Not at all," she replied, favouring me with a peculiar glance. Her expression seemed to read: *Why doesn't that surprise me? You're creepy on paper anyway, so what's the difference if the words come out of your mouth instead of your typewriter.*

I puffed myself up. "Would you have dinner with me tonight?"

Eve froze. It was a disheartening sight. Was that really the effect I had on women? Then she checked herself, trying out of politeness to at least sound vaguely interested. "Why should that be creepy?"

"There's a reason why I'm asking you out on this particular date. But I can only tell you over dinner."

"Why not now?" she pressed, hoping to determine the worthiness of the invitation, the appropriateness of it. Or, if needs be, give her an excuse to decline my offer of a date.

"No, it has to wait. Then you'll understand."

Eve deliberated for an endless, awkward minute, weighing up the pros and cons, and eventually came to an informed decision. "I don't know…"

I could see her struggling inside. "Nothing romantic, I assure you. Just a one-off dinner date. And all shall be revealed."

The promise of romance—or, more likely, the lack thereof—appeared to relax her. "Okay, I'll give it a shot."

"Great, seven-thirty at PASCAL'S."

"Connor, shall we swap numbers in case one of us can't make it?"

"No need, Eve…" I said, since I knew her game. "So I'll see you there!"

2

The Scribbler

Marianne Keene had remained the Editor-in-Chief at HAMBLEYS PUBLISHING since its founding in 1985. It was Marianne and, to a lesser extent, her husband, Leonard, who first set up the establishment, after coming into a little money, in the hope of attracting new writers. There was "a legion of them out there", according to Marianne, those ambitious dreamers whose sweat-and-toil deserved a chance at print when facing rejection after rejection from the cruel, snooty-nosed, more upmarket publishing houses. HAMBLEYS had certainly grown over the years—employed more staff, moved into bigger premises—but it still remained a small-time enterprise. More importantly, regardless of its modest status, working for this particular literary house was like being part of a family. Every member, whether on the permanent staff or a temporary employee, was considered precious. Marianne saw to it. There couldn't have been a friendlier or more understanding boss to work for. With her flowing white hair, flowery dresses and colourful stockings, she gave the place a fashionable air and a much-needed touch of class. She made everyone feel at home and went to great lengths to peruse through every unsolicited manuscript delivered to her door. Not because it was her job, but because reading was her "first love" and the writer was always "sacred". Leonard Keene, by contrast, was a serious-minded, tweed-wearing gentleman, whose inherent officiousness rendered him ideal for the role of Assistant Editor and Fact Checker. He also dabbled in a little historical drama.

The Scribbler was their baby, the flagship of the company, a monthly magazine packed with literary articles and short stories, penned by both permanent staff and the first-time writer looking for that all-important big break. It maintained a reasonable circulation. The best short fiction from *The Scribbler* went into a quarterly collected volume with such catchy titles as *Based on a True Story... Or Thereabouts* and *Here Are Some Stories We Prepared Earlier*. The primary aim of these compilations was, of course, to increase the profile of those newbie writers.

Alexander Regan, Gary Chapman and myself — Connor Holden — were the regular contributors to the magazine, aside from Marianne's editorial and her husband's sideline in historical fiction. She called us the Up-and-Comers. We'd been Up-and-Comers for several years now. Each of us churned out a short tale a month. Our different specialties gave the magazine an eclectic feel.

Alex, the Ginger One, was an author of romance who believed that writing was like "stroking a woman's thigh": an erotic, titillating experience. Not surprisingly, he moonlighted as a porn writer outside our inner circle. Old Salt-and-Pepper-Head Gary wrote speculative fiction whose peculiar ideas came directly to him from the Hits from the Bong. He often gave everyone the impression (whether deliberate or not) he had stepped straight out of *The Twilight Zone*. My forte was horror: tales about vampires, witches and haunted houses. Like my two Partners-in-Crime, I had other projects on the side, a novel to be more precise, a rollercoaster piece of fiction about a serial killer in the same vein as Hannibal Lecter, which had so far taken me five years to write and would probably take another five years to finish. Such was my slacker mentality, I was satisfied with producing only one short story a month and living off the steady income it generated. I began working full-time for Marianne in the fall of 2003 and never looked back. All three of us Up-and-Comers could have moved on to greater things, but together we decided against it. We owed it to Marianne, who gave us an office each and made us the staple writers of the magazine.

Even when HAMBLEYS faced a possible take-over bid in early 2007, Marianne kept her nerve and chose not to be a class sell-out. With her curious, discerning nature, she gladly went back to enjoying the slush-pile that arrived on her office desk daily. And she continued to encourage a homely atmosphere around the workplace. I guess that's what we were: one big, happy family.

Marianne popped her head round the door, the same August afternoon I'd asked Eve out on a date. "Hello there, Connor," she greeted me. "Hope I'm not disturbing you."

"How can you be?" I placed the kiddie-sized basketball I'd been idly shooting hoops with next to the blank screen of my PC. "You know I'll always have time for you."

She wandered into the office, which was a shrine to untidiness, and grabbed a chair. Her eyes chanced upon the brass plaque on my desk, bearing the legend: I LOVE MY PIGSTY. "Cute," she commented, then got swiftly down to business. "I was wondering if I could have a quick word with you."

"Certainly," I replied, crossing my feet on the desk, lacing my fingers behind my head. "You seem to be in an awfully good mood."

"I'm very excited..." she said with a natural sparkle.

Seeing fifty-seven-year-old Marianne as excited as a little girl receiving a pony for her birthday was not an uncommon sight at HAMBLEYS. Dressing like a little girl was an equally daily occurrence. Today, she had plumped for a purple mini-dress with pink stockings. At least she wasn't wearing the very embarrassing, gauzy, see-through white number she had worn at the Christmas party last year. I could not help but marvel at her fashion sense. "What's the big occasion?"

"I met with Marketing this morning," she informed me. "They're very keen on showcasing your talent."

"I thought my talent had already been showcased... in *The Scribbler*."

"This is a little different. You've given us enough material for a book. Our readers will be interested to know that we plan to select your twelve best works and put them into an eponymous short story collection."

I let the news sink in. "That's great!" I eventually said. "What changed your mind?"

Marianne grew thoughtful. "I know you pitched this idea a few months back, but I was sitting on it, waiting for the right hour. And the hour is now upon us..." She caught my baffled expression. "Believe me, you deserve it! You may not exactly write like the dickens, but you've met all your deadlines on time and, moreover, produced some fine work for us over the years, kept our readers spooked and coming back for more. You shouldn't be wasting your life on our rag."

"I don't mind wasting my life," I replied, reaching forward and patting the basketball. "I take great pleasure in it."

"I'm sure you do. But there's a whole world out there, a world for your taking. All you need is the right exposure. Who knows — you could become the next Stephen King, attract a movie deal and garner awards."

"Wishful thinking… Careful, or you're liable to be disappointed."

Marianne continued, "I decided we'll get this campaign up and running for this coming Halloween. Beginning with a proper preface from yourself followed by a promotional book-signing at midnight, JK-style. I could even show off my new pumpkin-coloured puffball dress. How do five thousand copies sound?"

Her suggestion elicited a brief, uncharacteristic exclamatory whoop from someone normally as cool-headed as myself. "*Wowser*! You're going all-out on this one!" I was suddenly struck by an unquiet thought. "But what about Alex and Gary? I don't want them to feel left out." I considered for a moment. "What the hell — let them get absurdly jealous until they hatch a plot to assassinate me!"

"If our little experiment is successful, we'll do the same with their works. We might even branch out into novels."

"Sounds like a plan," I said, in full support. I should have been delirious with Marianne's disclosure that there might be a book in it for me, that I might actually be going places. No point being published, I always believed, if you weren't established. Joining the pantheon of the world's gifted horror writers was my ultimate goal, but my efforts rarely if ever matched my ambitions. Even now, hearing what Marianne was proposing, being a self-confessed Champion of Sloth precluded outright delight. Instead of ecstasy, I felt ambivalence. I was too stuck in my ways, contented with my lot. Besides, I knew short story anthologies did not sell half as well as novels. Still, I supposed, it was a start.

"Then we're agreed?" Marianne concluded, getting up and shaking my hand in a congratulatory gesture. "I'll draw up a new contract." Just when I thought she was going, she sat back down again. "On another note..." she said, switching subjects. "Eve mentioned you asked her out."

"Guilty as charged."

"Came out of the blue, quite unexpected for her."

"Really?"

"I don't know what your motive is, and it is not my place to ask," she explained, going on to remind me, "but you know I encourage rich, fulfilling relationships amongst my staff. Being a fairly liberal-minded girl myself, I don't forbid intimacy between colleagues if the feeling is mutual, as long as it doesn't spoil the finer workings of this company, both in terms of productivity and camaraderie. I abhor disharmony." She went directly to the crux of the matter. "Eve came to me for advice. Since she's only been working here a short time, she wanted me to tell her what kind of person you are. So I fibbed and told her you're an absolute gentleman."

"And that bothers you?"

"Eve's a sweet, wonderful human being. I'm telling you as a friend, not as your boss, I don't want to see her hurt."

"How can I possibly hurt her?"

"If truth be known, you're not entirely a horrible person, a bit Jekyll-and-Hyde perhaps, which I suppose goes with the territory, perpetually bored, doing just enough to finish the job. But it's your struggle with the demon drink that concerns me."

I felt a little hurt. "Oh, I wouldn't call it a struggle."

"*Pleeease*, I've seen you drunk! You're wilder than a night out with Russell Brand."

"I like getting wild," I said truthfully. "Alleviates the boredom. Lubricates the senses. Gives me inspiration. Anyway, some of the greatest writers in the world enjoyed a small tipple. Take Jack Kerouac, for example. Consider F. Scott Fitzgerald who philosophized, *First you take a drink, then the drink takes a drink, then the drink takes you.*"

"Didn't both of them die in their forties from cirrhosis of the liver?"

"Yes, but Ernest Hemingway believed that *a man does not exist until he is drunk.*"

"And he shot himself in the grip of an alcoholic depression. You're not winning the argument, here, Connor."

Marianne was right on the money, as usual. I guess I needed to moderate my drinking unless I could figure out a way of managing myself in a civilized fashion while intoxicated. "You've got to admit I have a reasonable case."

"Try not to screw it up this time," she advised. "Go easy on the drink. I don't want a repeat of the getting-drunk-and-urinating-in-the-kitchen-sink incident."

"Why won't anyone ever let that rest?" I sighed in despair. That notorious, cringeworthy episode would haunt me to my grave. Not my finest hour, I admit. Drunk by four in the afternoon when I'm supposed to be hosting a dinner party that same evening. My girlfriend at the time is slaving away in the kitchen as the guests arrive. For some inexplicable reason, I take off all my clothes and saunter into the kitchen, while the guests watch on in absolute shock, as I relieve myself in the sink. Then, I go upstairs and collapse on the bed with absolutely no recollection of the incident the next day. I can positively pinpoint the beginning of the slippery downhill slide in our relationship to that day. "Fine, I won't get razzed."

"Treat Eve with more respect than you showed Marla."

"You have my word as a gentleman and a scholar."

Marianne seemed satisfied. "Other than that, I give you my blessing and I wish you the best of luck."

"Most gracious of you," I responded, with a bow of my head. "She'll be home by eleven, Ma'am."

"She'd better be or I'm setting the dogs on you."

With that humorous threat and a cursory farewell, Marianne, who acted and dressed forty years younger than her age, left my office.

I reflected on our amicable exchange and Marianne's desire to play happy families, suddenly feeling hopeful. Then, rapidly descending into chronic boredom, I went back to bouncing my basketball against the wall in a calculated bid to irritate Gary in the next room.

3
The Date

Eve Skellern arrived at seven-thirty on the dot.

When she sat down at my table in a quiet corner of the restaurant, I stared at her in astonishment, as if she were some kind of apparition. I almost didn't recognize her.

"What?" she asked, puzzled by my wide-eyed expression.

I chose my words carefully. "Great you could make it. I didn't expect you to show. I thought you might stand me up or ring me saying you had other commitments."

"Ye of little faith," she said in a manner which suggested I might have already offended her by questioning her reliability. "Besides, I can't ring you – I don't have your number, remember?"

"Point well taken," I said sheepishly.

Eve noticed the two empty wine glasses on my side of the table, their contents drained. "How long have you been here?"

"Just half an hour. I like to get a head start." As Eve was settling down, I asked her if she would like something to drink. I called over the waiter and requested another glass of red for myself while Eve went for a white wine spritzer.

"Nice restaurant," Eve said, scanning the room, taking in the atmosphere of the place. PASCAL'S was only half-full with more customers drifting in to the mouth-watering mix of aromas from the kitchen and the melody of accordion music on the overhead speakers. Trompe-l'oeils of traditional rustic life hung on the walls, paintings of wheat fields and lemon groves and vineyards, idyllic scenery reminiscent of *Jean de Florette*, so sharply-rendered they appeared to leap straight out of their respective frames. There seemed no escaping the Gallic charm of this bistro-style restaurant. "Do you come here often?"

"Sometimes, if the mood takes me."

She glanced at the menu. "My parents have brought me here a few times. I can't really afford it myself."

I put her mind at ease. "Remember, this is on me. So order anything your heart desires."

"I think I will take you up on that offer," Eve said with a bright smile.

"I didn't see you around much this afternoon. Where did you disappear to?"

"Marianne was kind enough to give me the afternoon off so I spent the last four hours at the hairdresser's."

Good old Marianne, I thought, *always looking out for us kids*. Indeed, Eve looked as lovely as ever. In contrast to my casual black shirt and jeans, Eve was dressed in a trendy white top and matching skirt, rounded off by an elegant white ponteroma jacket and sneakers, which together accentuated her perfect figure and gave her an almost angelic glow, save for the Union Jack she sported around her neck like a scarf in proper air hostess fashion. Angel or air hostess, her normally short brown hair was dyed platinum-blond. "Four hours of treatment in a health spa I can understand, but I can't imagine it can take so long at a hair salon."

"Oh, everything is so relaxed there. The pace, the conversation, the scrutiny of my hair — the place is an oasis of calm. They even offer you coffee or a glass of wine between takes."

I nodded in partial understanding. "Hey, whatever you do in your own time…" I left the comment unfinished, hanging in the air.

"Shall we order?" said Eve, faking a smile. I was certain she was thinking: *eat and be done with as quickly as possible and get out of here before it's too late.*

"Good idea."

We ordered, skipping starters. I requested a bottle of Charles Lafitte.

Eve looked at me with a wrinkled brow. "What are we celebrating?"

"The bigwigs in Marketing had a meeting this morning. They're in the process of signing me up for a book contract. I wanted to share this moment with someone."

"That's terrific news," she said, genuinely pleased. "And you thought to share it with me? I would have thought Gary and Alex would have been better bets."

"You've done me a great favour coming here. Means a lot to me. But that's not the total reason why I invited you out to dinner. I'll tell you when we're eating."

Eve appeared more confused than ever.

"Don't look so bewildered. I prefer to see you intrigued rather than mystified."

Her anxious expression smoothed out. "I suppose I can wait to find out what gruesome fate you have in store for me."

"Your accent," I asked, curious, "is it Cornish?"

"That's what a lot of people think. No, I was raised in the Channel Islands before my family moved to Chertsford when I was twelve. And yourself... where do you hail from?"

"I spent my childhood among the hills and valleys of South Wales... *Doctor Who* put it back on the map again."

"So you're a Welshman."

"It would appear so. Though my mother, who was a massive tennis fan, named me after Jimmy Connors, her all-time hero. Certainly made my father jealous as hell."

"You don't sound Welsh."

"I saw a Speech Therapist as a kid because I had an awful stammer and no-one could make out what I was saying, my accent was so thick. She recommended I read the newspaper aloud for half-an-hour a day. It fixed the problem eventually, although if I'm ever drunk or stressed-out my Welsh accent has a tendency to break through." I was keen to learn a little about her folks. "Your family, where are they?"

"Oh, they live locally. I stay with them. My Dad's an Accountant and my Mom's a Biomedical Scientist."

"Brothers and sisters?"

"One brother, younger than me, works as a valet at a golf club."

"Do you get on with them?"

"Very much so. I love them to bits." She reciprocated interest. "Where are your Mom and Dad?"

"Still back in Newport."

"How often do you visit them?"

"Not often. My father's still pissed at me for failing to keep up with family tradition and work on his farm. He never understood my preoccupation with horror."

"I wouldn't understand it myself, writing to scare people. What made you take up horror?"

"The first-ever movie I watched at the cinema as a growing lad was *Raiders of the Lost Ark*. Remember what happens at the climax of the film?"

Eve recalled, "The spirits of the dead rise up and consume the Nazis?"

"Exactly! Well, from that point on, I had found my calling."

"But, still, considering what passes off as literature these days—"

I was in my element. "There is a simple honesty about the genre, a virtue if you will. You deal with themes most people don't want to know about, let alone discuss: fear, pain, death, disease and madness. Love and romance and social commentary are all very well, but isn't it true that our time on earth boils down to we are born, we suffer, we die?"

Eve didn't seem so convinced. "I think that's a very extreme and bleak interpretation of the human condition."

"But nonetheless true."

"Doesn't your work ever get to you? I'd go tooting if I was writing that kind of stuff, day in, day out."

"I must admit I do sometimes get sick of the sound of screams."

Eve gave me a sympathetic glance which I greatly appreciated. Jokingly, she remarked: "Hey, whatever you do in your own time..."

Her attempt at light relief caused me to chuckle. "Touché!" I carried on down the same old beaten track. "Do you write much? You do realize you have the home advantage working in a publishing house."

She deliberated a moment whether to tell me, worried in case I might plagiarize her idea. "I do have something in the pipeline."

"So our Copy Girl is an author in her own right! Good for you!"

"Nothing fancy, of course," she explained. "A comic piece about a group of mates (not much unlike you, Gary and Alex) who get completely whammed during a Stag Party, and in the spirit of the thing, leave the bridegroom stranded and naked in the Outer Hebrides. The story follows his misadventures as he tries to make it on time to his wedding in London."

"Sounds like a potential bestseller."

"That may be so, but it's always down to the ability of the writer to pull it off."

"Do I detect a note of uncertainty?"

"I don't think I have the word-power, the confidence or the style."

"Don't sell yourself short," I counselled her. "I reckon you're a better writer than you give yourself credit for. Everyone has a book inside of them, whether it's fiction or non-fiction. It's about writing at whatever pace you're comfortable with—doing a small amount daily but consistently. Every writer is different, approaches the task from their own unique perspective. Some authors bring out three books a year, others manage only a couple of sentences a day. Joseph Heller took over a decade to pen *Catch-22*, but look where it is now. Reprinted every year since its publication in 1961 and voted as one of the greatest novels of the twentieth century. James Joyce's undoubted masterpiece is *Ulysses*, a whale of a book, the events of which are nearly all set over the space of one day. Joyce had a habit of picking out each individual word carefully because he was always searching for the right word. One particular time, his friend asks him how much he has written that day. Joyce tells him he's jotted down seven words. His friend goes on to say that you must be thrilled you've done quite a lot today. Joyce's reply is: *But I don't know which order they go in."*

Eve laughed. "Thanks for the inspirational pep-talk."

"I could help you develop your story. All you need to do is ask."

At that juncture our meals arrived, along with the champagne. Eve had gone for coq au vin with seasonal Mediterranean vegetables whereas I'd plumped for Duckling à l'Orange on a bed of arugula salad. The restaurant was filling up nicely; food, conversation and music surrounded us. We continued our banter.

"I'm leaving HAMBLEYS at the end of September," Eve was saying.

I tried not to sound crestfallen. "So what do you plan to do?"

"I've got a place at the College of Performing Arts."

I congratulated her, adding: "It will be a terrible loss for us. You have no idea how much I'm going to miss you."

"I'll miss you guys too. But I've always wanted to do drama. I was working at HAMBLEYS to pay my way. I've got to say I've really learned a great deal there."

"Any experience is good experience."

"I'm a lot like my grandmother. She was in the Performing Arts. Her crowning achievement was playing Ophelia at Drury Lane."

"Poor Ophelia… divided from herself and her fair judgement."

Eve kicked me under the table. "Trust you to quote her state of mind!"

"Any actors or actresses you particularly aspire to?"

"Will Smith," she said instantly. "I've seen everything he's ever been in a dozen times over. I just can't get enough of him."

"A toast, then," I announced, raising my glass. "Here's to drama school… and to Will Smith! May he never stop saving the world!"

Eve followed suit. "To your new book!"

We clinked glasses and drank.

"You promised you'd tell me over dinner," Eve reminded me, continuing with her meal.

"I guess I should," I said, improvising. "Okay, I wanted to get to know you so I could put you in a horror story and do horrible things to you."

It was meant to be a joke, but Eve looked positively shocked.

"No, how about if I hoped I could gather enough material from this date to stalk you?"

Eve didn't seem to consider my humour particularly funny. "Gary is just plain weird. But you're actually quite creepy."

"I'll take that as a compliment," I said, grinning broadly. "Maybe I took you out because I fancied you."

"I thought this wasn't supposed to be a romantic date," Eve said, beginning to get annoyed.

"Only teasing," I replied, deciding to get serious. "Right, I'll give you the real reason. I was in a relationship for fifteen months with an older woman called Marla. Towards the end, things weren't going well. One night I got drunk, I rang her and started raving on about how great a girl you were. I have no recollection of that telephone conversation. Marla told me what I'd said the next day. She mentioned that I was always at my most honest when I'd been drinking and that I secretly harboured feelings for you. She dumped me shortly afterwards."

"I'm so sorry," Eve breathed, pure, troublesome guilt suddenly written all over her face. "All because of me? I can't help but feel responsible in some way."

I couldn't believe it. Eve was actually blaming herself for my defunct relationship. Could she be any sweeter? "Please, it's not your fault so there's really no need to apologize. My relationship hit the rocks a long time ago. On hearing that I'd been praising you like some lovesick poet, I just felt I ought to take you out and see what all the fuss was about. Get it out of my system, find some form of closure."

"And have you found closure?" she asked, my motive now crystal-clear.

"Sort of." In many respects, no. In the presence of Eve, the night held certain possibilities, of friendship, of romance. Except I couldn't go back on my word. Not now. The last thing I wanted to do was to scare her away. I took another sip of champagne. "I'm so tempted to write about our date and send you a copy of the final draft as a farewell gift."

"I would like that," Eve said with a gentle smile.

"No ghouls or monsters, I promise."

We finished our meals, quaffed the last of our champagne, and went straight for dessert in the shape of a Black Forest Gâteau. Coffee followed as Eve and I talked like old friends.

I asked her about boys. She informed me that she wasn't in a relationship at present because she wanted to focus on her career. She, in turn, questioned me regarding my huge appetite for alcohol.

I answered metaphorically. "Alcohol is like a mistress to me. She never argues with you and is always available on demand, quenching secret desires."

"I had quite a reputation as a drinker myself," Eve disclosed.

"Join the club..."

She went on. "I used to get so smashed in my teens that I wouldn't be able to tell the cabbie where my home address was. These days, drinking doesn't sit well with my daily fitness regime."

"Gary's seen you jogging on the Common a few times."

"Gary's always boasting how many times he's destroyed you at squash."

I suddenly remembered something. "You must come down to the pub with us tomorrow. Gary and I are having a drinking contest. There's one sport I can destroy him at. Besides, it's also karaoke night."

"I'll check my schedule," Eve replied, "but, provisionally, count me in."

"Cool..."

"Before we wander off into the night, may I try something, just out of curiosity?"

"Indeed you can."

"Well, it's something we used to do at school, just a bit of adolescent fun. It was called a Compatibility Rating. I'll show you..." She got a pen and jotted down some numbers on her napkin and, releasing a momentary gasp, passed the results over to me.

I examined her scribbles:

CONNOR HOLDEN
LOVES
EVE SKELLERN

33151
6466
101012
11113
2224
446
810

91%

I managed to figure out the formula and how the final score was calculated. "So we're a ninety-one percent match." I looked back at her, wondering why she had suggested this little Love Tester. However, the surprise had vanished from her face, replaced by calm indifference. I could tell she had made up her mind. I therefore had to keep to my promise, tell her what she probably wanted to hear. "Never gonna happen, I suppose, but good to know."

I paid the bill and ordered a cab. We got our coats.

"I think I'm... drunk," she said with an endearing daintiness. "You're not hiding any bad intentions, are you, like taking rakish advantage of a lady in her squiffy condition?"

Was that an invitation? I doubted it. "None whatsoever," I reassured her.

I dropped her off at her place. Eve did not invite me in — why should she when this was supposed to have been nothing more than an unromantic one-off dinner? She told me she had enjoyed the meal and the company. I told her I had a splendid time and thanked her for choosing to grace me with her presence.

"It may not be the same as dating a doctor, but you, dearest Eve, can now proudly boast that you went out with a horror writer and survived."

Then, a silence descended between us, comfortable rather than awkward. I desperately wanted to kiss her for a lovely evening, yet neither was I keen for her to misinterpret the sentiment. The opportunity slipped me by and she disappeared into the house, probably not entirely disappointed.

Standing under the white spectral glow of the street lamp, I looked back on a pleasant Thursday evening, including our score on the Compatibility Meter, with a strange, daunting realization. I watched Eve turn on her bedroom light and draw the curtains before I climbed back into the cab and carried on with the rest of my journey.

Thirty-eight years on this lousy planet and I realized I had never fallen in love.

Until tonight, that is… with a sweet, wholesome twenty-three-year-old English rose.

Some people considered Love a universal emotion, others thought of it as a foolish anachronism in today's fast-paced society. Scientists believed Love was a simple hormonal distraction, like eating loads of chocolate. Whatever it was, I was in love for the very first time in my life.

Passions astir, rumours afloat, I felt like Middle-aged-Bloke-who's-dating-some-Young-Hot-Totty in that hilarious Harry Enfield sketch: *She's only twenty-three! TWENTY-THREE!*

4
The Drinking Contest

We Three Up-and-Comers dropped by the OX AND LAMB after work the Friday evening for a drink and a feed and to clear up some unfinished business. We considered ourselves writers foremost before sundown, exchanging ideas and talking shop, and case-hardened drinkers at night, who strove to, in the elegantly-put words of Sir Walter Raleigh, *delight in the depraved whims of beastliness.*

Celebrations seemed in order. Marianne came by my office with the new, modified contract which I duly signed, feeling an empowering sense of accomplishment. It confirmed the release date of my twelve-story anthology as this coming Halloween. Two months hence.

We got down to the drinking straight away, in the beer garden at the back of the pub, amidst the good-humoured hubbub of conversation between the various other patrons — couples, friends and families — who had come out in their droves to enjoy the fine weather, the local brew and one another's pleasant company. We basked in the summery fragrance of lavender and sweet william and wild sage. Every so often, a wasp would buzz around our table in idle curiosity, only to be batted away if it started to pester. The westering sun painted the heavens in mellow shades of red, a cool breeze springing up to soften the incumbent heat.

Both Alex and Gary had brought their respective girlfriends (me without any muse of my own) and, over a jug of Pimm's-and-lemonade, proceeded to cross-examine me on my date with Eve. I offloaded every sordid detail, while afraid of getting a ribbing from the lads. I chain-smoked three cigarettes in the process.

Alex was beaming at me when I finished my account, like a father seeing his son complete his Bar Mitzvah. "What do you think of Connor's balls of steel?" he asked the others.

"I'm deeply impressed," said Sasha Atkinson, Alex's half-Brazilian squeeze. "I didn't think he would go through with it."

"Okay, Alex, hit me with your rhythm stick!" I requested.

Alex gave me his inscrutable romance-writer's analysis. "Are you deliberately trying to screw this up?" he critiqued. "Let's see if I've got this clear: you don't take her telephone number when she offers it, you rule out any relationship by saying there's nothing romantic, you don't compliment her on her hair when she's spent four hours at the hairstylist for you, you give her some psycho-talk about wanting to stalk her, and worst of all you rattle on about your ex — as if she's still a part of your life... God, you can't make this up! You're like a runaway train, ploughing through building after building... and yet the funny thing is: everybody survives intact!"

"I had to keep all proceedings gentlemanly and above-board," I said, by way of explanation.

"You like this girl, don't you?" pressed Sasha. "You want to see her again, don't you?"

"Of course I do," I replied truthfully. "I just don't think we were meant to be together."

Sasha didn't seem entirely satisfied. "That's a pretty radical statement. What makes you say you don't belong together?"

"I'm over fifteen years older than her... I drink, I smoke... I'm lazy, work-shy, stuck in a rut... and the real bummer is: I'm a fucking horror writer!"

"What's wrong with being a horror writer?"

I thought of Alex's exquisite culinary skills and strong romantic sensibilities (despite the financial incentive to write porn) and felt a pang of envy. Sasha was a very lucky lady. "Girls prefer a good meal to a good horror story."

"Why can't she have both?"

"Eve's in her early twenties, good-looking, clean-living. She should be enjoying what ought to be the best years of her life, playing to packed audiences and travelling the world and meeting new people, without some old lug like me holding her back."

Gary emerged from his drug stupor and joined in the conversation. "If I might be so bold, are you saying she's out of your league?"

"What if I am?" I said.

"Someone, give this man a slap!" he said with a groan. "She's about to start a new life as an actress. She needs someone to be there for her, looking out for her, guiding her in the right direction. I mean you're both practically in the same profession. The Arts *are* the Arts, whether it's acting or writing."

"Your age and experience should prove invaluable," Sasha told me.

"She could star in your films," suggested Noamie Renoir in her sexy French accent.

It struck me as Noamie spoke how was it that someone like Gary, a habitual stoner, could court a stunning former beauty queen from French Guyana when I was miles off the dating radar? Was there something inherently wrong with me? "It ain't gonna happen."

"And why not?" challenged Sasha. "Your book might jump to the top of the bestseller list, and a few years from now, Eve could become an A-list Hollywood actress."

I remained distinctly sceptical. "Let's get sensible. Everyone knows fame is often fleeting."

"I can tell you're a glass-is-half-empty kind of guy," observed Gary.

"Now that you've taken the first step, what do you plan to do next?" inquired Alex.

"Nothing," I replied frankly. "As the Sloth said: *Patience*."

"Patience?" he said, astonished. "What are you being patient for? Playing hard to get after one date? Unless you want Eve to assume you're just not into her, you must make the next move."

"What do they warn you about the perils of office romance? Besides, she'll be leaving soon."

"All the more reason to make the most of your time together," Alex insisted. "Give her a proper send-off."

"Nah, relationships are a waste of time, energy and resources," I opined. "That time could be better spent... like watching a horror movie!"

"Oh, you're a right bundle of laughs!" remarked Gary. "How you managed to spend a whole year with Marla is beyond me."

"What the hell do I do, guys?" I exclaimed in dismay. "I think I'm developing feelings for Eve!"

"So you *are* human after all," said Gary, amused.

"Nurture those feelings, let them grow," Alex encouraged. "Before long, you'll be feeding off the ripened fruit."

"Listen to the Love Doctor," Gary seconded, "He may look like a ginger-bearded reject from the set of *Braveheart*, but believe me, when it comes to affairs of the heart, he is rarely ever wrong."

"And she's *only* twenty-three!" I said in mock-disbelief. "*Twenty-three!*"

"Use some of those irresistible vampire charms you keep writing about," Alex maintained. "Get her under your thrall—"

"Or, if all else fails, you could always go for Rohypnol," added Gary as an afterthought and received one of Noamie's looks of disgust and admonishment.

Alex continued to dispense his advice. "She's twenty-three, she's young, she's fertile, she's got a good many years of babies ahead of her! She could produce an entire clan!"

"She could be a regular baby-factory, *Alien* Queen-style!" re-phrased Gary, cracking up into zany laughter with Alex.

Sasha punched Alex in the arm, who kissed her back. She managed to squirm out of his embrace. "Men can be so cruel..." she uttered in exasperation. "Please get serious! You're talking about a girl Connor loves."

"I wouldn't go as far as—" I began.

"For the sake of argument, let's suppose you do," Sasha said on a sensible note. "You do plan to see her again? You did invite her to our little get-together, didn't you? She is coming to this thing, isn't she?"

"I did mention it in passing, yesterday," I reassured her, lighting up another Silk Cut.

"Good, so you'll need to act cool," went on Sasha. "Show interest, fuss over her when she arrives. Make her feel special."

Alex, who had stopped laughing, interjected with authority. "To really catch her attention, do something spontaneous, noteworthy... *extemporaneous.*"

I foresaw a hideous obstacle, the aforementioned unfinished business. "You're forgetting there is the small matter of the drinking contest. I can't communicate with her if I'm pissed. What kind of impression will that leave?"

"Hey, man, you promised," Gary reminded me with uncharacteristic seriousness. "You can't welch on our agreement."

"But what about Eve...?"

"Eve can see you get DES-TROYED!"

I suddenly wished I hadn't challenged Gary to a drinking contest. It had happened at last year's office Christmas do when Marianne had been wearing next to nothing. Utterly intoxicated at the time, I told him I could drink him under the table, that I could effectively *destroy* him. He took me up on my challenge, and since I had deferred the event four times over the course of the year, one more postponement meant he would win by default. I would have to go for it, I supposed, since Welsh pride was at stake. Reluctantly, I muttered: "Okay, I'm in..."

"Perhaps a few shots inside you might give you the Dutch courage you need to tell Eve how you really feel about her," suggested Alex.

"That's the least of my worries... Upchucking, being unable to stand, losing the precious gift of sight..."

We discussed the preliminaries, Alex chairing. Should we eat? *Better not... or maybe some light snacks to settle our stomachs...* Thai fishcakes were ordered and consumed. The general consensus was that Jack Daniels should be the drink of choice. Lines were drawn. The winner would be crowned the Ultimate Destroyer, the loser would have to go to the local gay bar and pick up a date.

The sun had nearly set, a sunken red disc on the horizon, and the stars were coming out. The temperature had dropped a few degrees, as the summer breeze blew fresh and vital. The festivities continued around us, unabated, in the beer garden.

I bought the first round, consisting of eight shots of gulping whiskey. I placed them on our table in the open air, dividing them between Gary and myself.

"Let the games begin..." announced Alex, sipping his rather harmless Pimm's.

"Gentlemen, on your marks... Get set... *Go!*"

Gary and I downed our drinks in less than a minute. They went down smoothly.

"You can't beat a good Pan-galactic gargle blaster," Gary said, quoting Douglas Adams.

"Puts fangs on your chest," I said, grimacing at the taste.

Round 2: Gary was buying. Again, four shots apiece.

We knocked them back, to the astonishment of the two ladies in our midst, slamming our glasses on the table when we were done.

I coughed and spluttered. Gary burped.

"Both Even-Stevens," observed our umpire, Alex. "Beware, gentlemen, it'll take at least twenty minutes for those shots to hit you."

However, I was already feeling a little inebriated. After a moment's breather, we jumped into our third round of drinks.

Once again, we proved our mettle. I gulped down my shots, the dark liquid sliding down the back of my throat and starting to burn my gullet. I felt hot.

"I need a smoke," I said, certain of this one fact. I lit up. The nicotine steadied me.

"Oh, look who it is!" exclaimed Sasha, all of a sudden.

Sure enough, there was Eve walking towards us, carrying a glass of Chablis. I cannot describe the emotions I felt. They were akin to infatuation and adoration. She looked like a million bucks and yet at the same time accessible, wearing a pastel green dress, studded with silver butterflies, a red rose planted in her cropped blond hair. She approached our table, moving with soft graceful steps. I was completely smitten. I wanted to marry her.

She introduced herself to the two girls at our table and sat down next to me on the bench, somewhat tentatively. She must have seen my stupid-eyed grin. "What are you guys up to?"

"Drinking contest," said Gary as a matter of course.

A look of concern crossed her face. "How many have they had?" she asked Alex.

"Twelve each, so far, and still going strong."

"Do you think it's wise?"

"Some mightn't think so... but me, I survive on the humiliation of others," Alex quipped, going on to quote an extract from Lord Byron, somewhat in keeping with his Catholic faith. "*Let us have wine and women, mirth and laughter / Sermons and soda-water the day after.*"

"Isn't Marianne going to join us?"

"We didn't invite her. She wouldn't approve."

"And with good reason."

I finished my cigarette. I gazed up at the stars, tiny twinkling beacons in the dusky sky. A cold rind of crescent moon peered down through tattered clouds. "*I was in love with a beautiful blonde once. She drove me to drink. That's the one thing I'm indebted to her for,*" I recited from that perennial alcoholic comic genius, WC Fields. "Bathroom break," I stated. "I have an urge to dream the lizard."

"It's getting a little chilly out here," indicated Sasha, shivering a little. "We should go inside."

We did as she suggested. I took myself to the GENTS and did my business. I returned to a table my colleagues had secured, close to the stage. The inside of the OX AND LAMB wasn't as packed as the outdoor seating area.

The stage was where the local bands would normally play. Tonight, it served as a karaoke night-spot. Every so often people would go up on stage and sing a tune from the karaoke machine. Most of the performances were pretty dire and out-of-key, although one woman did an excellent Whitney Houston.

It would take twenty minutes for the alcohol to kick in, according to Alex... and boy did it kick in! The world seemed to spin and I felt on the verge of throwing up. But I was also riding on a high. The thought of this fine girl by my side kept me in line, at least for the time being. I decided I would do something spontaneous.

I staggered up on stage to a short rally of applause. I scanned the playlist on the karaoke machine for a suitable song, a song that I might actually be able to sing in my condition. I excluded the Lemars, the Take Thats and the Gloria Gaynors before my search yielded something half-decent and appropriate.

I grabbed the mike. "This one goes out to a special lady," I announced, my speech noticeably slurred. "It's all about Eve, all for you, baby..."

And with that I sang, trying to read the lyrics on the screen. I sang as though I had been summoned by the Rock Gods themselves. I sang about the potential in all of us to search within ourselves and change in the name of love, suffer and survive the heartbreak that follows. I sang that old alternative rock gem from across the pond, *Now I'm a Fool* by the Eagles of Death Metal.

And as I waxed lyrical to my girl under the blinding glare of the spotlights, a hundred nameless faces stared up at me in rowdy accompaniment—and judgement—and according to the resounding welter of applause that followed my performance, I must have succeeded. Most people who get smashed sing badly. *So very badly.* But not I. I had hit all the right notes with real aptitude and perfect aplomb.

I went back to our table as another girl stepped up on stage to perform Sophie Ellis-Bexter.

"How's that for spontaneous?" I said to Alex. "Extemporaneous enough for you?"

"Great entertainment, mate," replied Alex, "true showmanship. Who would have thought? A rocker *and* a horror writer... cooler than Jesus."

"And what did the lady in question think?" asked Sasha.

Eve was strangely quiet. Finally, she gave her opinion. "I think it was... *moving.*" She suddenly got up. "I have to go."

"You're not leaving already?" Gary said, surprised. "We're still in the middle of our drinking contest."

"I've got a few things to sort out," she told him.

I sensed her humiliation. "Have I upset you?" I asked, standing up.

She gave due consideration to her reply. "I'm touched by how you feel, but you know damn well I'm not in that place right now! I don't need a relationship!"

"But, Eve, I only—"

"Please don't follow me!"

I watched her depart, my mouth agape.

"Go after her," urged Sasha.

"Not a good idea," warned Alex. "She's made her feelings quite clear."

I sat back down, crushed. "What did I say?"

Alex's tone was grave, sympathetic. "Mate, hard luck…"

No-one spoke for a while, giving me the space and silence I needed. The lively bacchanal which filled the pub suddenly seemed hollow and obscene. I experienced an overwhelming desire to inflict my misery on all those jolly punters.

Gary eventually put a consoling hand on my shoulder. "Cheer up, old buddy. I understand right now it feels like she's driven a stake through your heart, but there's plenty more fish in the ocean, as the saying goes. A couple more drinks should address the issue, take your mind off it."

He was right. I should drown my sorrows. I looked at my problem from a different, less emotional, more rational angle. I hadn't cried when Marla left me, so why should I mope over Eve when I had only dated her once? Besides, I was supposed to be a horror writer for chrissakes with an in-built power to scare, not an incurable romantic like Alex. Leave romance to the experts.

"*Let's do this thing!*" I said, slightly more brightly. I admit I had sobered up but not significantly.

We resumed our drink-off. It could only end in disaster, I heard Noamie say, worried for our well-being. But we were men, blokes, dominant alpha males — we could handle it!

After the fifth round, my memory gets hazy. I have vague recollections of growing increasingly drunk and finding it difficult to focus or raise my head due to the accompanying dragging stupor, of the conversations between us melting into an unutterable language and the wider laughter inside the pub acquiring an erratic, whirling, loony quality. Our alcoholic onslaught turned us into a pair of loose cannons, a random set of variables. I was convinced my body was shutting down, organ by organ.

Apparently, we managed twenty-four units each in a single sitting. The last of these drinks broke the camel's back. Alex terminated the contest when Gary vomited down the front of his shirt. I was declared the winner by default, with Gary left to play gay some day.

But it didn't end there. Gary, gutted by his unceremonious defeat, decided he could defeat me in a "willy" contest, measured flaccid as well as fully erect. He explained that the male organ came in three classifiable sizes: *prick*, *dick* and *cock*. What dimensions did he have tucked down his pants? I wondered, rising to the challenge. So we stood up on the table, pulled down our trousers and started comparing penises. Until the landlord intervened and threatened to call the police while the other customers, having overcome their initial shock, threatened to beat us up.

We were forced to do the moonlight flit.

Noamie escorted Gary home, but not before he allegedly pissed in the local cemetery, lay down in the middle of the road and accosted various passers-by, both male and female, exposing himself and demanding to know how big their penises were. Extraordinarily enough, he somehow evaded a patrolling police car.

I vaguely remember Alex and Sasha carrying me home. I stumbled several times and banged my head on the ground, but they got me to my apartment relatively safely, albeit with a slight gash on my forehead. They cleaned me up, undressed me and tucked me into bed before going on their merry way.

I did not realize the full extent of the damage from our night of binge-drinking until the next morning. What I had considered was normal, laddish behaviour for us Three Up-and-Comers—We Three Infernal Masters of Short Fiction—soon took a sinister turn.

I found out the cost of our little bender the hard way.

5

The Mourning After

When I awoke on the Saturday, I couldn't have felt more proverbially fucked. My body cried agony like the first time I'd ever played squash, my stomach burned with a molten, acidic fire and my lungs felt as though they'd been through a cheese-grater. The hangover was the worst part. When it came to hangovers, I'd read the book, watched the film and bought the T-shirt. But this particular hangover seemed like the very apotheosis of hangovers. It was like a symphony of the damned screaming inside my head — real crazy-making stuff.

Never again, I promised myself, knowing full well that it was probably a promise I wouldn't be able to keep.

I took a moment to orientate myself. The clock on the bedside cabinet told me it was just past noon and, sure enough, sunlight spilled in through the half-drawn curtains, illuminating the dust-motes in dancing, glittering specks of blue.

I could have gone for a longer lie-in, but I thought I ought to get up and start the day. Maybe celebrate my victory over Gary by cracking open a few cold ones. Groaning like a feeble old man, I climbed out of bed.

Throwing on my black bathrobe, I staggered to the en-suite bathroom, each step sending a mad shooting pain directly to my temples. A shave, a shower and a shit (and not necessarily in that order) and I thought I would be partway back to my normal self. A dose of paracetamol should do the rest.

I flicked on the bathroom light, took a glance at myself in the mirror... and stopped dead.

I stared at my reflection in jarring alarm and horror, the fog lifting from my mind in an instant. What the *fuck* was going on?

I knew, though. The frightening yellowness of my skin and the dark urine colour of my eyes could mean only one thing. I simply had to think of Ollie Reed, Dicky Harris and, of course, Georgie Best to put two-and-two together. The pint of brain-rotter I'd consumed last night might as well have been floor polish.

Either way, it had damaged my liver. Damaged it, *irreparably*.

My temples pounded. My stomach heaved, causing me to retch. I stared at the ghastly image in the mirror, taking in my jaundiced condition. I noticed, then, the stench emanating from me like a black cloud. Amidst the smell of stale alcohol arose an evil foetor, of dead mice and gaseous decomposition.

An imaginary newspaper headline formed in my head: *Calling All Dunderheads! World's Laziest Horror Writer Fucks Up His Liver!*

Livers are for weaklings!

Acute liver failure, I thought, the truth hitting home with a stark, tragic inevitability. One of the most resilient and hard-working organs in the human body had died on me overnight, without so much as a by-your-leave. What kind of rampant night of excess could completely shut down the liver when it normally possessed an incredible capacity to regenerate? This could only be punishment for my sins, the ugly aftermath of the drinking contest. It seemed as if my crazy, hell-raising days were over. And my life would be over, too, if I didn't do something about it soon.

I acted with a sense of urgency. I returned to my bedroom and grabbed my mobile phone.

As I began punching in the number for the Emergency Services, the doorbell rang.

I paused. Who the hell could be bothering me at this time?

I decided to ignore them, hoping they would go away.

The doorbell went again.

No chance. I had to answer it. It could be Alex checking on me, making sure I was okay. Wouldn't he be in for a surprise when he saw I had turned yellow?

I walked to the door of the flat and opened it.

There stood the last person I was expecting to see.

"Hello, Connor," Eve greeted me. "May I come in?"

I did not speak for a moment, at a loss for words. Then, I gestured for her to enter.

Eve wandered in and I took her into the lounge. She seated herself on the couch. "We need to talk."

I sat down in an armchair. "So it would seem…"

She glanced around the lounge. The place was a tip. Books and paper were strewn everywhere. Dust was collecting in thick, unsanitary layers.

"I normally hire a maid to tidy up once a month," I informed her, almost apologetically. "Unfortunately, she's on maternity leave."

"I guess so…"

It occurred to me that she did not seem particularly fazed by my grotesque appearance. My mustard-yellow colour must have registered by now, surely. "So what brings you to this neck of the woods?" I asked, all too conscious of my disgusting, mousy breath.

"I have a confession," began Eve.

"Go ahead. I'm listening."

"I hope you didn't mind me leaving the pub so abruptly yesterday," she said, struggling with something inside her, perhaps her conscience.

"Why should I mind?" I lied. "It wasn't personal."

"I was upset," she said, justification for her walking-out on us. "I was appalled by what you were doing to yourself and, I guess, a little embarrassed. I knew I couldn't change anything. Can you forgive me?"

"I already have," I said absently, returning to a more pressing matter. "Now if you don't mind I'm in the middle of a medical crisis. I must call for an ambulance."

"You can't!" she burst out, mysteriously. "I mean it won't make any difference."

I stopped dialling and put down my mobile phone slowly. I wished for her to elaborate. "What exactly do you mean?"

"You haven't got long to live."

"No kidding."

"You're not hearing me."

"Then, pray, enlighten me."

"Your liver's packed in, the result of years of hard drinking. Your irresponsible drinking session last night was the final straw. Your body won't be able to recover. You're going to die."

So she *had* noticed my sickly-yellow condition, the fetid smell of death. I didn't know whether to be glad or scared. "All the more reason I mustn't delay. The doctors could stabilize me with drugs." George Best again came to mind. "Give me a liver transplant."

"No matter what the doctors do, you'll be dead by ten this evening."

This was turning into a distinctly freaky conversation. "How could you possibly know?"

"You still haven't heard my confession," she said quietly. "Like the rest of my family, I have psychic abilities."

I tried to understand what she'd mentioned, feeling oddly disjointed. "Pardon me, I'm not exactly firing on all four cylinders... Psychic, you say? You mean you can read people's minds, predict the future, and all that crap?"

"My gift allows me to see into the future, yes."

She had certainly grabbed my attention. I studied her to determine if she was exaggerating or having me on. This social butterfly with her designer platinum-blond hair, enigmatic smile and gentle, enchanting manner. Now garbed in seductive black silk, like a mourning Scottish Widow, or some angel in disguise as I had once previously alluded to. She was an angel alright, I thought... the soul-harvesting Angel of Death. "And you see me die?"

Eve nodded.

"I don't buy it!" Except by her earnest, sympathetic expression, I knew she wasn't delusional or trying to bullshit me.

"There is nothing you can change," Eve maintained solemnly. "It is already written."

"What if you're wrong? You expect me to just sit around and die a lonely death?"

"What you may not know is that drinking contest will go down in legend," Eve explained. "You and the other Up-and-Comers will be remembered for a long time to come."

"Whatever for? We're simply small-time writers for a low-key literary magazine."

"Your deaths will catapult you to stardom. You'll develop a cult following. Your stories will sell millions. They'll even make movies."

"You're forgetting that Alex and Gary are still with us." I suddenly wished I hadn't made that assumption for I experienced a feeling of dark dread.

"Noamie woke up this morning to find Gary beside her stone-cold, having choked on his own vomit last night. His dog was by his bedside, licking the sick from his pillow." Eve paused to let me digest the grim and shocking news before continuing. "Alex and Sasha went clubbing last night after they left you. At the BARRACUDA, Alex got involved in a fight where he was kicked repeatedly in the head, fracturing his skull in several places and causing a serious brain haemorrhage. Despite draining the bleed, he is presently lying in a coma in ICU on a respirator. He will die in the next few minutes."

"*My God*—" I muttered, stunned by the succession of revelations, feeling as though Eve had dropped an anvil on my head. I couldn't believe that someone like Gary, who was constantly whacked-out on weed in a quest to further the creative process, could have perished in such an undignified way, let alone Alex, who was a stalwart at the magazine, a moral compass and a towering pillar of strength. They were both dead—or as good as. I felt like crying. "Why are you telling me all this?"

"You have one final task to perform before you, too, die," Eve declared. "You must write down the events of the last three days — your greatest piece of work."

The situation was getting weirder and weirder. My colleagues had bought it big-time and I, too, existed on the edge of death. And, according to Eve, it was my destiny to produce my last piece of work from scratch in the short allotted time I had left on this earth. Fact was demonstrably stranger than fiction. "You want me to write?"

Eve nodded.

"You will watch me write?"

"Like a guardian angel to your story," Eve confirmed, "I am here to see that it happens."

"Can you grant a dying man his final wish?"

"I suppose I can."

I rose from the armchair and grabbed Eve by the hand, pulling her up from the couch. I placed my arm around her swanlike shoulders, and tipping her head gently back, crushed my lips against hers with all the passion I could muster. "I always wanted to do that," I said, releasing her.

"I kind of figured..." she said, grimacing at my fragrant death breath.

I went into the study and switched on the computer. Eve, my graceful harbinger of doom, my own regular Cassandra, followed me in. I decided to do this thing sober, without the usual disinhibiting effect of alcohol. This would be, in all likelihood, my last duty to my readers. Distil the last seventy-two hours of my life, including the night three writers met and drank themselves to their graves. So deliciously gothic, almost on par with Byron, Shelley and Coleridge on that fateful night at the Villa Diodati, Lake Geneva. I had learned an invaluable lesson: that the price of winning sometimes resulted in losing more than you gained. I felt compelled to jot down my experiences more than anything I had ever done in the past. I had a deadline to beat — my own impending death — and apparently, once completed, it would be a dead sell. And, with it, should come posthumous acclaim as well as provide perfect iconic material for Halloween. Did I want to be immortalized in this way? *Fuck, yeah!* After all, I had told a certain someone that fear, pain, death, disease and madness were my business. I had already even chosen a title for my finished manuscript: *Deadliner*.

Relax. Take a deep breath...

I began to write.

August 2009-October 2009

Hiding in the Light

"I listened to her as she spoke in her beautiful voice, spoke of things which even now I would not dare whisper in the blackest night… for all I can say you may have heard the talk of the vilest, but I tell you, you can have no conception of what I know, not in your most fantastic, hideous dreams can you have imaged forth the faintest shadow of what I have heard – and seen. Yes, seen. I have seen the incredible, such horrors that even I myself sometimes stop in the middle of the street and ask whether it is possible for a man to behold such things and live."

The Great God Pan (1894)
Arthur Machen

I would like to relate to you one of the saddest – and darkest – chapters of my life. It's taken a while – a whole decade – for me to put my thoughts down on paper, but something happened recently that tripped those grim memories, brought them flooding back to my conscious with stark vengeance.

I'd really want to talk about Aidan Sayles. Because, you see, me and him were the very best of friends in those olden days. More modern vernacular would have used the term 'bromance'. But it was Chertsford in the 1990s, and Grunge had arrived on the scene. Grunge kicked ass, Chavpop dint. Nirvana's *Come As You Are* became our secret tune.

Aidan spoke his mind and, in my opinion, that made him honest. His parents weren't well-off (unlike mine), always scrimping and saving, attending Church every Sunday, come rain or shine. Besides providing spiritual counselling one evening a week on a voluntary basis, Aidan's father worked for the tax office, in a super-honest line of work, so I suppose that's where Aidan's honesty sprang from. With a dash of moral pep gained from the oft-watched regulars of *Have I Got News For You*, which Aidan had religiously watched since it first appeared on our screens in 1990 and which has since become—bear with me—the longest-running, wittiest, satirical, current affairs quiz show in the world—an *institution*—Aidan quickly adopted its straight-for-the-jugular, tell-it-like-it-is approach and from it, I suppose, forged a reputation as a prankster—or piss-taker.

Aidan loved a good piss-take.

I remember when we first met in English Lit class in Sixth Form, and Aidan caught a whiff of my name. *Henry Schofield? What are you—your own grandfather?*

Call me Hank... I suggested, preferring the cooler nickname so as not to be thought of as an old fart.

What are you? A Yank?

When I told him what my father did for a living, without sounding like some upstart, he remarked in the same vein: *What is he—Gordon Gekko's lapdog?*

You cannot imagine how refreshing it was to hear such an insult.

I suppose my father was a lapdog in many respects, for whom making money—and tonnes of it at that—served as *his* religion. He was an investment banker and he never stayed in one place for longer than a few weeks. In fact the longest, I remember, he stayed put was six weeks when he had that skiing accident and broke his arm, forced somewhat reluctantly to convalesce in a private Swiss clinic. He had high hopes for me, decided I should follow in his wealthy footsteps at *Heymans, Staples & Schofield,* but shunning any more mouthfuls from the silver spoon, I dropped out of boarding school and took my A-Levels at Oaks Fold Tech, just to spite the old man for being such an unloving, greedy bastard. I wanted to be a writer.

Aidan, I guess, was a godsend—if the fellow had believed in God—and his take on life a breath of fresh air. And, while he introduced me to the delights of stand-up comedy, he was kind enough to refrain from calling me Hank the Wank despite the obvious temptation.

One of his favourite targets was the local supermarket where every week he caused one hell or another. He hated the way the corporate greed of the supermarket was ruthlessly squeezing the local honest, hardworking shopkeeper out of business. I remember Aidan leaving a trail of tomato ketchup all the way to the LADIES. I can still see him hiding in the clothes rack, and as people browsed through his section of the rack, he'd jump out and shout: *Choose me! Choose me!* He caused such a shock to one woman she fainted. When an announcement came over the loudspeaker, he assumed the foetal position, acting distressed: *Oh no, it's those voices again!* He was the kind of cool dude who would take a box of condoms to the Customer Services desk and ask where the fitting room was. Another time he actually hid in the fitting room, and after several minutes of silence yelled very loudly: *Hey, there's no toilet paper in here!*

Outstanding!

And as any stand-up kind of guy, he'd apologize to the staff for his antics and be on his merry way. Until next week, of course…

No legal action was taken against him by the shopping chain, and he was never reported to the authorities. Neither was he kicked out of the restaurant when he poked a finger up his nose and scooped out a hard, crusty one attached to a length of nostril hair while others tried to eat, even when he kept flicking his bogeys here, there and everywhere while complaining out aloud that the water was 'too dry', and does anyone mind if he puts his hands down his pants and adjusts his balls? Nor was he arrested when he mooned the pigs out of the passenger window of a car that I was, in quote, 'driving like a mong'. The police let us go since we were celebrating our A-Level results and I seemed sober enough, confidently passing the breathalyzer and getting away with the spliff I'd smoked just prior to sitting behind the wheel. Aidan always survived the flak because he could smooth-talk himself out of any tricky situation – it was always meant to be taken in good humour rather than descending into anything obnoxious, and 'because I'm so awesome'.

Aidan enjoyed cow-tipping, an activity we'd respectfully observe at midnight, running up to a standing, sleeping cow and pushing them over.

Some of the quotes that defined him included such priceless observations as: *Floss my teeth? Man, whatever smells down there at the back of my mouth comes out after dark.*

When he passed wind and stank out the college library: *You boffed, Aidy.*

To wit he replied while feigning perplexion: *I don't know if I did! I was confused! Damn my interminable flatulence! Must have snuck up on me! Alas, I have turned into something I didn't want to be: a stinky, fart-man!*

He once asked a posh tart outside Harrods: *Fifty quid for tickets to* Les Miz *or a half-ounce of weed?* She chose the bag of weed.

Aidan was one for hash cakes for breakfast because it was 'a slacker's way to start the day'.

Stoned out of his head one evening, he jumped up from his seat and declared loudly: *I am The Superintendent of Everything.*

What the hell does that mean? I asked him.

Exactly! he replied emphatically.

Aidan would deliberately confuse feminism with lesbianism, and vice versa, just to get on Germaine Nothing-Is-Ever-Good-Enough-For-Me Greer's tits.

Of genuine Z-Lister, Katie Price, he observed: *The woman doesn't just need a facelift but an entirely new face as well as a brand new personality, so as not to be confused with a loud-mouthed slapper with a boob-job that could compete with a bouncy castle.*

Of Robbie Williams's belief in his own musical abilities: *Confident – or deluded? Necessitating a compulsory ego transplant? Or just shooting the damn fellow for inflicting his tone-deaf, karaoke style of wailing on the world?*

Opinion on Simon Cowell, who at the time was making waves and whom Aidan prophesized would one day go on to greater things, later *X-Factor* judge? *Old Cowell the Bowel? Because he's so full of crap!*

Regarding the past Turner prize winners? *People sure have a thing for crap!*

He once sent a mock-scientific letter to a retired Arthur Scargill, informing him that 'human beings evolved from miners' and that he, Arthur Scargill, was the 'missing link'.

When the 'Noughties came round: *Why did George Dubya never join the Church of Scientology?* He's way too smart for their Lincoln Logs and, thusly, Tom Thumb.

Another great put-down, courtesy of Aidan: *You can dig Peter Ustinov out of his grave and film his remains on TV and he'd still be a more effective communicator than Rooney, you know, the footballer who could pass himself off as Shrek's Runt of the Litter.*

When Aidan was slammed in the back of his car — ironically, it was not his fault on this occasion—and the engineers decided to write his car off because it would have cost more to replace the bumper than the car itself was worth, he proved once again an expert at dishing out insults, this time having a go at the insurance firm in Blackpool who should have received his letter, signed and dated, agreeing to the financial settlement from the third party insurers. His insults flew thick and fast, such as: *It's bad enough that my car is now considered salvage because those lazy sods can't be bothered to fix it but then to incompetently deal with the administration side of things? The letter's probably got lost in their internal mail. I might as well have taken the train up there and delivered it myself. I bet that's how they do things in Blackpool—no, 'Black Poo'. So utterly useless at their jobs, more likely than not out gambling!*

Aidan was honest, outspoken and an excellent piss-taker. He had his own inimical style, relied on a well-developed repertoire, an acerbic wit that could have even made generations of Blackadders green with envy. *A real gem in a pile of dung*, I might have said of my buddy, taking a leap from his lexicon.

Together, we were a double act, more like Waldorf and Statler, less Mike Judge's sneering, sniggering cartoon slackers who seemed permanently glued to their TV set.

While I went off to Chertsford University to study Literature, even an idle stoner like Aidan, who lacked any decent academic grades, went to work, for the *Big Issue* as a support writer, because he did not 'wish to sink so low as to scrounge off the State like the Royal Family' or 'join the government statistics of common layabouts who pretend to do something useful by just living off the dole, sitting on their arses, drinking Special Brew, and watching self-righteous narcissists lamely posing as defenders of family values and social morality such as *The Jeremy Pratt Show* or the sheer volume of daytime quiz-shows like *Crap In The Morning'*. He'd visit me on campus and we'd either go out on a bender or just lounge around at the digs on the stone, watching pirated copies of *Saturday Night Live*. Maybe we were those sneering, sniggering slackers, after all. Aidan took me on a jolly to the world-famous Comedy Store in Piccadilly Circus, and we travelled up, knowing we could never be disappointed, to the Edinburgh Fringe.

Then, Luna came into his life, and I came to realize that not even the most Goddamnedest prayer in the world could save him.

*****

How do you describe colour to a congenitally blind man? Aidan was carving SEX IS ACE into his desk in junior school and making hugely inappropriate jokes about tampons when he graduated to secondary school. I suppose he didn't know the first thing about the fairer sex. He was as hopeless on the subject as much as he excelled at lampooning others. His inexperience might even be considered amusing if it wasn't so serious.

I remember a conversation he had with a fairly good-looking girl in a bar:

"Maybe I'm just too intellectual for you," Aidan was saying.

"You calling me thick?" the girl ventured suspiciously.

"No, I think you're a very intelligent girl with a very intelligent body..." I heard him tell her rather leerily. Of course, he got a drink in his face.

To him, a girl with a 'nice personality' meant she was 'Bull Terrier-ugly'. Aidan dreamed of playing with a 'lovely bird's coochy-coo' as he put it euphemistically, and he thought that Margaret Thatcher had more cobwebs than Miss Havisham.

He met Luna Thessaly at, of all places, the supermarket when they bumped aisles, and he responded to her sudden interest in him with the shy awkwardness and nervousness of a girl phobic. Their relationship, however, gathered strength from that first encounter.

The change in him was astonishing. For a guy who made a lot of noise, he became unusually calm and focused and, need I say, genuinely overawed. He was like a housecat that probably doesn't believe its luck: all the doors are open and it's [accidentally] been given two pouches before ten a.m.

He spoke about Luna all the time which irritated me to an extent and made me jealous sometimes.

I am your man and you are my babe, I remember him saying to her once when we were out on a double date. I suppose she was a bit of babe whose body no sane man would have refused to ravish and worship. A short black bob cropped an oval face with dark, expressive eyes and a full gorgeous smile. She was always adorned in the best designer clothes and owned a swanky flat in Friarsgate, part of her inheritance, she claimed, from a rich uncle. She claimed she worked as a party organizer though I never saw her work. The thing that particularly sticks with me about her was her voice, the husky Tara Reid quality of which could mesmerize and make someone feel special. Even horny.

They got engaged very quickly and wedded soon after. Almost as fast as a shotgun wedding.

I did get the old Aidan back for a disappointingly short period. *Us getting married?* he told Luna one time during a — mind I say — *very infrequent quarrel. What on earth for? Waste of my bloody time. I'm giving you the chance to back out now.*

Luna didn't back out and they did get married, expediting their wedding, and I was the Best Man. And as Best Man I wished them well: *May your lives together be blessed with love and happiness always.*

His parents didn't attend as they didn't approve of him marrying an atheist. Neither did Luna's parents, whom Aidan never met, agree with her choice of husband, allegedly. As Aidan said during his Reception speech traditionally following on from mine: *Shame our parents didn't feel the occasion worthwhile to come. That blows. Their decision, their loss...*

We welcomed all and sundry, but only the curious came. But at least all the ladies looked ornate and the gentlemen dapper, as they should. The day passed off without a glitch. And the weather held against all the Met Office's expectations: it didn't rain on that grey, overcast September day.

They honeymooned in the Scilly Isles where, according to Aidan, they made hot, steamy love and ate a lot of fish, and when they returned, he appeared more affectionate. Devoted. All rainbows and kittens. Smitten. He could have gladly eaten her bogeys, and her farts must have surely smelled like perfume. He said she had made an honest man out of him. I should have been happy for him, but a nagging doubt lingered in the back of my mind that something wasn't entirely authentic here: the supposed-innocent way she had appeared on the scene, the ease by which she had seduced him, the speed at which she had persuaded him into marriage and how she had unconditionally and disquietingly gained his obedience. His *unquestioning* loyalty and obedience.

She could appear all smiles and kisses and platitudes, but I had a curious sense that there was something bogus about her, almost predatory, as though she had specifically singled out my hilarious but vulnerable friend for some dark purpose that was yet unclear. Even the way he was piling on the pounds, from a relatively weedy kind of fellow, no pun intended, to someone growing podgier by the day, I regarded as highly suspicious. *As though he were being deliberately fattened up.*

And he didn't suspect a thing.

Maybe only I saw through that illusion of conjugal bliss. There was no doubt in my mind that she wore the pants in their relationship and had controlled the pace their relationship progressed from the outset.

In the weeks that followed I saw less and less of Aidan. I myself was emerging as a writer, wrapped up in my first book deal. I would ring him up but for some reason he'd be unavailable. Of the couple of times I did manage to catch him he seemed anxious and said some peculiar things which I didn't feel it my place to explore with him: *She's either wandering around naked or I'm playing with himself... I asked her if that's the grope and feel I get for the day...*

That sort of thing. Odd and ominous.

That was just before he appeared at my Italianate apartment in the small hours, having braved a violent storm in his nightwear, genuinely distressed and scared.

"Luna is not who she claims she is..."

I tried to make sense of what the man sitting before me had just uttered, couldn't quite get my head round it. All I felt was a deep understandable concern for my friend, my good friend, Aidan Sayles, who had pitched up at my apartment at two in the morning, in a raging November storm, barefoot, wearing only a dressing gown and pyjamas. I thought the guy must be desperate or, worse, undergoing some kind of nervous breakdown. His night clothes were drenched through, the thinning hair on his head in wet tangles, and he was shivering. I worried he might catch hypothermia so I gave him a towel to dry himself with, lit up the hearth and poured each of us a generous tumbler of scotch. We seated ourselves in opposite armchairs in front of the fireplace.

"What exactly do you mean?" I said, quizzically.

He glanced around nervously before whispering conspiratorially. "She's plotting my downfall..."

"What gives you that idea?"

He paused, pondered how to proceed, lest he should be thought of as crazy, perhaps.

"Please, Aidy, a problem shared is a problem halved," I reminded him, *pressed* him.

It was all the encouragement he needed. He blurted it straight out. "Luna *isn't* human."

"Not human?" I said, slow on the uptake, wondering what he was driving at. "If Luna's not human, what else could she be?"

"I don't know," he said distractedly. "I thought she was a witch at first with all those books — *grimoires* — she keeps on her shelves, but she's something much worse. An ancient manifestation of evil. *She hides in the light.*"

"Hides in the light?" This would take some comprehending.

"It's an old Biblical term. Non-canonical. From the Gospel of Thomas, Logion 5: *And Jesus said: Now what is before thy face, and what is hidden from thee shall be revealed unto thee; for there is nothing hidden which shall not be made manifest.*" I looked at him peculiarly, wondering at what point did he start reading Scripture — and why? But he went on to explain, "It basically means where something is so obvious that you don't see it or pay any attention to it or it doesn't even cross your mind." His eyes widened with a frightening memory that he was evidently struggling to block out. "*But I saw her for what she really is!*"

The fire roared and crackled in the hearth, the snug heat of which I relished on this cold, damp autumnal night. I'm sure Aidan appreciated it, too. I sipped from my tumbler to supplement the warmth.

Something had definitely been up between him and Luna, I knew now for certain, I'd always suspected she was a controlling woman, but I wasn't expecting this. I didn't know what to say. "Hey...?"

The doubtful, almost disbelieving, look on my face must have infuriated him. "You think I'm barking, don't you?" he remarked with unexpected resentment. Then, he threw his head back and erupted into a siren of laughter, deeply removed from his naturally humorous disposition and so close to insanity, it brought gooseflesh prickling to my skin.

A knot exploded in the fireplace, making me jump, sending bright, orange sparks up the flue. Outside, the sky continued to jettison its load, a furious downpour that tattooed against the pane. I took several more sips of my scotch to steady myself.

Aidan continued, more morosely this time, accusation and self-pity in his voice. "You sold me down the river, man. Why didn't you stop me from marrying her?"

"That wouldn't have been up to code. I thought you were happy," I said truthfully, and thought of the most obvious course of action. "You might as well stay here tonight. We can go to your place tomorrow morning and assess the situation, objectively. Confront her."

Aidan heaved a weary sigh, accepting my offer of a warm bed and close companionship. "No, I don't want to go back and *confront* her. There's been something brewing for days—I don't know what—but I think I'm going to find out tonight."

I didn't ask what he meant. But that thought popped in my head again: *he's being fattened up like a pig.* In life, Aidan had been a lanky, self-assured fellow, but at that precise moment, hunched-up like he was and regardless of the weight he had put on, he looked small and old and tired and miserable. Fragile. *And horribly afraid.* There were bags under his eyes as though he hadn't slept in days. Madness lurked just around the corner.

"Thank you, Hank, for hearing me out. You're a damn fine person and the best damn friend I ever had!"

His gratitude touched me, almost brought a tear to my eye. I remembered those wonderfully amusing, gag-filled days of old. *HIGNFY*, Waldorf and Statler, and all that jazz. I never minded being his sounding board. "Likewise, buddy, likewise. Any time…"

Aidan shook his head with even greater weariness. He downed the rest of his scotch. "*Needs must*, as they say."

The apartment buzzer rang. Aidan quailed before the sound, his colour draining instantly. A fresh and wild dread widened his peepers.

Who could it be at this hour?

But it was abundantly clear he knew. So did I.

Sure enough—*speak of the Devil*—Luna stood outside the door. *Stellar timing, babe.* She made no attempt at a greeting. "Where is he?"

"He's here," I replied, matter-of-factly, "but he's not in the best of shape. He's agreed to stay over."

Luna's voice remained cold and level and blunt. The voice of a woman scorned, seriously pissed, a woman whose authority is rarely, if ever, challenged. "He will do no such thing! He's coming with me!" When she saw I wouldn't be letting her come in, she started calling his name from the hallway. Her jet-black eyes fired daggers at me. "Aidan! Aidan! Come out this *instant!*"

Aidan's voice drifted up from the dark somewhere behind me. "Don't boss me around, woman!" *Good for you, my fine fellow!*

"Come here this instant!" Luna repeated, louder still, growing more impatient and frustrated, a school ma'am scolding a misbehaving little child, or a dog. "We're not finished yet! The Master is expecting you! Otherwise you're going to see the wrong side of me, *again!*"

The emphasis on that last word — *again* — made me think of Aidan's paranoid talk about his wife, the craziness of his explanation: *An ancient manifestation of evil. I saw her for what she really is.* What had he seen? What might her wrong side consist of?

I didn't much care for what she had done to Aidan, the way she had reduced my jolly, fine fellow-of-a-friend to a pathetic, quivering wreck. "You can't threaten him! Or get near him without getting past me first! He's my friend and a grown man capable of making his own decisions! He needs time apart from you! If you don't leave right now, I'm calling the pol —"

I felt a gentle tap on my shoulder and, as I moved aside, Aidan wandered into the hallway, taking me by surprise. The fear had fled from his face, replaced by an air of acceptance and resignation apparent in his stooped, pottering gait.

I begged him, dismayed. "Aidy, don't do this. Please stay…"

He kissed me. The soppy sod kissed me! Kissed my cheek in a tender, poignant gesture of brotherly love! "Man, I got to go. I have to do this. It's happening tonight…" he said quietly, humbly, serenely, putting paid to my request. I caught an awful sense of finality in those words, felt a hideous foreboding. "It's out of my hands now. I won't be coming back…"

[*May your lives together be blessed with love and happiness always.*]

I wanted to cry.

Luna wrapped Aidan in a mac and scarf and fitted some shoes on his feet. She did not hug or kiss or show any affection to her husband, did not ask how he was. She was as cold as ice, compassionless to the point of inhuman. I wondered what Aidan must have endured during his time with her; I could imagine her being an absolute nightmare to live with.

"Move!" she snapped, as though ordering a prisoner. "You have important work to do…"

As Aidan said his farewells to me and turned to go while I pushed back tears, Luna whispered triumphantly, chillingly, into my ear. "What Luna wants Luna gets." Yet, at the same time, there was also something raunchy, provocative — *arousing*, even — in those low, gravelly tones.

Then she was on her way. Aidan did not hear or notice the disturbing remark. I watched her escort her husband — my friend — down the hall and depart into the wet, blustery night. Then, I grabbed my long black coat and, against my better judgement, followed them, fearful for my friend's welfare, recalling the dire manner he had presented himself to me that night, the soaking, wild-eyed, absurdly-underdressed condition he'd arrived in. I would soon learn my fears had been justified.

She bundled him into the passenger seat and drove off. I tailed her through the dark, damp, deserted streets of Chertsford, keeping a respectable distance. Not that it mattered. She must have known I was following her. Nothing moved but us. Besides, my headlights must have been a dead give-away in her rear-view mirror.

Luna brought us to an old, abandoned quarry on the fringes of town, its mother lode of granite extracted long ago. She parked up, and with Aidan in tow, clambered out of the car. I, too, crawled to a stop some distance away, instinctively, so as not to be seen.

The storm had broken, the rain had let up. The air was still, condensed by the cold night into a low-lying mist.

I wondered what business Luna might want with this lonely place. *With Aidan.*

Here he was, tramping around an isolated, disused quarry in his night attire on the very edge of winter at four in the morning. She had him by the short and curlies. She had glamoured him like a vampire, enchanted him like a sorceress. *Bedevilled him.* Whatever she had in store for him, whatever agenda she was working on, I knew I would find out soon.

She walked Aidan across the derelict open-pit mine, strewn with chunks of rubble, curling tendrils of mist rising up from the ground, shimmering pools of water reflecting the disencumbered, shrunken rainclouds and the moon they obscured. She took him towards a dark opening, shaped like the arch of a small viaduct, bored into the farthest quarry-face.

I kept low and crouched, in tentative pursuit, my heart pounding, my breath coming in frozen gasps, apprehension building up inside me, threatening to explode.

When the moon did finally emerge from behind a shifting congress of night-clouds, I witnessed something I didn't think possible in our sane, ordinary world.

Luna looked over her shoulders and her eyes met mine as I sat, hunkered-down behind a moss-covered boulder, peering over the top. My question was answered: she had known all along I was on her heels.

But that wasn't what startled me.

It was her face. It was no longer young and wickedly-alluring. In that brief instant, as the full moon lit up every rock, boulder and contour of the quarry-field like a floodlight and gave the creeping mist an eerie, sickly-wan glow, I was staring at a countenance so ancient and scarred and unspeakably grotesque it will haunt my hours till the day I die. Moonlight gleamed waxy from her utterly-bald, keloid-ridden scalp. The eyes of the demonic creature I recognized — and, yet, did not — black pits of the purest evil, matured over the ages and all-pervading.

And Aidan did not protest, appeared oblivious to the nameless monster in his midst, merely toddled along obediently and simplemindedly beside her, fully compliant, acknowledging, whether consenting to it or not, her dominion over him, as she led him to meet the Master. Aidan, whose personality and wit Luna had crushed, turning him into a mirthless, feeble-minded individual. How had he come to this? Overfed, plumped-up just right, ready for the slaughterhouse.

I thought of Hella, one of Woland's diabolic retinue, and Margarita, riding her witch's broom in nocturnal search of her absent lover, himself committed to a mental asylum after burning his manuscript which doesn't stay burned.

I daren't imagine what Luna's Master — perhaps, her cruel, maleficent, sacrifice-demanding god — must look like.

Then, as they approached the arched, blackly-yawning entrance to the tunnel, both Aidan and Luna vanished.

I never saw my friend again.

That song keeps repeating in my head: *Come As You Are*, courtesy of Cobain, Grohl and Novoselic.

He was never found. Both he and Luna disappeared that night as if the earth had swallowed them up. I gave the police an account of everything I witnessed that same night. They rationalized it away: it was late, I was tired and maybe what I saw must have been due to a trick of the moonlight. Without belabouring the point, you can call me mad and lock me up, but I will defend to the hilt what I saw. The police search yielded nothing. Even that rock tunnel had ceased to exist when they went to investigate. The whole episode shook my faith in human nature and gave me my first glimpse beyond the veil that separated our reality from the obscene, seldom-penetrated darkness of another and the terrifying alien deities that dwell in that place, passing unmerciful judgement over the degenerate bestial hordes they govern.

Who — or *what* — was Luna?

She remains a profound mystery. She is no longer the woman — the control freak — who came between two men and deprived me of my closest friend, but something much more repulsive and sinister. I do not know what kind of abomination she is. I can only assume she is an inhabitant of that other twilight world.

This is now over a decade later, and his case remains open to this day. The police suspected he and his wife did a bunk abroad and are now living a life of leisure in some foreign idyll. I hope, and sometimes convince myself, that that's what happened than try to imagine whatever unimaginable fate he suffered. I try to imagine he thinks about me sometimes and the brotherhood we once shared as much as I think about him.

Wherever you are, Aidan, my thoughts go out to you. I miss your acid wit, your outrageous comments, your snappy comebacks, but most of all I miss your friendship. I wake up every morning and am saddled by guilt, and regret, that I could not save you, and the scary, sucking black hole of grief that goes with it.

His parents never recovered from their loss, either. They are still alive but in perpetual mourning. I sometimes drop by their house and reminisce on how outstanding a fellow Aidan was. They are immensely grateful for my visits. These days, the Internet Revolution provides a considerable source of material to work with. Take nipple and labial piercings and the whole concept of body modification, for instance. Or, for that matter, the fun we could have had with Nigel Farage of UKIP, a real so-and-so. Or the irreverent digs to be had at SuBo, short for Susan Boyle. Even Benedict Cumberbatch. *Are you telling me that the guy who plays Sherlock Holmes is named after a massive sausage roll?* Aidan might have said in his infinite wisdom. I watched *Spamalot* recently at the Playhouse Theatre and thought of Aidan, and despite commendable performances all-round, Les Dennis and Bonnie Langford, in my opinion, do not Monty Python make.

I have created a Twatter account, a page devoted solely to my erstwhile mate, called *Sayles Says* which I update daily with a Rant For The Day, generating side-splitting discussion and feedback. Even after two whole decades, *HIGNFY* is still going strong, without losing any of its unique edge, as fresh as ever, doing their bit against pomposity, hypocrisy and corruption, ripping the piss out of those who deserve it.

I made it as a writer, and now one of my novels, *The Master and Luna*, is due to be adapted for the small screen, a semi-fictional, darkly comic tale inspired by the events of that fateful night, and its title and certain plot devices unashamedly borrowed, for obvious reasons, from one of the greatest books of the twentieth century since *Catch-22*. Simon Pegg and Nick Frost are rumoured to have read the script. My truffle pig of a father, who never had faith in my creative abilities, fled to the Dominican Republic when the banks went tits-up and he was implicated in a pensions' scandal. My mother grew senile, obsessing over black fluffy bits on the carpet and the need to empty the dishwasher, fixating over the tiny dents in the Bosch kettle and incessantly scrubbing the kitchen floor to a mad mirror-shine, despite the live-in housekeeper in her payee, than playing with her own grandchildren, of which there are two little girls (aged eight and five), during the three-year spell when I married and divorced my literary agent.

I suppose what jogged my memories and made me write about my old buddy was something that happened while I was out shopping on the High Street last week. I had just stepped out of a bookstore when, opposite me, I saw a woman looking into the window of a dress shop. She seemed strangely familiar, and when she tilted her head softly to the side in apparent conversation with a gentleman who accompanied her, I recognized her profile, and I was struck by a tremendous flashback of her walking my unfortunate friend across the misty, moonlit quarry to wherever she had sent him to, whatever terrible doom she had planned for him.

Yet she had not aged a day. The same smooth, olive skin, the same lovely black bob, that same delicious, strawberry pout. She still looked just as chic and foxy and desirable as she had done ten years ago. The same royal babeness. Only I bet she was using a different name.

The man who escorted her I thought for a moment was Aidan, my heart leaping. Except I saw that from his ginger hair and the significant portliness of his frame that it wasn't. I saw the wedding ring on his finger, and the expression of the gentleman, relaxed, happy, in love, and an intense, burning hatred gripped me. The execrable, two-faced bitch had ensnared another poor soul [*What Luna wants Luna gets*] with her artifices and diablerie, another man who in all likelihood didn't know that it would not end well for him.

I felt the compulsion to walk up to her new husband and warn him that Luna, apparently untouched by age, regardless of the passing of over a decade, was not a woman, but an ancient, sublimely-evil hag whose raven-haired beauty was nothing short of an illusion, hiding in plain sight, blending in with her surroundings, in order to supply a constant stream of victims to the Master, probably tasked with this despicable responsibility over countless ages. But I froze in alarm when she turned and, as people walked by, caught my gaze as though she knew I was there. Time seemed to slow down. I read her expression, and something unspoken passed between us. I saw the dark warning in those eyes, the menace and the malevolence it inferred, and I knew that an even worse, more grisly, unknown fate than the one my missing friend went through awaited me if I dared interfere. I was dealing with powers that no human could ever conceive and walk away from with their sanity intact. I thought better of my confrontation.

Then, as though nothing had happened, she went back to talking and laughing with her man, keeping it light, casual and carefree, and the moment was gone. Her gentleman had failed to notice her short, reproachful glance behind, and continued their conversation, adoration in his eyes, hanging on to her every word. Then, they strolled away and disappeared into the moving crowd.

My paralysis broke. A tear trickled down my cheek. I only felt pity for the fellow, mouthed a small prayer for him. The poor mug didn't have a clue that he belonged to her now—she owned him, body-and-soul—and it could only end badly for him. *Just like it had done for Aidan Sayles.*

I think of an art class where the students are asked to paint a beautiful nude model. The teacher asks them to draw her how they see her. Everyone draws the female form in all its exquisite, naked loveliness, except for one student who paints a monstrous creature, claiming to see through her disguise, apprising her for the abhorrence she really is…

I must go now. My laptop's got asthma. I ought to buy a new one. God knows I can afford it.

Please, all I hope for with this tragic tale is for you to understand what a splendid fellow—and joker—Aidan was and how I miss him dearly. And I would be greatly remiss if I didn't take into consideration your thoughts on the matter.

I still don't know what became of him, can only guess.

Someone once said that the sacrifice of hiding in the light is living with your shadows.

September 2013

Neighbourliness Unto Edification

"I want you to be concerned about your next door neighbour. Do you know your next door neighbour?"

Mother Teresa

"Because all cottages have names," Pamela Haber piped excitedly, in response to her husband's inquiry as to why their new house did not have a number. She wanted to say all *true* cottages but she didn't wish to disrespect other houses *pretending* to be cottages.

Gabriel Haber accepted her explanation as gospel while they stood on the threshold of their new dwelling, on the cusp of officially moving in, with their two little ones in tow: Susie, aged four, and her eleven-month-old baby brother, Dalton. Dalton sat gurgling contentedly in a push-chair, while Susie, stood next to her father holding her favourite plaything, Ben the Brown Bear. The young family, for Gabriel and Pamela were only in their mid-twenties themselves, took several long minutes to study the exterior of the cottage, just as they had done when they first viewed it all those weeks ago, as though it were a house they had built with their own bare hands and they were proudly admiring the finished work. Or maybe they hoped to see enlightenment in the mortar-and-stone, bring them closer together or help them belong.

ROSEDENE was a picturesque Edwardian cottage, its stonework pebble-dashed and painted pristine white. Built in 1908, it was a traditional spacious two-up, two-down, with exposed wood beams and rafters and a fully-functioning log burner in the sitting room, suggesting cosy winter nights-in but presently lying redundant in the baking summer months. The cottage had been recently restored and extended with a lovely conservatory, a distinctive modern touch, but there could be no escaping its inherent old world charm and lived-in feel.

The Habers now had a place they could call their own, unless they believed the cynically-minded who might claim that it still technically belonged to the bank for another twenty years, sooner if they ever defaulted on any of their monthly mortgage repayments. They were immensely grateful they had made it on the property ladder, courtesy of a sizeable nest egg, a damned sight better and cheaper than continuing to rent, not believing their luck especially when taking into account their property was located immediately on Chapel Mead Preservation Society land, with the rambling woods only a quick flit down the gravelly lane, descended upon by the village community and perfect for long evening walks and communing with nature. The unpacking had been done to everyone's satisfaction, the removals guys well-paid and long since departed, headed for the local pub, THE HOGSBACK. The family took a short, sun-shielding gander at their near-identical semi-detached whitewashed counterpart, apparently called BLACKWOOD due to its dark front door and window trims and showing evidence of weathering and occupancy—no sign of their neighbours yet, though—before they stepped through their polished oak door, its stained-glass window splashing vibrant cathedral colours onto the lounge hardwood flooring.

The conservatory along with the side-gate opened up onto a burgeoning garden, a 'cottage' garden in the aesthetic sense of the word. The covered patio, garden dining furniture and log store gave way to a modest lawn that was bordered by ornamental shrubbery and resplendent flower-beds of roses and evening primrose, foxgloves and lily-of-the-valley, the rich nectar of the buddleia luring in the butterflies. Honeysuckle climbed the trellised fence, and a variety of flowering herbs, such as lavender and basil and sage, grew in fragrant abundance with a small but flourishing vegetable patch, consisting largely of tomatoes and courgettes, further along. Rosedene had been aptly named, it seemed, for there was a secret hollow at the bottom of the garden, never filled with earth, beneath the shade of a crab apple tree, next to a cramped corner shed. The garden bloomed with grace and beauty and summer life, Pam promising to maintain its upkeep as a labour of love.

Gabe and Pam Haber couldn't have asked for more when they moved into their picture-postcard cottage in a secluded rural idyll.

Their housewarming that weekend went off without a hitch, a general family get-together with lashings of beer for the blokes and wine for the ladies and barbecue roast for all, tempered only by a slight disappointment that their neighbours didn't honour them with their presence, despite Pam's ever-frantic attempts of knocking on the door in order to introduce herself and her family, eventually giving up and dropping an invitation card through the letterbox.

Perhaps their neighbours were private people, not one for socializing, and any visitors were considered an imposition. The newcomers tried to ignore their desire to meet their elusive neighbours as best they could and focus on enjoying their new home, hoping though for at least a fortuitous glimpse of whoever lived next door. But humans are curious creatures, prone to being nosy, and their curiosity would soon stake claim to them, spiralling into a strange and overwhelming and disturbing obsession…

How much time he saves who does not look to see what his neighbour says or does or thinks, Marcus Aurelius once philosophized. Gabe and Pam paid little attention to their neighbours once they realized they were making no headway in meeting them, carrying on with their daily lives, settling swimmingly into their dream home. Pam sometimes imagined she heard voices from next door as faint as whispers on the wind. She tried to centre in on them, but nothing coherent transpired.

Gabe worked as a senior computer analyst in a successful IT firm. Pam stayed at home to look after their baby boy, run Susie to and from the local nursery and do other housewifey things: bringing home the shopping and tending to the general housework, making the place spotless and liveable. She did all the cooking, producing delicious home-made meals in the manner of an all-round domestic goddess who would have made Nigella proud, as well as pottering around and showcasing her green fingers in the garden, guiding it to its absolute splendour. She periodically visited her in-laws who lived in the next village, some afternoons she stood on the lawn, brush-and-palette in hand, masterfully reproducing aspects of the garden on canvas.

Then, one particular afternoon, while idly flicking through a magazine in the sitting room after putting away the easel, as the baby slept, Pam heard the first strains of conversation from next door.

You're home early, said a distinctly male voice.

Early shift, remember? replied the woman.

Must have slipped my mind. Every day merges into one when you work from home. How are the old codgers?

Well-behaved, for a change.

The man sounded amused. *Not dropping their pants every five seconds?*

The woman kept it professional and respectable. *Fortunately, not today,* she said wearily. *Dementia care has its ups and downs.*

I envy you, Jacqui. Either you're a true humanitarian or a complete chump. I couldn't do it, myself.

Suddenly alert, interest piqued, Pam experienced the almost overpowering temptation to go next door and make the necessary introductions, but she resisted the impulse. Instead, she listened on.

I think there's something tragic about living a long and fruitful life and losing your marbles in your golden years, Jacqui continued rather sadly. *That's what attracted me to nursing the elderly. I want to make their last few days on this earth comfortable.*

Yeah, you're a regular Mother Teresa.

You started drinking early, Jacqui observed, slightly accusatorily.

Just a couple of tumblers of scotch. I'm still sober as a judge.

That's a matter of opinion. How's the book coming?

Painstakingly slow, thank you for asking, my darling. But I should get there. There was a slight pause, then the man spoke in soft, solicitous tones. *You look particularly gorgeous today.*

So I don't look particularly gorgeous other days? What do you want?

I was thinking. As you're still in your uniform, would you mind if we get it on?

Tad, I'm very tired.

Come on, babe. Want to put your hands down my pants and have a fiddle? You know I'm just your horny little devil, however greatly misunderstood.

The woman thought about it for a moment before agreeing. *Okay,* she said, sighing. *Hopefully, it should help me nap.*

Good girl!

And, before Pam knew it, her neighbours were firmly in the sack, loud as sin, a wall separating her from the heavy moans and grunts of their sexual congress. She didn't want Dalton to hear, in case it corrupted his innocent little brain, but thankfully he was still asleep. At least now, she knew the names of their neighbours. Tad Quayling, it turned out, was a writer, and Jacqueline [the Scottish spelling] Richmond a nurse. And weren't they just a little bit naughty? Checking her watch, she realized it was nearly time for the school run. Waking up and dressing Dalton, planting a bottle in his mouth, she vacated the house as quickly as she could, hoping her neighbours would be finished by the time she got back.

Wouldn't Gabe be surprised?

Pam told Gabe about the conversation she had overheard through the walls when he got home from work and what had followed.

"The walls must be paper-thin," Gabe commented. "You get that with old period homes. You didn't decide to pop your head round, introduce yourself?"

"How could I? They were rather... *busy*," Pam replied euphemistically, slightly embarrassed.

Gabe laughed. "They're an ordinary couple like you and me," and thought no more of it until later that evening.

That night, whilst dozing off in the summer humidity, kids tucked into their respective cribs, he and Pam were roused by a loud, unexpected exclamation from the neighbours' bedroom.

OH MY GOD, YOU'RE NAKED AGAIN! exclaimed the man, whom Gabe assumed was Tad.

I just came out of the shower, Jacqui said matter-of-factly.

Why do you do these things to me? said Tad, purposefully sounding as though he were wrestling with emotions related to the sight of his girlfriend in the buff.

What things? Jacqui said absently. *You couldn't massage my feet? They really hurt.*

And what lovely feet they are, too, complimented Tad. *Fancy a toe-suck?*

Stop teasing and get on with it!

The massage or the toe-suck? There was a moment's hiatus before Tad spoke up with a lecherous proposal: *You look particularly accessible and accommodating tonight. Mind if I use and abuse your beautiful body tonight?*

Yes, I think I might just be able to accommodate you, Jacqui invited, tongue-in-cheek.

Against their own conservative Christian sensibilities, Gabe and Pam listened silently and unashamedly to the couple having sex for a whole hour, no temptation on their part to do likewise, or compete.

"They're very explicit," observed Pam, "and deeply passionate."

"And oversexed, don't forget," Gabe added his opinion without judgement or outrage. "Twice in one day. That's more times than we ever did on our honeymoon."

A high, climactic squeal from Jacqui signalled the conclusion to the late-night loving session, next door.

You must have been a right little raver at nursing school, speculated Tad, evidently satisfied and smug.

I had my moments, recalled Jacqui contemplatively.

I could lie here and gaze at your heavenly body adoringly all night.

Stop being crazy and go to sleep.

I do love you, you know?

I know…

Maybe you never really loved me, Tad said with mock-spookiness, *and I hypnotized you into believing you did.*

Maybe you never hypnotized me, Jacqui said, implying something, then cautioned lightly. *Don't start with that nonsense. I'm not one of your characters of your novel.*

Yummy dreams, my darling. Dreams you can eat.

Scrumptious.

Scrummy.

And they did it a third time.

The days remained hot and blistering. *Expect a long and lustrous summer,* promised the weatherman. Pam continued with her daily routine, changing the baby's nappies, ferrying her eldest to and from nursery, visiting relatives she'd inherited and painting still-life watercolours of the garden, but her mind grew increasingly fixed on the neighbours and their unsociable nightly behaviour. She and Gabe would lie in bed, making random, sometimes humorous comments on the sexual athletics carried through the bedroom wall, finally drifting off to sleep in the small hours of the morning. Tad must have been an exceptionally good lover since he always drove his partner to the peak of ecstasy, culminating in her uttering a high-pitched, banshee-like shriek, completely satisfied and set to whisper sweet nothings into his ear. Pam was reminded of a George Eliot quote: *People are almost always better than their neighbours think they are.*

They're just like every ordinary couple, she remembered Gabe saying.

Aside from the notion of just another couple in love, why do they have to be so damned loud? thought Pam, mildly exasperated.

Jacqui seemed to spend most days at work while her partner stayed at home, probably drinking and working on his novel.

All alone, on another glorious afternoon, she had stepped back in the conservatory after hanging damp clothes on the washing line when she noticed curious murmurings coming from somewhere nearby. Initially, she thought Dalton [*such a quiet, contented baby, not in the least bit loud and wild*] had awoken and discovered, afraid, nobody in his vicinity, but when she checked on him, he was still asleep in the crib in the lounge.

She pressed an ear against the wall, listened intently. No, the mysterious sound emanated from next door. She identified it as a dull moaning, belonging to a man and born of excitement.

It sounded like Tad, and she realized, instantly startled, she could hear him masturbating.

She couldn't believe her ears. His uniform fetish, foot love and sexualized language aside, she could actually hear him playing with himself. She should have moved away from her spot and got on with her to-do list, given the man some privacy to do what ought to have been essentially a private activity, but she was strangely drawn to the heavy breathing like a Labrador to a dog-whistle, alarm soon melting into outright fascination.

Oversexed, was how Gabe had described their neighbours.

Damn tooting! agreed Pam, presently. *Does masturbation count as cheating? There's Jacqui tirelessly working another shift at the care home to make the surviving days of its elderly residents worth living, help them maintain some quality of life, and here's her so-called boyfriend seeking gratification without her.*

Astonished, she continued to listen to the low, distasteful moaning as Tad continued to flog the bishop. She even thought she could picture him, perhaps sitting in an armchair, rhythmically tugging at his member in the manner of a mac-donning flasher possessed.

Tad suddenly delivered a risqué remark that caused Pam to jerk back from the wall: *Love thy neighbour, especially when the husband's away!*

Was that smutty comment meant for her? Did he know she was listening? Had he been secretly watching her in the garden?

She should have felt violated or deeply disgusted, or creeped-out at a bare minimum, but the shock of him possibly perving over her wore off quickly, and she went back to eavesdropping on her neighbour as he carried on with his sordid business, his efforts growing gradually more frenzied.

The man wasn't just oversexed, thought Pam, not understanding how she could be compelled to listen and not feel outraged. He was positively a sex maniac.

She heard Tad climax, manifested as a loud, whooshing intake of breath followed by a slow, wordless, relinquishing groan. He gave a sharp, fiendish chuckle.

I hope it was worth it, she wanted to ask him, reading his mood, inferring satisfaction sublime.

It was only at that point that it occurred to her she had, in her own Christian way, creamed her panties.

Pam did not mention to her husband the incident of her neighbour wanking in the spirit of neighbourliness, lest Gabe should be offended or feel inadequate. Their own lovemaking was a wholesome, hygienic affair while their neighbours came across as a very active couple for whom sex and passion formed the bedrock of their relationship, and who were not afraid to experiment with objects of incontrovertible kinkiness: handcuffs, stilettos and blindfolds, and the suchlike. Pam had to admit she found their intimate nocturnal escapades vastly stimulating, but she personally decided not to tell her husband that, even if a part of her wished to do some experimenting of her own in order to enrich their own love life. She supposed it went to prove the Devil always had more fun.

Events, however, were about to take a sinister turn.

The first inklings suggesting the neighbours' relationship was far from immaculate arose one evening out of the blue.

The TV was set on mute, and Pam and Gabe were listening in through the wall. They asked Susie to hush up when she casually sauntered over to request whether they could join her in playing *My Little Pony*. "Can't you see Mommy and Daddy are busy?" Pam told her, annoyed at the interruption. Susie wandered off, looking decidedly disappointed.

The moment Jacqui arrived home, Tad was on her case like the world's worst boyfriend.

Where have you been? he demanded to know.

Out with friends, Jacqui replied casually.

You don't have any friends! he contended.

Of course I do! Jacqui protested. *I do have a life, you know! I don't just sit around all day, getting lashed-up and pretending to write!*

So pray, tell me about these special friends you claim to have... Any of them man-friends? Tad snarled back.

Oh, please don't start, Tad... That's why I don't like you drinking! Makes you suspicious, temperamental, unstable!

The green-eyed monster that doth mock the meat it feeds on, Pam recalled from her days of amateur dramatics before she had kids, before she even got married. *Jealousy, that dragon which slays love under the pretence of keeping it alive*, from one Havelock Ellis, physician and psychologist on human sexuality.

My drinking has nothing to do with you finding a fancy man... You think you can use me as a secure base to explore other men?

I'm not doing any such thing, I swear! Jacqui maintained, at the end of her tether. *Your morbid jealousy is tearing my mind apart!*

But it seemed Jacqui knew she couldn't win. She could never allay Tad's drunken, irrational mistrust of her fidelity. *Bullshit!* he bellowed furiously. *'Fess up, you lying bitch!* and the Habers heard a loud *thwack!* There was no doubt in their minds that Tad had struck Jacqui with an open palm.

Jacqui began to weep, her crying rising in pitch and hysterics.

Shut the fuck up, you CUNTING TWAT! Tad screamed, and there followed the crash of shattering glass. He had smashed his scotch bottle against the wall, and he stormed off in a retreating stomp of steps.

Jacqui wailed harder.

"This is getting crazy," Gabe said, concerned, the spell broken. "The guy's a nutter!"

"I'm going to check on Jacqui — see if the poor woman's okay," Pam said, and disappeared into the dusky evening.

Jacqui's classic yellow Citroen C5 was parked outside next to the Habers' black Volvo. Pam banged desperately on the door. The loud, miserable wailing ceased all of a sudden. The lights were on, the curtains drawn, but nobody came to the door. Or *refused* to come to the door.

Pam wondered if she should open their side-gate and go round the side of the house.

You mean trespass? she asked herself.

Yes, she dared herself.

You can't trust what the man's going to do if he catches you interfering in his business. Safer to call the police and report a domestic disturbance.

Determined to follow through with this particular course of action, the only course of action that made any sense, Pam returned to her house.

Gabe greeted her, grinning. "I really don't believe those two."

"What do you mean?" asked Pam, puzzled.

"Listen..."

She did. And realized their noisy neighbours were having make-up sex.

Pam invited the in-laws and a couple of friends to Dalton's first Birthday party.

Unfortunately, her parents couldn't attend, since they were in the midst of a Mediterranean cruise. One might have called the weather in Chapel Mead 'Mediterranean': clear blue skies and a scorching, midday sun, with temperatures expected to soar to the mid-nineties in this drought-stricken part of Middle England. Another day for another juicy, sizzling, flaming barbecue and all the beer and wine one could consume.

The small gathering of guests was content to be present on this fine Saturday to celebrate an important day in a child's calendar, even if the child in question preferred to spend the time dozing like a cat and didn't know what all the fuss was about. Erasmus and Cressida Haber were greatly pleased to see their adorable grandson, showering him with gifts that one day he might appreciate.

Same-old Dalton, thought Erasmus proudly. *The most contented baby in the world. Goes straight after his Grandad.*

However, it soon became apparent to the retired couple that their son and daughter-in-law were not themselves. Gabriel and Pamela seemed curiously distracted, listless, not entirely *there*.

Erasmus put a fatherly arm around Gabe's shoulder and took him aside, both fellows carrying fresh bottles of Bud. "How are things going these days, Gabe?"

Gabe answered immediately. "Oh, fine."

"I heard you've missed a lot of work lately, and stopped going to Church. Should I be worried?"

"Nothing to trouble you," Gabe replied chirpily. But, as his father took note, it was a forced chirpiness. "Got too many things happening at the moment."

"Like what, exactly?"

"Oh, you know…"

"No, I *don't* know."

"Oh, it's just the neighbours," Gabe admitted, tentatively at first. "They can be loud at times, fighting or fornicating, but they make very entertaining listening. Like some soap opera on the radio."

"Is that why you and Pam look as though you haven't slept in days? And why our grandchildren look scruffy?"

"You've got to hear our neighbours, Dad," Gabe said excitedly, "and perhaps then you'll appreciate what I'm talking about."

"We don't hear anything."

"You ought to stay the night. Our ears have become attuned to their voices and grown accustomed to their conversations."

"I can talk to them for you about keeping the noise down," Erasmus suggested helpfully.

"Thanks for the offer, Dad, but I wouldn't want to bother them."

"No trouble…"

Gabe continued to flat-out refuse, growing increasingly irritated at his father's pressurizing and desire to interfere. *Will the old man stop pestering me?* "No thanks, it's fine, *really...*"

Erasmus tried to bring home the message. "Word of advice, son: it's all very well looking out for your neighbours, but you should put your own house in order first."

"I understand..."

"No, I don't think you do," warned Erasmus, patting Gabe sternly on the shoulder. "Stop shirking your responsibilities, son, and get your act together!" He paused. "And Gabriel?"

"Yes, Dad?"

"Get some rest."

As Erasmus re-joined the Birthday celebrations, it occurred to him that Gabriel hadn't said anything meaningful during their father-and-son exchange, except some redundant claptrap about the neighbours. Unnecessary stress can affect the strongest of minds, and sanity can begin to slip without the person even realizing it, and Gabriel and his wife appeared to be under a lot of stress, but for the life of him, Erasmus couldn't figure out where this additional stress was coming from. More profoundly, though, he had a sad and disturbing vision that this would be the last time he would ever see Gabriel and Pam and the little ones together as a family.

Relations were strained between the couple next door. Their love-hate relationship, hot-and-cold feelings towards each other grew more extreme as the weeks progressed, enough to drive anyone mad. Gabe and Pam dropped everything to listen in, like secret agents indulging in a little espionage. They remembered how yesterday Jacqui came home and Tad abruptly demanded, screaming, she leave as he was, in his drunken state, convinced she was having an affair. Shocked by the sheer depth of his fury and conviction, Jacqui nearly packed her things on the spur, bawling her eyes out and afraid what he might do to her, but she bravely held her ground, and they had yet another blazing row, which ended in a lot of expletives and the crash of something breaking. Their fights—and subsequent fallings-out—were becoming more notorious by the day. Today, while *Houses* by Great Northern played softly on the radio, Gabe and Pam waited on tenderhooks for their neighbours' conversation to start up. Would it be discord or harmony?

I'm done with the novel, Tad finally said, that fine evening. *I will give my book a straightforward title:* The Neighbours. *Time to celebrate!*

Congratulations, Tad... Jacqui said, less than enthusiastically. She was still sour over the row they'd had earlier, again the product of Tad's suspicions, accusing her of having an affair.

You don't sound particularly thrilled...

I'm happy for you. I hope The Neighbours *makes it on the bestseller list.*

Gabe brought the title of the book sharply into focus. "How can he be writing a book that has already been published years ago? Is he crazy? Or blatantly plagiarizing?"

"What's the book about?"

"It's supposed to be a psychological drama about a murderer who puts a hypnotic spell on the neighbours after killing his wife, causing the neighbours to go mad. It was bugging me for so long, but I now know why the name, Tad Quayling, seemed familiar to me. He wrote *The Neighbours.* I always wondered what became of him. I can't believe he's living next door."

"Maybe he went on sabbatical and he's writing a sequel."

"That might explain everything, my love. Good call."

"Mesmerizing stuff, indeed..."

You always seem to use me in your books and do the meanest, most horrible things to my character, Jacqui complained.

You inspire me, my darling. You are my muse.

You shouldn't be messing with the neighbours, either, just for your book.

What's that supposed to mean?

You only write about stuff that you've already done or consider doing.

Like hypnosis? Murder?

No, but you've definitely thought about it.

So what if I have? I have to channel my urges in some way. It's about writing from experience, then using my imagination to complete the picture, applying creative license to take the scenario to its absolute extreme. That jeering old devil, Aleister Crowley, once opined that there was something supremely satisfying about despising your neighbour, accounting for a lot of religious intolerance and a consoling, universally-held belief that the people next door were destined for Hell.

Aleister Crowley is it, now? Where do you get off? It wouldn't surprise me if, in your drunken state, you acted on your sick fantasies.

Don't say that, my darling. Even I have to have limits...

So was Tad messing with them? And they were destined for Hell? This was getting awfully fascinating, Gabe informed Pam, who nodded in rapt agreement.

Pam did not feel a need to tend to the house anymore. She found gardening no longer relaxing or therapeutic, letting the flowering plants as well as the weeds proliferate and overrun the garden in riotous, jungle-like profusion, the tomatoes in the vegetable patch left to over-ripen, drop to the ground and rot. Gabe lost interest in his daytime job, calling in long-term sick before deciding it would be best to resign. Pam and Gabe started neglecting their children so they could spend more time vegging out by the wall and snooping on the neighbours, raising them up to the centre of their universe, as though hypnotized—or hexed.

The plumbing was as old as the cottage. Nobody noticed the stopcock below the kitchen sink had begun to leak.

Obsession became addiction.

Gabe and Pam remained riveted to the voices of their noisy neighbours broadcast through the walls. Gabe wished he'd invited guests. This made first-class entertainment.

Mind if I fondle your Abi Titmusses and play with your favourite place? Tad asked his girlfriend as she came home from another exhausting shift at the care home. *Is your pussy open for business again?*

Absolutely incredible! Jacqui screeched, the sound of a woman harassed once too often. *I am still waiting for this amazing loving session you've been speaking of since we first met, constantly promising me all the absolutely incredible things you'd do to my body that nobody else can!* Never happened baby!

Tad was taken aback, stung by the obvious venom in her voice. *But I thought —*

But you thought what? Jacqui snapped. *Dozy parrot, you don't get it, do you?*

Get what? What have I done?

Drinking and fucking and writing, that's all you do! I bet you're drunk and hard as a poker right now!

Tad giggled drunkenly and mischievously. *Maybe just a little…*

Well, no more! Jacqui announced determinedly. *I'm not taking this lying down anymore!*

Tad tittered at a potential double entendre, like some immature teenage boy. *Lying down…*

Jacqui came out with it. *You were right to be suspicious. I am having an affair, and there's nothing in hell you can do about it!*

The disclosure dispelled Tad's giggles in an instant. There was a short silence during which Gabe assumed that Tad might be stewing. *Now that the cat is out of the bag, how long has it been going on for?*

Just a fortnight, Jacqui confessed. *I hoped you'd bring girls home in the afternoon when I was at work and cheat on me, so I'd have a reason to leave you. But you can't even do that even though you're always home! Considering you don't trust me anyway, I thought I might as well do exactly what I'm constantly accused of. And you know what, fuckwit? I love her!*

Her? It's a her?

Yes, one of the female resident's granddaughters whom I've become close to.

Tad was quiet for a while, then like any wicked libertine, tried to find a lusty, debauched angle. *Any chance of a threesome?*

She's not interested in men.

Tad said something that exemplified his selfish, sexist nature. *I could cure her of her affliction.*

She doesn't need men, let alone you! Neither do I! *Tad by name, Tad by nature!*

Her undisguised hatred and unreserved insult to his manliness proved to be the straw that finally broke the camel's back. Tad went nuclear. *You're not good enough to EAT MY SHIT, you whoring cunt! I THINK YOU DESERVE A GOOD RAPING TO!*

Jacqui was suddenly afraid: *What the hell are you doing?… Don't you dare come near me! Please, don't!* The sinister sound of tearing fabric, the ripping off of her underwear, accompanied by her desperate pleas as Tad made good on his threat.

Is this what you want, you cheating DYKE? Tad snarled contemptuously, getting into his stride. *I shall be the last man who ever FUCKED you!*

Oh God! Oh God, NO! And her voice was reduced to muffled, tortured moans as he clamped his hand tightly over her mouth.

Jacqui did not physically struggle any further, took her punishment passively.

Gabe and Pam listened with bated breath to him degrade his girlfriend against her will, judging by the piggish, thrusting noises he made and her low, sniffling misery, as she hopelessly implored him to *stop, please, stop, please, no more —*

— The sound of a hand rummaging through a desk drawer.

Then a gunshot as loud as a bazooka blast, followed by the sound of a second shot.

Silence — tangible and vast and interminable.

"I thought he might beat her up," Pam chimed blithely. "I certainly wasn't expecting *that!*"

The police broke down the door half-an-hour later.

Detective Inspector Beale of the Child Protection Unit, his two constables and the duty social worker stared in stunned silence at the catastrophic state of the house before taking a few minutes to confront and acclimatize to the foulness sufficiently enough to introduce themselves. The leak from the old plumbing had magnified until the pipes burst, flooding the floor and growing mouldy things as well as providing the perfect breeding ground for the summer mosquitoes. Rotting vegetation as well as a ragged brown teddy-bear floated in the stagnant water, stinking to high heaven.

Lord knows how long this had been going on for, thought DI Beale. The couple sat by the sitting-room wall, dangerously malnourished, emaciated, terribly ravaged, dressed in soiled clothes, with the same identical gormless looks on their faces that had haunted the previous owners of the house no less than six months ago, as though caught in the wake of the same curse. *Like déjà vu all over again.*

"Did you know your daughter, Susie, ran from your house, and was found wandering the street, filthy and starving, in the small hours of the morning? A group of clubbers were kind enough to call it in."

Pam laughed off this disturbing information in typical loony fashion. "Oh, I was wondering where Susie had got to!"

"*Oh my God!*" the social worker yelled by the crib, forgetting her professionalism momentarily, aghast.

DI Beale went over to investigate, stood beside her. Sure enough, the baby was dead. The poor thing had probably been left unfed for some time and forgotten. He must have died several days ago since his miserable, helpless corpse was grey and mottled and gathering flies. The small, mouldering presence in the cot reminded DI Beale of the frayed remains of a ragdoll that has somehow survived a plane crash. DI Beale somehow maintained his own professionalism, despite the tingling revulsion that gripped him. Of all the grisly horrors he'd witnessed throughout his police service, it was always difficult to stomach the senseless loss of innocent life, particularly of one so young. *God give us strength and deliver us from evil.* "It is my sad duty to inform you that your son has passed away."

"Oh dear, is that why Dalton's been so quiet?" Pam exclaimed vacuously, undistressed. "I would never have guessed." Pam zeroed back in on the wall, dismissing the utterly sickening news as either unimportant or none of her business, showing a chilling lack of motherly love for her dead twelve-month-old baby boy. DI Beale shuddered. "Talking of quiet, it's gone strangely quiet in there since he raped and murdered her and shot himself," she stage-whispered. "Shh, I think I hear something!"

"Mr. Haber, what do you have to say to all this?"

Gabe turned his head with a ghoulish creak of the neck. "*I will not think ill or evil of or bear false witness against my neighbour,*" he quoted Romans 15:2 reverently but irrelevantly. "*Let each of us please our neighbour for his good unto edification.*" Then he noticed the bottle of Corona he held in his hand. "The wedge of lime is supposed to keep the flies out."

Now both of them were looking up at DI Beale with only craziness in their expressions. They had gone invariably mad, just like the last owners, focused as they were on what was happening next door.

But *that* was the maddest thing. There was nothing happening next door. DI Beale didn't wish to dig up ancient history, but the original neighbour of Blackwood—some writer fellow—had murdered his girlfriend before turning the gun on himself eight years ago. The gas from the stove he'd turned on earlier had ignited, incinerating their bodies, burning the whole house down to its foundations. So there wasn't even a house next door, only a few ruins. Thus, for this particular Haber couple to be acting as goofy as the last owners, who even today still languished in the nearby mental health facility, had to infer something not-quite-of-this-earth.

DI Beale didn't put much credence in the supernatural but the police psychic had suggested a theory. What if the Habers, and their predecessors, had become receivers, picking up a transmission of the dead couple next door, experiencing them play out their lives straight through to their deaths, like a recording from the past, an echo. But for the ghostly manifestations to be brought into existence, to be sustained in this way and to gather strength and replay their final moments on this earth, they needed to feed off the *energies* of the living, draining the psyches like a battery, until the listeners' minds unravelled and lost all sense of reality. Just a theory, a dumb theory…

With a curt nod of the head, DI Beale signalled for the two police officers to apprehend the lunatic couple, who had apparently lasted only six weeks in their new house, their stay culminating in the sheer neglect of themselves and their children to tragic, unimaginable proportions in favour of homing back in on the wall, listening avidly to something that no longer existed in the physical world. He decided to address them, let them know — if they still possessed an iota of insight inside their delusional minds — what would happen from this point on. "I'm afraid, Mr. and Mrs. Haber, you are going to be leaving your pretty house now and taking a short trip with us down to the station."

"This is a cottage, not a house," Pam registered, hurt. "And not one of those mock cottages. Because, you see, all true cottages have names."

July 2013

Hartigan Strange

"Where there is no imagination there is no horror."

Sir Arthur Conan Doyle

I will continue to trawl through the archives and present to you the mysterious case of Hartigan Strange, which coincidentally happens to be Case #13 in my memoirs and, I suppose, aptly so, as well as one of the last cases I ever investigated before I retired. I didn't include this as the thirteenth entry deliberately but it seemed to enter the frame by chance as I sorted through the paperwork.

You may have heard of Hartigan Strange if you enjoy reading about the sinister or the terrible or the macabre. Hartigan Strange was a horror writer of modest reputation — not quite making it to the Hollywood lifestyle Clive Barker is accustomed to but neither was he some bargain-basement Clive Barker — and his death was as peculiar as his name or the mad characters he wrote about.

When I was called in to his one-million-pound mansion in Oaks Fold by my police colleagues, it was a dark, stormy night on, of all nights, the 6th June 2006. Can you Adam-and-Eve it: 6/6/6? The Number of the Beast — you can't make this up! His literary agent, Vivian Bassett, had contacted the police, as he had not heard hide nor hair of him for over a month and Hartigan Strange had missed the deadline for his latest manuscript. No-one had answered, and the police were forced to break down the front door. The house was in total darkness, except for a visible slit of light from under the study door. As there was still no response, our brawniest men disposed of that door, too. On entering, we discovered the light emanating from a single, slow-burning candle on the mahogany pedestal desk at the far end of a room wallpapered in the darkest velvet, making me feel as though I was in the black heart of the house. Behind the desk sat Hartigan Strange, forty-odd and dressed in black, head flung back in his chair, face as pale as death, eyes bugged and glassy, mouth drawn in a disturbing rictus of terror. It was my immediate impression that he had died from absolute fright as though his old ticker had suddenly seized up after witnessing something dreadful and unspeakable. In his hand he clutched a photograph, which the forensic team later removed and dusted for prints. The degree of lividity informed me he had died around seventy-two hours ago as was the fact he was in the grip of rigor mortis. I could not believe I was in the midst of a 'locked room' mystery, a rarity in police detective work, since it transpired the only key ever forged to that study Strange carried on his person like a good luck charm.

Horror fiction is not my cup of tea. I consider it trash. As you've already seen from my previous entries, I've seen my fair share of horror in my line of business. Besides, there's that old adage about life proving much stranger than fiction. But, as a form of expression, the horror genre still has its virtues. There is a kind of brutal honesty to horror. Every talented horror writer speaks his mind without pussyfooting around or ducking the issues. Besides their outspokenness and candour, they take everything to its extreme: family drama, crime, love, etc. Your traditional horror family will be dysfunctional and incestuous and abuse-ridden. The horror writer can do things — horrible, horrible things — that most crime writers couldn't even conceive of or dare to include in their work in case of offending their faithful readers. Romance in horror is classically dark, twisted, doomed. Yet, most of all, the horror writer excels in the ability to scare and shock and repulse. They see the worst in everything, like any decent cynic. Believe me when I say pessimism is closer to realism than goggle-eyed optimism, learning to mentally prepare yourself for the worst eventuality possible so that anything less than that comes as a pleasant surprise. That's how most experienced policemen operate in their day-to-day duties, not because they've seen so many unpleasant things in their time, but it helps them get through the day with their minds intact. You're primed and ready for the worst shift in history and you're eternally grateful you're not insane by the end of the day. So, despite viewing horror as trash, I have a secret respect for the horror writer since they portray the world as it is, the aspects of life and human relationships that most of us avoid or gloss over or brush under the carpet. Reading Hartigan Strange in order to get into the mind of the victim, I understood why he'd made it into print. He had an uncanny knack of dealing with the sinister, the terrible and the macabre in an intelligent, no-holds-barred, grab-you-forcefully-by-the-throat-and-shake-you kind of way. He apparently once claimed that he could not function in normal reality as effectively as in the world of the dark fantastic. Fear, pain, death, disease and madness gave his life meaning. He wrote about all manner of unsavoury characters, from psycho-pimps and date rapists and child killers to shadowy, well-funded organizations or the morally-bankrupt Wall Street CEO who likes to torture teenage girls, and Strange had his own formulaic take on more mythical fare, such as vampires and werewolves and zombies intent on bringing about an apocalypse on Man in the sequential format of a thriller. Strange's preoccupation with these nonsensical monsters goes to prove that horror writers have never forgotten to be kids. Robert Bloch, author of *Psycho*, once said he had the heart of a child which he joked he kept in a jar! Such was his very erudite style of writing, Strange could spin out a tale effortlessly and balance the ultra-ordinary with the infinitely bizarre while never once making the reader suspend their disbelief. He could create an unsettling effect on the reader with the minimum of descriptive prose, hence the rather short length of even his longer novels.

Some might have considered the entire circumstances of the crime scene—the death of a horror writer from unutterable shock locked inside his private study in a gothic mansion, with the only key to the room still on his person, on a dark and stormy night on the sixth day of the sixth month of the sixth year—a publicity stunt if it weren't for the fact that a man had actually died. The thing that sticks to mind was the ever-growing nameless fear I felt standing in the flickering gloom of that perishing room, despite never one for being anxious. The other police officers also reported similar dread feelings. What had this man—this consummate author of dark imaginings—witnessed at the moment of his death?

I am loth to remember the world's shortest horror story ever, composed by one Frederic Brown: *The Last Man on Earth sat alone in a room. There was a knock on the door…*

We began rounding up the suspects, of the few we had. Hartigan Strange must have been fiercely protective of his study because the only fingerprints detected belonged to him, or maybe the alleged perpetrator had removed theirs. Vivian Bassett the Agent was immediately ruled out. He took his gay lover out to dinner, his alibi corroborated by those in the restaurant that night. On closer questioning, he seemed to have nothing to hide or grumble about. He'd been on good terms with his client, receiving a rather substantial fifteen-percent cut of all net earnings. But might he have been sexually attracted to Strange and made a pass at him? Then killed Strange in a fit of passionate rage when rejected? I didn't think so; the man was clean. The wife, however, was a different kettle of fish. The relationship between her and her husband was severely strained, and Delia Strange was in the process of seeking a divorce as well as requesting a large alimony. There were no dependents – she bore him no children due to his infertile nature. She claimed on that fateful night she was out with her circle of ladyfriends. Her alibi did not check out, though. Her friends gave inconsistent accounts of her whereabouts that evening. One particular striking testimony suggested she was visiting her family doctor. It soon transpired, after an intense grilling at the station, that she was having an affair with Dr Payton. It seemed the good doctor was doing more than just dispensing sound medical advice to the family. Could she – or in collusion with her GP – have done the dirty on her soon-to-be ex-husband? But how had she killed him? What had frightened him to death?

A post-mortem report cited the victim had suffered a fatal heart attack and excluded alcohol or illicit drugs in the bloodstream, surprising for someone who often advocated psychoactive substances in his books, his favourite drug of choice being ketamine and the experience of 'getting lost in the K-Hole'. No, he had apparently led a teetotal life since quitting drugs almost ten years ago, not even dabbling in legal highs of which ministers were yet to pass a bill in Parliament banning them, unable to keep up with the new ones that magically appeared overnight. Except Strange had been an avid adrenaline junkie, enjoying such psych-out activities as rock climbing, rollercoasters, bungee-jumping and sky-diving, etc. In the meantime, the Forensics mop-up crew examined every inch of that house, and mass spectrometry picked up traces of Beta-carbolines in the study. The toxicology screen would have turned out negative unless you were specifically looking for Beta-carbolines. Sure enough, a re-test revealed large doses of Beta-carbolines in his system.

A receipt of purchase from a pharmaceutical company showed up, signed for by Strange himself. Now, you may not know what Beta-carbolines are. They are related to tryptamine and widespread in nature, present in South American jungle vines and the sting of a scorpion's tail, the seeds of Syrian Rue, certain varieties of tobacco and the passionflower as well as those marine tunicates that fluoresce when exposed to blacklight. Roasting coffee beans release Beta-carbolines as a by-product. Beta-carbolines induce anxiety and fear, i.e. having the opposite role on the brain receptors as Benzodiazepines, such as Valium and Ativan, which mediate a calming effect. At higher concentrations, Beta-carbolines cause outright panic in the individual, progressing on to vivid hallucinations — nothing recreational about them — and eventually bring on violent convulsions. Hartigan Strange had overdosed on them. It would also explain the awful, uncharacteristic disquiet myself and my police colleagues experienced when we arrived on the scene, suggesting we had been exposed too, albeit in trace amounts.

The stuff had been sprayed liberally across the room, and the offending can was discovered, spent, in the trash can, bearing only Strange's fingerprints. The wife might have known about the Beta-carbolines, and conspiring with Dr Payton and using gloves to conceal her presence, administered it around the study before wearing some freaky mask to make sure, murdering her husband for his small fortune. Yet, despite my suspicions, I did not believe she dunnit; call it a policeman's hunch.

Because, in the desk drawer beneath the receipt, was a manuscript, the same manuscript Strange had been due to submit to his agent. The book went by the title: *A Study of Fear and Other Terrifying Things*, a first-person account of a fictional character experimenting with Fear... or maybe not so fictional. It has since been published posthumously, managing thirteen weeks on *The Times* Bestseller List and his most popular book to date and culminating in a resurgence of public interest in Strange. I gained permission to include an excerpt here, the most telling piece of evidence:

Aren't we proud of the tolerant society we live in, you and I? A society where you can have sex with somebody and marry someone else? Where you can fuck another once wedded and be granted your freedom at the drop of a hat? Where women are allowed to have children from five different fathers? Where fathers have no choice in who raises their kids, even if it might be a total stranger, with a criminal record? Where our disenfranchised youths seek intimate comfort in their stepsiblings? Where grandparents are dumped and left to fester away their golden years in stinking hell-holes called care homes, the providers of which are only out to make a quick buck? Where professional footballers are viewed as role models and worshipped in place of God, earning astronomically more than those who care for the sick and dying? Where our politicians start wars on a whim or a lie, instilling fear and panic in those they are supposed to serve, creating a pervasive, unhealthy atmosphere of paranoia across the nation, perhaps to keep themselves in office for longer? For the only thing to fear is fear itself, as one great but rare statesman declared. We have been desensitized to the injustices of the world to a point that fear no longer has meaning in our lives. The child soldiers in Africa cause us to go through the motions of momentarily tutting in sympathy, offering superficial platitudes that we do care, before eagerly moving on to the next horror story. We turn a selfish blind eye to the unwashed homeless and the certifiably insane, not wishing to cross paths with them, consoling ourselves that it is not us on Skid Row.

But we should be afraid. Inherently afraid, as we wait in blissful oblivion for Society, like the origins of the Universe, to implode apocalyptically on itself.

Psychologists speak of **stimulus preparedness**, *where our genes still express the fear of snakes and spiders that our cave-dwelling ancestors experienced.*

Fear is an emotional state which has got lost in the small print, and which I intend to rediscover with a vengeance, whatever it takes. Even the stoniest, most doughty dreadnought is now searching far and wide, and **beyond**...

The manuscript had been right under our noses, a voice from the grave, one man's last confession underlying the social commentary, life imitating art, or vice versa. Hartigan Strange, I suppose, had grown weary of his life, its absence of fear and excitement, the lack of any 'kick', forcing him to explore further afield in the spirit of *The Seeker*, as defined by The Who. He had eventually succumbed to the fear-provoking drug, achieved his desire to be scared, at a cost. Maybe he had harboured a death-wish, we shall never know. The Judge ruled it 'Death by Misadventure'.

If you remember, I mentioned a photograph earlier on at the crime scene, which Hartigan Strange had been clutching, and which required Forensics to prise open from his cold, dead hands. It was less an exhibit in the case, more a curio. Nobody really understood its relevance, deemed nothing more than circumstantial. I—Sanford Wolfe, aka 'The Bloodhound'—had seen nothing like it in all my forty-three years of police service but remain firmly convinced it is a missing element in the investigation, may have in some way played an important part in his demise.

I accepted the photograph as a retirement present rather than let it fade away in the evidence locker.

It was a snapshot of an eye, taken close up, belonging I think to an animal of some kind. Surrounded by sleek black fur like that of a panther, the eye is a dull yellow and glaring and all-seeing, the pupil narrowed to a red, almost reptilian-like slit, appearing to follow you around the room. Except for the life of me, I still cannot tell what creature it belongs to. The lab authenticated the image, confirmed it had not been doctored, and, even after consulting various animal experts, I am none the wiser.

As I sit here, writing up this case, with thunder bellowing outside and November rain lashing at the window on another dark and stormy night, candle guttering, I stare at the photograph, horribly intrigued, at the grotesque, glowering eye as it watches me as a predator watches its prey, sizing me up, scrutinizing me for any signs of weakness. . .

Oh my God, it *blinked*!

July 2013

Charterhouse Road

"To fall in love is to create a religion with a fallible god."

Jorge Luis Borges

MANNING & IBBOTSON *offer to the market an elegant, detached three-bedroom Victorian period home set in a quiet and sought-after cul-de-sac just off Charterhouse Road, within easily-walkable reach of the local schools, amenities, transport links and Oaks Fold village green. Tetherdown retains strong character features, doubly suited for family life or the discerning executive couple, comprising an entrance hall with an understairs storage cupboard/cloakroom, two separate principal reception rooms with limestone fireplaces, a spacious kitchen/breakfast room, and two impressive bathrooms, including an en suite attached to the master bedroom. There is enough parking for 3-4 cars in the gravelled frontage. This desirable property has been thoughtfully extended to incorporate a modern light and airy conservatory which opens onto a south-facing terrace garden considered quaint and unique, deceptively so, and to die for. Viewings are highly recommended.*

Guy Hastings sat puffing away on a JP Special, casually glancing at the apparently-unremarkable, grey-bricked Victorian building listed as TETHERDOWN from his black Hyundai coupe across the road. He recognized the house from its image online, but the FOR SALE sign outside lent confirmation of the right address. Although there were no other vehicles in the driveway, he had seen two separate people walk into the house but neither had re-emerged so far. His own appointment was set for four o'clock sharp, less than five minutes away. Was this meant to be an open house or strictly by-appointment-only gig?

Turning off the stereo where Iron Butterfly were offering to take his hand and walk him through this land, Guy clambered out of the car, dressed in characteristic black, to match his short, dark designer hair and stubble, despite the humid August afternoon. He was immediately struck by a stifling wall of heat. The air was stagnant; a breeze would have been much appreciated.

This was a peculiar neck of the woods. Guy had read somewhere that Oaks Fold was an odd place, posh and prosperous to the innocent observer yet if you scratched the surface, a neighbourhood where queer things randomly occurred... or, perhaps, not all that randomly. Maybe there was a conscious plan to every queer event in Oaks Fold. It was the same place where that playwright went crazy, convinced that his girlfriend had taken on the characteristics of his dead wife—how queer was that? The latest queer event, as evidenced by the flyers posted on the trunks of the sycamore-lined road, was the unexplained disappearances of ordinary people. A dozen or more people, who had gone missing, continued to baffle the police, the only consistent feature of the victims being they were all professionals but unrelated to one another in any other way.

Still, if there was some murderous crackpot out there, killing for kicks, or even an organized gang of criminal kidnappers, who were yet to demand some serious regal ransoms, Guy would flip them the middle finger, and advise them to go screw their mother, sister, wife and daughter, otherwise he'd do it for them, including dig up their grandmother's remains and rape her skull. He prided himself on being a cool fuck who took no shit from anyone. Not even from his fucking girlfriend...

Guy strode with the arrogant swagger of a Rock star towards the mahogany door, gravel scrunching underfoot, the chrome-gilded sun in the cloudless, sapphire sky keeping close watch over his deliberate steps. He pushed the doorbell with a similar sense of purpose, unhesitatingly, impenetrably.

The chimes of Big Ben echoed throughout the rooms and passageways of the house.

Before Guy even thought about hitting the bell again, the door abruptly swung open and a blond, blue-eyed pretty-boy presented himself inside the hallway.

"You must be Mr. Hastings," the young man presumed, extending a hand in greeting.

Guy got over his initial start at the sudden appearance of this person and cautiously took the proffered hand. "Indeed I am. Call me Guy. And you are?"

"Curtis Manning," the blond fellow announced, "at your service."

"As in *Manning & Ibbotson* Estate Agents?"

"The one and the same," Curtis responded.

He wasn't quite what Guy was expecting. Curtis looked way too young, less a big shot with an exclusive estate agency, but rather a kid on work experience. Perhaps his grandfather or great-grandfather had co-founded the firm, subsequently turning it into a family business. The white, deep-collared shirt and red, mock-Ivy-league, silk tie and glossy, blue trousers — all Armani — seemed strangely at odds with his blond curtains and boyish good looks, just as to him, Guy must have seemed out of place in a velvet shirt, distressed jeans and Cuban heels — all decidedly black — on a day like this. "Pleased to meet you, I'm sure. Shall we get on with it?"

"Why, of course," Curtis replied, acknowledging Guy's desire to hurry through the viewing. "Correct me if I am wrong, but I can already see you are a man not accustomed to small talk, chit-chat or any other form of light banter." He graciously gestured with a hand for Guy to enter.

Guy accepted the invitation, crossed the threshold. "You're not mistaken. Small talk is pointless, nonsense, trivial, a waste of time that could be better spent doing something more *constructive* and *productive.*"

"And what do you do, if I might be so bold?" Curtis ventured.

"I make films."

"Anything I might have watched?"

"Only if you like pornography," Guy said deliberately, studying Curtis's face closely for a reaction. "Do you?"

"Not quite my cup of chai," Curtis said politely. If he was shocked, his voice did not betray it. However, Guy thought the young estate agent's expression registered his earlier droll attempt at an in-joke, his intentional emphasis on the words 'constructive' and 'productive', and the innuendos therein. Curtis proceeded to brush it aside, though, continued to engage Guy in decent, unobjectionable conversation. "If you don't mind me asking, why black?"

"Black is fashionable in every season," Guy explained willingly. "It epitomizes the cool and the dark, the sensual and the sinister. I like to be different, hence the black garb. Whereas every other dick is driving an Audi or a Beamer or a Merc where I currently inhabit my swanky chalet bungalow in Upper Nasebury, I own a car no-one else would dare buy. Before my F2, I drove a FTO, another import—speedometer was in kilometres instead of miles, catch my drift?"

"I can tell you have hidden depths," Curtis considered, although the manner in which he delivered the compliment suggested he thought Guy was as superficial as the films he shot and possibly even starred in. However, he recovered quickly before Guy even noticed anything awry. "Hence your interest in this house?"

"Glad you can guess where this is all heading."

"You will not be disappointed," Curtis assured him, raising his eyebrows knowingly and producing a grin with teeth that were just too bright and too white for his mouth. "I shall therefore endeavour to furnish you with the salient points. No nonsense."

He began his sales pitch in the rather ordinary-looking hallway. "Tetherdown dates back to 1872. My firm has managed the property throughout, whether letting it or drawing up the conveyance documents to potential buyers. The house has exchanged hands a few times. As you can see, it has been fully refurbished and has leaded windows and oak flooring." Curtis showed his client the two reception rooms with their generous room proportions, the typical high ceilings and, according to Curtis, working dolomite fireplaces. The floors were fitted with polar-white shag piles, sensitive to footprints like snow.

Curtis then took a slight detour upstairs, following the mahogany staircase with its wrought-iron banister. There were fitted wardrobes in two of the bedrooms, each occupied by a king-sized brass bed. The previous owners had put bespoke furniture in the third and smallest of the bedrooms in an attempt to convert it into a study. Both the en-suite and family bathrooms were ample and decked out in Egyptian marble, each separate shower and bath replete with dark Corian surround. The latter of the bathrooms housed the airing cupboard with its combi Worcester boiler.

Curtis led Guy downstairs again, maintaining the 'salient points', as he called them. The kitchen possessed terracotta-tiled flooring with underfloor heating, granite worktops, integrated dishwasher, and washing machine, a Belling cooker with ceramic hob, a top-of-the-range microwave and American-style fridge/freezer. The glazed door from the breakfast area folded open into the roomy, hardwood conservatory, which admitted a great deal of natural light and could give a sense of a sauna in the summer.

Guy had a small trifling question at the back of his mind. He had glanced around for the others who had entered before, but they were nowhere to be seen.

"They must have slipped out whilst you weren't looking," Curtis replied rationally, "except I must warn you that some people claim this house is haunted."

Guy was suddenly intrigued. "Haunted, as in ghosts?"

Curtis nodded. "The deeds to the property have been passed down from owner to owner, and everyone who has lived here has heard or witnessed something unnatural. Mysterious lights, vague, moving spectral figures, terrifying loud thuds in the dead of night, or inexplicable cold spots in the heat of day, and the all-pervading stench of putrefaction that comes and goes at will. I don't wish to frighten you away, but are you aware of the number of people who have vanished around these parts, so close to the centre of town? Pseudoscience has spoken of 'thin spots' in the fabric of reality."

"I don't frighten easily..." *And, yes, I am fully aware of those multiple disappearances you speak of.* The alleged, unaccountable visitations, however, were new information to him. Horror films often depicted the haunted house as dark and cold and attractive to ghosts and other supernatural entities. There was nothing presently in evidence to suggest any spooky goings-on. Nevertheless, Guy couldn't deny feeling impressed. "Hell of a house. Maybe I could Facebook the spirit world."

"Not many houses can boast such a colourful history."

There, the positive spin on a possibly scary deal-breaker, thought Guy, with a degree of admiration. Curtis might be just a boy, but he talked the talk and walked the walk. There were certain professions Guy didn't trust. He put estate agents in the same league as bankers and lawyers and politicians and used-car salesmen. He remembered

Stephen Fry comparing estate agents to an unlanced boil. Then, there were all those old, unflattering jokes: *What do you call fifty estate agents chained together at the bottom of the ocean? A damned good start. Why is sex between an estate agent and his client frowned upon?* Because it risks the client being billed twice for what is essentially the same service. But presently Guy felt that Curtis was doing a splendid job proverbially selling the place. The man was slick.

"I'm curious: why the sudden impulse to buy another house if you already own a fine chalet bungalow in an enviable location?"

Guy was surprised by the forwardness of the question. Or perhaps it wasn't all that forward. "You really want to know?"

"Yes, I do. Honestly."

"Then brace yourself," Guy began, giving fair warning before plunging straight in. "It's my girlfriend, Krista Avery. She's an actress of some distinction in my popular erotic homemade flicks—very Bree Olson/Ashlynn Brooke. Face of an angel, a body made for sin, sexy beyond all reason and common sense. Able to perform some of the down-and-dirtiest things imaginable, but nobody's fool when it comes to putting her feminine wiles to use, always to her advantage, and a shrewd businesswoman. You can understand why Charlie Sheen went crazy and imploded." Guy noticed the blank look on Curtis's face. Unless Curtis was an adolescent boy with a good grasp of porn and the accompanying sleazy gossip, he wouldn't know what Guy was referring to. So Guy kept it as frank as he could. "You see, I'm sweet on Krista. She's a very sexual girlfriend, and very accommodating. But unfortunately I cannot seem to satisfy her. Which is just so unusual for someone as primed, ready and willing as me, who's supposed to have led a life as debauched as Jack Nicholson in his heyday, notorious for frequently sharing his trailer with a steady stream of wild and willing women. I've had a lot of hot babes in my time, both in front of and behind the camera, and I love challenges. But Krista has an unbelievable libido, tends to lose her clothes at the drop of a hat. Even loves a bit of anal. She never spurns the advances of most well-endowed men—as I said, very accommodating. Gets carried away, satisfies her man every time, and it gets under my skin. I want us to be exclusive, but she won't have it. Makes me want to find a rock to crawl under and die. I guess what I'm trying to say is that I have a girlfriend, albeit a raving nympho, no-one has—but possibly *had*, in common parlance—and drive a make and model of car that nobody would ever consider buying, so I would like to own a bigger place—a house, as the case may be—that is as different as the above. My own personal pad, while Krista keeps the trendy chalet as a token of my affection for her."

Curtis listened to Guy's intimate confession in the attentive manner of an old friend. "Quite the bind you're in," he said when Guy had finished. "Although, kudos on a wise gambit to gift her with the chalet. She will feel forever obligated to you." Then, Curtis flashed his white, pinball smile again, reciting pleasantly. *"The best investment on earth is earth."*

"Excuse me—?"

"Louis Glickman, one of the greatest real estate investors in the world." The tour of the house's interior ended with Curtis flinging open the conservatory French doors on to the garden terrace. "Onwards and upwards."

Guy remembered the quirky wording of the blurb advertising the garden on the website. *A garden to die for*, it had said. It ought to have hopefully been the star attraction of the residence. Guy, however, was greatly disappointed. On first impressions there was nothing noteworthy, hip or enchanting about the garden. It would have been rather appropriate to describe the garden as more of a yard, and a long one at that, with no end in sight. Beyond the nondescript patio furniture on the sun terrace with its brick-built barbecue and the easily-accessible log store opposite, overseen by dormant London lamps, a knavish design of vintage flagstones formed a path down the garden. There was hardly any grass in evidence, only a few straggling weeds in the cracks between the stone-crafted pavings, and a series of flowering acacias that grew against the tall, timber fence on either side and lined the route towards the concealed foot of the garden. Between two acacias was an arbour loveseat. Beside it, someone had planted a pole in the ground crowned by a man in the [crescent] moon.

Very cute and soppy, thought Guy drily. *Not my type, mind.*

He resumed silently along the snaking path, Curtis in tow, and arrived at a wooden park-style bench over which loomed another traditional lamp-post. It was at this stage things got interesting. The bench seemed to mark the junction between the acacias on one side, with their pretty yellow flowers, and the yew trees yonder, with their distinctive, upside-down hanging foliage. Yet, the path showed no sign of letting up.

Guy wondered as to the purpose of this peculiar demarcation point. *A game of two halves, perhaps?* He took a brief recess and considered. "Is there any wiggle-room around the asking price?" he asked, sweating against the humidity of the sunny afternoon. Rain would have been a welcome relief, to cool and purify the air, but there wasn't a cloud in the sky. "I mean I can buy a small castle in the Scottish Highlands for a quarter-of-a-mill."

"We can negotiate," Curtis responded, once again revealing that toothpaste-ad sparkling grin, "but what was put down on paper is an accurate valuation. Although I still do believe in the principle that a house is not how much it is worth but what people are willing to pay for it."

Should this possibly [*deceptively so*] be the house and garden nobody else owned?

Thinking otherwise, Guy started walking again, following the course of the path. The farther he journeyed, the more crooked, gnarly, sinister the yew trees became, until he no longer recognized their shapes. He might easily have been looking at an improbable, yet-undiscovered wooded species, as the trees took on unfamiliar, weirder and more fantastical characteristics. In this part of the garden, the light continued to grow murkier, as though the sun, in spite of its glaring presence overhead, could not penetrate the possibly denser air, giving Guy the sense he was gazing up at the sky through a soft filter. Sound, too, seemed muffled, strangely muted—no busy drone of insects or rich birdcalls—like listening to everyday noises through water. Feeling increasingly like Dorothy in the Land of Oz, Guy kept going. He was beginning to wonder where the old grey path was leading him when it finally drew to a close, terminating in a ringed cobblestone pentagram. No tool shed was located down at the bottom of the exceptionally long garden, only a tremendously striking, ominous pergola over the pentangled, occult circle. Tremendously striking, since the exaggerated architecture of the shaded pillars and crossbeams, constructed in purest granite, did not meet any conventional, earthly design, and ominous, because creeping vines seemed to *move* black and snakelike over the trellised framework and one another. Prior to the mysterious configuration, a black rock protruded up from the ground, waist-high, hewn and polished and inscribed with the same indecipherable glyphs as the vertical columns. But, perhaps, the most perturbing feature about this particular aspect of the garden was how it lacked any identifiable, quantifiable boundary and seemed to stretch off into yawning, rippling infinity, if such a thing were possible.

Guy had never seen anything like it before. If he didn't know better, he thought the insect-shaped pergola, esoteric pentagram, jutting quartz monument and enigmatic inscriptions together comprised some sort of ancient shrine... but what of this awesome spot at the borderless base of the garden where reality seemed to break down, this shimmering, singular phenomenon which was testament to an unperceived, immeasurable force that had effectively punched an impossible hole into our world?

His step faltered. Guy turned to ask Curtis to explain what he could possibly be seeing. "I don't underst—"

"Frightfully sorry to do this, old chap," remarked Curtis darkly, and gave him a violent shove in the chest. "Ta-ta!"

Guy didn't realize what had happened when he unbalanced and staggered backwards, but bewilderment soon turned to alarm as he learned of his fate, instantly sucked into the unfathomable rip between worlds.

Now I did not see this shit coming!

Guy did not know where he'd landed—or *arrived*—or whatever served as the correct term to describe that instantaneous mode of transport. One minute he was in that offbeat garden, the next fraction of a second *here*. But *where* was here?

Checking his senses, Guy discovered he'd been unceremoniously dumped in a land he could never have conceived of in all his time on earth. Not even at the extremes of the earth.

This place did *not* make an iota of sense.

Guy found himself sitting on the crest of a dune in a desert of sand dunes—nothing unusual in that, most would have thought. Except the sky was coral-pink, as though poisoned by methane fumes, and crowded with a vibrant medley of heavenly bodies—moons and asteroid belts and crazy constellations of stars—that didn't respect any natural laws of physics. Even where he sat, he felt there was something strange about the coppery sands. He got a sense he was sinking, as though seated in quicksand. The texture of the sand, too, was all wrong as though the particles hadn't fully taken to the siliconization process, giving them a squishy, semi-gelatinous quality.

What the hell kind of place is this?

Gathering himself up, Guy realized he was not alone.

He spotted two other people down below. Guy waved at them and trudged down the slope towards them, fighting against that nauseating, sinking feeling with each step, like walking through mud.

The balding, grey-suited gentleman introduced himself as Oscar, a tax auditor, in his late fifties. The name of the floral-dressed thirtysomething woman was Yolanda, candy-store owner and all chestnut curls. She looked flustered and understandably scared, as opposed to the meek, perplexed expression residing on the other fellow's face. It occurred to Guy that these were the same people he had seen go into the house before his own viewing but had not come back out. The three of them shared their similar experiences, the one common feature between them being Old Slick, aka Curtis Manning. The estate agent had sent them here—whatever this weird wilderness was—against their will, [*Are you aware of the number of people who have vanished around these parts?*] but to what end?

He drew everyone's attention to an isolated building glimpsed on the distant horizon, obscured on occasion by the fast-moving sandstorms that swept the surface. Something told him the answer to every pressing question lay there.

His new acquaintances agreed.

They made the journey on foot under a rose-tinted, moon-congested sky. Every stride seemed to attract the grains of sand like a magnet, which actively, almost consciously formed and reformed around their shoes.

The shifting, titian sands gave way to cracked, parched earth that somehow nurtured life. The initial shoots of supposed vegetation sprouted randomly up across the dirt pans, in a cluster of long narrow leaves radiating upwards and inwards with their tips touching at the apex that made Guy think of dead, curled-up spiders. Then, the further they trekked, the more definite became the physiognomy of the plants.

Except the outsiders soon realized that these weren't an unknown species of spider-plant at all, but a more advanced form of life.

Within touching distance of the dark tower, Oscar pointed towards one of these peculiar germinating things and the others crouched round to examine it. If Guy thought that the trippy spectacle of celestial objects congregated in the pink void overhead or the almost organized, spongy properties of the sand was absurd, then he was looking at a quiescent, sleeping creature that was growing out of the ground like the Vegetable Lamb of Tartary. It floated, curled over on itself in the foetal position, inside a transparent, fluid-filled sac, suspended from a stalk, as heavy-duty as mountain rope, by its umbilicated belly like some hanging egg chair, drawing up nourishment from the dry, compact dirt. While there were other embryos tethered to the ground in different stages of gestation, resembling obscenely bloated tomatoes, this particular specimen, deep within its diaphanous cocoon, was fully grown and its stalk, sprouting up from the desert beneath and normally perpendicular and robust, was now bowed and heavy. The trio moved in closer to determine the nature of the maturing life in their midst when the unborn creature began to jerk violently and desperately, roused unexpectedly from its slumber and possibly drowning in its life-giving fluids, panicking and bouncing against the turgid membrane, causing its human observers to step back. The distended sac detached itself from the stem as a ripe apple would, perhaps indicating the moment of birth, and fell to earth, splitting open like a monstrous cyst and splattering its messy contents in a thick, noisome gush, bringing its nascent issue into this world. The peduncle snapped back upright and slid down into the ground, disappearing with the slow, mechanical grace of a retracted car aerial.

The nameless spawn uncoiled and tore through its protective sheath as easily as cellophane, springing from its womb, newborn and dripping clear, embryonic goo that, presently, on contact with the surrounding air, instantly vaporized, as did the semi-aqueous pool on the ground, sizzling untraceably to steam. The emergent being rose up and breathed in a whistling lungful of air. It stood well over seven-feet-tall and gangling, more bone than flesh, the colour of dark ash, covered in a roadmap of black, pulsing veins as though coursing with crude oil. Leathery wings unfolded from its back, fanned out to a great span, then closed back again, as the lanky creature tested them. It was difficult to ascertain its gender, devoid as it was of any obvious reproductive organs.

Its head, too, was bald and cadaverous and veined, practically a skull, and several sizes too large to maintain on its spindly body, risking flopping forward, but the creature managed to hold it upright with no apparent difficulties. The countenance possessed two air-holes where its nose should have been, and grinned a hideous Chelsea grin, exposing teeth comparable to a cannibal's, filed down to points and efficient and deadly. But the most disturbing aspect about the face was its eyes. The right eye was substantially larger than the left, huge and round and grotesque. Both rolled around in their sockets, independent of one another. This winged, wiry otherworldly demon with its needle-sharp teeth and preposterously-uneven set of eyes, Guy had to give a name. He thought 'Greyyun' might be a suitable descriptive.

Presently, the creature took in its surroundings and both of its ill-proportioned eyes stopped swivelling crazily around and came to focus and rest on the small group of humans, staring up at it with a mixture of awe and dread. They could see themselves reflected in the dilated pupil of its freaky, oversized right eye. It began to growl and bark in a language Guy could not make any recognizable sense of, sounding clumsily and unsuccessfully like a bulldog trying to speak. It must have been some legitimate arrangement of communication, for it alerted more of its kind as they made an abrupt appearance, descending in dark, flapping droves from the sky. The skeletal flying things gained purchase on the desert sands, surrounding the human interlopers ominously. They bore similar frames to the now erect, newly-emerged creature, sentient, warrior-like and aberrant-eyed.

"I think the game's up," Guy remarked lightly. Fear was thankfully diluted by fascination. He did not know what to expect next, what designs these creatures had on them, whether his little troupe would be torn to shreds by their vicious teeth and eaten alive or set upon by their formidable claws and mauled to death, or executed in some other horrible fashion, but at that moment, he did not care.

His two fellow humans did care, though. "What are these things? What do they want with us?" Yolanda muttered, holding on to Oscar for dear life. She did not seem to notice he was trembling nor had she yet caught sight of his stricken expression, neither of which would have inspired much confidence.

But the legion of Greyyuns took them prisoners instead, and conducted them towards the mysterious tower that dominated the horizon like an alien sentinel, possibly the hub of this landscape. They made the rest of the short journey in silence, apprehension increasing the nearer they got.

Guy had already seen too many implausible things in this outlandish place—the exotic sky and shifting sands, least of all this breed of bipedal beings, currently escorting them and capable of flight, that the desert that had given birth to, in the absolute literal sense, and to which they owed their very existence—but as the company approached its destination, he blinked again and again, not quite sure what he was looking at. He stared at the imposing structure, which in spite of its sheer scale and architectural alienness, was, he figured, essentially a fortress or keep. It did not give the appearance of having been constructed from a zillion quarried blocks of stone, but rather seemed to have arisen from the ground like some mad Arabian fairytale citadel or been carved from a single, immense mountain of rock. Its sandstone walls, set at bizarre geometric angles, shimmered like a mirage, punctured with multiple small holes and manifesting only two genuine windows, arched and massive and made of some reflective material. Steps led up its facade to create terraces above the said-substantive windows in the manner of a ziggurat. Together with the portcullis, apparently raised in anticipation of their arrival, the entire lunatic-angled edifice resembled an enormous lopsided, leering face, intimidating and sinister, maybe a remote, age-old sanctuary for disembodied alien spirits–*who knows?* Guy might have even gone on to call it an 'eyesore'.

While this was the place where the three prisoners had initially hoped to seek the answers to their present predicament, none of them were now keen to go on. But they no longer had any choice in the matter. Their reluctance to move was met with animalistic grunts from their lofty, skeleton-like captors, commanding the humans to tread forward, the perpetually-querulous snarl of an entrance swallowing them up.

Inside, Guy lost his orientation. Pitch blackness flowed impenetrably in every direction, save for the middle of this incalculably large room where a solitary, crooked staircase wound its way upwards and may or may not have fulfilled the visual paradoxes of Escher. They began to climb the dizzying stone steps, the grotesque progeny of the desert spreading their wings and flying alongside them like vampire bats, further contributing to Guy's sense of dislocation and the very real danger of falling and disappearing into the stygian abyss below.

Guy didn't know how long they had been climbing through this unestablished black nothingness, concerned only with the self-prescribed mandate not to look down, when they perceived light from up above, and they soon clambered through a wide, uncovered trapdoor into a cavernous, dimly-illuminated hall.

Their eyes adjusted to the curious gloom of the chamber, picking up a hive of activity.

The beanstalk, so to speak, had led them to this magical kingdom in the clouds. Sure enough, a giant dwelled on the throne, in the company of more of the cinereal, desert-sired demons. The eerie, blue-violet light was provided by a myriad of strategically-positioned floating orbs, which the giant would leisurely rotate and tap. Guy reached for the nearest wall. The wall rippled to his touch, like poking between the ribs, and it was scarred by the same runes that had brought him here. It occurred to him that this keep was never built — it was *grown*. Dark fluid circulated through the veins of the organic material, suggesting the whole building might actually be alive.

What of this giant... this fairytale *ogre*?

At first glance, the giant appeared to be anatomically different from its underlings, if Guy could call them that. The giant was taller than a double-decker bus, of significantly heavier, almost corpulent build, with rubbery, globular features, somewhere between Jabba and Kong, maybe the abominable troll of Norwegian folklore. Except Guy had a nagging feeling that the giant wasn't entirely a different race of being, but a distant, more superior relative. He could see the family resemblance: similar ash-grey skin, the folded wings on its back, the glaring Cyclopean right eye, the other peeper a vestigial but still working remnant that seemed to give him a disfigured Quasimodo look. Guy could not determine whether this living colossus was male or female since it possessed peculiar, cobwebby growths where its genitals ought to have been, their function unclear. Maybe these creatures were asexual.

The Colossus noticed their presence immediately as though it had been expecting them, both eyes spinning round and fixing intently and disconcertingly on them. "Come...!" it bellowed. "Hungry...!"

Its retinue of Greyyuns pushed a terrified, wildly protesting Oscar towards the giant. The Colossus grabbed and lifted the cowering man as an adult might pick up an infant, and in an instant, before Oscar had a chance to scream, crunched through and spat out the top of the skull with its razor-sharp teeth and sucked on the brain as one would a lollipop, making greedy, guzzling noises. Relatively satisfied, it tossed the limp body like a tattered ragdoll into the corner of the chamber, where, for the first time, Guy spotted old, discarded skeletons piled up high and dusty.

Their purpose here had become all too clear, like that *Twilight Zone* episode, *To Serve Man*.

Christ on a Cross! Guy thought, revulsed, keeping down the urge to upchuck. He had long since stopped praying to God—God rarely figured in his line of business—but right now he could have happily spent the rest of his life hiding away in a monastery. He needed His Divine Intervention right now.

"I want girl!" the Colossus demanded, licking its dinghy-shaped lips with its anaconda-sized tongue. Oscar, whom Guy had barely spoken to, had already caught a cropper. Now it seemed it was Yolanda's turn to rendezvous with the slaughterhouse, and as the Greyyun guards ripped off her clothes, the Colossus hoisted her up, swiping its huge, serpentine tongue along her plump, naked body, coating her pale skin in a trail of sticky, gummy drool. "I desire her!" the Colossus announced, dementedly, and instead of shoving her head into its dripping mouth, it placed her, shrieking hysterically and helplessly, into the spider's web-like organ attached to its groin. The strange apparatus snapped shut like a Venus Flytrap, encasing her completely.

Yet Guy could just about see what was happening within the lucent membrane, vaguely reminding him of the Excessive Machine Jane Fonda's Barbarella was forced into, risking death by pleasure. Tubules snaked and entwined, seeking out every available orifice, mimicking some kind of perverse sexual congress, the copulating organ vibrating, its fronds fluttering like jellyfish, engorging, turning red... then Yolanda was expelled from it. She splashed to the floor in a pool of gluey substance, discarded like a used condom. Her flesh was grossly distended, pulpy. But Guy noticed that, regardless of whatever sick, unspeakable ordeal she had gone through, she was only unconscious and still alive and breathing...

The giant has a serious soft spot for the ladies, I see, thought Guy grimly. Kong and the Hutt again sprang to mind. Guy nearly choked on the musk the randy custodian emitted into the vast chamber at the point of climax, a sweetly-cloying and overpowering invisible miasma, before it gradually dispersed.

The levitating globes continued to cast a strange, bluish luminescence in the giant's sovereign court. They captured images of alleyways and subways and motorway underpasses and dubious gardens, which the giant closely monitored, predatory ground where unsuspecting people disappeared and leaked through these fractures in reality. For space was multi-dimensional, and human existence ephemeral and futile and insignificant in the wider, abstract Universe with ordinary life hiding all manner of forgotten gods and cosmic horrors that could drive the ordinary person insane if they dared to grasp the bigger picture. That talk with Old Slick Manning came back to Guy, and now he gained some insight at the expense of his own fragile sanity. It was an audacious set-up. Old Slick Dick had an excellent racket going on in the designated patch of earth he patrolled, a place commonly referred to as Charterhouse Road by the public. He lured a constant supply of potential clients—or victims—whom he dialled into the portal, whisked them across the stars or through tangential dimensions, or both, to this very outpost. Or, perhaps, it was vice versa, and Earth served as an outpost for this race of titans. The Colossus—or Sexed One, for that was what it was—fed on the nervous tissue of men whereas it raped and impregnated the women prisoners in the most unimaginable way possible. That sense that this planet—Sexus, as it was called—was alive and heaving, and everything was connected occurred to Guy again. The castle walls that were reminiscent of a ribcage, the desert that was populated by legions of winged grotesqueries, nothing more than servants bound in worship to their satyr-like deity, even every grain of sand, were different facets of a single, much larger, prodigious organism: this very planet, Sexus. *A Being Unto Itself.* He knew that Yolanda would soon burst open, releasing the orgasmic load that swam inside her swollen, twitching body, seeding the planet and propagating the species.

Guy didn't particularly fancy having his skull cracked open and his brain glugged down like an oyster. He opted for a different tact, wishing not to suffer the same abject fate as his fellow humans. He approached the Sexed One and pursued the only idea he could conceive of—for what it was worth. "Hello, you must be Ibbotson, I presume…"

He materialized back in the garden at Tetherdown. It was still not yet half-four; he had gone to hell and back in a matter of a few seconds.

Curtis Manning was taken aback, still standing at the black quartz dialling console. "Nobody's ever made it back before."

But Guy had brought something back with him from that warped place: second sight. His mind bulged with arcane knowledge, and he saw the world in both its normal spectrum of colours and beyond, in trails of flamingo pinks to hallucinatory blues. And Curtis for what he really was, just another of that eldritch life, a Greyyun, complete with wings, volcanic-ash skin, a stooped, spindly physique, and two frighteningly dissimilar eyes, pointy, piranha teeth where his fake, bright-white smile had been, and dirty pauper's rags instead of a lustrous designer suit.

I got your number, pal, thought Guy. *You're just another drone, serving as gatekeeper to the Sexed One.* "Bet you weren't expecting to see me again?"

"Why did my master let you go?" the raggedy creature, posing as Curtis, asked.

Guy had to consider himself a sleazeball, admittedly a piss-take of everything that was good and honest. He made cheap skin flicks, which didn't require much artistic integrity but still demanded hard graft. Besides a desire to direct a movie on par with *A Serbian Film*, of course, he had everything he desired, a schlong he could swing like a truncheon, all the pussy he could eat, including GILFS [Granny Slappers], except perhaps the only girl he had ever coveted and could not make entirely his, a girl who was frustratingly yet to fully succumb to his cockapotimus self. A girl who did not have it in her lexicon to say 'no'. A girl whose body men had befouled and filled with their presence a thousand times over—maybe more. A girl whose latest craze was eating quinoa, because it was a superfood, and because it made anal easier. A girl with whom he had once joked about what she would do if she got raped, and whose honest reply was: *Enjoy it! Always nice to have sex with someone who can keep it up!* A girl who was forever accessible and accommodating and forthcoming, who always satisfied her man. A girl whose films he had stopped spectating on because of stupid romantic notions he never thought he was capable of. Guy had bargained with the Sexed One, struck a deal. The trade-off? Krista Avery's life in exchange for his. Guy considered it resourcefulness rather than cowardice, something constructive and productive, an intriguing sacrifice only he was in the position to make. He was holding the winning ace. Change of plans: Guy Hastings would keep the chalet as his own personal pad... and Tetherdown? *Well—*

"I'll take it."

June 2013-July 2013

Picturing the Unimaginable

"There's something those fellows catch — beyond life — that they're able to make us catch for a second."

Pickman's Model (1927)

H. P. Lovecraft

1: A History of Dark Art

The first snow of winter fell gently on the hillside as the handful of guests arrived for a private viewing of the works of Haston Sant-Cassia. The sheer, powdery white of the slope seemed to glow in the witch-light. The wind gusted down from the hollow sky intermittently, its queer wailing like the wonting cry of a loon. Upon the summit of the hill, close to the French Pyrenees, sat the old chateau, dark, brooding, a keeper of arcane secrets.

The chateau belonged to one Jacob Erlebach, millionaire industrialist and recluse and avid art collector. No-one had seen him for years and Hendon Flack — modern Rock legend and one of the select few invited to this little soirée — speculated on as to what could have brought about this sudden change of heart. Not that Flack would have refused; the invitation had mentioned that he, like the other guests, would have ample opportunity to see Sant-Cassia's actual paintings for himself. Over the years, Erlebach had snapped up the entire back-catalogue of Sant-Cassia and decided against sharing it with the rest of the world. So tonight promised to be an utterly unique experience.

Someone claiming to be Erlebach's lawyer ushered the guests one-by-one through the oak doors, out of the winter chill and away from the loon-calling wind. Niall Dalrymple—for that was his name—led the four visitors to the reception hall and asked them to help themselves to refreshments.

The red velvet decor of the great hall was not wholly unfashionable, but Flack suspected he knew the reason for the enshrouded furniture.

In the opulent warmth of the chateau, they sipped their champagne, nibbled on the finest caviar and entered into a formal round of introductions. Just as they were getting comfortable, Dalrymple called them over.

"Gather round, everybody," Dalrymple requested, tapping his champagne flute with a spoon.

His guests summarily obliged.

"You may be wondering why you were invited here," Dalrymple began in all seriousness. "This, as you may have guessed, is not a social event. We are here to do business."

"If this is nothing less than a business meeting, why wasn't I informed?" Sterling Bryce, the investment banker, demanded. "I make it my duty to know what I am to expect so I can be ahead of the game."

"What kind of business are we talking about?" Meredith Rae—three-times widowed and wife of the late shipping magnate, Blake Thompson Rae—inquired.

"Soon all will become clear." Dalrymple continued. "Sadly, Mr. Erlebach can't be with us tonight. As you may or may not know, he passed away several weeks ago. However, since he has no living relatives, it was his undying wish to bequeath his priceless collection of Haston Sant-Cassia paintings to those who might appreciate the anatomy of horror and the physiology of fear."

"When you say bequeath," Bryce interrupted, "you mean hand them over to the one deemed the most worthy? For nothing?"

"Not for nothing," Dalrymple corrected him. "They come with a price. That price you must decide."

"Sounds all very Faustian to me," Meredith Rae remarked.

"You would *know*... !" Charles Gravestock, a judge on the High Court circuit, told the Black Widow, chuckling.

Rae turned on him, not caring for the insinuation. "What is that supposed to mean?"

Dalrymple directed them back to the matter at hand. "Please, this is a meeting of minds, not a forum for character assassination. Believe me, the vetting process wasn't exactly easy. I researched each and every one of you thoroughly, and I can state with absolute confidence that you are all well-rounded individuals and best-placed to acknowledge the twisted genius of an extraordinary artist." He took a step back, indicating towards the double doors. "Behind these doors are images that will fascinate and horrify, tantalize and sicken in equal measure. I shall be shortly taking you on a guided tour of the gallery. But first, may I take this opportunity, on behalf of the Erlebach estate, to once again offer my gratitude for honouring us with your presence!"

Hendon Flack developed an interest in the occult at a very young age. As a kid, he would snigger at the madcap antics of Shaggy and Scooby and be instantly transported by the often-unnerving adventures of a mysterious time traveller from Gallifrey. Accompanied by Connor Holden, his chum from school, Hendon Flack's first-ever cinematic experience involved the hell-raising horrors of the Lost Ark.

Then, in the age of Buffy, Flack would be drawn into the whole Goth subculture and dabble in drugs, bondage and Suicide Girls. He came out the other side in one piece as the lead singer of a cult rock group, deliberately and to hilarious effect called Buggered Rectums. His band of rockers quickly entered the mainstream and, by his mid-twenties, Flack had become somewhat of a Byronic hero. The power to shock was essential to his act, but his liberal use of expletives and showering the concert-goers, en masse, with lubricating jelly soon wore thin. Following constant internal wrangling, the group disbanded, and now Flack worked as a solo artist, albeit without heaping the same success as when he was figurehead to a tribe of subversive rock musicians.

Myth, mysticism and the macabre continued to fascinate him. Most critics would describe horror as trash, but not Flack. Like most of his kind, he saw only its positives, its biggest virtue being that the genre operated by taking everything to its extreme, be it emotion, romance, family drama, crime or art.

Flack's tastes grew more refined as the years progressed until he evolved into a collector of dark art.

Hieronymous Bosch set the wheels in motion, so to speak. *Death and the Miser* was a morality tale from the Early Renaissance. In the painting, the naked miser is unprepared to give up his worldly possessions, even on his deathbed. His hand reaches for the bag of gold offered by the demon, as his guardian angel desperately draws his attention to the crucifix in the window, from where a beam of ethereal light shines through, implying that it is never too late to seek the path of salvation. The Grim Reaper puts in a leering appearance from around the door, his arrow pointed squarely at the sick man. The miser, shown a second time when he was once in full health, drops a gold coin into the strongbox. He is humbly-dressed since he hoards instead of flaunts his spoils from the Crusades to the grinning satisfaction of the lurking demon. A rat's tail is seen disappearing underneath the strongbox, suggesting that the miser has been struck down by the Black Death. Another demon peers down from above the bed, expectantly awaiting the last breath. Can the dying man redeem himself in his final hour or will temptation damn him to the eternal torments of Hell?

The late eighteenth century produced Henry Fuseli and his most famous work, *The Nightmare*. A woman lies asleep on the bed, her head draped over the edge, her slender neck exposed and vulnerable. She languishes in a state of unquiet dreams whilst an incubus crouches on her chest, peering gleefully at the viewer. A nag's head pokes through a parting in the curtain with blank, unseeing eyes. The picture is obviously inspired by Germanic folklore, particularly from stories associated with witches sending demons to rape those sleeping alone. It is a symbolic representation of subconscious fears: the sleeper's universally-held perception of a suffocating weight bearing down on the chest, sleep paralysis and a profound, nameless dread.

Francisco Goya is regarded by most as the last of the Old Masters. From court painter for the Spanish monarchs, Goya journeyed to darker, more disturbing realms during his much-discussed Black Period. Left deaf and mentally unhinged by a brain fever, he expressed his enormous distress through his work. *Courtyard with Lunatics* is a searing indictment of the widespread alienation and punitive treatment of the insane. *The Disasters* show the savageries of the battlefield as an outraged conscience pictorially denounces the Peninsular War. *The Witches' Sabbath* features several repugnant-looking hags paying audience to a goated Devil. *Devoration* sees the Roman god, Saturn, feasting upon his son in an act of shocking brutality. He has already devoured the head and right arm and is presently on the verge of biting off his cannibalized child's remaining arm. His hair is wild and his eyes bulge horribly as though murdering his own son, let alone in such a vicious manner, has driven him absolutely mad. The prophecy predicting he would be displaced by one of his children would come to pass, when Jupiter, his sixth born, eventually overthrew him.

The Scream is an Expressionist work by Edvard Munch at the height of his powers as an artist. It depicts an agonized soul overcome by a fit of existential angst. The strange, sexless appearance of this figure makes their pain all the more explosive. The blood-red sky — probably inspired by the volcanic eruption of Krakatoa a decade earlier — imbues an unnatural vibrancy to the painting, an almost synaesthetic quality, where a clever interplay of light and colour creates the impression of sound. Whether or not it represents an infinite scream passing through Nature is a different matter as the latest theory dictates that the person doing the actual screaming cannot be seen and the figure in the picture has clamped their hands over their ears to block out the noise of that very scream.

Gustave Dore and Sidney Sime have both stood the test of time as literary illustrators and should not be ignored. Dore was commissioned to illustrate the works of Balzac, Milton, Dante and Lord Byron, whereas Sime worked closely with Lord Dunsany. Dore's stand-alone piece, *Cupid and Skulls*, is his most thought-provoking. A plump, cherubic Cupid sits on a pile of human skulls, po-faced, contemplating the romances that did not work out in spite of his intervention. The skulls symbolize those relationships which have withered to dust for whatever reason, let it be incompatibility or jealousy or the lack of affection through ennui. Sime's involvement on an article by H. E. Gowers about Hashish for a respected medical journal demonstrates his considerable versatility and enduring, outlandish vision. *Seeing in Himself the Drug He Had Chewed* finds our protagonist experiencing a drug-induced hallucination, his pair of orbiting eyes beaming down on the jewel of their dreams, sharing a bizarre mindscape with a flamingo, a raccoon and a tall mandrake plant.

Who hasn't admired *The Persistence of Memory* at some point in their life, a desert landscape of softened, melting pocket-watches? Salvador Dali was a consummate genius with a prolific output, painting whatever surreal fancies took him. He was equally adept as a sculptor. *The Premonition of the Drawers* is the epitome of craftsmanship, an amalgam of his previous, commonly-employed archetypes. A man with a clock for a face reclines on the ground with a series of drawers protruding from his chest. The sculpture warns of the coming of the atomic age with little hope left for Humanity. The clock is ticking, time is running out. The anthromorphic drawers, which only a strong will can open, reek of the foolish complacency of Mankind. The bean balanced precariously on the man's head denotes the anxieties of living in such an uncertain era.

One of the greatest fantastic realists of the modern age is Ernst Fuchs. *The Angel of Death over the Gate to Purgatory* provides a hideous interpretation of Death. He is flanked on one side by hooded, harp-playing angels and on the other by a heap of crawling, panic-stricken humans astride a huge bowler hat, signifying that no-one no matter how civilized or well-off is immune from mortality. A solitary figure stands in the witness box, awaiting judgement. Central to the picture is the singular manifestation of Death, an ancient, towering, grotesque-looking demon with two sets of mismatched wings, a spindly, skeletal body and a long horizontal head, the face smooth and minimalistic, little more than a set of jaws. This nightmarish creature is considered by critics to have inspired the design for H. R. Giger's chest-buster in the film, *Alien*.

Prints of these chilling, classic works Hendon Flack acquired and derived great pleasure from, but he was always on the lookout for more.

Haston Sant-Cassia was a name whispered in underground circles. A Frenchman, Sant-Cassia had existed in the early part of the twentieth century, overlooked in his time. He shunned the literati and artistic luminaries of Jazz Age Paris, an era fondly remembered as *Les Années folles*. Interest in him only developed after he mysteriously disappeared in 1927; no-one to this day knew what became of him. He had always favoured the supernatural, and old library records claimed that most of those who had glimpsed his work had either killed themselves or ended up in a lunatic asylum, such was the disturbing nature of his work. Through his established wealth, Jacob Erlebach would later stake ownership of Sant-Cassia's entire body of work, keeping it out of the public domain… until tonight.

The promise of art with the power to terrify and shock was motivation enough to attend this evening's function. It all sounded too good to be true, accepted, but moments from now Flack would know if his presence here was justified, whether he would be exploring the darker aspects of the human soul or merely contemplating a damp squib. *The anatomy of horror*, he recalled Dalrymple pitching, *and the physiology of fear.*

Flack could feel the anticipation rising inside him as he stood on the threshold of macabre treasures unseen and unspoken. He thought of the song *Shine on Brightly* by Procol Harum and grinned and hoped.

2: The Thirteen Paintings of Haston Sant-Cassia

"Are we all ready?" Niall Dalrymple asked.

His guests murmured their affirmatives.

"Then may I welcome you to the world of Haston Sant-Cassia," Dalrymple announced, throwing the doors wide open. "Ladies and gentlemen, enjoy!"

Expectantly, the group of people stepped into a large, similarly plush-decorated, chamber. Paintings, lit up by spotlights, hung on all four walls. A door at the far end of the room seemed to lead to some secret inner sanctum. Immediately striking was how the marble floor was inlaid with a pentagram the size of the room, made of polished strips of brass.

"Nice touch," commented Sterling Bryce.

Dalrymple shepherded them to the first painting. It was titled *The Thing in the Cellar*, and set the tone for the evening. It depicted a traditional mid-western homestead on a dark, stormy night. Rain lashes down from the bruised, swollen mass of thunderclouds overhead. The farmhouse appears deserted, except for the light coming from one of the upper-storey windows. The silhouette of an old woman — a deduction made from the bonnet she is wearing — stands by the window. The light falls on the cellar doors, raised open from the ground, and the writhing tentacles emerging up from the darkness within.

Bryce summed up his opinion, "Worrying."

Hendon Flack could clearly see the Lovecraftian influence, subtle yet effective. He took a closer look at the painting and made an astute observation. "Doesn't the lack of surprise or fear in the old lady's posture suggest the tentacles might belong to her?"

"Don't say such things," Meredith Rae said, shuddering.

"I think you're reaching," Bryce told Flack.

Judge Gravestock remained unmoved, however. "Kind of picture you'd find in a penny dreadful," he said pompously. "Cheap, sensational and utterly pointless. I hope the others are less dubious and better conceived."

Dalrymple said nothing, instead led them to the next painting called *The Girl in the Mirror*. The subject was a voluptuous young model, clad in a figure-hugging red satin gown. With her back turned and her alluring face in profile, she gazes absently into a cheval glass. In the image reflected back, she wears the same dress... but the fabric seems to bulge at the seams. Her flesh has taken on a pink, bloated quality and is covered all over in a light dusting of spidery webs. Likewise, her head has grown decidedly wedge-shaped, with her snout elongated and puckered into some kind of proboscis, as she casts a baleful stare directly at the observer with the sole purpose to unnerve.

"You go out with a beautiful woman," joked Bryce. "Then she turns out to be a dog."

"I wouldn't mind taking her out to dinner myself," Gravestock remarked, showing marginally more interest, "as long as I keep her away from a mirror."

Whether the reflection captured the model's true appearance was a matter of debate. The spell, Flack concluded, was indeed broken. "The mirror never lies."

"Perhaps it relates to the darkness inside all of us," Mrs. Rae offered as way of interpretation.

They drifted over to the third painting in the gallery. *The Well of Ashoka* was the artist's attempt at a seldom-spoken segment of Indian history. Emperor Ashoka, before he would rise to greatness by embracing Buddhism, rounded up all his concubines and incinerated them in a gigantic man-made well. The unfortunate women, impossible to count, are crammed into the well as a vat of molten copper is poured over them. Some are seen shrieking, others trying to flee while the majority instantly drown and disintegrate in the seething liquid fire, undeserving victims of a wroth, paranoid king who came to believe, rather irrationally, that one of them was plotting to poison him.

"That's awful," Mrs. Rae stated in dismay. "Poor creatures… Punished for their love and loyalty to an imperial fiend."

"A man after my own heart!" exclaimed Gravestock, getting into the spirit of the thing. "He certainly knew how to put a woman in her place! If the threat of a swift slap on the cheek doesn't shut her up, then burning her alive definitely will!"

"Don't be obnoxious!" Mrs. Rae snapped.

"Look at the brushstrokes," said Bryce, deeply fascinated. "Sant-Cassia must have painted it like a man possessed. The vigour, the energy… you can practically feel the Emperor's cruel rage."

They moved to the next exhibit.

Gravestock was suitably impressed. "Now that's more like it!"

The Excommunicated Priest was a painting straight out of silver-proof lore. A priest, attired in a black soutane, sits on a stool in a modest log dwelling, undergoing a startling metamorphosis. The full moon, visible through the window, governs his physical transformation as his face, already contorted in pain, becomes distinctly lupine, growing animal hair and sprouting fangs. The eyes take on a feral glow. His hands are furring over and developing claws. Except the horror comes not from the accursed priest, but from the half-dozen naked children, chained and manacled, huddled up against the wall around him. Their captor's preternatural conversion to a wolf is only partial so far, and the children watch in abject terror, knowing what must surely follow.

"I can see why he was excommunicated," Bryce remarked wryly.

Mrs. Rae found the suffering of the children at the hands of this bestial man unsettling. "What does he want with the children?"

"Supper," Flack replied candidly.

"You mean he's going to eat them?"

"He's a lycan," Flack explained, surprised by her naivety. "Lycans eat people. You talked about the darkness inside all of us. Here's a fine example."

"Well, it doesn't bear thinking about," said Mrs. Rae in a huff.

Gravestock sounded thoughtful. "A disgraced priest flaunting his unholy miracle to a congregation of kidnapped innocents almost suggests paedophilic tendencies. I guess the fellow *can* paint after all!"

Their tour of the gallery continued with the next work, *Night at the Morgue*. The scene, as the title suggested, is one of a deserted, dimly-lit morgue approaching the witching hour as the clock on the wall will testify. Despite the clinical setting, the shadows creep and the atmosphere thickens. Gurneys, each laden with concealed corpses, provide the only trace of what once was human life. Along the far wall, a bank of storage lockers, all fastened shut, hide their own frozen, gruesome secrets. But is the place really deserted?

"There," indicated Bryce, excitedly, "do you see it?"

The others looked to where he was pointing.

In the top corner of the picture is a figure, half-obscured by the surrounding shadows, crawling on all fours along the ceiling. Ragged clothes hang loosely from skin-and-bones. Gimlet eyes survey the bay of fresh corpses voraciously.

"What is that thing?" asked Mrs. Rae.

"I might be mistaken," contemplated Flack, unsure. "Possibly a ghoul — a devourer of the dead."

"It's certainly in the right place," Gravestock said, with a charnel-house grin. "A smart solution to all your disposal needs. When the pathologist's finished his dissecting, he could donate the cadaver to that thing to scavenge on. I mean, why should dead humans go to waste when they could feed the hungry?"

"You're a regular ghoul, Judge," quipped Bryce.

Gravestock gave a cheeky bow. "Thanking you," he said, taking the comment as a compliment.

Another painting, another story. *The Changeling* portrayed a young woman breastfeeding an infant. The woman looks down with pride and maternal affection at the baby cradled in her arms. Her left breast is exposed, the baby suckling eagerly upon the teat. What immediately strikes the observer is how the elegantly-dressed mother — obviously a lady of fine breeding and sophistication — is in stark contrast to the sheer monstrousness of the child with its troll-like features, reptilian ridges and tiny claws.

"Why doesn't she notice?" Mrs. Rae demanded, appalled. "Is she blind?"

"Maybe she thinks she sees a normal, healthy, bouncing baby boy," Flack suggested. "An illusion of the senses, like hiding in the light."

"A cuckoo in the nest," Gravestock uttered in agreement. "Brilliantly deceptive."

"Her baby shower must have been a hoot," Bryce said, injecting some black humour, "attended by every creep and weirdo from Hell."

"Or maybe," Flack continued, "she made a pact with whatever demonic being impregnated her to raise the child on her own."

"Must you be so morbid?" Mrs. Rae objected, chastising Flack.

"Why don't you get with the programme?" Gravestock intervened, annoyed by her tiresome skittish attitude channelled through her constant sanctimonious criticizing. If she didn't have the stomach for it, why was she invited to this event in the first place? "We're analyzing the mind of Haston Sant-Cassia. Expect horrible things."

"Anything goes," Bryce warned with relish.

The Magician's Oath seemed to be set in a Victorian theatre house. An unnamed magician is in the midst of a show-stopping performance. A small orchestra plays below the stage, generating a steady drumroll. The audience watch, rapt, as the magician rips off the sheet covering the glass cage, revealing the evolutionary aberration he has somehow conjured up. A merman, wearing a coat of scales and all webbed hands and feet, floats inside the watery tank. Pharyngeal gills flap lazily, moon eyes regard the crowd with an air of filmy vacancy. The magician's female assistant, apparently unacquainted with the act, screams.

"A freak of nature to rival any Siamese twin or Elephant Man," pondered Gravestock.

"The carnival sideshows will never lose their appeal with the public," Bryce interjected. "People will always pay good money to see them."

"Who's to say it's not some guy dressed in a fish costume?" dismissed Mrs. Rae.

"Do you have to destroy the magic every time?" Gravestock asked her gruffly.

Mrs. Rae went silent. She glanced at him dourly as if warning him not to push her.

Flack could date the scene depicted in *The House of the Spirits* to Edwardian times. A séance is in progress in the lowly-lit parlour. At the table, each participant holds their neighbour's hand to form a perfect circle. The medium's face is blurred as though overlapped by other countenances. It seems she has succeeded in tapping into the ether because rising up from the waxy smoke of the extinguished candle is the half-coalesced image of a wraith-like entity. The apparition she has summoned has not yet fully manifested itself; only the misty outline of its upper torso and its angular head are apparent. From a distance it vaguely bears the characteristics of a gigantic sphynx cat, except for the eyes that glare at the observer with a fierce, sinister intelligence.

"It's almost as though it knows you're watching," murmured Flack with a faint smile.

"Just when you thought all psychics were charlatans!" retorted Bryce. "Even the faceless ones!"

"She's achieved something quite momentous," Flack enthused. "Not only has she managed to communicate with the other side, she has above all else reached into a world even further beyond and brought back one of its original residents."

"How many more of these are there?" Mrs. Rae inquired, referring to the paintings.

Niall Dalrymple, who had not entered into any of the verbal exchanges thus far, spoke up, "Five more to go." He had noted her disinterest throughout the viewing. "The paintings don't meet your expectations, madam?"

Mrs. Rae gave a contemptuous snort.

"I find them riveting," exhorted Flack. "Imagination can be such a powerful tool."

"Not my cup of tea, I'm afraid," Mrs. Rae finally said. "I'm just doing a friend a small favour."

The following picture was called *By the Sleep of Morpheus*. A gentleman in a red smoking jacket literally steps out of a brick wall. He checks his pocket-watch, which contains odd-looking ciphers instead of Roman numerals. The ground blossoms with poppy flowers as far as the eye can see. A four-legged creature with a spiral horn emerges from the gossamer clouds as it gallops headlong at the man, deprived of its hide, its exposed, livid, tumour-raddled flesh perspiring sprays of noisome pink fluid, possibly blood. Its eyes blaze with a sick, blinding rage.

"Once it was a unicorn," said Flack insightfully. "Now it's a skinned, rotting thing, imbued with unnatural life. Trust Sant-Cassia to come up with the idea."

"As surreal as anything Dali produced," compared Bryce. "Remember the burning giraffes?"

"Makes you want to ride that beast," Gravestock said, impressed as ever, "no matter what the consequences would be."

"I think what we have here is a lucid dream," explained Flack, "where the sleeper realizes they are dreaming. The clues are all there: walking through walls, strange characters on the watch, a field of opium plants, the mythical, if not degraded, unicorn."

"Who was Morpheus?" quizzed Bryce.

"The Greek god of dreams," answered Flack, "the gatekeeper to fabulous visions."

"Why couldn't he have just painted an ordinary unicorn?" bemoaned Mrs. Rae, not understanding their admiration. "I would have liked that—beautiful, white and sinewy."

"What would be the fun in that?" Bryce expressed in a purely rhetorical sense.

Lurking Beneath brought a subterranean flavour to the proceedings. The backdrop for the painting is a set of dark, rat-infested catacombs. Water drips from the ceiling. Two men, wearing slickers and galoshes over their Parisian police uniforms, stand over a motionless figure, smoking pistols in hand. One of the policemen raises his lantern to get a better view of the creature they have just shot. It lies on the ground, a short, hairy, inbred mutant. Unbeknownst to the men, more of these degenerate midgets emerge in their scores, shambling and dragging their knuckles, from the tunnel behind them, murder in their savage, fevered expressions.

"Very *Rue Morgue*," alluded Gravestock, "except with crazies instead of apes."

Bryce stated the obvious, "I don't like the look of that angry pygmy demi-mob. Those cops are serious goners."

"Murder, madness and monsters feature prominently in Sant-Cassia's works," mused Gravestock.

"Essential ingredients to horror art as a whole," replied Flack. "If it produces shock, fear or disgust in its audience, then it has achieved its purpose." He casually shifted to the eleventh painting. "What else do we have here?"

The Brain-Eaters proved a treat for the horror voyeur. A dinner party is in progress. The guests at the banquet table are enjoying their main course of roast pheasant and spring vegetables. The scene would be an accurate glimpse into the lives of the upper classes if it were not for the alarming condition of their heads. The backs of their heads have split open, each providing egress to a loathsome, cranium-dwelling species of worm.

This is particularly evident with the hostess, who is seated at the end of the table, closest to the viewer. Her skull reveals an empty, ragged cavity inside because her own squirming abhorrence has already gestated, fed on her brain and moved on to fresher fare. Yet the presence of these brain-chewing, vermiform parasites goes largely unnoticed by the dinner guests as they tuck into their meals as if nothing happened.

"Gives a whole new meaning to the term 'airhead'," said Bryce, amused.

"Could pertain to the vacuousness of the aristocracy," suggested Gravestock, "their constant inbreeding or their persistently greedy nature, gorging on society's wealth."

Flack agreed with him. "Makes sense in a roundabout kind of way."

"I think it borders on bad taste," opined Mrs. Rae, grimacing at the painting.

"That's the whole point," Bryce reminded her. "Like Mr. Flack here mentioned, it's all about provoking an emotional response: fear, shock or, in this case, disgust."

Picture #12: *Minions of the Ancient One*. Skyscrapers shoot up to the heavens. Factories belch industrial smoke into the murky air. Hovercars struggle along the congested skyways in single file. At the centre of the metropolis rises a granite pyramid, milling with people in flowing robes, honouring their call to prayer. Outside this temple stands the golden statue of their veneration, a giant, globulous Cyclopean being—

the eponymous Ancient One.

"What does it mean?" puzzled Mrs. Rae.

"Must be our artist's take on the future," replied Flack. *More shades of Lovecraft.*

"Mankind certainly seems to have progressed," deliberated Bryce. "Second-class citizen on a polluted, overpopulated planet."

"Yes, but *what* is this Ancient One?" demanded Mrs. Rae.

Flack borrowed from his stock of esoteric knowledge. "Some legends go that the world was once ruled by a race of eternal monsters before man even learned to walk upright. Then something happened and they fell into a deep sleep, dreaming of the day when they would reawaken and re-claim the Earth. Through the aeons they have supposedly been worshipped by almost every civilization, from the ancient Babylonians to various fleeting cults in our time. The Ancient One is regarded as a greater deity in the hierarchy of these evil gods, much older and more powerful than the Olden Ones."

"Explains why there're no churches in the picture," noted Bryce, sighing. "I guess the Ancient One finally awoke and enslaved the human race."

"Such puerile, pagan nonsense!" cried Mrs. Rae, putting her usual negative spin on the debate. "What was wrong with the awe-inspiring beauty of Christian art? Give me the Sistine Chapel any day!"

The last painting in the gallery was simply titled *Self-portrait*, providing the summoned guests with the opportunity to see what their mysterious painter actually looked like. It was a straightforward portraiture of a man in his late-thirties. All agreed that Haston Sant-Cassia must have indeed been handsome in life. However, in the painting, he is unshaven and unkempt with long, straggly hair and possesses a besieged, haunted look... the look of someone who has stared too long into the dark and begun to see what lies there.

"So this is the fellow," reflected Gravestock. "I detect a state of derangement."

"I don't think you're far off," attested Flack. "His demons seem to have caught up with him. It's as though he knows he doesn't have long left in this world." He scrutinized the signature, looking for confirmation. "The painting is dated 1927, the very year he disappeared."

Bryce gave them his version. "Is it just me or do you also find those brown eyes hypnotic? The rich flourishes, the sharpness of definition, the honest realism, the staggering energy of the painting—how it leaps out at you from the canvas."

"Well, ladies and gentlemen," declared Dalrymple, clapping his hands for attention, "each of you has had a chance to see and admire the works of Haston Sant-Cassia. Now I must ask you each to take out your cheque-books and bid for these pieces."

"I think I'll just stick with *The Girl in the Mirror*," stated Gravestock.

"I can't allow that," Dalrymple replied firmly. "The paintings mustn't be separated. You either bid for the entire collection or not at all. It was Mr. Erlebach who stipulated the conditions of the sale."

"Seems a bit excessive, doesn't it?" protested Gravestock. "What if we don't want all of them?"

"Then you have every right to abstain. I would therefore ask you to wait in the main hall whilst the rest of us get on with our business."

Gravestock sounded disgruntled. "Alright, I'll stay..."

"Then shall we?" asked Dalrymple with the authority of an auctioneer. "Remember, from this point forth, you are now in direct competition with each other. The paintings go to the highest bidder."

"You're bidding too?" Gravestock said, astonished to find Mrs. Rae opening her cheque-book. "I thought you didn't like the damned paintings."

Mrs. Rae maintained her staid manner. "As I communicated earlier, I have a friend who might find them interesting."

"Shall we begin?" Dalrymple requested briskly, indicating to his watch. "You have exactly five minutes to decide what these thirteen pieces are worth. You can go round and examine the paintings again to help you with your deliberations." He checked his watch again. "Your time starts... *now*! Good luck!"

Apart from Mrs. Rae who scribbled down a figure immediately, the guests went their separate ways, taking up positions around the gallery. Judge Gravestock certainly seemed attracted to *The Girl in the Mirror*, for he did not budge from the painting for the entirety of the designated period. The malevolent glare of the proboscidate reflection held him in thrall.

"Makes you wonder where Sant-Cassia drew his inspiration from," Flack heard Bryce murmur as he passed him by.

Flack, himself, did a quick sweep of the exhibits. In today's age of Schadenfreude and torture porn, he thought, Sant-Cassia's work came as a refreshing change. *He doesn't have to be Picasso conveying many sides of the same object at the same time or Pollock with his frenzied, abstract use of colour – Sant-Cassia is as unique in his field as any convincing artist. Vivid, stylish renderings of a wide range of horror themes, traditionally underpinned, painstakingly realized, meticulously defined and, oh so, strangely lifelike, as though the artist created them from first-hand experience. A genuine meta-education.*

The seconds spun out into what felt like an eternity. The eyes of all the subjects, particularly those of the haggard-looking self-portrait, seemed to leer at the guests around the room with a ravenous intensity, disquietingly so. From somewhere faraway came a peculiar sound, like the faint, incoherent whisperings of forgotten tongues, which Flack quite rationally put down to the low babel of a sedulous wind on an ice-cold winter's night.

"Your time is up," Dalrymple eventually announced. His guests gathered in the pentagram, handing him their precious slips of paper. Dalrymple unfolded their cheques one by one while they watched him with tense anticipation. He soon informed them of the result. "It seems we have a clear winner! Mr. Hendon Flack, congratulations! You are now the proud owner of the works of Haston Sant-Cassia!"

All of a sudden, chaos ensued.

"You must be kidding!" Bryce exclaimed unexpectedly. "You're going to give those paintings to this... this mascara-wearing, velvet-dressing *Goth*?"

"Goth I might be," retorted Flack, taken aback by the aggressive outburst, "but I am a celebrated member of the Ministry of Rock and Roll. And that makes me an extremely rich goth!"

Bryce implored Dalrymple. "You can't give them to him! Those paintings should go to someone who'll appreciate them... like me! I'll double his offer!"

Dalrymple didn't intend to overturn the decision no matter how much he felt tempted. "Mr. Flack was the highest bidder. He won them fair and square."

"The paintings are *mine!*" snapped Mrs. Rae.

"Like hell they are, you gold-digging tramp!" exploded Gravestock.

"Excuse me?"

"Yes, we all know you murdered your husband with the help of your Brazilian toyboy! We just can't prove it!"

"That's a lie! I've never been more insulted in my life!"

"*Cut the crap!*"

Mrs. Rae spewed out some of her own vitriol. "And didn't you, Judge Holier-than-Thou, sentence a top-ranking policeman to prison for perverting the course of justice so you could start an affair with both his wife *and* his underage daughter?"

Bryce burst out laughing. "You two are fucking crazy!"

"You find something funny?" Gravestock roared, turning on him. "Do you think you can just push your colleague out of a high-rise window and call it suicide?"

The laughter instantly ceased, the colour drained from his cheeks.

Gravestock's belligerence didn't stop there. "And *you*, Mr. Rock Star! What crime have *you* committed?"

Flack looked him straight in the eye. "Oh, the usual: taken every drug under the sun, slept with a lot of pretty young girls, trashed loads of hotel rooms and generally given people like you, who represent all that is woeful about the Establishment, the middle finger!"

The bare-cheeked insolence of the remark empurpled Gravestock. "How dare you? You're the last person in the world who deserves such exquisite artwork!"

"Ladies and gentlemen, please!" Dalrymple intervened, not altogether shocked by the series of disclosures. He needed to bring a modicum of order to a situation that was spiralling out of control. "I feel your passion, but there is still such a thing as good sportsmanship!"

Judge Gravestock carried in his pocket an [illegal] instrument of justice. Before the others realized what was happening, a semi-automatic was pointed at them. "If the paintings ought to belong to anybody, they ought to belong to me…!"

There followed a long, dreadful hush.

The paintings leered. The lights of the gallery winked momentarily.

Then, Mrs. Rae broke the silence. "What are going to do? *Shoot us all?*" she challenged him hysterically.

"This is just fucking great!" muttered Bryce, aghast. "We're all going to die!"

"Now, now, Judge," Dalrymple said, assessing the dangerousness of the situation, "you don't want to do anything hasty."

"I want those paintings," Gravestock insisted—except his voice, as well as his resolve, was already beginning to falter.

Dalrymple spoke as coolly as he could muster. "Judge, you're supposed to uphold the law, and we're all aware you're a courageous champion of the cause."

"Yes, but the paintings..." he agonized weakly.

"Now, I want you to lower your gun slowly. You can still leave here the man you are, feared and respected by the public."

Gravestock seemed on some level to comprehend the error of his ways. His brow furrowed and a sad, bewildered look overtook him. His eyes glazed over. His body sagged and he fell to his knees, the gun clattering on the floor. Sanity departed. "I didn't mean to..." he uttered, sobbing. "Impulse... It was all about the paintings..."

Crisis averted, everybody heaved a sigh of relief.

"I'll take that, thank you," said Dalrymple, snatching up the gun and shoving it into his pocket.

"The old judge really lost it, didn't he?" said Bryce, sounding perplexed.

"That's enough excitement for one night, I hope," Mrs. Rae said, still shaking.

"I want you two to take Judge Gravestock back to the main hall," instructed Dalrymple, "and wait for me there. Help yourselves to more champagne. I've got a few financial details to finalize with Mr. Flack."

"I'm not going near him," Mrs. Rae remonstrated, eyeing the Judge with suspicion and disdain, as though he were a leper. "What if he attacks us?"

"I can assure you he's quite harmless," replied Dalrymple wearily.

Taking him by the arms, a reluctant, resigned Bryce and Mrs. Rae led a confused, stupefied Judge Gravestock to the main hall through the door which they had entered.

When they were alone, Flack asked Dalrymple: "So what do you need to know?"

"We're not quite finished yet," answered Dalrymple. He gestured to the door in the far wall. "Beyond that door lies the Black Room. Inside are treasures more shocking than anything you've seen tonight. Mr. Erlebach requested in his will that whoever inherited the paintings should not leave without viewing the contents of that room. And come up with a suitable offer if they so choose."

"The Black Room?" said Flack, more intrigued than ever. "Lead on, good sir…"

3: The Black Room… and Beyond

When he stepped through the secret door, Hendon Flack did not know what to expect. The thirteen paintings earlier, now his to keep, had been a real eye-opener, vindicating Sant-Cassia's position in the pantheon of pioneering horror artists.

The tentacles rising up from the fruit-cellar.

The medusa's-stare of the monster in the mirror.

The awful, fiery execution of an emperor's entire harem of concubines.

A disgraced, child-snatching priest's transformation into a werewolf.

The arrival of a ghoul in a deserted morgue at night.

A mother lovingly breastfeeding her demon-spawn.

The revelation by a stage magician of a prehistoric fish-man.

The summoning of a malignant spirit from beyond the ether during a séance.

The last act of a disintegrating unicorn to spear its lucid dreamer before it dies.

The shooting-dead of an ape-like obscenity under the streets of Paris.

Brain-suckers crawling out from the heads of guests at a dinner party as they eat on.

A vision of the future centred around the worship of a multi-millennial god.

And, of course, the artist himself, suffering for his art, tortured by his horrible imaginings.

Diseased flights of the imagination that deserved a wider audience. Their classical feel, enhanced by a deliberate dash of stylishness and emboldened by a sense of realism, almost gave them the appearance of coming out of the frame—*Trompe-l'oeils* in many respects. Their power to unsettle, at the very least, and capable of sending the excitable mind over the edge—Gravestock being a case in point. Yet none of those masterpieces compared to the collection of fascinating artefacts Flack found in the Black Room.

The Black Room was so-called because the walls were composed of pure obsidian as though it had been carved straight out of the hillside. The low-wattage light-fixtures only inspissated the sepulchral gloom of the place.

Flack saw before him a self-contained museum of sorts, home to some singularly breathtaking items. Among the dusty shelves of curios and oddities, he spied Chinese puzzle-boxes and finger-traps, a pair of customized ivory fangs once belonging to the late great Max Schreck, shrunken human heads of old, hoodoo tradition, poppets allegedly confiscated from a witch hanged in Salem, the bound conically-shaped skull of a Toltec Indian, a Ouija Board used by the Hermetic Order of the Golden Dawn, the mummified remains of a monkey's paw, an original copy of the fabled sixteenth-century grimoire *Pseudomonarchia Daemonum*, a Seal of Solomon signet ring, painted pebbles from the Pictish period, a bag of punched "good luck" coins, an Eye of Horus amulet and a Kabbalistic prayer shawl. There was an assortment of small polished rock carvings of strange, frightening creatures. These nightmare-hewn effigies—of life not of this earth—had queer-sounding names Flack could barely pronounce: H'ISP-HORA, LAO-MOGHET, TAUJ'OMHI, BEKAZOP'TAC, KHAZEMAT'HOR, N'HEBP-MIZ'KROUN, ZA'LEKAL'ROHBA-YO'MODIN. They must represent, Flack suspected, the gods of old, worshipped long before the Age of Antiquity.

Overall, a den of priceless treasures, thought Flack, astounded. If people like Gravestock could kill for those paintings, imagine what they would do for this clutter.

Flack came across a section devoted entirely to congenital malformations. A library of specimen jars containing preserved, non-viable foetuses. There were cyclops babies, babies with eyes where their ears should be, babies conjoined from the waist up, babies sharing the same brain, babies with misshapen bulbous heads, legless and armless wonders, an anatomical horror with no face except a mouthful of needle-sharp teeth. Flack stared at these pickled miscreants, their freakish development showcased, with a mixture of disgust, fascination and pity. Maybe they died prematurely or came out stillborn, or perhaps their mothers, sickened by the sight of their crippled, twitching offspring, demanded the backstreet abortionist finish the job. Erlebach must have had an unquenchable morbid streak to keep these specimens when any medical school would have paid handsomely for them.

Tacked on the obsidian walls were charcoal drawings which Flack almost missed, sketches of scenes that defied normal convention and strived to alarm. The figures in these pictures were, like the foetuses before, blasphemies of the human form. A couple with horribly disfigured features engage in sexual congress amongst the headstones in a cemetery. A cruise-liner full of hysterical people is set upon on the decks by a horde of loping, lurching, lunging subhumans. Flying at an altitude of ten-thousand feet, a pilot stares goggle-eyed at the unnameable hellion clinging perilously to the lower wing of his biplane. A naked virgin, tied to a pole by a tribe of savages, faints at the sight of the giant, slavering, misproportioned face emerging from the entrance of a cave. An explorer flees the ruins of a fallen temple, chased over the desert by a swarm of grotesque, shambling things. A dapper gentleman tends to his broken-down motor-car on a remote moonlit country lane as huge tentacles reach for his ankles from the nearby woods. A soldier in the trenches of Ypres is bound tight by a twisted skein of barbed wire, the vicious hooks digging into his bleeding flesh, his eyelids stitched shut and his lips sewed together.

Sant-Cassia had outdone himself. Flack marvelled at the bold artistry, the remarkable ease by which Sant-Cassia managed to unease. Could it get any creepier?

Flack delved deeper and picked up what he thought was a scrapbook, bound in leather, badly scuffed and titled: *From a Brownie*. Should he expect more sketches, more shuddersome gems to quicken the heart?

Except, when he opened it, the truth behind Sant-Cassia's iconographic creations came crashing home.

"*My God...!*" Flack murmured, confronting the inconceivable.

Earlier on, Bryce had wondered from where Sant-Cassia got his inspiration. The answer, Flack discovered, lay within the yellowed pages of this volume. Flack had firmly believed that Sant-Cassia had combined his unique perspective on the human condition with his knowledge of the occult to scare up the imagination and govern his brush. But now Flack knew Sant-Cassia was a graduate of Still Life, fully schooled in the scientific method.

For Flack found photographs pasted into the pages of the book. Page after page of faded brown photographs, each an event in itself as rare as a solar eclipse or the parting of the Red Sea. Flack saw a photograph of the dead, crooked body of a vile ape-thing, riddled with bullets, on the floor of a catacomb. On the following page, he recognized the single larva slithering out of each of the guests' heads at a formal dinner function from a painting he had already seen. He regarded an eerie close-up of a half-formed spectral entity rising up from the mist as summoned by a medium. Another photograph showed an overweening mother offering her abomination of an infant her bare breast. Further in the book was snapped an opportunistic photo of a ghoul feeding on a luckless cadaver in a benighted morgue. Several images captured the full scale of a magician's prestige as a simple minnow in a water-tank miraculously and sequentially transformed into a gilled, amphibious man through some weird mode of evolution. Flack speculated over the flayed, decayed unicorn in the picture of a dream—possibly a sleep thoughtograph. And he studied the disconcerting photograph of a provocative young woman, peering at her repulsive reflection—the poses of the model and the tubular-snouted grotesquerie glaring directly at the camera were a perfect mirror image to their counterparts in the painting. There were other pictures in the album, of more unclassifiable, inhuman creatures caught on camera, not yet reproduced as art.

What Sant-Cassia had committed to canvas, it seemed, was not some cleverly thought-out mental construction, but a snapshot of reality. These original, undoctored photographs apparently provided the source of his inspiration and the very templates for his paintings. In short, Sant-Cassia had painted from life itself...

Flack gawked at the implications thereof. How had Sant-Cassia obtained these impossible shots? Did such monsters actually exist? The evidence he held in his hands was indisputable, the groundbreaking contents of his portfolio of the damned staring him straight in the face.

"We're not quite done yet," Niall Dalrymple said matter-of-factly.

Stone the crows! thought Flack, struggling with the mind-blowing impact of these photographs. *How much more can there be? Any more surprises and my head might* actually *explode!*

Dalrymple led him round the last tier of shelves to the grand prize dominating this final section of the storeroom.

Rising well over ten feet tall and dwarfing the two men stood a statue of the Ancient One. Fashioned from gold, the shining, shapeless idol glared inscrutably ahead with its one giant eye. The base of the statue was emblazoned with indecipherable alien hieroglyphics.

Monument to an unhallowed god rumoured to be older than the Dark Ages, the time of Gilgamesh, the invention of fire, older than even Mankind and History itself. Flack deliberated, overawed. "It must be worth millions, the crown jewels of this momentous evening."

He moved forward and touched its cold, polished surface. The statue thrummed with a mysterious energy as though fed by a hidden generator. Voices came from the statue, sinister whisperings and unsouled titterings.

"Look..." Dalrymple said, gesturing to a place beyond the statue.

And Flack saw it, too. Sure enough, where the back wall should have existed was the black gulf of space. Crazy, whirling constellations of stars filled the illimitable blackness. Flack could sense the distant howling and motion of unspeakable winged creatures that reminded him of the Nightgaunts of Lovecraftian lore flying through the fantastic ultra-cosmic void.

Flack turned to Dalrymple, excited as a kid in a candy store. "Name your price. I would gladly stake my entire fortune on everything I've seen in the Black Room."

"That is extremely generous of you," replied Dalrymple. "But I do not ask so much. Double on your bid for the paintings and Mr. Erlebach's entire secret stash is yours."

A thought occurred to Flack. "How did Erlebach die?" he inquired, curious.

"His time was up," Dalrymple explained and pointed towards the dark, dimensional rift. "*They* came for him. The Guardian of the Abyss can only protect you for so long."

"And Haston Sant-Cassia?"

"No-one knows," Dalrymple said with an unnatural calm. "He tapped into the unguessable and glimpsed the unthinkable. Mr. Erlebach claimed he received a visitation from Sant-Cassia before he died."

"Dark night of the soul…"

"Still, Mr. Erlebach lived well past a hundred. Longevity of life is overshadowed by the prospect of eventually succumbing to whatever lies beyond the forbidden gateway."

Flack remembered Sant-Cassia's haunted expression in his self-portrait. An artist upon whom his admirers had piled markedly more layers of myth than even the seventeenth-century Dutch painter, Godfried Schalcken. "Horror with no limits. I'll go for it…"

Sterling Bryce plummeted to his death after falling out from his twelfth-storey window in the business district of Manhattan. The Medical Examiner suspected suicide if it weren't for the claw-marks on his neck. Traces of hair were embedded in the wounds and, when tested, found to contain wolf DNA.

Meredith Rae was discovered dead by her lover in the banquet-hall of her Colorado mansion. Something had chewed its way out of her skull, leaving a brainless excavation site. She had gouged her eyes out and, using her own blood, scrawled on the walls: I CAN STILL SEE.

The alarm was raised when Judge Charles Gravestock did not report for Sessions. When the police broke down the front door to his Kensington apartment, they found his old, corpulent corpse on the couch in the sitting room. He was wearing only a bathrobe. His exposed penis was bruised and stretched and swollen as though a suction device had been applied to it. All the mirrors in his apartment were smashed.

Following his own dark night of the soul, Hendon Flack disappeared off the musical radar and, when last heard, had moved to the South Pacific. In the secret vaults of his island home, he took up worship of the Ancient One, the infinite and invincible interdimensional god who guarded the Gates to the Back of Beyond. Although satisfied with his newly self-imposed isolation, he was forever conscious of the invisible threat that lingered over him like a shadow—he could keep back the pressing wall of space with his prayers as long as he had breath in his body, but he knew, one day, the honeymoon would be over and the other dimension would come spilling through into our world.

As High Priest, he prayed and chanted and sang and gave thanks to the glory of the Ancient One in return for Its everlasting protection.

And lived to be one hundred and thirty.

November 2008-February 2009

BOOKEND: TALES TOLD A THOUSANDFOLD (FINITO)

Even before the last yarn has been spun out, I have caught on to the dread, diabolical nature of the tales I have listened to, the hopelessness and sin within, the bleak despair and bitter aftertaste, and I finally come to see this place, this dark, smoke-filled place – and the punters within – for what it really is. That nagging sense of foreboding materializes into complete comprehension, a 'moment of clarity' as every half-decent alcoholic calls it. In horrible dismay, I realize there is nothing 'magical' or heraldic about this inn, this decrepit den of iniquity, for it is built solely on illusion, constructed by the perception of each person, each personal hell as separate and unique as the other fella's, since this hangout, dressed up like a watering hole, is older than Antiquity itself, something goat-old and a place of pure evil, dating as far back as the Fall of Man.

These people with their tales to tell are all cursed. Damned. *Either they don't know they're dead or they are in denial of their own demise, trapped in this nightmare sphere of existence. For they are without repentance, salvation or hope, and they await a fate worse than death. Damnation Inn, it seems, serves as the stopping point, a pit-stop, before these people continue their onward journey to Hell itself. Yes, Hell, full of burning souls, where the wicked are punished by the minions of the Devil.*

The sunset does not paint the firmament outside with that lurid redness but it is a sky rendered ablaze in Dantean fury by being situated on the outer fringes of the Inferno, destined to get only hotter the further one goes towards the constant, sinister glow in the distance. By the quayside, the sea bubbles and spits, releasing noxious fumes of brimstone, awaiting its next ferryload of condemned souls.

"Last orders, anyone?" the Innkeeper, still looking vaguely like Epstein, announces, ringing the bell.

The *Legends of Rock* ignore the decree and continue what they're doing, but a certain company of men rises up from a corner table and proceeds to the bar and, once it has detached themselves from the shadows, I notice, without experiencing any profound shock – for I am past the stage of shock, or fear – it consists of the Emperor Nero, the Marquis de Sade, Adolf Hitler and Louis XVI. Nearby, Rasputin and Aleister Crowley look on, wavering between finishing their glass and buying the last round or staying put, with what they've got. At the adjoining table, Reverend Jim Jones, carrying off his usual lame, bloated Elvis impression, folds his hands in prayer, perhaps to atone for his terrible sins, while on either side of him Ted Bundy gives me an all-knowing salute and Charles Manson furnishes me with a nefarious grin, informing me that it is time to drink up and go, prepare to meet the First Evil.

"Are you ready?" emerges a shaky but very friendly and familiar voice from over my right shoulder. Dennis 'the Menace' Hopper is standing right beside me, probably still waiting for Old Jack Nick to turn up.

"I guess I am," I reply, nodding slowly. "Anybody who goes by the name of Ixidorr Hack is always ready."

"Good luck, man..." Dennis Hopper offers in encouragement, tipping me a cheeky wink.

"I don't need luck where I'm going," I remind him, confidently. "I should fit right in. I shall gladly endure every torment Hell has to offer. I might even teach Lucifer a trick or two. But first God must explain Himself, be held accountable, for forsaking the earth and His people for so long."

I heed the commandment of the Rolling Stones from the jukebox – the Cheaters of Death – bidding us to **Paint It, Black** as the song plays a thousandfold. And another thousandfold. And another.

I suppose the secret lies with the tales. These tales that have been told a thousandfold. And shall be told a further thousandfold. And a thousandfold after that. **Ad infinitum.**

And, just as I have listened to these tales of the damned in this unholy place called Damnation Inn and passed them on to you, any who dare read these tales are forever **damned...**

HACK TRACK LISTING

(songs from which I derived dark inspiration…
and in no particular order)

Paint It, Black	The Rolling Stones
This Ain't The Summer of Love	The Blue Öyster Cult
The Seeker	The Who
In-A-Gadda-Da-Vida	Iron Butterfly
Puppet Man	Tom Jones
Cold Day In Hell	Gary Moore
Come As You Are	Nirvana
There's No Other Way	Blur
Now I'm A Fool	Eagles of Death Metal
Houses	Great Northern
Ring The Bells	James
You're The Voice	John Farnham
Africa	Toto
Kashmir	Led Zeppelin
Hellraiser	Motörhead
1492: la Conquista del Paradis	Red Banner
Mr Sandman	Blind Guardian
Wish I Had An Angel	Nightwish
Bela Lugosi's Dead	Bauhaus
Mass Destruction	Faithless
Dream A Little Dream Of Me	The Beautiful South
Shine On Brightly	Procol Harum
End Of The Line	The Traveling Wilburys

www.ingramcontent.com/pod-product-compliance
Lightning Source LLC
Chambersburg PA
CBHW030928020726
47498CB00001B/156